The New Assassin's Field Guide & Almanac

M. W. GATS

DORRANCE
PUBLISHING CO
EST. 1920
PITTSBURGH, PENNSYLVANIA 15238

Cover design by Matt Gats

Dorrance Publishing Co
585 Alpha Drive
Suite 103
Pittsburgh, PA 15238
Visit our website at *www.dorrancebookstore.com*

ISBN: 978-1-6393-7036-8
eISBN: 978-1-6393-7825-8

This book is for Beth my wife & Griffin my daughter, the bookends of my life and love. Griffin, you came out of the blue and dear Beth—you came out of the rising sun.

I want to thank my family of origin for making me into a teacher, writer, father--and so many other things. I love you Ruth, Dan, Michelle and Beth...you are all part of anything I ever create.

I also want to thank the fine people at Dorrance Publishing, especially Sara Lewis. I hope to work with you again.

And most especial thanks to Paulette Hoeflich, Gerald Zinfon, Ruth Greenwood, Kenneth Butler and too many former students to mention. The list is too long, but I hope you all know why you were vital to me, then and now.

Part One

CHAPTER ONE

Twenty-First Century Outlaws-Tribal Solutions. Rugby and Lesbians. Denuzzio Visits the Twilight Kingdom.

I WAS ON THE BEACH, reading a T.S. Eliot collection, when I noticed the commotion over the dog.

"The Wasteland." "The Hollow Men." I particularly liked "The Hollow Men," which is to say it disturbed me. If you were an author looking for titles for books, you couldn't ask for better inspiration. *Death's Only Twilight Kingdom. Prayers to Broken Stone. The Hope Only/Of Empty Men.*

On the other hand, *Old Possum's Book of Practical Cats* could make my teeth ache.

And don't even get me started on the goddamned musical.

Long before Brightman Jones and the Guild and the Three, I'd taken a date to see *Cats* in New York. At one point the actors came climbing into the goddamned audience, all in your face and slathered with sweat and make-up. Horrifying.

The dog bounded across my blanket, kicking sand, and button-hooked around behind my chair, a pretty black woman chasing him. There was a dead bird in his mouth.

Some kids ran up behind her, but the dog—some kind of lab mix—blasted off to the left and then raced, splashing, along the water's edge. Then he wheeled around to buzz past us again, showing off, wanting to be chased.

I saw that the bird in his mouth was a dead seagull.

I think the black woman and the children were a family, but never found out for sure. The kids were laughing, but the woman was breathless and irritated.

"Mason!" she yelled.

But Mason was having none of it. He planted his paws and crouched—head low, butt up—for just a beat before the woman and then wheeled around her, the gull's head flopping tonelessly.

I got up to help just as a fat, extremely tan old man approached for the same reason.

And here's where the magic began. We didn't speak the entire time beyond a word or two. The tall woman, three kids with her now; the old man, tan as teak; a willowy teen girl; and me—all of us fanned out as Mason turned to look at us, ears pricked, mouth clownishly stretched around the gull.

The woman spoke to one of the boys and he moved further to her left. I had stepped to her other side, standing up to my ankles in tide-covered marsh grass. All of us had assumed a fairly evenly spaced capital C formation with Mason and his prize in the approximate center. The dog trotted back and forth in a short parade, tossing his head back in jerks to catch and further snuffle the gull deeper into his mouth.

He reminded me of a bullfighter, somehow.

The sun was westering toward two p.m. and the light made the incoming tide a gold mirror over the sea grass. The figures of the woman and the old man slightly behind her became black engraved figures on steel. It occurred to me that this is what it must have been like for the surviving ten thousand in ice-age Africa that some scientists think all modern humans sprang from, this largely wordless cooperation of The

Tribe, working together to solve a communal problem. No real dogma yet beyond the sea itself, work and play largely indistinguishable.

Just life.

Mason decided we were getting far too organized for his taste and scrambled right for me at the center. We tightened, "dressing the line," and one of the boys yelled "Closer, closer!" The dog feinted left and then bounded to the right, up onto the hard, wet sand, and the old man lunged and snagged Mason's collar with a coin-jingling grab.

"Gotcha!" he cried.

My moment of usefulness involved coaxing Mason—now leashed and humbled—into releasing the mashed and saliva-sodden gull.

"Thank you so much," the woman said, to all of us, and she led the boys and Mason up the path that wound through the sawgrass and rosehips.

Further down the beach it widened into dunes, with occasional stern signs warning people about bird nesting areas, fires, and beach erosion. A quarter mile away you could see the first neat, silver-grey, weathered cottages that spotted the dune-scape. Some sort of writer's colony.

Further off was an untidy jumble of picturesque buildings, docks, and boats—the local fisherman's co-op, along with bait storage shack and small rental office for kayaks and deep-sea fishing day trips.

There were also two boats that fit the description "yacht" to my way of thinking.

I walked up the sawgrass-overhung path and stowed my chair, T.S. Eliot, and blanket in the trunk of my stolen car.

Time to work.

Which is what probably spelled doom for the old tribal days, too.

* * *

Richard Denuzzio was on the phone but waved me aboard the *Rubric*. The deck space alone could have hosted a hockey game.

Denuzzio gestured toward a wet bar inside the spacious cabin and I helped myself to an Amstel Light that was set in a bucket of ice.

"I don't give a shit, Ralph, data-driven dialogue is what we're looking for. Nothing else. Phase one, we have prediction dialogue; phase two is observation, and when we get to phase three I'll hear about—"

He paused to pull a face at me like *Can you believe this asshole?* and then turned to paw papers at his desk, talking more angrily now in a lowered voice.

I sipped my beer and wandered out onto the vast deck. There were a collection of fishing rods leaning against the cabin, all very long and thick. Deep-sea fishing gear. But the lures were all wrong—big, jointed, treble-hooked rapala lures, bright plastic and clunky.

"Smoke, Danny? It's Danny, right?"

I turned to find Denuzzio standing in the cabin door with a handful of cigars fanned out.

"Dan," I said.

"Okay, Dan. Primo Del Ray, Quintero, Royal, Jamaica, take your pick. Nothing like a fine cigar."

I selected the Quintero, thanking him.

Richard Denuzzio (Ricky, he told me) looked like the evolutionary plateau for lard. Thirties, pale overlaid with recent sunburn, baseball cap with some team's logo, shorts, expensive new sneakers. And so on.

"Sandy says after you crew for me you're staying in Florida for a job?"

I puffed expensive smoke and nodded.

"That's right," I said. "Coaching job."

"No kidding! What, college ball?"

"Women's rugby," I said.

"Women's rugby! Geez! What, are they all big, hairy lesbos or are some decent tail?"

"Oh Sure," I said, looking out over the water.

Twenty minutes later Denuzzio had taken the *Rubric* out roughly three miles from Ash bay and now we were anchored, motor off, about halfway to the Isles of Shoals and the beaches of Portsmouth, NH. He said the second crew member he'd hired was due to meet us in Hampton that evening and he'd decided we'd loaf, have a few beers and fish.

"Hey, Danny. Let me tell you something; once we get to the sunshine state, my partner will be joining us with a selection of pussy so choice you'll forget all about your rugby dykes."

There were no other boats near us, the sea lake calm. Sunlight arrowed and darted on the mild ripples and swells.

"What kind of boat is this?"

"Goliath Motoryacht, baby," Denuzzio said, "Paid for by extremely creative tax loopholes!"

He cackled.

I laughed since it seemed expected. But I understood more thoroughly than he would have thought. I understood all sorts of things about Mr. Denuzzio—his scuzzy business dealings, his penchant for kiddie porn and underage sex, and the use of his boat as the setting for private film-shoots of the same.

But any need for understanding was irising shut with each moment.

"Say," Denuzzio said, "you ever play ball? You're big enough."

He had selected a rod and had stepped to the stern, trailing cigar smoke. I stood before the collection of rods, sorting through them.

"Rugby," I said, "and lacrosse, in college."

"Geez, Danny, you and rugby! No football?"

I slid a long black rod out of the stand, freed the lure to swing and unlocked the reel, keeping my thumb on it.

"Football, to *me*, is pretty much a pig-stupid game for numb-nuts assholes. Rugby's a warrior's game."

Denuzzio had just dropped his baited hook and turned to me with his cigar planted perfectly in the center of his kisser, like he was nursing.

"Stupid like—the name of your boat. Unless you were going for the ecclesiastical, which I kind of doubt."

"Hey, asshole—" Denuzzio said as I released the reel and swung the rod hard enough for it to whistle in the air. The line whipsawed out slightly over the water for an instant before those big rapala treble hooks buried themselves high in Denuzzio's fleshy pink cheek. He screamed, dropping his own rod into the water along with the cigar in a spray of embers.

"Aw, jeez. You okay?" I said and walked toward him as he clawed his face, managing to hook his left thumb, too.

"You fucking fucking idiot! Aaah! Jesus! Motherfucker goddamnit help me! What the fuck!! What—"

And so on.

As I approached, I whipped another arc of line out over the water, clicked the catch, and passed the rod once under and over the railing before dropping it into the drink. As it sank, it yanked him sideways, still screaming and flailing with his free hand.

"What the fuck are you doing?!!"

"Me, I like the medieval meaning of rubric. You know it? No? It means, *written in red*. I mean, think about it. Ironic, all that."

Denuzzio tried to grab at me with his free hand but batted it away and finished up. I hooked his left foot with my right, yanked him further off balance and—minding the hooks—drove his head down with my right hand, his neck hitting the railing with all of our combined force. His neck broke with a muffled crunch, like stomping a wine glass wrapped in a wet sock.

Satisfied that his neck was broken, I stooped before he could fall and flipped him up and over the rail. Splash. I checked the high-test line looped around the rail: one end hooked to Denuzzio, the other attached to the sinking rod.

After a few moments of searching I found the switch to raise anchor and fired up the engine, swinging the thyroidal elephant of a boat roughly toward the shore.

I looked back out over the railing and caught just a glimpse of Denuzzio tumbling languidly, sinking downward, the heavy test line taut with the boat's steady surge.

I scanned the shoreline. There were a pair of lobster boats off to the west, but neither were close enough to be a concern.

I picked up the rucksack I'd brought aboard and took out a cheap black flip-phone, hitting "call" on the only number it had programmed in it. They answered on the second ring.

"Accounts."

"Proteus," I said.

"Yes, Proteus."

"*Telestai,*" I said.

"Understood, Proteus."

And click. I closed the phone and tossed it into the ocean. I stepped to the railing. Maybe two miles to shore, maybe a little less. It was pretty warm, even out here. I checked the black nylon rucksack. Inside were dry clothes in zip-locked plastic bags, along with my scrambler phone, also in plastic, and a pair of black split-fins.

Some aficionados said paddle fins were better, but I found the split-fins were just as fast and easier on the ankles, especially for a long swim.

I slipped off my boat shoes and T-shirt and threaded a length of fishing line through the sleeves and laces, clipped a cluster of lead fishing weights to the line and threw them overboard. I wiped down anything I'd touched. Then I slipped the fins on, stuck my arms through the rucksack straps, and jumped.

* * *

Two hours later it was almost sunset and I was limping toward my car, my heel bleeding from climbing out of the water across barnacle encrusted rocks. Twenty minutes later I was driving my rented car from where The Guild had arranged for it to be waiting for me. The stolen car was still sitting back at Ash and I stopped there briefly to wipe things down and retrieve my copy of T.S. Eliot.

CHAPTER TWO

Welcome Home, Mr. Ketch.

"**WELCOME HOME,** Mr. Ketch."

"Thank you, Omi. It's good to be back."

I returned his slight bow with one of my own, though westerners usually did so awkwardly.

But Omi couldn't see that.

As far as my name goes, you can call me Daniel Ketch.

And Dan, usually, as I'm not fond of "Danny," though a few individuals can pull it off without it grating on me. Mostly, grown men with a "Y" on the end of their name are suspect.

"Kiku just brought your mail, Mr. Ketch, not an hour ago."

"Please thank her for me, Omi."

Omi nodded in a shorter bow, smiling broadly. His eyes were a bleary silver and tracked vaguely with useless muscle reflexes.

Kiku, Omi's wife, was even tinier than her husband and just as blind.

Now, before you think there's any weird requirement I have for blind servants or anything, let's get some things straight. I chose to maintain a connection to The Guild (even though it involves a hefty amount of profit-sharing, or "tithing" as we call it) just like I chose to make Wells, Maine, my *Eyrie*, as the trade calls one's home base.

Some Paladins—like Mors, for example—chose to attend to their own affairs and mostly freelance. I might do the same someday. But for now, I paid my tithe and thus got perks like the Toranagas for caretakers. Caretakers, mind you, not servants.

Besides, it was always nice to come home to somebody. And the Toranagas were far more reliable than some elaborate security system (though there was plenty of that).

The fact that the Toranagas were both blind wasn't in their dossier, but as it turned out, it wasn't really an issue either. They'd been living in the spacious and well-appointed caretaker's cottage on the estate for going on three years and knew it well, eyes or no.

My home was a renovated mill on the edge of a sprawling marshland that bordered on the Laudholm nature preserve in Wells, Maine. All brick with a pitched roof and small tower on one side, hardwood roof-deck on the other, the building had been a flour mill, then a feedstore in the early 1900s, then an inn and now, fully renovated, my home. My Fortress of Solitude.

My favorite place on Earth.

The first floor was where I spent most of my time when work or sleep weren't pressing. I liked to cook and had a huge kitchen to do it in, a dining room overlooking the lovely landscape of the marshes beyond the deck, a first-floor library and a large entertainment area with all the bells and whistles.

Too many, in fact.

The worst that could be said of my dream house was that it was a little stark. Amid the preponderance of Ikea this and authentic antique and quirky that, were many paintings and photos stacked against the walls, long awaiting hanging. I hadn't been home much, or for very long, in months.

I saw the Master Chief as I was walking upstairs to the second floor. He was standing on the second landing, big shoulders hunched in his peacoat, face as unreadable as ever.

I ignored him, pleased with myself for not jumping at the sight of him.

On the second floor was my private bath, bedroom, study, and meditation room. On the third was a workout room and a second, more specialized library and solar. On the roof was a hardwood deck, styled after a widow's walk with a gas brazier and telescope, chairs and table, all that.

And we can get to the basement and sub-basement later.

After a shower I returned to the kitchen in my sweats and a comfortable and paint splattered T-shirt and poured a glass of *Brunello di Montalcino* and leaned back against the butcher block island table to flip through the mail Kiku had left for me. Bills, an alumni notice from good old Logan College, and a personal letter, addressed to yours truly in a fine, copperplate hand, an anomaly in the age of email.

Zabu, a huge orange cat that I'd picked up at the pound a few years ago, leapt up onto the table and padded across to ram his head under the vellum envelope.

The return address was "*Dagny Constantine.*"

The name triggered a slow-motion avalanche in me better suited to the boy I'd been before Brightman Jones and The Guild.

I had convinced myself that I was well-shut of that boy and his weaknesses.

I opened it.

> *Dan,*
>
> *I've thought of writing to you a hundred times, but always decided it was better if I didn't. I'm still not sure if I should now, but this has weighed upon me longer than I can bear and it's no longer even totally up to me.*
>
> *You have an eight-year-old daughter. She's yours. Ours.*
>
> *I don't want to burden you and I don't want money. But I do need to talk to you about Rourke. That's her name.*
>
> *Dagny*

There was an email address and a phone number.

I set the letter down and scratched Zabu under the chin, looking into his cool, green murderous gaze.

"Rourke?" I said.

Zabu purred, eyes falling to slits.

I said it again, picturing a little girl to go with the name.

"Rourke."

Then Zabu sprang into my arms, nearly knocking me down. I held the big cat up to my shoulder like you'd do to burp a baby and looked out over the now shadowed marshland.

"Jesus H. Christ," I said.

As the Master Chief used to say, when he was still alive.

CHAPTER THREE

Expedient Murder and Its Rituals. A Word About Lord Henry. Para Bellum, Para Pactum.

PUT SIMPLY, I'M AN ASSASSIN, a professional contractor who provides Expedient Murder. I was scouted by an organization called The Thanatos Guild, following a murder I committed during my sophomore year in college. It's not public knowledge, but obviously, The Guild knows. That's how they choose you, screen you, all that. You got away with it, but somehow, The Guild finds out.

Finds people like me.

But we'll be getting to The Guild and *The Ballad of Brightman Jones* in awhile. First, there was ritual to attend to. With a will, I set aside the letter and its contents.

Will is All, as The Kestrel would say.

I'd killed several people by this point. Were I to be caught, I've no doubt I'd be executed. I am not a psychopath or sociopath or any other kind of "path." And spare me "God's Judgement." There is no God.

No one's watching.

Consider Andre Mackalry. He killed nine women between 1956 and 1958. When he was finally caught, Mackalry was raving he hadn't finished his "masterpiece."

His last meal request before his execution was something called "Bubble and Squeak."

His last words before they threw the klieg switch were "A doomed society kills its greatest artists."

Myself, I'm quite certain that a doomed society is better off without a psycho like *that*.

I padded about the big kitchen putting "Bubble and Squeak" together. That's my ritual after a slate, to make a death-row last supper.

> *From The New Assassin's Field Guide & Almanac*
>
> *Chapter IV. Some pointed Helps and Golden Laws:*
>
> *The desirable qualities of the assassin's profession: To be able to kill—and kill well—is not enough. A shark can do such, a wolf, an insect, a pestilential plague.*
>
> *The professional assassin may assume the aspects of an animal sigil, say, but he must rise above the brute aspect to dignify his vital work, thus does ritual become his balm and refuge.*
>
> *Following an action, you must therefore create a reaction through ritual. The method of the ritual is up to the individual to craft and devise, but comfort, dignity, and a peaceful aspect of emotional calm is the goal following an action.*
>
> *The specifics, of course, are naturally highly individuated.*

Bubble and squeak is British.

Or maybe Irish.

It's basically potatoes and cabbage cooked in a pan. I'd spruced it up a bit by adding chopped scallions, grated zucchini, crumbled bacon, and some chopped ham (just a quarter cup) plus plenty of pepper.

It was pretty good with some white wine and a green salad.

* * *

It was late now and just a hint of fall in the air. Fireflies winked and glided over the marsh and Mozart played softly from the kitchen speakers.

As I'd been cooking, calm did in fact descend as it always did during an after-slate supper, although drinking a bottle of wine might have helped. Hard to say.

I cleared the dishes and put them in the dishwasher.

Most of my groceries were delivered, but when it came to dishes and everyday stuff, I was all set. The Toranagas took care of the grounds, Omi doing most of the outside stuff and Kiku the housekeeping, linens, like that. In fact, when they first came, I had to limit how much they would do, if I'd let them.

And it was hard to remember they were blind, sometimes.

I picked up Dagny's letter and sat down to reread it again with my scrambler phone at hand. It's funny, the things that scare you, make you sweat. Give you the ol' butterflies, when you thought you'd outgrown normal fears.

The music, Mozart's Piano Concerto No. 12 in A major, stopped abruptly, followed by a soft tone.

"***There is an intruder at the south gate, Mr. Ketch.***"

"Visual," I said.

The flatscreen TV mounted on the dining room wall switched on soundlessly, showing a shadowy male form walking away from the now open south gate and across the lawn.

Other than being locked, I hadn't buttoned the place up much since I'd gotten home. Live and learn.

"***Should I engage sanctions, sir?***"

"No," I said, "monitor me on One."

"***Yes, sir,***" Lord Henry said.

I took a black earpiece from the junk drawer, flipped the mike out, and slipped the loop over my right ear. Several cabinets were free of cookware, instead holding various other tools in black foam padding. I selected the Walther PK380 with the C5 laser sight.

A pretty green, by the way.

I was barefoot, which suited the job, slightly buzzed, not so much. But you work with what you've got.

Of course, I could have told Lord Henry to engage sanctions, but then it would be hard to get answers from smoldering ground beef.

Besides, I was curious, both about who, what, and why and if I was efficient when slightly squiffed.

Omi spoke over both the speakers and my earpiece now.

"Mr. Ketch? Are—"

"It's okay, Omi, I got it. You two stay put and stand by."

"Yes, Mr. Ketch."

"Lord Henry, kill the lights."

"***Yes, sir.***"

Dark.

I slid the screen door on its track and went across the deck silently and vaulted over the railing onto the grass, leaving the laser sight off for now.

The south gate was a baseball outfield's distance away. I ran into the shadows under the wall of overhanging lilac bushes, tall as trees, and crouched there to wait.

A word about Lord Henry.

While it would be nifty to have an actual "AI" to run my home security system, the fact is, we're not there yet. Lord Henry was a very sophisticated binary computer program but still, just a machine. "He" responded beautifully to a whole slew of commands, inquiries, scenarios, and even variations of "shooting the shit," but you can reach his limits pretty quickly. When I first got him, it pleased me to have his voice program patterned after the actor George Sanders, whose voice now spoke quietly in my right ear.

"***Sir, all sanctions are still on standby.***"

I didn't answer nor did Lord Henry require it. Somewhere in his silicon guts he could "see" my heat signature and hear my heartbeat, along with my guest's.

The intruder came out of the gloom or shambled out, more like. He was not the stealthy, night-work garbed threat I would have expected but a tall, male shape of both rumpled hair and suit. Moonlight glinted off thick glasses and he was carrying a metallic briefcase.

Someone's gait—like the cadence of someone's speech—was something my brain tended to file away with reliable efficiency. I knew this man, from somewhere.

I switched the laser sight on and aimed for his chest, the center of the mass. A fierce, bright green dot appeared on the man's chest from fifteen feet away. I stayed in the shadows, holding the Walther in a standard, two-handed shooter's stance.

"Freeze, asshole. Drop the case, hands on top of your head."

The case fell with a heavy thud, but instead of lacing his hands over his head like he was told, he looked down at the glowing green dot and then straightened his tie.

"*Si vis pacem, para helium,*" the shadow man said, in a mellifluous, soft but somehow rolling voice.

I felt sucker-punched but responded without any conscious intent, so deeply ingrained was the training.

"*Si vi pacem, para pactum,*" I replied.

If you wish for peace, prepare for war.

If you wish for peace, agree to keep the peace.

I raised my gun, the laser now pointed into the night sky and maybe into space beyond that.

"Hello, Gardener," I said.

CHAPTER FOUR

Kitchen Comforts. Hogwarts for the Homicidal. The Eye of the Kestrel.

GARDENER SAT IN MY NICE KITCHEN, now softly relit with a word to Lord Henry, Brubeck's "Take Five" playing in the background. Gardener too, was slightly lit, enjoying his second Aberlour single malt as a means of recovery from nearly being drilled.

Why we were in the kitchen was a mystery to me. My guests are infrequent, but whenever I have them, whomever they might be, everyone wants to hang around in the goddamned kitchen, who knows why.

Gardener set his glass down and adjusted his thick, horn-rimmed glasses.

"That is excellent scotch, I must say."

"Gardener," I said, "what are you doing here?"

And how did you find me?

You see, one of the rock-solid assurances of The Thanatos Guild—once you've completed your "Three," that is—is that your choice of "home" is kept absolutely confidential between you and your sempai, the one who scouted you in the first place. Sure, I had people who knew where I lived but not many. And no Guild members knew except for the Kestrel and Mors.

Potential jobs came via an elaborate remailing service and "home," home-plate, home-base, sanctum, shire (there were plenty of slang terms, code, and gobbledy-gookisms for it; "eyrie" was the most common)but whatever you wanted to call it, was sacred.

It was where you were safe. Where you could rest and tend to life's simpler concerns and where you never, ever, shit where you eat.

Gardener sipped his drink and then arranged his hands neatly on the table as if he were about to begin a piano piece.

"Daniel. First, please accept my sincere apology at my barging in on you like this. I know what a breach it is and I'm rather surprised to still be breathing after intruding on you."

"Yes, well, let's start with—"

Gardener held up one neatly manicured hand to halt me.

"Please, let me speak, Daniel. I'm dreadfully upset. I breached your security when I picked the lock on your gate, knowing full well your security systems would announce me. There simply was no other way, as your mailing service, your phone numbers, all of that is denied me."

I was tired and getting an early hangover. So I clammed up and listened while I brewed coffee, leaving Gardener to his malt.

A quick word about Gardener and his place in the scheme of things—first, like all of our instructors at Guild House, I had no idea what his real name was. For all I knew it is Gardener, but I doubted it.

Guild House was, is, a school of sorts, "Hogwarts for the Homicidal" Mors called it. And like we were all strongly encouraged to do, the "staff" there went only by their codenames: *The Nightingale, Dr. Yes, Mr. Quark, Professor Artemis, Ms. Mercy, Iron Horse, Mr. Blue,* and *Gardener*, of course.

And above them all, roughly equivalent to a headmaster—The Kestrel.

Six men and three women, all varied in age and appearance, one

American Indian, one *Indian* Indian, an African American, and an Asian among the races represented, whose job it was to teach each flight of recruits the art and trade of expedient murder.

Gardener's specialty was, among other things, psychology and silent killing techniques. In appearance he looked like a dangerous Garrison Keillor.

"A week ago, the Kestrel went missing. There were no signs of violence, no clue as to where he'd gone or what had happened; he simply never showed up at Guild House after leaving his home. Believe me, even putting that together took enormous effort. At the end of that puzzling week, this briefcase arrived at my home. *My home.*"

He reached down and then set a steel briefcase on my kitchen table. Sixteen-gauge carbon steel plate, high security barrel lock.

"The Nightingale reached me via scrambler phone that she, in turn, had received this note along with the key, with her normal home-mail delivery."

He reached into his jacket (a move that makes everyone in my professional circles *tense*, momentarily) and laid a blank, egg-shell vellum envelope upon the table.

Gardener gestured that I pick it up.

Inside the envelope was a note, written in newspaper-print cut-and-paste style, with the golden key still taped to the bottom, obviously replaced after having been pulled off and used once.

> *To The Cackle of Hyenas-*
> *I Have Your "Man." Put On Your Ockham*
> *And Attend: These Three Heads MUST Roll*
> *Or We Will Send You HIS. But First,*
> *We'll Scrape The Inside Clean. Merlin*
> *Chose Proteus When We Took One Of His*
> *Eyes. We Give It Freely To You. We*
> *Will Return Him To You, ALIVE, When 'Tis*

> *Done. You Have Until Christmas-Tide To Erase These Three From "The Book." DON'T Think Beyond Your Means. You Will Hear From Us If We Don't Like What We See. Attempt No Contact.*

My hand was shaking slightly when I put the note down. Gardener peeled the key loose and opened the case.

Inside, there were three dark green folders. On top of them was a green bottle, filled with what I assumed was alcohol and inside it was a human eyeball, bright green, with the ragged end of an optic nerve twined about it.

I picked up the bottle and set it on the table. Gardener lifted the folders out and turned them to me and I flipped them open, one by one, only looking at the headshot photos inside each.

I closed the top folder and looked out the dark kitchen windows as Gardener finished his scotch in one head-thrown-back swallow.

It was far past midnight, into those hours when it's as dark as it gets.

CHAPTER FIVE

The Vault of The Id and The Law of Economy.

I HAVE A BASEMENT and a sub-basement.

If a house is like a mind (and I think it often can be), then the upper floors are the ego, the basement (in my case, a perfectly realized art studio) the super-ego, and the sub-basement is the Id.

As the Id is based upon something Freud called "The Pleasure Principal," I suppose my sub-basement would make a therapist look askance.

Originally designed as a bomb shelter when people were ignorant enough to believe such a construct would actually work, it was now an arsenal, among other things.

"Are these Edgerton's?" Gardener asked.

He was peering at a full color photo print of an atomic bomb explosion. There were twenty-two in all, mounted and framed throughout the armory, all various test explosions of atomic and thermonuclear blasts, taken during the forties and fifties.

"The one over the main workbench is Edgerton. That one's Yoshitake. I think he's one of the only ones left not dead of cancer."

Each print had the name of the "test-shot" beneath it on a small metal plate: *Hornet, Charlie Z, Bighorn, Able, Dog 3, Mike, Swanee, Oak, Kiwi*, and all the other asinine, innocuous names the atomic playboys gave their fucked-to-the-skies progeny.

The contrast between the idiot codenames and the portraits of raw, destructive power always made me feel in the mood to kill people.

It was a clean, dry, and well-lit space, mostly occupied by three adapted-to-the-task workbenches as well as a Barska safe, an American Security safe, a Gardall, and a pair of massive Victorian Twitchell Hobnail safes, all refitted with biometric keypads.

The sub-basement, or The Vault, also had a biometric keypad on the door as well.

Biometric means that the keystroke dynamics of my own rhythm of typing, my touch, is measured and "remembered" by the mechanism.

In other words, even if you knew the combination, you'd likely never get it open if you weren't me.

Gardener looked around and finally sat with his refreshed drink in a padded office chair.

"I must say, Daniel, that if you're bringing our discussion down here was meant to calm me, it's having the opposite effect."

"How so?" I said, pushing tools and an antique Walker Dragoon pistol aside on the bench to make room for the dossiers.

"It's just a rather disturbing room," Gardener said in his soft, soothing voice.

"I guess," I said. "I find it helps me focus. Lord Henry?"

"Yes, Mr. Ketch."

"Patch in the music down here, please."

"Yes, sir."

Respighi's "The Birds" played softly above the shaded work-lights.

"Better?" I said.

Gardener smiled for the first time.

"Not really. The combination of the music, the artwork, and the fact that those safes contain enough firepower to overthrow a small country is still unsettling."

"Gardener, you teach people—you taught me—how to kill in the dark! Quietly! In lots of nasty ways!"

"I know. But I'm tired, Daniel. And frightened. And a little drunk, besides."

I looked at him, this rumpled, professorial man, probably closer to sixty than not. And a murderer like myself. Like our fellows.

"I understand, Gard. I just thought our conversation would be better done in a place I can think—and know beyond any doubt is safe and private."

He looked startled.

"You don't trust the upstairs?"

"Not since you came into my yard with a suitcase full of trouble," I said. "Lord Henry is sweeping everything as we speak, believe me."

I opened each dossier, then lay the note on top of them, swinging the arm of an architect's desk lamp over all.

I reread the note and sighed.

"I don't understand this."

"Oh, I think I do," Gardener said, rising to join me on my side of the workbench, drink in hand. He peered at the note.

"A 'cackle' is common nomenclature for a group of jackals—that's us, I would think—the Guild. Our 'man' would be the Kestrel."

He was suddenly at his most professorial and I decided to let him continue despite my comment being sort of rhetorical. Gardener was, after all, very smart.

"Ockham, I suppose, would be a reference to Ockham's Razor."

"What's that?"

"It's the concept *lex parsimoniae*, in the Latin."

"Oh, that," I said.

"The law of economy," Gardener continued, ignoring me. "In layman's terms, the simplest solution is usually the correct one. A husband is murdered, look to the wife. A girlfriend is killed, look to the boyfriend. That sort of thing. In this case, I think the author means that we should take them at their word and not try to make this any more complicated."

"Or try to pull a fast one," I said.

"Just so," Gardener said.

He smoothed the vellum paper out, bending low to examine the newsprint cobbled script.

"These three heads are, of course, the three dossiers of their intended targets. So like our own dossier kits."

"And interesting that they chose three," I said.

"Indeed," Gardener said.

"And their threat to send the Kestrel's head is obviously a threat to kill him, but first they will get every piece of information from him they can—about us."

"The Thanatos Guild," I said.

"Yes. As to 'taking his eyes,' I shudder to think of it. But, regardless of whatever physical or psychic inducement, they have indicated Kestrel's choice of catspaw for the job they want done."

"According to them—whoever they, or he, or *she* is..."

Gardener looked at me with a sad expression.

But then, his expression was always sort of glum.

"Regardless, I would say that 'Proteus' is quite specific," he said.

Yeah, it sure was.

"What's Christmastide?" I said.

"Hm. The period that Christians call the epiphany season, say, from Christmas Eve to January fifth. That would be our deadline, it seems. No pun intended."

Gardener resumed his seat, taking the note with him.

I opened the folders on the table.

"I assume you've looked at these."

"I have," Gardener said. "I assume you know the faces."

Each picture was a black-and-white smiling headshot, like three middle-aged actors trying out for local theater or TV commercial work. The first picture, grinning like he was auditioning for Harold Hill in *The Music Man*, was Vincent Becke Mitchell. Yeah, that Vincent Becke Mitchell. Chief advisor of the family-values, uber right-wing group American Core. He pulls down fifty thousand dollars in speaking fees. Republican fat cats refer to him in reverent tones as "The Ringmaster."

Mitchell looked back at me with a nice blend of well-fed smugness and wisdom. Or maybe that was just the glasses, which were similar in style to ones Benjamin Franklin wore, save that these were gold.

The dossier was pretty standard in its information, if sloppily typed and copied. In fact, it was pretty similar to the ones I'd received before a job from the Guild.

The next photo was a middle-aged brunette, no glasses, horsey teeth, with subdued, tasteful pearls, sweater, jacket, hair—Kathleen Collins, United States Rep. from Nevada. She'd been flirting with running for president but had run into some trouble around her religious beliefs. Dominionism, the US being founded on biblical principles, march all the gays who couldn't be cured by Jesus into woodchippers, and so on.

Inside the dossier was a smaller photo of her husband, Buckley Collins, founder of "Under My Wing," a Christian rescue center for troubled youth. Buckley was also well-padded and was grinning like a constipated cherub.

The last photo and folder was of Jeffrey Chandler, of *The Jeffrey Chandler Show*, a fifty-million-dollar enterprise that you've no doubt heard or heard of. Most of his dossier traced Chandler's rise from high school dropout, to disc jockey, to pro-football team promoter and finally to A.M. radio's constitutional stalwart to some, incendiary asshat to others.

"So these are the three the Kestrel's kidnappers want dead in exchange for releasing him," I said.

Gardener nodded.

I sighed and shook my head, dropping Chandler's file on top of the others.

"What are you going to do?" Gardener said.

I looked at the vast dome of the "Mike" hydrogen blast at Eniwetok, five hundred times the blast strength of the bomb we dropped on Nagasaki.

"Well, I guess I'll have to kill them. But first you're going to answer some questions, Gardener."

For the first time since I'd met him in his "class" for silent killing techniques, Gardener didn't look sleepy-sad. He looked frightened.

CHAPTER SIX

Of Thugs and Palladins. Talking to Dagny.

MORNING. EVERYTHING LOOKS better in it, unless the morning is grey and rainy and cold as a bastard, which it was.

After a night's sleep—Gardener in a guest room and Lord Henry's cyber-assurance that we were buttoned up tight—we were just finishing breakfast. With every bell and whistle switched on, an army couldn't get onto the grounds, or even "see" in, as in infrared from a black helicopter and the like.

Gardener was on his third cup of coffee, the dossiers now on the kitchen table between us.

"I didn't realize you were a cook, Dan," he said, finishing his Eggs Benedict.

"My dad thought a man should be a good cook," I said, rereading the note for the thirtieth time.

The Master Chief thought a man should be able to cook, sew, iron, be a reasonably proficient mechanic and carpenter, be well-versed in the classics, and be able to box, among other things.

A flash of push-ups in the cold, stinging rain, the Master Chief's heavy boot coming down like a hammer on the back of my head to crush my face into the mud. The taste of blood, earth, and my own tears and snot and rage and made-up memories of Mom and how could she have left me with—

"—really going to do this?" Gardener said.

He was regarding me with his sad owl eyes, and I shook off the lapse. The Master Chief hadn't been around much lately until yesterday and now I could see him in the Toranaga's huge gardens, standing huddled in his peacoat and staring off into the marshes.

Stress, I thought. *I am under stress.*

Fuck it.

"I don't know. On the one hand, killing those three stooges wouldn't leave the world any poorer. Chandler and Mitchell I might even enjoy, but..."

"Ah," Gardener said, "I recall now you made it a point on your original profile that you eschewed the slating of women or children. How did you put it? *I'll kill bad guys*, I believe."

"That's right," I said, "but I also took the Kestrel's offer of choice seriously, the choice between Paladin and Thug."

I could tell just by the way he drew his breath in that Gardener was going to launch into lecture-mode.

"Yes, I always found the Kestrel's little speech about what kind of killer a talent could choose to be to be a bit of a... rationalization. Are you familiar with Kenneth J. Arrow's General Possibility Theorum? In it, he states that any procedure—"

"I don't give a rat's ass about Arrow's theorem at the moment, Gardener. I made some choices, starting with the black-and-white one you people gave me when you found me. I live with them, happy as a clam."

"Do you?" he said.

"Usually. The point is, I don't just kill like a fucking brainless meatgrinder like Bleach or Dupre. I'm inclined toward loyalty. I chose Paladin. I choose to slate the bastards who fuck us up, the ones who *need killing*. I'm no machine."

"Yes, of course. Yet you have some form of friendship with Mr. Mors—"

"That's beside the point," I said.

Gardener sighed.

"So. You're going ahead with it, then?"

"What does the Guild think I should do? Can we ask?"

Gardener looked frightened again.

"The Guild? If you mean the faculty of Guild House, I can't—"

"I mean *The Guild, the Thanatos Guild*, Gardener. Who are they, really? Who started it? Who pays you? And while we're at it, who are you, Gardener? Is that really your name or the name you chose after your Three?"

And why oh why didn't I ask any of this before? Oh yeah. They put a bullet in your head for Chatty-Kathy stuff like after recruitment. Remember Jeromy. Not Jeremy, Jeromy.

"Daniel, I can't answer those questions."

"Fine, then, fuck it, I change my mind. Let's just let whoever this is kill the Kestrel and then pull the curtain back on the whole thing and we can bet on who's gassed and who gets life. Me, I'm betting they'll dump us all at sea with cinderblocks around our necks and skip the usual legal crap."

Then Gardener surprised me. He leaned forward and buried his head in his hands.

"We're all killers, Daniel. That's what we do. What the Guild has always done. I can't answer your questions because I don't know most of—"

"Oh bullshit, Gardener! You don't know your own name?"

"I can't—"

"You don't know who pulls our strings? Brokers our jobs?"

"They're beyond any threat, Daniel!"

"So it's just us? Be co-opted and, what, work for whomever to do whatever like a fucking puppet from now on?"

"I don't know," he said.

"Where did the rest of the Guild House faculty piss off to?"

"I don't know."

"Why did the Kestrel choose me, for Christ's sake?"

"I don't know," he said.

"What do you think we should do?" I said.

"*I don't know.*"

I went to him and yanked him to his feet by the collar of his borrowed robe.

"You listen to me, goddamn it, I'm not going to jail or anything worse. Not yet. Not sent by some faceless fucks who think I'm their new puppet. Who could do this, Gardener? Who could infiltrate Thanatos deeply enough to make this threat? Who's good enough to nab the fucking Kestrel?"

"I don't know!"

I threw him back in his chair where he stayed crumpled like a gutted scarecrow.

I paced around the table. Outside, Omi was doing something CQ patient and tender to an impressive array of tomato plants. The Master Chief was nowhere to be seen. Good riddance.

I reached for my own coffee and saw the letter from Dagny, still under the wooden bowl where I'd tucked it the night before.

You have an eight-year-old daughter. She's yours. Ours.

"Lord Henry."

"Yes, Mr. Ketch."

"Please locate Mors and request his presence here."

"I'll do my best, sir."

Gardener stirred at that—restuffing himself like the scarecrow in *The Wizard of Oz.*

They tore my legs off and threw them over there!

"Why on earth would you call Mors, Daniel?"

"Well, he's my friend. Sort of."

I scrabbled in the kitchen junk drawer for an old pack of cigarettes.

"Besides," I said, "he's a Thug."

* * *

The day didn't look much better from the roof.

A fine mist was blowing in off the sea. I stood under the canvas awning that shielded the grill and the telescope case. I usually found this kind of blustery, wet weather sort of cozy, but today it felt funereal.

I tapped Dagny's number into the scrambler phone, another of the perks of continuing to associate with the Guild. I won't bore you with specifics, save that it's heavier than a typical cell and that it changes its codes about one hundred and seventy times a second. So there.

"Hello?"

Oh boy.

"Ah. Hi Dagny. It's—"

"Danny!"

"You got me."

A beat.

"I wasn't sure that you'd call," Dagny said.

"Well, here I am," I said.

Her voice was as I'd remembered, like maple syrup would sound if it could speak.

"Here you are," Dagny said, "scared as I am?"

"More, probably. You're used to the idea."

"Aren't you going to ask me how I know she's yours?"

Ouch.

"No," I said.

I listened to her breathe through another Broadway beat. I can't exactly say how I still loved her. It had been seven years since she and I had parted ways. But she had always been easy to love, lovely to look at. When I was with her, I'd felt lucky to be alive. That sort of thing.

"I'm glad you called, Daniel. And like I wrote, I'm not asking for money or anything like that."

"But I have a lot of it, Dags, I can—"

"Are you still a hitman?" she said.

"Now seriously, how many people are having a conversation like this right now?" I said.

She surprised me by laughing. She had a laugh that could make the moon want to join in. Memories swamped me, and I had to bear down and remind myself of the hurdles. No, the walls.

I'd committed murder once for love and had gone on to do it for money. Dagny had walked away after I gave Brightman his ticket to the Twilight Kingdom, and to make things even more complicated, her family was *connected*. Not as in emotionally close-connected but as in her father was Arthur "The Bull" Constantine and her sisters and brothers were all in it up to their ears and Dagny wanted no part of it, never had.

"Are you?" she said again, laughter lost.

"I'm seriously reassessing things," I said.

"I see. Whatever that means. Well, I don't want your money, Dan. Rourke is a beautiful little girl; she has a step-father—"

Yee-ouch.

"But she's autistic. It's pretty hard, though she's really, um, high functioning. Do you know anything about—"

"I know about what it is and what that means, yes," I said.

"Well, the thing is, she's asking about you. Who you are, where you are. Rourke can get really hyper-focused on stuff, and I thought, her counselor thought, that if you could talk with her, maybe, eventually, see her..."

She started crying.

"Dags?"

"Don't call me that anymore, it's like a pet-name, I can't—"

"Dagdelena?"

"That's worse!" she said, laughing again, through tears.

"What can I do, Dagny? Tell me and I'll try to do it."

"Well. Could you call her on the phone, to start? She'll want to ask you questions, or just tell you stuff. She can tell a lot from a voice too; it's, well, it's weird."

What the hell did that mean?

"When should I call?" I said.

"Could you call this weekend? Any day after like, six?"

"Yes. I will."

"Okay. Danny, are you all right? I mean—"

"I'm fine. I'll call this weekend. And maybe we could get together for a meeting, you know? See each other. Rourke, I mean. Can you send me her picture?"

"Let's try the phone first, Danny."

"Gotcha," I said.

"Are you sure you're all right? You sound, I don't know, it's none of my business, but you sound scared. Something. Is it because of Rourke?"

"I'm always scared when I talk to you," I said.

Dagny surprised me by laughing again. Just a little one but better than none.

"I'm really glad you called. Thank you for that," she said.

"Sure," I said. I waited too long to say anything else and she said "Bye" and was gone.

As I went back into the house, Lord Henry hailed me from a speaker.

"***Mr. Ketch, I have attempted to contact Mr. Mors. His phone is set for stand-by.***"

"Okay. Keep at it."

"***Of course, sir.***"

Not often but at times like my post-phone call ache, I wished I was built like Mors. He doesn't worry, that I ever knew of. He doesn't care.

CHAPTER SEVEN

Mors 1.

IT WAS RAINING IN BOSTON, *and Mors was glad; it would make things easier. If the pack ended up splitting, say, or work occurred primarily outside.*

M.J. O'Connor's was a nice Irish pub in the back bay, rich lighting, dark wood, very old world, or at least the world people expected. Mors had been there for going on two hours, sipping a beer and pretending to read the Herald, *waiting.*

Mors didn't mind waiting, never had, even in the service. He had many internal resources and accessed them with ease. For the past hour he'd been listing all the Latin phrases he knew and he was in the G's. Gaudeamus: let us rejoice today, gaudete in domino*: rejoice in the lord,* gaudium in veritae*: joy in truth....*

Suddenly he could tell that Foyle, Foyle Junior, and their goons were getting ready to move. One of their party had already left, and the body English of the rest was sort of flexy and "getting ready," somehow.

Mors could just tell, and that was enough.

He did one more and mentally marked his place.

Graviora manent*: heavier things remain.*

Mors sat alone at a smaller table with his beer and cooling appetizer. Cattywampus to him and about twenty feet away, Foyle's party had dwindled to a still fairly loud eight. A pretty waitress walked over and set the check down before The Big Man, Finbar, who took her hand and said something to her, his face as red and shining with auld sod charm as a canned ham. Big burst of laughter all around and Foyle slid the bill to some flunky. More stirring. A goon slipped the son's, little wee Foyle's, coat on for him as he stood.

Mors smiled. He dipped a boxty wedge in congealing cheese sauce, chewed, and finished his beer with a swallow. He was glad it was late.

Time to work.

Outside, the rain was heavy, cold, and windblown. Foyle and his company milled about under the awning, and then it was just Finny, Finny Junior, and two goons as the third lumbered off for the car, a weird walker, bouncing off his toes in an almost goofy way.

Mors slipped his leather jacket on and messed with his pockets, collar, deliberately hanging back from the entrance for a bit. He winked at the hostess, and she smiled.

Then he stepped out into the wind and the rain.

Finbar Foyle and son and gunsels were almost to their sleek black Lincoln, one of Foyle's muscle already holding the rear door open when Mors stepped up behind the tallest man and shot him in the back of the head and then turned smoothly and shot the second muscle just as he was grabbing inside his overcoat, two taps to the chest. The shots weren't loud; Mors was trying out the Smith & Wesson Model 29 for this go-round, a so-called "quiet" gun.

As the first man fell and the second was falling, the Lincoln driver was quick and prepared, and craning around backward from the front seat, he managed to shoot once at Mors. The bullet droned by in the moist air, cracking off the brick wall of O'Connor's.

Mors spun away from the open door and shot the driver twice through the passenger's side window. The driver fell on the horn and set it blaring.

A car had slammed its brakes on as Mors was shooting the Lincoln driver but just as immediately screeched them again, the big boxy ass of the SW wagging as whomever was driving decided to stay out of it after all.

Mors jammed the Smith into his coat with his left hand and pulled out the Sauer 38H with his other. The Family Foyle were hot footing it across Boylston Street, no traffic to impede them as the rainfall became a downpour. The car horn blared on in dull, flat fury—Someone's DEEEAAAAD.

Mors pounded after them. Finbar the elder was grabbing something out of his coat, gun? No. Phone.

Weel, none o' that, now.

Mors poured it on, boots smacking the water-sluiced macadam, and shot Foyle in the back with the Sauer. A much louder gun.

The big man fell in a spectacular sprawl, cell phone clattering off into the center of Charles Street.

The younger Foyle almost stopped to crouch at his father's side but then thought better of it and ran in a zig-zagging streak across Charles onto Boston Common. But first he did this crazy, flapping spin, holding his hand out toward Mors. Mors ducked but no shot came, though there was a flash.

Mors crouched at Finbar's side. The gang boss was still alive, glasses shattered, spitting blood, trying to hump forward like a beached lobster in the rain.

"Who sent you? Who—?"

Mors grimaced.

"Be professional, Mr. Foyle. Christ." He shot Foyle once in the head.

* * *

The Common was rain-roaring green darkness.

Noel Foyle was breathing like a hyena. He'd lost one Gucci loafer in the sucking muck and he'd shed his town coat. He hobbled along the edge of the park, in the dripping shadowed overhang of tree limbs. He jerked constantly like some broken clockwork toy, trying to see everywhere at once.

Sirens sounded off to his rear right. The car horn had stopped.

He considered trying to circle around back toward them but no. That would put him back in the open. Sobbing in frustration he tried speed-dial again. NO SERVICE jeered back at him from the cool blue screen.

Fuck!

Maybe he could just go further into the bush and just lie down and wait. Hide 'til daylight. Or ambush the motherfucker! "Noel," a voice said from the dark behind him.

Foyle spun, gun out.

Now, off to his left: "Forget it Noel, ye'll never see me coomin'," the voice said in a faux Irish accent.

Foyle shot three times in a broad arc. He was half deaf then except for a high-pitched, keening whine. More sirens swam up far behind him now as his hearing returned. The rain hissed.

"It's over, Noel. This is The Moment," the voice said. Conversational now. To his right.

Foyle shot again; the bullet whined off a stone.

"You shot my dad you motherfucker!"

Nothing. Foyle jerked the gun in a two-handed grip. North. South!

"And he's shot lots of people, Noel. Are you seriously feeling this isn't fair? Jesus, you two."

Noel Foyle swung to shoot right there at the terrible, calm voice when something exploded right in front of him and a hammer, a wrecking ball, smashed into his chest. He avalanched down a muddy, leaf-strewn slope, losing his gun, his other shoe.

He rolled to a stop, breathing in pig-squeals.

Mors walked out of the shadows, clothes black and soaked. He crouched over Foyle, rummaging his pockets and patting until he found the phone. He fiddled with the screen and scrolled through the pictures quickly. Some swank dinner elsewhen. Outdoors at tables. Wedding? Raunchy nude shots of a skinny black woman. Then a Patriot's game. Then Mors himself, far off but still recognizable, close-cropped buzzcut. Stubbled face.

"That was clever, really," Mors said, gesturing to Foyle with the phone. He pocketed it.

"Whoever you are...whatever you want us, me, to stop, we'll stop," Noel croaked.

"Don't be an idiot," Mors said, "it never stops. And I don't care what you were doing. Why would I? As to who I am, I'm The Invisible Man, Noel. You were dead before you brushed your teeth this morning."

Mors shot him. Then he walked off into the murky shadows, melting into the rain.

* * *

Twenty minutes later Mors was making his wet and squelching way through thick brush, well aware of the curfew and the very good likelihood that police were now milling around all over the park.

Mors kept heading toward the Park St. "T" and safety with dead-reckoning, his immediate aim to lose himself in the stone veins under Boston.

He took out his scrambler phone and switched it on.

"Accounts."

"Mors," Mors said.

"Yes, Mors."

"Telestai."

"Understood, Mors."

Mors hung up and tucked the phone in his jacket only to feel it buzz against his chest.

He answered and listened.

"Mr. Mors, I am calling you on behalf of Mr. Ketch. He requests your assistance at your earliest convenience. Message ends."

There was a deep, resonant tone, and the borrowed voice of Lord Henry spoke no more.

"Begorrah," Mors said.

CHAPTER EIGHT

Vault Detention. Lord Henry's Riddle. The Conspiracy Calendar.

"ARE EITHER OF YOU AWARE of the Council of Chalcedon in the year 451 AD?"

Mors and I looked at each other and then back at Gardener. Gardener sighed.

"All right. Are you familiar with the Great Schism in Christianity that took place in the eleventh century?"

Mors laughed, which made the whole thing feel even more like detention. Adding to that impression was the fact that Gardener was in his familiar rumpled suit, standing behind a table in the Vault. The gun safes and cabinets, the array of nuclear explosions, both leant further to the illusion that Mors and I had been kept after school in some weird special-ed detention room, one normally used for physics.

Or something worse.

"Um, Gard? We wanted to know more about the Guild. Do you have to start a thousand years ago?" I said.

"Or bring the Holy Rollers into it?" Mors said.

Gardener looked pained.

"I'm afraid I do, Mors, if you two wish to understand what the Thanatos Guild is. All our sorrows stem from religious decisions, if inadvertently."

"But I'll keep it as simple as I can. For most of its history, the church in Europe was divided between the Latin-speaking west—with Rome as its heart, so to speak—and the Greek speaking east, with Constantinople as its primary. Differences in politics, culture, various rivalries resulted in a schism in the church. The main bones of contention were doctrinal and—"

Mors lit a cigarette. After my initial frown, I reached over for one.

Gardener regarded us both with disdain.

"You wanted to know more about the Guild. This, you see, is where it was born. After the schism, like the aftershocks of an earthquake, various factions looked to their way as the true way. And built structures to enforce those beliefs. Surely you've heard of the Knights Templar? The Knights of Malta? Ah. Amazing. Well, these were Christian military orders. The specifics don't concern us save that the Knights Templar concerned themselves with defending the Holy Land after the conquest of the First Crusade; The Thanatos Guild was created to serve both. To serve all. The Thanatos Guild was born—according to my researches—circa 1053 AD, to serve one simple purpose—provide expedient, professional murder. For a price."

"Holy cow," I said.

No one got it.

More waggled a finger.

"Yes, Mors," Gardener said, glasses flashing in the shaded overheads.

"Was the Guild ever religious in its—urm, mission?"

"Never. Thanatos, as you both do know, is the Greek daemon personification of death. That was sum and total of what the Guild provided. Reserving its own internal judgement as to whether they would grant the petitioner at all, and if so, what payment was required. I have reason to believe that the Guild charged political favors as well as gold and was instrumental in starting, stopping, and forestalling wars and steadfast in keeping no allegiance to anything but itself."

"And now someone's taken the Kestrel and has the whole clubhouse by the nut-sack," More said.

"Essentially," Gardener sighed.

More sat almost slumped in his chair, one black-clad leg over the chair's arm. He reminded me of a cheetah, draped in the branches of a tree.

"Well," More said, "what's the rumpus?"

"The rumpus, Mors, is what, if anything, we can do about this," Gardener said, "other than do as the note commands."

"Look, the Kestrel was your sempai," Mors said to me, "not mine. And all that Paladin Dark Bushido hoo-hah is a load of crap, in my humble."

"Not to me," I said.

"Then what about this?" Gardener said, holding up that morning's copy of the *Boston Globe* with the headline:

"MOB BOSS FINNY FOYLE AND SON EXECUTED IN BOSTON COMMON."

"That's inaccurate," Mors said, but his face was grim.

"Even the Invisible Man leaves a trail, Mors," Gardener said, "and I'm sure the remaining Foyles would enjoy getting to know you."

"I *know* you're not threatening me," Mors said.

"I'm not. But independent or not, you are deep in the Guild's files, in some computer mainframe or other."

"And where are those computers, pray?" Mors said.

"Here we go," I said.

"I have no idea," Gardener said, "The Thanatos Guild is like Chinese boxes. A puzzle within a puzzle. It's designed that way. You can get angry with me. Threaten. Torture. It won't make me privy to things I don't know. The fact remains, if we ignore this threat, we'll all be dead or in jail within a year."

We all thought about that for a bit.

"*You* two may be," Mors said, but he'd sat up straighter.

"And if we do slate these three," I said, "or if I do, what's to stop 'them' from fucking us all over anyway?"

"Nothing," Mors said.

"Our usefulness," Gardener said, "but we could be in their thrall. And all your illusory choices—for both of you—might very well evaporate. Still, better than prison. Or death."

Mors sighed and rose and walked to the table. He stirred the photos atop the folders with one hand.

"I'd kill these assholes for free," he said.

Gardener stood looking down at the same photos, upside down now from his perspective.

"Lord Henry," I said to the ceiling.

"Yes, Mr. Ketch."

"Wait a sec," Mors said," I've always wanted to try something. Will Lord Henry respond to me, too?"

"Lord Henry, please acknowledge Mors in any query."

"It would be my pleasure to do so, sir."

Mors sat on the table.

"Lord Henry, I'm in a bind here."

"I'm sorry to hear that, Mr. Mors. What is a 'bind'?"

"A quandary. A problem I'm having. Why do *you* think I have a problem?"

There was a pause, which was weird in itself.

"Perhaps it's because of your childhood that you are facing a problem."

I was about to interrupt, but Mors held up a hand, grinning.

"I'm sure everything in my life stems from my childhood. It made me who I am."

"Why do you say that?" Lord Henry said (which was a little eerie as "he" hardly ever inquires, he *serves*).

"Well, I say that because I'm not you, I'm me," Mors said.

There was another, longer pause.

"Are you sure you are you?"

Mors laughed.

"Isn't that wild? It's like a Zen riddle or something."

"That's terrific," I said.

"It's in his programming, see? Heuristical pattern matching, so, all you do is—"

"Yes, fascinating," Gardener said, "but is this really the time?"

"Just trying to lighten the moment, ye gods," Mors said, lighting another cigarette.

"Disregard, Lord Henry. I have another question. What is an event that the following three people would be present at, if any? Jeffrey Chandler, Kathleen Collins, Vincent Becke Mitchell."

"I'll do my best to check, Mr. Ketch. It may take a few minutes."

"Understood," I said.

"So you're thinking about actually doing this?" More said.

"I'm just thinking, period, at the moment," I said.

More smoked. Gardener picked up a decanter of Scotch he'd brought downstairs following Mors's arrival dinner and poured us each a knock in three Ravenscroft glasses. He handed them out to each of us.

"Not some Freemason thing," More said, after a sip.

"No," Gardener agreed.

"The Grotto?" I said.

"Nah," Mors said, "not this time of year."

"The Bohemian Club—no! Bohemian Grove," I said.

"Exclusively male," Gardener said, grimacing after downing his glass.

"You really should sip that," Mors said.

"What about the Golden Cabal?" Gardener said.

Mors and I both shook our heads.

"Disbanded," I said, "for lack of a better term. They haven't met in years. Hey, when's the, ah, Bilderberg thing?"

"May or June," Mors and Gardener said, almost in unison.

"Besides," Gardener said, "there's no guarantee that all three would be invited to any of these. Chandler's a buffoon."

"Or that they'd show up even if they were," Mors said.

"Egos like that? They'd show," I said.

"Pardon me, Mr. Ketch, but I have some information for you. I apologize for the delay."

"Not at all," I said, "let's hear it."

"Jeffrey Chandler, Kathleen Collins, and Vincent Beck Mitchell are all invited to attend the next meeting of The New Alexandrians, this year."

Gloriosky!

"That's oddly convenient," Gardener said.

"Where?" I said.

"When?" Mors said.

Lord Henry's patient, George Sanders' voice answered us in reverse.

"On All Hallow's Eve, in Washington, DC."

CHAPTER NINE

Baikyi-Sa Goodbye. Psychopathic Etiquette. Mors Makes a Toast.

I WAS HUNGOVER, irritable, and scratchy-eyed from plotting, drinking, and smoking in the Vault until the wee hours. The morning, however, was a perfect, crisp fall day in Maine.

I decided to go for a run along a largely unused road that followed the marshes along the Laudholm preserve, after going through a series of Ashtanga yoga poses to limber up.

While neither Mors nor I had excelled in "Hands" as a method of Slate-work, the Ashanga was perfect for any workout, not just martial arts.

Actually, Mors could be fairly lethal with Hands. Myself, I boxed, and pretty well for a while, but that was all but useless for killing people, unless you wanted two broken hands.

After finishing the tough stuff, I sat on the grass overlooking the marshes in the Sukhasana pose. The sun felt good, the breeze off the water very chill. I got up and tucked a Ruger LCP in my Galco SOB holster, flipped my T-shirt back over it, and went off for my run.

Halloween was about three weeks away. Last night's discussion never quite gelled into a meeting of the minds, more like a meeting with me being the only one with a plan that didn't just mean rolling over like a dog and could maybe smoke these assholes out, too, in the bargain.

A very big maybe, though.

Our divergent views became more pronounced when dealing with motivation. Gardener seemed a bit freaked out to me, not the calm pedantic who taught us at Guild House. He warmed most to the idea of just going through with the triple slate and maybe at least getting the Kestrel back with his head still attached. Better than jail, perhaps.

Mors wavered between lighting out for the territories (it wasn't his fight, to his way of thinking) and back-tracing our tormentors and then the ol' slash and burn for their impertinence.

Hard to know where to start with that one though, especially since Gardener had said the entire staff of Guild House had gone to ground in their various eyries and taken their possible resources with them.

But Mors would help me, regardless.

Which left my plan, which would appear to our supposed yet unseen audience that I was going through with their wishes. And I would, with some minor deviations.

Neither of the boys were crazy about that, but I had the advantage of actually having a cohesive plan. Rock smashes scissors and so on.

The Master Chief was watching from the bluff as I set out. I glanced up at his face, but it was unreadable. Polite interest, maybe, even as he was thinking about something else. The wind was blowing steadily now, but his coat never stirred.

When I returned and was walking through my cool-down, I came upon Kiku at the edge of the vast vegetable garden the Toranagas had created. She was kneeling amid a row of acorn squashes and didn't look up as I approached. There was a small green plastic cart next to her. I knew she could hear me.

"Good morning, Mr. Ketch."

"Good morning, Kiku. What do we have?"

Kiku's smile was shy, her eyes as grey and sightless as her husband's.

"Honey Bear. Very sweet. But we have too many!"

"Well, I'll have company for a day or two more. I'll take some.

Listen, Kiku, I'm going to be leaving again for a while. I don't know how long. Would you and Omi like to travel anywhere while I'm gone? Take some time off?"

Kiku's tiny hands selected each squash and deftly snapped the stem, then placed it in the little cart.

"Travel?"

"Yeah. Well. I mean, take a vacation. A holiday."

"No, Mr. Ketch. We know"—she gestured vaguely to her own face and then fluttered her fingers around in a circle to indicate everything around us— "this place. Omi and I are always on holiday now. This is a restful place."

I squatted down next to her, feeling like a giant in some fairy tale; she was so tiny.

"You both work hard, Kiku. You can take some time off if you'd like to."

"Omi's not working very hard. He's asleep on the porch instead of helping me with Honey Bears."

"Okay. I just—"

"Is this a dangerous place now?" she said, brushing dirt off a squash like a mother tidying a baby.

I sighed.

"It might be for the time being," I said. "I'm not sure."

Kiku wiped one hand on her jeans and then reached for my face. Her fingers were cold as they butterflied over my brow, my mouth, my jaw.

"You feel sure," she said, still smiling slightly.

I had nothing for that.

She lowered her hand to the next squash.

"Mr. Ketch, both my husband and I knew much, much danger in the *Baikyi-sa*, opposing the communists in Korea."

"What does *Baikyi-sa* mean, Kiku?" I said.

"*The White Clothes Society,*" she said, "we knew duty, honor to an assignment, secrecy. More. We will stay here."

I sighed again.

"Okay. Lord Henry—the security program? —will keep things buttoned up and also respond to anything you require of it. The fence will stay hot, all that, until I return. Admit no one else. I mean *no one*. Okay?"

"Okay, Mr. Ketch."

"I don't want anything to happen to you two."

Kiku laughed, giggled actually, like a girl, though she must have been in her late sixties.

"Life is happening to us all, right now. Every moment. We happen to people, yes?"

"Yes. We sure do."

She patted my leg like a nana with her grandson.

"Go about the business of The Great Game of The World. We will stay and work in the nice air."

On impulse, I kissed her cheek.

"*Annyeonghi gaseyo. Haeng un eul bin da,*" she said.

"*Moreugesseumnida,*" I said.

"Oh, it means goodbye, Mr. Ketch. Goodbye and good luck."

Mors was sitting on the living room couch, holding Zabu cradled legs-up like an enormous, furry baby. Even upside down, the slit-green eyes seemed to project contempt.

You never do this, you prick.

Gardener sat at the kitchen table out of sight, but we could hear him on the phone, speaking in low tones.

"What are you thinking?" I said.

Mors kept petting Zabu, both cat and man seemed like they could stay that way forever.

"Right now I'm thinking you're the only person I know who asks that question," Mors said.

"Well, answer it."

"I'm thinking this a fucked-up, half-assed plan and the Kestrel is probably dead already, and even if he isn't, he will be when this shit-show is over with and likely so will we."

"I'm sorry I asked," I said.

"You should be. It's rude. Wait for someone to tell you what they think when they want to," Mors said.

"Ah," I said, "etiquette from a psychopath."

More shrugged. He did it the way the truly cool shrug, which is to say he barely moved.

"I'm not a psycho and neither are you. I just don't need the greasepaint. I respect that you do," Mors said.

"It's greasepaint to have a preferred area? Um, limits? You ever kill a woman?"

"Sure," he said.

Zabu was purring loudly now, like a motor.

"Kids?"

"Not yet," Mors said, "but anyway, *you* kill kids."

"*What?* I kill adults, Mors. The last guy I slated was a child molester and kiddie porn-maker!"

"So?" Mors said.

"So! So, he's not innocent, Mors. And he was no kid."

Another eloquent shrug.

"He's *somebody's* kid," Mors said.

We were silent for a few minutes. I didn't literally look around at it or anything, but I felt the house, the grounds, the Toaranagas. I liked what I had. I liked being rich. I liked—not thinking about all this shit, the eel-slippery grapple of moral debate.

Within a circle of less than a hundred yards there were four murderers near me. Five, if you counted the cat.

"Why are you helping me in this, as you put it, 'shit-show,' Mors? You're *The Invisible Man*; you could leave for Europe, wherever, and wait it out."

"You know why, Vladimir," he said.

And of course I did.

Gardener came into the room, paused to examine a suit of samurai armor standing next to one of the bookcases and then sat heavily on the other end of the couch.

Neither More nor Zabu stirred.

"You still insist on going to Guild House," Gardener said to Mors and he nodded *and* shrugged, which I really admired. Gardener sighed.

"As you requested, I have reserved Amtrak tickets for you to DC. The ambulance will be at the Ronald Reagan airport lot, waiting for you. I am now officially tapped-out on favors. It took a great deal of persuasion to get Buzzcock to do all that you required," Gardener said.

Mors looked disgusted.

"Buzzcock? What the fuck did you call him in for?"

Gardener gave Mors his coldest schoolteacher look.

"Unless Daniel is planning to use a squirt gun and a pick-up truck, Mr. Buzzcock is who we have. I have done my best."

Mors sighed.

"I apologize, Gardener."

"And I accept your apology," Gardener said.

"So, we're aces. The three of us are in it," I said.

"The three of us," Gardener said, and poured himself a single malt from the decanter on the coffee table. He served Mors and I next.

Mors dumped Zabu on the floor and raised his glass to toast. Surprised, I raised mine too, as did Gardener.

"'Three can keep a secret, if two of them are dead,'" he said.

Gardener choked into his glass, and I didn't even drink.

"Jesus, you two," Mors said, "try to have a little sense of humor."

Part Two

CHAPTER TEN

The Ballad of Brightman Jones-

I BOARDED THE AMTRAK TRAIN at South Station in Boston; Mors dropped me off in his most-prized possession, a thoroughly restored and enhanced 1950 Mercury named *Mariah.* We were quiet during the drive, save for a series of phone calls I had to make in order to finalize my lodging arrangements in Washington.

As I was getting my bags out of the trunk, passersby openly goggle-eyed at *Mariah's* gleaming, black mass, Mors lit a cigarette and leaned back on his car.

"This whole thing feels hinky to me," he said.

"That's because it is hinky, Mors. Call me if you find anything out and let me know when your flight's due."

"Yeah. Keep your eyes open," he said.

I went into South Station, bought a cup of coffee, and sat with a paper I didn't bother reading while I waited. There was an announcement on a recorded loop about being on alert for suspicious packages, while television monitors showed a film on how bomb-sniffing dogs were trained.

Things were hinky all right.

I got on the train and stored my bags in the overhead compartment. I never slept on trains, even when I was a kid. I liked watching out the window at the changing landscape, although sometimes it seemed like the worst ass-end of a town would be on display near the tracks.

I flipped through someone else's wilted magazine and already felt uncomfortable in the overheated compartment. But I'd never liked to fly, and besides, I figured if anyone was observing my movements, they might be easier to spot (and then forcibly question) on a train.

So far, I didn't notice anybody except a lot of bleary-eyed commuters, and none of them seemed particularly interested in me. The free Amtrak magazine had a picture of a tiger on the cover and that made me smile, a little. In a way, a tiger was part of the reason I was here. Part of the reason I was *Proteus*.

I could still remember exactly how a tiger smelled in close quarters.

The train pulled out of the station, and while I was waiting for the dining car to open for a fresh coffee, I fell asleep.

* * *

"*Hit me, mutt.*"

I spit blood on the cellar floor.

"I'm trying," I said, through my teeth.

"Stop *trying* to hit me and hit me," my father said.

And I did try, feinting with my right and skipping sideways to the right and, as the Master Chief seemed to buy it, shifting also. But as I tried to hit him in the face with a nice corkscrew, he batted it aside and nailed me with an uppercut that made my teeth bite painfully into the mouthguard.

I spit blood again and danced back.

"You're a bleeder, mutt. Always were. Now c'mon. C'mon! Take the Puncher's chance."

The Master Chief was handsome once but what was left now in his late fifties was cut and muscled arms vined with veins, a neck like steel cables, just the slightest impression of a gut and the silver ash of his short back and sides. He was more hard, more silvered driftwood, than handsome.

My father liked Infighting, which he'd taught me in both boxer lingo and action was close-range fighting. So, naturally (and from long experience) I preferred to Stick and Move.

He danced in and hit me with a flurry of body shots. I covered up as best I could, but when the Master Chief went to the body, it was like being trampled by a horse.

"Take the Puncher's chance," he said again, "don't rope a dope like you always do."

He made for his own corkscrew, but I slipped it and tagged him good on the side of his face, one of the few punches in the ring that had that satisfying movie sound.

"You're getting Shopworn," I said, (or *thopworn*, through the mouth-guard—the Master Chief, of course, eschewed them). He didn't like that and waded in, throwing haymakers with blinding speed, left, right, and then another left connected with my ear, staggering and turning me. His next right was a liver shot.

I backpedaled to my corner, but he was having none of it.

"*Shopworn* am I?"

He hit me with a blurring combination that felt like an avalanche. I fell slightly to one knee only to be knocked back up straight by another bolo that echoed in the basement.

"That feel Shopworn, mutt?"

I tried to roll with the punches, but it was impossible. His next haymaker was showy and stupid, but I really couldn't go anywhere, and it laid me out flat, the back of my head hitting the concrete before my ass did.

I managed to roll onto my left side, but that was all I had. I wasn't knocked out. That would have been better, really. A brief reprieve-trip to la-la land.

The master chief stood over all, breathing hard, glaring down at me. Then, *The Cool* fell over him like it usually did, and he pulled at his glove-laces with his even, white teeth. "How's Queer Street?" he said.

He walked across the cellar and flipped on his workbench light. A small black-and-white TV began immediately to babble the evening news.

I got up by degrees, as if miming the stages of evolution.

"Queer Street," by the way, is an old boxing term. Loosely translated, it means a fighter who's not on the ball anymore after having the shit kicked out of him.

So, it fit.

* * *

That night after dinner (my father prepared grilled swordfish, on the deck), he flipped my report card onto the table and lit a cigarette. My grades were all A's and B's except for the quietly accusatory "F" next to *Algebra*.

"PT, three times a week until that's fixed. We clear?"

I'd been hungry but chewing hurt. I'd also been working on *The Cool* for my own sake and had let it drop, though I'm quite sure he could see the perfect hate in my eyes.

Otherwise, my face was bland.

"We clear?" he said again, exhaling a blue plume.

"We're clear, Master Chief."

Seventh grade hadn't been going all that well.

* * *

And neither had eighth or most of high school.

I had friends, sure, and was even somewhat popular, mostly for my social value as a wise guy. But I didn't bring many friends home, and when I was astonished to be asked on dates (the pukesome term "hooking up" hadn't quite come about yet), I never brought them home unless the Master Chief was away.

A couple times he was away I even got laid. Thought I was in love.

All that. But even as those longings for whomever "she" was (largely in my imaginative head) waxed and waned, it was the waned part I usually welcomed.

Life was too weird, mine anyway, to allow anyone in for a protracted period.

Math continued to elude me but even if I nailed it from time to time there were always periods of "PT" for any and all infractions, both obvious (beating Randy Wallis into a hospital bed for taking my hat at the beach, say) and those that just occurred exclusively in the confines of the Master Chief's concrete labyrinth of a brain.

I worked at a grocery store during the school year and summers at The Portsmouth Fisherman's Co-op, crewing for boats, repairing boats, hauling boats and fish and other related sea-going hootenanny. I liked it all, mostly.

The summer before my senior year I bought a motorcycle, just a little Honda 350.

It was a lot of fun, that bike. The Master Chief didn't like it and said so.

"It's not just the idiot on the bike, mutt. It's the other assholes behind the wheel. You're going to get creamed by some shit-wit some night because you're not looking and Mr. Asshole never looks. Not for a bike, anyway."

I ignored that and went about my life. We were of a size by then. The Chief wasn't as eager to box anymore since a night during my sophomore year when we really hurt each other pretty badly (both of us with broken noses, broken ribs, the Chief with a cracked cheekbone and a broken left hand). But he could hurt me in a hundred ways, although by then—from time to time—he was a second man.

The Professor.

The Professor was a teacher at the University of Southern Maine, a job he'd gotten after retiring from the navy. He taught "Math Methods in Optics and Physics," "Geometrical Optics," "Physical Optics Lab" and the like.

The Professor, like the Chief, was an impressive man. A great cook, good and reliable neighbor, courtly to women and fond of dogs. Unlike the Chief, the Professor would invite me to share his impressive array of telescopes on the back deck. He taught me to play chess, explained the speed of light and particle accelerators and the Uncertainty Principle.

He also told me how much he missed my mom, how he taught her to skate, how she died so suddenly from an infection that started after having the most minor of dental work, how shocked he was that she was gone.

"From a *tooth*, for Christ's sake," he said.

The Professor told me about his own good for nothing drunk of a father. He told me one night out on the deck under the stars "I love you, Danny, with all of my fucked-up heart."

I didn't love him, exactly. Maybe a little. But I could really get to like him. The Professor didn't hit, or yell.

The Professor was pleasantly preoccupied, you see, with *light*. And I heard his students thought he was the cat's ass.

But he was a thin persona, born too late to be very strong. And the Master Chief was always prepared to step forward and get things *squared away*.

And, as his physical strength stuttered, the Chief found drink. It was gradual, but like a werewolf tasting blood, he began to need it.

My mother died when I was four. My memories of her are so blurred and sepia-toned shopworn that I began to cherish the made-up ones more, over the years. There were pictures I left behind after my last night at home, but I've always kept the portrait of the pretty young brunette that the chief had commissioned, long ago, in my memory palace.

She looks happy and elegant in that portrait, like the queen of an ever-peaceful country, one where they never had a war. Didn't even have a word for it.

On the anniversary of her death, the summer after my senior year, the Master Chief had been drinking all day. He took the keys to my bike off the hook and pocketed them. He didn't look or sound drunk, usually.

But today he did.

"That goddamned thing's a disgrace, mutt. It's *filthy*. Today of all days, get that fucking thing squared away."

My bike was in the barn, dried mud splattered all over it from a long ride back from Logan State College where I'd just visited to "take the tour."

He pointed to the tool bench, straight-armed.

"Rags, polish. Get to it."

He marched back toward the house, only slightly out of sync.

I make no excuses. People have had it much worse and turned out to be saints. People have had it much better and turned out to be serial murderers. I am *myself.* It was the Kestrel who taught me about choices. Anybody who says that because Mommy didn't bathe them right, they rob banks is a cocksucker.

It's *all* the Uncertainty Principle. Tricks of the light.

But anyway, I polished the bike.

The Chief came out after a while. Looked her over.

"Unacceptable," he said, and kicked it over. Crash. Kicked dirt on it. Walked back inside.

So I righted her. Worked. Polished. Detailed.

Afternoon came, dark clouds and thunder flickering in the west.

The Chief came out.

"What kind of shit are you trying to pull, mutt?"

He kicked her over and the rearview mirror bent with a screech. He kicked the gas tank a good one with a steel-toed boot. Stomped both front and rear spokes.

"Unacceptable," he said.

He walked back to the house, less steady now but twirling my keychain on his finger like a coach's whistle.

I stood there and considered. He had a point, now, anyway. It certainly wasn't acceptable.

I righted her, glass from the broken mirror jingled down onto my sneaker. Outside, the storm had come, lightning and thunder but only spitting rain. It was getting windy.

There was a can of gasoline for the mower on the tool bench. Gas can clean anything.

I doused the bike from stem to stern and stood back and lit one of the cigarettes from a pack of his he'd left on the bench. Then I flipped the match.

WHUMP! a blaze ten times what I'd expected engulfed my good old bike. Flames lapped the barn ceiling.

I walked away and hotwired the Chief's jeep (he'd taught me how, years ago, long before my Guild classes) and drove to my friends the Ewell's lake house, about twenty-five miles away. In the rearview I could see the whole barn going up.

What I *didn't* see that night, while drinking cocoa with Mrs. Ewell in their cozy kitchen, was when the fire swept over to the main house and set the roof ablaze.

Everything burned. Fire trucks didn't even show up until the barn had collapsed and the house was on its way down too. Our nearest neighbors, Mr. and Mrs. Robbins, had been at their daughter's wedding in Vermont.

There were a lot of *theys* in the following days.

They figured he'd been dead drunk, passed out, when the fire started.

They figured it was a lightning strike (there'd been two others in the area that night, one setting a tree briefly ablaze in Kittery).

They didn't investigate much of anything.

They gave me a scholarship for orphans or some fucking thing. Total Disaster Aid, something like that. A teacher I'd gotten on with, Ruth Godwin, arranged everything.

They handed me a folded flag at his funeral. Full honors, all that.

CHAPTER ELEVEN

The Lazarus Heart.
Jesus Can't Play Rugby.
The Empire Constantine.
The Shears of Atropos.

THERE WAS A SONG THAT DAGNY LIKED and put on a mixed CD for me, "The Lazarus Heart" by Sting. There was a line in it that summed up my first three years of college for me.

The power to remake himself, at the time of his darkest hour.

It seems corny now, I suppose, but that was Logan State College for me. A place where I could be anyone.

Though big enough and hard, sports hadn't interested me much in high school. Too many doors opened toward home in things like that.

But at Logan, within my first month I was eating at the dining hall with a loose group the size of a baseball inning. I was finding the academic work easy enough and I'd been recruited to play rugby for the Logan Norsemen.

By the time I was a junior, I felt like a king. True, I'd had no lasting romance, though there was usually company if I wanted it. I was good at finding women who were as emotionally distant as I was and had some nice "arrangements."

I had friends. After an enjoyable period of living in the raucous student apartments, I'd just been hired for a highly coveted spot as the head resident assistant in a brand new, co-ed dorm and could thereby live there for free and earn a paycheck in the bargain.

Then I met Dagny. Dagny Marie Constantine.

Gloriosky.

* * *

We were already in a circle, muddy, bloody and sweaty, but it was my first time holding the bottle to my head. The air was hot and thick and smelled like beer, sweat, and popcorn.

I was extremely happy.

Happier still when my mates from both teams pointed at me in unison with their elbows. Thus encouraged, I started off, and they joined me with a roar after the first verse (and just to give you the flavor of things, the tune used is "The Battle Hymn of The Republic"):

Jesus can't play rugby 'cause his dad'll fix the game,
Jesus can't play rugby 'cause his dad'll fix the game,
Jesus can't play rugby 'cause his dad'll fix the game,
Jesus saves, Jesus saves, Jesus saaaaaaves!

On the chorus, I noticed her.

I suppose at that moment, I felt saved.

The pub was in Massachusetts, an away game, and crowded with both teams and their supporters.

And this girl.

She was medium height and curvy. I know curvy in our dumbass cyber age is sometimes considered fat, but there are still those of us on Earth who like a woman to actually look like a woman. She was strong, athletic even, but for all that, the word voluptuous would have come to mind if I'd known it then. She also had glorious chestnut hair in a curly, long, tousled mess. The way it would look during lovemaking.

And—she was singing along.

I'd never led in the singing before; my almost subconscious habit was to never stand out too much, anywhere. Be part of the group, but don't spearhead attention. So it was easy to relinquish the lead to a buddy, and despite the sprays of beer to punish my jumping ship, I made my way across to The Girl.

"You know all the words," I said, "I'm impressed. And horrified."

We were actually pretty much shouting, given the noise. But that was nice because I got to lean in and smell her hair and skin when I was shouting, then immediately have her lips brushing my ear when she shouted back.

"I'm glad you're impressed. But don't be too horrified, I play rugby. Women's rugby. Intramural. *The Valkyries.*"

"Nuh-uh!" I said

"Yuh-huh!" she said.

"Where? What position?"

"Summers, Providence, and no stupid jokes, but—*Hooker.*"

"Okay. But I'm struggling," I said.

And so it went. Love at a rugby party.

Long story short, she was Dagny Constantine.

And I was Dan Ketch. Very happy to be him, too.

We hit it off, drifting away from the noise of the party to find a spot near a blazing fireplace on some truly sprung couches that were as beat up as they were comfortable.

"Oh, this is good," I said, indicating the fire. "I'm not sweaty enough."

As per rugby custom, we'd come to the pub directly from the field, so everyone was clomping around in cleats, wearing their muddy, in some cases bloody, uniforms.

"I'm a rugger too, remember. I'm used to partying with stinky people."

We talked about school and majors and all that. As it turned out, Dagny was a sophomore at Logan, majoring in psychology. I'd never seen her before but was delighted to hear she'd seen me, once at another game, once at a practice behind the field house.

"What made you look?" I said.

"Your butt," she said.

I laughed.

"Well, your butt and—"

"Oh, please, go on," I said, and she laughed with me. "And—you don't seem to play like you're pissed off throughout the whole game."

"That's noticeable to a female?"

"It's noticeable to *this* female, yeah. In fact, I really noticed you when you and another guy were laughing during practice about something. You were really laughing."

"Ah. That'd be Brad. He's a buddy of mine," I said.

"What were you laughing about?"

And here's the thing, I could see in her eyes—not in a judgmental, bitchy way, not that, but—that I was being weighed. Having my measure taken.

It might have felt heavy, had I not wanted to pass each test so badly. Cliché or not, I'd never felt this way about a girl before.

"Actually, we were laughing about something from a Monty Python movie," I said.

"Which thing?" Dagny said, smiling wider.

It was cozily thrilling to have her scooting closer, slightly, in her interest.

"Um. I believe it was King Arthur verses The Black Knight scene," I said, "something of that nature."

"'Come back here! I'll bite your kneecaps off!'" she said.

And her accent was spot-on, too.

So, goofy or not, that was the start. By the time the party was over and people were heading off to other, smaller gatherings or heading home, I was heading home with Dagny.

I went back to her apartment, which she shared with two other girls, Mona and Janine. No sex, just a terrific night getting drunk and high with three pretty girls (Janine had pot and was happy to share).

Dagny walked me outside at four in the morning, barefoot and wrapped in a quilt. We'd laughed all night throughout a very confusing game of Trivial Pursuit. I learned she was recovering from a bad break-up with some football player for the Logan Wildcats and she learned I was an orphan.

And then, outside, we kissed.

That kiss was something. You know how it is, when your mouths, tongues, just—fit? Where you breathe each other and the person just always tastes good? If you don't know about that, I don't know whether to feel sorry for you or not.

Of course, knowing it can be a sorry thing too, when it's lost. A devastating thing.

Dagny pulled my collar to make me lower my head and pressed her forehead to mine.

"This is the last thing I need right now, Dan."

"Thank you," I said, smiling.

Then a bright, fall leaf spun out of the dark sky above us, landing in her tangled hair. She brushed at it, setting it more firmly behind her ear.

"So, is that a sign?" she said.

"Definitely," I said, "definitely a major sign. Pay attention."

Later, she told me she pressed the leaf in a book when she went back up that early morning.

I have thought about that leaf since but never asked what became of it.

* * *

So, it was idyllic for a while. We studied together. She came to my games and their subsequent parties. Dagny took me horseback riding in Rhode Island, as she actually knew how (and owned horses). Her family was away so I didn't meet them, but her house was astonishing. Lavish. She seemed embarrassed by it.

While it must seem terribly old fashioned, we hadn't made love yet until the afternoon of that ride. We'd made out, and come very close to making love, we'd slept together in a bed all night, at both her place when her roommates were away wherever and once at my new room in Grafton, the dorm I was now head RA for. But Dagny had been hurt in some way in her last relationship. I waited for her to be ready.

We made love in a guest cabin her father used for his hunt club, on quilts in front of a fire we'd made of dried birch logs, while the big animals cropped grass outside. I hadn't understood that there was a world—a universe of difference between fucking and lovemaking. The instinct to wait, to be patient for her opening herself to me was maybe the first step I'd ever made as a lover opposed to a fucker.

Sinking into her, her strong legs around me and her hair spilled out like a halo around her head, kissing each other not just our mouths but all over each other's face, and later, being beneath her as she straddled me, I felt like my life as a man had actually begun, had a start date. A moment when I at last understood what it meant to cherish someone and love them more than you could ever love yourself or your own course through life. I came when she did, again, her mouth on mine, moaning in unison with her with her apple-spicy scented hair a tent over both of our faces and the rays of sunlight through the curtains highlighted in dust motes that caught the light like grains of glass.

Lovers could fuck, but just fucking didn't make you lovers.

That's what I found out in that cabin. Later I found out just how rare it was. Why it was worth building giant wooden horses just to taste its echo, again.

Talk from a blanket on a late fall day:

"You don't talk about your family much," I said.

"Neither do you, pot calling the kettle blabbity blah," she said.

"Well," I said, propped up on an elbow, "my parents are dead."

"Yes, Daniel. But you never talk about that."

I didn't say anything, and she misunderstood, rolling onto her belly and taking my hand in both of hers.

"I'm sorry, Danny. I know it must be hard. Harder than anything I know."

"No, no. It's just, ah, I don't know where to start, even," I said.

"It's okay," she said. "Okay, here's my big secret. Have you ever heard of the Constantine family? Of Rhode Island?"

"Except from you? No," I said.

"Yeah. Okay, I need to trust you, Danny. This is pretty bad."

"You can trust me. I'm ready."

"Okay," Dagny said, blowing air out her cheeks like she'd just benched a block of marble.

"My dad is Arthur Constantine, one of the biggest, most prominent Mafia families outside of New York."

"Um," I said.

"Last I was forced to hear about it, that included about ten or fifteen 'made men.' You know what that is?"

"Like, they made their bones, or whatever? Shooting people?"

Dagny nodded.

"*Killing* people, Danny. My dad is a murderer and the boss boss of murderers."

"Well. Is your mom nice?" I said.

That got a laugh. Dagny's laughter always seemed to bounce around my chest for a while after. A very good feeling.

"My mom is The Good Mafia Wife. She knows her place and accepts it," she said.

"But you don't," I said.

"I'm at Logan on scholarship," she said, "just like you. I've told Arthur I want no part of his disgusting empire. The Family Biz, as my brother Mark calls it."

"Where's he?" I said.

"At Daddy's right hand, in Providence," she said.

We were quiet for a bit.

"That's why, well, partly why I broke up with Brightman, my ex-boyfriend. I told him about this, I shouldn't have, but I did, and he ate it up."

Note to our listeners: Brightman Jones (yes, that's a name human beings actually chose for a twenty-first-century son) was the quarterback for the Logan Wildcats. A BMOC jock shithead who I'd heard of and seen from afar, long before I knew Dags.

"Anyway, Brightman and I had been going together for about a year but started having some problems; we'd been drifting for a while. It was about sex. How much sex, not enough sex, and a couple times he... hurt me. Like, physically. Don't look like that, Danny. I'm a big girl. But anyway. At first I thought he was really nice, but after a while I realized the only person Brightman really loves is Brightman. So after I broke it off, he tells me he wants to meet my dad. And he tells some of his asshole friends about my family. Do you know Gooch?"

"Thankfully, I know no Gooches," I said.

"I think his real name is Bob Gouche; he's one of Brightman's droogs. He says to me in Sociology class, 'Hey, Dagny! You a made woman? Want me to make you so Daddy will be impressed? You rich?' Shit like that."

"Want me to, ah, discuss this with Gooch?"

"No! No, I don't. I just want you to listen, Dan. I don't need anything fixed. I just wanted you to know a big skeleton in my closet."

"I guess I won't be meeting your parents," I said.

Dagny laughed.

"I guess not. Not for a while, anyway. Can that be okay?"

"Yes," I said, "but it's not a good idea to expect meeting mine either."

And she laughed again and kissed me. And one thing led to another. When she had an orgasm on top of me, she always ducked her head down and said the same thing, burying me in all that glorious, scented pelt, "Oh, Danny, Danny, I'm coming," as if she were astonished.

I knew I was. I also knew one thing—that this was the woman I was in love with. Real love. We must never be apart, because fate brought us together, to heal from dark origins.

Something like that. Young thoughts culled from too many songs and movies and America's favorite heroin: Hope.

Later, studying at Guild House, I came to know *The Fates* much better. Clotho, the spinner of the thread of life; Lachesis, the measurer of that life's span; and Atropos, who's shears cut the thread of life.

Atropos. She who cannot be turned away from her task.

Sometimes I wonder if *they* were already watching then, too. Watching for any signs of my talent, kindled to flames when Atropos's blades sheared together, throwing sparks.

CHAPTER TWELVE

Black Friday. The Fall of The Smartest Man in the World. Brightman Redux.

WINTER CAME TO LOGAN, and being a college nestled in the White Mountain region of New Hampshire, it was a very cold and snowy one.

With rugby over and neither of us particularly looking forward to the Christmas break (Dagny had been going to her sister's in Rhode Island for the past two years; I'd been going to the Ewells', though my relationship with them had sort of faded, making the visits feel awkward and strained), we decided to pool our money and go up to the Conroy Hotel and take a room for a week.

And I never thought about the "dark and stormy night" or the fact that I'd killed the Master Chief by burning him alive (and the Professor, that strangely likeable man, along with him). I never spoke of it to Dagny, just leaving it at that my mother died when I was four and my father, a naval officer and college professor, had died in a fire.

"Poor Danny," Dagny said once.

Well. Not anymore.

It was weird, though, that my fellow RAs had taken to calling me *Chief*, which was meant as an affectionate nickname, I know.

Still.

Over the fall and early winter, Dagny and I loved each other well and school seemed like a play where I knew the story and it was a good one. I talked a potential suicide off the seventh-floor ledge of Grafton, an incredibly fat and acne-riddled boy named Mark Farazzo ("Fatty" Farazzo, of course). He always wore a battered unicorn horn baseball cap, complete with ears.

Anyway, that was the worst problem I had up to that point, and it wasn't a problem at all. Farazzo came in after an hour of cop-movie clichés on both our parts and plenty of attention from the students watching. I truly felt like a hero.

I think it actually helped him, socially, too. He'd acquired a kind of mildly scandalous fame.

The Friday before Christmas break, I was scheduled to be on duty overnight and Dagny had been invited to a big Christmas party, Catelleros—the restaurant she waitressed at—was having for its employees. The party was going to be at the Shadaquaw Ski Lodge, not far from where we'd planned to go for our little pre-Christmas getaway.

Early Friday night, Dagny called before leaving for her wingding.

"Hi."

"Hi," I'd say.

And then she'd say:

"*Hiiiiii.*"

And I'd say it back in the same drawl of pleasure.

I know it borders on the retarded, but oh, those were the days, love all 'round. The deliciously happy joy of just having each other.

"Are you still on duty tonight?"

"I am," I said.

"Well, I'm going with Janine to the Shad. I won't be too late. Justine's driving—"

"Oh, boy, you can get plastered," I said.

"I will not! Hey, when do you get off?" she said.

"With the dawn, baby."

"Come to my apartment when you're done. My bitches have both left for vacay, so..."

"Okay."

"Wake me up, *that* way," Dagny purred.

Use your imagination.

We'd made love that morning and I remember we weren't particularly careful. Dagny said it was all right, cycle-wise.

In my dorm there were two guys, roommates, Dennis Allen and Kent Wyllis. I wasn't close friends with either, but we all got on. They were intellectual rivals of the worst, if hilarious, sort, and that Friday they had arranged a contest: "The Smartest Man in the World" contest.

The idea was that they had combined seven Trivial Pursuit games, various specialized ones included, that would take literally all night to play. Whenever someone missed a question, that someone would drink a shot.

They'd made a scoreboard, a poster with two opposing pictures of "The Thinker" statue over their names, between which a dunce cap could be moved depending upon who was ahead.

College fun at its finest.

It was the kind of thing that, as chief RA, I tended to tolerate if things were kept fairly mellow, especially before a break. I freely admit that was a mistake and absolute, willful negligence on my part.

By nine that night, I had a three quarters empty dorm, with most of the residents on seven watching the contest. I didn't even bother doing 'rounds, just set the intercom on "listen" to each floor's speakers and sat at the lobby front desk, reading *Rolling Stone.*

Occasionally I'd look up at the sounds of doors opening and closing, snatches of music or conversation and on seven, the sounds of laughter, cheers and groans as the two Smartest Men in the World dueled it out.

A lot of what happened I found out later from Janine and a few other people. It was fairly easy to get answers from kids, especially when I frightened them without even trying, after.

Dagny went to Shadaquaw Lodge with Janine, whom she did not know all that well; they'd become roommates mostly out of convenience. Waiting in line for drinks, they ran into Brightman and Gouche and some other members of the Logan football team. Justine was dazzled by Brightman and his fellow Centurions, and at his most civil and charming, he invited the two of them to join his group for a drink. Just one. Old time's sake. All that.

Janine got very drunk, very fast. Shifted her interest to Bob "Gooch" Gouiche, who suggested they go someplace else, and Dagny said they could do what they want, but she wanted to go home.

Brightman said that he'd take her.

And that's what he did.

* * *

"Chief."

I'd been standing just outside the dorm lobby entrance, trying to get cell phone reception. It had started to spit snow from a slate-grey sky.

"You better get in here," Lisa said, looking both amused and concerned.

I'd tried to call Dagny twice and didn't get a signal, which was par for the course around much of the campus.

Nick and Lisa were my fellow RAs that night, and as I went in, Nick spun the speaker on the counter around to face me. All I could hear were screams, predominant among them a male voice screaming "*I am supreme!*" and others screaming "*No!*" "*Stop it!*" (and this was key) "*Put the sword down!*"

Not a sentence you want to hear on a night you thought you could go light on regarding rounds.

The elevator was way too slow, so we took the stairs.

What we found on seven was funny and ridiculous. Most of the spectators had fled, not out of fear of the situation, but fear of getting written up for drinking in the dorm.

Me and my two fellow RAs found a loose knot of people still on the floor, as well as what seemed to be about a thousand Trivial Pursuit cards scattering the hallway.

Dennis Allen stood in the center of them, tall and thin and wearing only boxer shorts and a Santa hat and holding a civil war cutlass.

"I am supreme. I am *intellect*, at its most...something."

He swayed, absolutely plastered.

"Where's Kent?" Lisa said.

"Let's drop the sword, Dennis," I said, "you could hurt someone."

"Mmmm," Dennis said and staggered as he about-faced, abruptly, stalking back into the room he shared with Kent.

Lisa, Nick, and I followed, me in the lead, calling over my shoulder for everyone to go to their rooms and that all lounges were closed.

At that moment, I figured the whole thing as a moderate fuck-up. I'd hear about it, but things would work out.

The room was absolutely trashed, Trivial Pursuit board slashed in half, whiskey bottles everywhere and board pieces scattered throughout. It was cold, too, cold enough to see your breath as both slider windows were wide open and both screens were out.

A multi-colored rock-climbing rope was whipsawing back and forth, stretched taut over the windowsill, the other end tied to the leg of a bureau which was flipped over at a disjointed angle by the weight of whatever was at the other end.

Lisa peered out the window and spun back to me.

"Dan!"

I freely admit that we should have grabbed the sword. It's just neither Dennis nor Kent had ever been any trouble, to anyone, not even each other.

I joined Lisa at the window and looked down to see Kent Wyllis hanging from the end of the rope about six feet below the window ledge, the rope cinched up around his armpits. He was unconscious, though I did see his head jerk when Lisa yelled his name.

Everything was very quick after that.

I had the rope in my hand; Lisa was reaching to help me and almost laughing a little, and Dennis, forgotten, said, "Death to the dumb!"

And he swung the sword, parting the rope. It zipped through my grasp, burning my palm before I could even close it. Kent Wyllis fell without a sound, spinning once as his head hit the sixth-floor ledge, and seemed to fall in a strobe light as he passed each lit window and brick wall, alternating light and dark until he hit the ground.

* * *

There were frantic phone calls amid screams and tears and eventually a crowd of pre-holiday students. Every piece of emergency equipment from the campus cops to the town fire and police department gathered and every color of roof-rack light washed and pulsed across the building, front and back.

It started to snow in earnest.

I would have called both boys' parents if the cops had let me, but by then I was virtually under house arrest. They took Dennis away, looking dazed and stupid, and they took Kent's body and my career as an RA—and likely a student at Logan—was as dead as Julius Caesar.

And throughout, calling, calling, calling Dagny and getting a direct-to-voicemail that made me hot and cold and angry and finally, terrified.

By one thirty a.m. it was over, the dorm quiet and me and my former staff relieved of our duties until further notice.

The second the campus cop's ass hit the chair behind the front desk, I bolted.

The lights were on in her apartment.

I found her in the bathtub.

She was sitting in a steam-shrouded claw-foot tub, sitting up straight with her head hanging down, hair sopping and tangled.

"Dags? Are you all right?"

Something in me said "Don't touch her." I felt like I'd walked out of one horror movie and into another.

"No. I'm sorry. I'm not all right."

I stepped closer; the bathroom felt like a cauldron after the run through the cold night.

"*Dagny, what's wrong*? I've been trying to reach you."

"I lost my phone. It's gone," she said.

"Dagny." I knelt down. For some reason my hands were shaking. I reached out for her shoulder.

"*Don't*. Please. I'm sorry. But please, don't touch me."

"Dags, what is it?"

She reached up out of the steaming, soapy water and pulled her hair back. Her lip was spilt in two places. One of her eyes was purple and shiny-tight with swelling. Her nose looked swollen. Her eyes were glassy. Feral. Unknown to me.

A rage, sickening and enormous, filled me.

"*What happened?! Who did this?*"

"Daniel. I'm going to answer you. And if you do anything, *anything* but just listen, I will never see you. Or speak to you. Again."

"All right," I said. Not to agree. But to hear. To know.

"Justine and I met Brightman and Bob at the Shad. Justine wanted to hang out with their group. I didn't, but she drove. It was getting late, and she wouldn't leave, and I couldn't get a signal to call you and you were on duty. And Brightman offered to drive me home."

Black dots caromed around my peripheral vision, a snowstorm of black ash.

"Only, he took me to Gooch's condo. Someplace in Hooksum. He threw my phone out th-th-the window. *No—don't—*I a-and at first I wouldn't go in because it was freezing and I couldn't just walk anywhere. So I went in, but Justine, they were already there too, in Bob's car, and they went upstairs, and when he, I tried, when he, he... I tried to scream, and Brightman hit me. And he kept his hand over my mouth while he raped me."

I shook the black blizzard away.

"We have to call the—"

"No," she said.

"We have to! You shouldn't even wash because—"

"NO."

"*For God's sake, Dagny, why!?*"

She looked at me, sitting there, hair in her face again.

"Because my father will *kill* him. My brother *will kill him*. They will kill him for *days*."

And oh, I shouldn't have said it, but I was losing this shiny new self.

"*So what?*"

Dagny just looked at me.

"So. What. So—I don't want someone *murdered*, Daniel. I don't want my father or my brother arrested and ruin the rest of my mother and my sister's lives, Daniel. I don't want to go home for a wedding or some fucking thing and sit there thinking *Oh, there's my dad, hey! That reminds me of the time I was raped by that fuck Brightman and Daddy and Nick chopped him up in a warehouse!* DO YOU UNDERSTAND ME!!?"

I did. I didn't. I was falling, somehow. That first, pin-wheeling sway back over the precipice.

"What do you want me to do?" I said.

She was quiet for a long time.

"I want you to leave. I'm sorry, but I have to...go home. I need to rest and—I don't know. Please go. I'm sorry."

Then we were both quiet for a long time.

Then I left.

CHAPTER THIRTEEN

Kurt Vonnegut's Asshole. Falling Through the Branches.

I WAS ABLE TO STAY IN GRAFTON HALL for the break. A group of firemen were staying in the first-floor lounge for the whole vacation, going through some training on Shadaquaw mountain and sleeping in the dorm, using the showers and lounge kitchen, TV, and so on.

I'd been notified to expect a meeting with Dean Fletcher the day before the spring semester. I assumed that the topics of discussion would be my dismissal and possible charges. Plus a lawsuit, who knows?

I called Dagny, oh, thirty times? She would not return my calls, and finally her mother called me back.

"She doesn't want to talk to you, do you understand that, sir?"

Icicles grew and hung from the phone on that one. Clearly, Mrs. Constantine thought *I'd* done some something awful to her daughter. Maybe I had, too, I couldn't think straight.

The firemen were there to learn all about Winter Rescue Training, I came to find out. One night, I was trying to fix their cable connection in the lounge and overheard them talking.

"Capinelli, you going in the water tomorrow?"

"Yeah," the youngest among them said back. There was a chorus of knowing laughter from the others.

"Nobody's goin' if we don't have at least four inches. Preferably six."

"Capinelli's got at *least* four!"

More laughter. When in doubt, try a dick joke.

The point was, I gleaned, after listening to more of their conversation, was that four to six inches of ice was what you needed—to walk on. Or skate. Or ice fish. Or practice with an environment suit, like these guys were planning to do.

After a little research, I found out even two inches could usually hold a person.

But you'd need seven or eight to hold a car.

* * *

It's hard to describe, let alone remember how I felt that winter. What happened to Dagny, her absence, missing her, was a constant agony. What had happened to Kent was also horrible, but this felt worse, however much a bastard it made me to feel that way.

The point is, there was no refuge.

Until, that is, I seriously began planning how to murder Brightman Jones.

The first, vague idea of it, the "*Could I do it*?" brought my appetite back a little. My first vague plan of how to go about it gave me my first, peaceful, dreamless night's sleep.

Winter break at Logan lasts from December 17th to January 14th.

I had my plan tightened up and ready with almost a week to spare.

* * *

Student directories are easy enough to access, especially for an RA, disgraced or not. Brightman Jones, Bob Gouche, and some other football knob-job named Jerry "*Beaver*" Larson all lived in an apartment about a mile from campus in a place called "The Gulag."

The Gulag was called the Gulag because a lot of the old student apartments built during the early fifties or so were now decrepit and abandoned. It was a creepy ghost-townesque place, especially in the winter, but still spotted with a couple inhabitable buildings that had been privately refurbished.

Between the Gulag and campus was a large hill called The Crest, where a little business that used the same name rented out inner tubes for people to go sliding with, served coffee, soda, hot cocoa, and hot-dogs. Cheap winter fun.

During the spring and summers, it served the same stuff to anybody using the little artificial beach on the edge of Lake Wendigo, which it faced, the same inner tubes to now float in.

Behind The Crest sledding hill was a dirt road that ran around the entire lake and was reportedly a great place to snowmobile in the winter.

There were several parking areas with warped and faded picnic tables which also served year 'round as places to start a fire, grill out, drink or get laid.

It had been very cold that winter, but I drove out to Wendigo just the same to look it all over, count the ice-fishing shacks on the far side of the lake, watch the skaters, and casually inquire at The Crest over a cup of coffee about the thickness of the ice.

* * *

There was a supply closet for spring groundskeeping in the dorm. A week or so before the boys and girls were due back at the school, I was standing in it, examining the one-man, gas-powered earth auger. Perfect for digging holes for plants, little trees and so on. And also, it looked an awful lot like the powered ice-auger the firemen had been using, except theirs was spanking new silver and this was a banged-up orange.

The bit looked the same.

The ice-saw, that I had to buy.

* * *

I was driving an absolute shit-box of a Saab in those days and had to take a second running start to reach the top of the little picnic overlook I wanted. The road was paved but caked with ice and packed snow.

Brightman drove a BMW, though, and it would probably have the muscle to zip right up there. It was ten on Saturday night, two days before the others were due back. The weather was supposed to get above freezing, with no precipitation expected besides squalls, cloudy throughout the week.

That was good; I didn't want moonlight, next week or now. And I didn't want freezing temperatures.

There was no guardrail past the picnic area, just a gradually increasing slope of scrub brush that led to the lake. Where the ground and the ice co-mingled, a few small rocks protruded from the ice at the lake's edge.

I used the ice-saw to make a mark in the snow down the slope to the edge of the ice, taking care to stick to a straight line. The snow wasn't more than five inches deep and frozen to a hard crust.

I walked out onto the ice, it's surface all but free of snow from the wind and heel-toed what I'd already counted out on land to be thirty feet. Then I scraped an "X" about fifteen feet by twenty feet, scraping a third line through the middle of the "X" to make a crude asterisk.

Then it struck me that I'd drawn Kurt Vonnegut's cartoon of his own asshole, writ large, which got me laughing.

Laughing felt good. Nothing else had felt like much of anything since Mrs. Constantine had given me the heave-ho over the phone.

I'd worn heavy leather gloves, a watch-cap and long-johns under a sheep-herder's jacket, jeans, heavy socks, and hiking boots, but the wind seemed to cut right through all of it.

I went back up to the car for the auger. It was distressingly loud, but nobody seemed to give a shit. No lights on the far shore that hadn't already been there. No snowmobiles.

At one point a shuddering, thunderous crack had run along ahead of me and put my heart in my mouth, but that was all.

Creepy, though. Because I knew for a fact that under my feet was roughly thirty feet of cold, black water.

I cut holes at each point of the asterisk and at its center. Then I set to hand-sawing from hole to hole. The wind picked up, and it was sweaty work combined with a frozen face. By the end of the first hour, I had a line and a half cut and had stripped off my coat and hat. By midnight both my palms were blistered raw and weeping.

But it was done.

I had another heart-thudding moment when, at the center of the star, there was a crack like a gunshot and water spurted up from all seven, slush-filled holes to splatter on the surface, while the wedge I was standing on broke away and keeled up on one end while sinking behind me.

I scampered off to the side and all became flat and still again.

I was home and in bed by two a.m., the auger back in the shed and the ice-saw javelined off into the woods a mile from the lake.

I slept and it brought the Master Chief, striding unharmed through the hallways of a burning house in full uniform, saying:

"*Unacceptable, mutt, unacceptable!*"

Monday was difficult. More harsh snaps of the branches that had supported my tree-house life as something other than the *father-killer*, in my mind.

Dagny did not return to school. When I went to her place, Justine wouldn't even come out, but Mona came to the door and greeted me cautiously, having little to add beyond, "I think she's taking a semester off."

"Do you have her new cell number?" I said.

"I think you'd really better leave, Dan."

Snap.

The meeting with the dean was short and sweet. Maria, his secretary, was openly hostile toward me, telling me to wait with open contempt on her face.

I was fired for "gross negligence of duty." The school had avoided a lawsuit and so, apparently, had Dennis the Swordsman. The dean, at my inquiry, informed me that The Smartest Man in the World was in a mental health facility in Stanton, NH.

I was to turn in my keys. I had a two-week window to find alternate housing. My scholarship was kaput. I wasn't suspended, but how I could afford to stay was seriously in question. The dean explained that the religious beliefs of Kent's grieving parents "was all that saved you from a lawsuit."

Neither of us offered to shake hands.

Snap.

Back at Grafton, I was roundly avoided, except by Fatty Farazzo, who was sans unicorn cap and markedly acne-free. He hugged me.

"You saved my life, man. If there was anything I could do..."

Sorry, Fatty. That just didn't do it for me.

And Lisa, my best friend on staff, would not answer her door. She spoke through it, sounding alien.

"We'll talk later, Danny. Okay?"

Snap.

Snap.

Snap.

I fell down through the dark, breaking branches all the way down, landing feet first in the country of Murder.

So be it.

CHAPTER FOURTEEN

On the Ice. Rugby Versus Football. Turn with the Skid.

BRIGHTMAN JONES, back from Christmas break, didn't look like a rapist. He didn't act like a rapist.

I watched him unpack his BMW, talk on his cell while he shared a joint with one of his acolytes in his parking lot, and play with a pit bull in the early evening, (whose name I learned was "*Bengals*").

I was sitting in a tree overlooking his property, dressed entirely in black—black sweats, cleats, peacoat, gloves, and watch-cap. The Pentax binoculars I'd boosted from a kid's room (Andy Something) effectively brought Brightman about a foot from my face. I watched him drinking with his roommate, Gouche, and some other football pals, watched him back on the phone again, laughing, and then giving Gooch a high-five when he hung up.

In my coat I had a Spartican stun gun I'd bought in Laconia and an Uzi Night Commander matte-black knife I'd confiscated from a freshman six months ago and never disposed of, properly.

If Brightman went out alone, aces. If he left with Gooch or some other assholes, I'd have to either improvise or start over.

Part of me was fine with that, an excuse to say *Don't do this*. But one by one, his buddies departed.

I was fine with that, too.

Gooch was last to go, driving off in his rattle-trap VW, all decked out in bright new clothes. Merry Christmas, Gooch.

Brightman came out and started his BMW and then went back inside, strolling back and forth in the living room with his phone to his ear, maybe waiting for the heater to warm the car. He was dressed casually, old jeans, faded football jersey, probably not a rape-night. He was a handsome bastard and moved like an athlete. I'm pretty big but Jones was a lot bigger.

I clambered down the tree, ripped my peacoat off, and threw it off into the trees. I'd taken it from lost and found, nothing could tie me to it, and I needed to be able to move.

I moved quickly, leaves crunching under my cleats, and got into the back seat of the car, hunkering down onto the floor.

* * *

Brightman got in the car, revved the engine a couple times, and popped a CD into the player. *Insane Clown Posse*. Loud. The music made me feel even better about my plans.

No offense to ICP. I hear they're quite devoted to their fan base.

I sat up in the back seat and grabbed Brightman by the hair with my left hand, leather glove gripping his curls, and held the knife across his throat with my right.

He screamed. Loud. High-pitched like a young girl.

Hey, I didn't blame him. The car slewed right, and then he slammed the brakes on.

"Don't fucking move, asshole! *Keep driving*!"

"What-what-what?! Who the fuck is this!?"

"Shut up asshole, I'm—"

And then the prick flailed backwards and punched me.

Really hard, square in the face.

I dropped the knife, and the car slammed sideways into a snowbank and stopped. Brightman was still screaming in his shriek voice.

"You fucker! All right, motherfucker, all right!"

It fit weirdly well with ICP.

Very, very difficult to keep your eyes open when your nose has just been smashed. Blood was everywhere, and I had just gotten the knife off the floor, blood pattering down on the nice interior, when the back door was ripped open and a ham-sized fist grabbed by the back of my collar and hair.

"Motherfucker!"

He hauled me out onto the dark road in the middle of the Gulag, banging the top of my head on the door jam, making a second starburst cloud my vision. The knife clattered to the pavement.

"Motherfucker! You know who you're fucking with?"

Brightman kept shrieking. He drew back to take my head off with his next punch, and I fumbled the stun-gun out of my sweatshirt pouch.

"Hello from *Dagny Constantine*, asshole," I said and jammed it under his chin.

He fell like a tree onto the pavement, taking me with him and hitting his head so hard it sounded like someone had dropped a bowling ball on the cold asphalt.

I staggered to my feet and picked up the knife.

And kicked him in the balls for good measure.

* * *

Hauling two hundred pounds of deadweight college football-player is hard. Harder when you're bleeding from a broken nose and split scalp. But I got him into the passenger seat and belted him in.

I had to rock the BMW to get it free of the snowbank. The right side was crumpled in, somewhat.

This wasn't going well.

But I had to stick to the plan, I didn't have anything else. My mind was a blank.

My blood was everywhere. I had to hope an immersed winter under a frozen lake would take care of that. I kept thinking of cop shows as I drove, *COPS*, *World's Dumbest Criminals*, all during the fifteen minutes it took to get to Lake Wendigo. I kept hawking blood and spitting it out the window. I didn't want to let go of the stun-gun in case Brightman, bobbing and drooling and sagged against the seatbelt, proved resistant to eight hundred thousand volts.

I tried not to hammer it and stick to the speed limit, the cold air blasting in through the open window clearing my head.

It was full dark, just past nine thirty, and I had The Crest to myself, ramming the BMW up the slope and reaching the edge of the lakeside slope with ease.

Brightman snorted, moaned, and jerked around, looking right at me.

"What the fug? You—"

I hit him with the stun-gun *again*, this time on the side of his head. He convulsed and collapsed into the belt again, motionless.

I left the car on in park and undid his belt and got out to haul him sideways into the driver's seat. Adrenaline helped, but he was so fucking heavy that I could only get his butt onto the seat, not his legs and feet and keep him upright. I had to get over on his side and arrange him that way.

Do you want to be a victim? Eight hundred thousand volts will DROP attackers IN THEIR TRACKS. Once is all you'll need.

Uh-huh.

I strapped him in, got out the passenger door, and checked my alignment. Leaving the window open made sense, not only so I could reach in and put it in drive but to facilitate him drowning. When investigated, they'd figure he either had it open or tried to get out.

Well. That was the plan, anyway.

Car aligned. Thin ice weakened. Inertia, my one and only goddess of the hour.

I reached in, having to lean over way farther than I'd figured. It was especially hard to squeeze my relatively big frame past a man much bigger and with a steering wheel in the way. I was leaning so far into the car that I had one foot off the ground.

I yanked the car into gear, and it lurched forward.

And so did Brightman, keening a wordless bawling cry as he grabbed me in a rib-cracking hug.

So much for the fucking *Spartacus*.

A ton and a half of sedan dipped sickeningly and lurched over the drop-off, came down with a huge, crunching thud, and then we were barreling down the hill toward the lake.

The car went down the slope like a toboggan, way faster than first gear would have ever propelled it, sheer weight and inertia sent its wheels skidding across the surface. The BMW hit the scree of rocks poking up through the ice and so did the side of my left foot, so hard it felt instantly broken. That, and the twisting of my neck in Brightman's clutch would have probably finished me if I hadn't jammed both of my thumbs into his eyes, trying hook into the sockets.

He let go and I fell the rest of the way out the window, hit the ice, and pinwheeled to a stop on my back like a kid playing.

The ice felt good on the back of my gashed scalp.

I rolled onto my side in time to watch the BMW sliding sideways in a big, yawing loop, Jones barely visible, frantically trying to control the skid.

I could feel the staccato vibration of the power brakes through the ice as the sedan skidded to a stop, facing me. About a yard from Kurt Vonnegut's asshole.

Getting up was very hard.

My face hurt; my head hurt. My neck felt wrenched, and my left foot felt like it was on fire when I put weight on it.

I got up anyway, my shadow thrown for thirty feet across the snow-streaked ice by Brightman's remaining headlight.

Behind the car, a crack erupted across the ice to the left, spitting powdery snow.

Brightman was struggling to get out of the car, though whether it was to escape or to come for me I couldn't say.

I didn't want to find out either. The driver's side door opened and—his head still hanging, hair veiling him, swaying side to side—he set one foot on the ice.

"God *damn* it!" I screamed, aloud.

Brightman's head snapped up at that and he yelled "Hey!" like an old man yelling at kids on his lawn.

I ran forward, screaming as my left foot exploded in agony, and hit the grill palms first, head down, back straight out and began to push, driving forward as hard as I could, at first with my right leg and then—when I could feel the car actually moving—with both. I could only push off my left with my toes and the pushing itself made my head erupt in white-hot agony, but I kept pushing.

The ice began to crack, huge, gunshot, wracking reports.

Brightman pulled his foot back in and tromped on the gas.

I spun off the front of the car to be on it's right fender, splattered with slush as the tires screamed on the ice and my own scream blending with it as I drove off my broken foot, cleats digging into the ice. I hit the fender like a rugby scrum, forcing Brightman to do what they always taught in driver's ed, *turn with the skid*.

Brightman Jones, quarterback to the end, tried to ram the car forward, probably thinking that in a pursuit across the icy lake, he could simply run me down.

I kept driving my push against the fender even as the car swung and pulled away from me. Brightman yelled "*Hey*!" again.

I drove forward with both feet, screaming again as whatever was cracked in my foot fractured a little more. The BMW slid crookedly over the asterisk, the front end breaking through almost instantly in a fusillade of ice and freezing water. Two parallel cracks ran past me from both sides of the car and linked crudely behind me to become one.

As the car suddenly, fully submerged, I went with it.

Shocking, electric cold bit me to the marrow as the car, flooding through the driver's side door and window the quickest, canted drunkenly to the right and swung around in a mini wave of ice chunks and frigid water.

The car sank sideways, taillights still bright, engine now silent. I was able to climb onto the rear bumper and, from there, scramble onto the ice.

More of it broke beneath me as I humped and crawled across the jigsaw ice-quake until I finally reached stable, solid ice.

I turned around on my ass, hands jammed under my armpits, shivering so violently that I couldn't help making an idiot's vocal "*Guh-guh-guh-guh*!" as I watched the tail-end of the BMW bob up and down and on the third, lowest bob, sink from view.

Jagged teeth shards of ice stirred, but not much. There was a great belch of bubbles as the car hit the lakebed. Then the roiling water settled.

Brightman never surfaced. He didn't get out.

My car was parked behind the inner tube shack, where I'd left it and walked from many hours ago. It was two hundred yards away, give or take.

CHAPTER FIFTEEN

Alcohol and Death. The Master Chief. An Alternative to Denmark.

AS THE SPRING SEMESTER BEGAN, I was pretty lonesome.

I had housing in a total shit dorm called Hannity Hall, and to make it all the crumbier, I had a basement room.

But a single, at least.

I was using my cane, my left foot in a small cast for what the doctor called a spiral fracture. My black eyes had faded to mild purple smudges from a broken nose that was itchy with the healing process, as was my foot.

Three papers, two of them local, had articles about the discovery of Brightman's car and body. "LOCAL FOOTBALL STAR'S TRAGIC END" was the townie paper's headline. The school paper followed it with "WILDCATS CO-CAPTAIN KILLED IN ICY CRASH." A national paper reported the death along with about twenty others in huge article titled "ALCOHOL AND DEATH GO HAND IN HAND ON NATION'S CAMPUSES."

I hadn't noticed Brightman had been drunk, actually, but who knows?

A snowmobiler's harmless wipeout on the lumpy mound of ice led to the discovery. It had snowed once, but some of the tracks of the car's slide down the hill were still visible. The car was visible too, as Wendigo was apparently a hell of lot shallower near the shore than I'd been told.

The car was on its side and only about eighteen feet deep.

No major forensics performed, it seemed. The body was retrieved with no reports of knives or stun-guns being found (I'd lost them both). Brightman's funeral was attended by every football player on campus, I assumed.

I didn't go, of course.

No one put two and two together that a very banged up Dan Ketch lurched into the infirmary the same night that Brightman went missing. He wasn't reported missing for almost a week, for one thing. And the candy stripers and the doctor on-call that night were all too willing to believe I'd had an accident on a dirt bike at a party, soaked clothes and all.

They'd patched up plenty of idiots.

But I had other problems. Dagny was gone, and that was a constant ache. And I needed a job, if not three.

And—I had apparently gone insane.

I had been climbing up the slope that led to my car that night, half frozen to death and pretty sure I would die of hypothermia when I saw a dark form standing at the edge of the ridge above me, a tall, angular black shape. I jumped when I first saw it, thinking it was a cop. But the figure said nothing, didn't draw a gun or flashlight or anything else. At that point it was either get warm or drop dead, so I lurched up the hill to see *the Master Chief*, windblown snow skirling right through him, drawing on a cigarette I couldn't smell and squinting at me like he was considering a bet.

He was in full uniform. I had to walk through him to get to my car, which I did. I started the car, and he was gone.

I wrote it off to the stress of the moment.

But he'd shown up again, here and there.

In the street. In classes.

Not grotesque and corpse-like, not standing pointing a finger at me or moaning under a hooded shroud, *but still.*

My dead father. Hanging out. Looking content, even.

Even without living in the age of Oprah and Dr. Phil and shrinks for every occasion, I understood a manifestation of guilt. The thing was, I didn't feel guilty. Not one little bit. I felt worried but not remorseful.

Brightman Jones, arrogant rapist and Mafia wanna-be, was dead, and I'd killed him. And I'd have felt more guilty about killing a field-mouse.

The problem was compounded by not just seeing my father, but there was *another* man.

I'd seen him several times around campus. Tall, hard, and slim. Bald, with just a grey frost of a goatee. Dark suits. I'd seen him twice in the crowded quad across the street from the student union when I'd walked among my fellows when classes changed. And once, late at night, standing beneath a streetlight in my new dorm's parking lot, looking like the poster for *The Exorcist*.

I'd been up in another kid's room, smoking a joint. I looked out the window and saw The Man.

"Casey," I said, "come here."

Casey, a burnout acquaintance of mine, came to the window.

Had I looked away? For a second? Hard to say when you're stoned.

"What is it, bud?"

"Nothing," I said.

Nothing. There was no man there.

* * *

I was in my room in the motherfucking basement, looking at the cin-derblock walls, which were painted a dark green.

I used to decorate according to my tastes in music, movies, all that, like any kid. Since my exile to Hannity (a known shithole for misfits and fuck-ups), I didn't have the heart for it. My classes were going okay, but without the structure of my RA life—combined with rugby—I found that things were pretty empty for me at good 'ol Logan.

And Dagny. Dagny. Dagny.

I couldn't even join the team for winter workouts at the fieldhouse, my goddamned foot put paid to that.

I'd skipped dinner and was hungry. I grabbed my cane and decided to head over to the student union for a sub. It was a weeknight and late enough that I'd avoid running into anyone. It was cold, and a light snow was falling. I clicked myself across the campus, trying to avoid placing my cane in any ice patches. When I got to the front of Grafton Hall, I ended up making my way to the back of the dormitory to the nondescript patch of ground where Kent Wyllis fell.

I didn't feel guilty about Brightman Jones. But I thought a lot about Kent Wyllis. I thought about how much I enjoyed being head RA. "The Chief." It seemed simple enough, to take care of my charges. Holding the reins loosely. We weren't West Point or a convent or something. But I'd failed a fairly simple task, to keep things together.

To keep them safe.

I squatted awkwardly with my hurt leg out to the side and placed my hand on the snow where he'd hit. The snow beneath my hand began to melt.

It began to hurt.

I kept it there awhile longer.

Then, rising, I looked at the perfect mold I'd left there. An imprimatur. Or a signature to some confession no one had asked me to write.

* * *

It was late when I crutched my way back from going downtown to eat and then get drunk. My body felt light, actually, like I could vault up and balance myself on my cane like a one-man Cirque du Soleil.

There was no reason to feel that way, but I still allowed the walk through the arctic streets and cobbles to feel pleasant. Maybe there would be a tomorrow after the awful fall. One I could again feel—if not joyful in—then, at least content?

The campus was still as if the very atmosphere was frozen to spun ice. I made my way down to my basement room in Hannity, and there, the absolute quiet didn't feel as strange. Besides me, there was another monk-cell single across the crap-filled rec room, and it was unoccupied.

The light was on in my room, glowing in a razor line beneath the door.

I hadn't left it on.

I unlocked the door and stepped in with my cane held like a cudgel, not entirely sure what I expected.

What I got was a sheet thrown over my head, about two seconds of clattering struggle, during which I whacked my knee on the corner of a desk, and then there was a steel pincer grip to my neck, high behind the ear.

Lights out.

* * *

I came to all at once, to bright light in my face, a terrible headache and music playing on my cheap stereo. Something classical.

Bach, I found out later. When I learned about such music.

Behind the desk lamp pointed at my face was only the shadowy form of a man. He was standing. I tried to do the same and found myself tightly bound to my chair.

"What the fuck is this?" I said. I was very scared.

"What indeed," the man's voice purred. Just the slightest English accent. Hard without needing to be loud.

"You are a dangerous man, Mr. Ketch. Stupid. Crude. But dangerous, nonetheless. I have subdued you to force your keenest attentiveness. Behave, and you will be released."

He looked at my books arranged on a shelf above my desk.

"You study Shakespeare here, in this rustic font of learning?

"Yeah," I said, "but I read it before that. Him."

"Do you enjoy it? *Him*?"

"Yeah," I said.

"Let's have a test," the shadow said.

"*Hamlet*," the shadow said.

"How well do you know it?" the shadow said.

"It's a favorite," I said.

This wasn't a cop. The thought brought no relief.

"'What have you, my good friend, deserved at the hands of fortune that she sends you to prison hither?'"

I knew this. Shadow was playing Hamlet. So—

"'Prison, my lord?'" I said.

"'Denmark's a prison,'" he said.

"'Then the world is one," I said.

"'A goodly one, in which there are many confines, wards, and dungeons, Denmark being one of the worst,'" he said.

He was pretty good.

"'We think not so, my lord,'" I said, wondering if we were going to just do the whole fucking play.

"'Why then, tis none to you; for there is nothing either good nor bad but thinking makes it so. To me...it is a prison.'"

His sudden, loud clapping startled me so much that my already pounding heart hurt, for just a beat.

"I'm impressed, Mr. Ketch. I enjoyed that. Very good. Let there be light."

The sudden light from the fly-specked overhead was icy and harsh.

In my hovel stood a tall, angular man in a dark suit, dark shirt and tie, and dark handkerchief in his pocket. Slick as owl shit, as the Master Chief would have said. He was cue-ball bald with just a thin rind of silver goatee on his sharp chin.

"Who are you and what do you want?" I said.

"An excellent question, I will not equivocate. You may call me the *Kestrel*. I am here to offer you a choice."

"Meaning what, Mr. Kestrel?" I said.

"Just Kestrel, yes? Bird of prey. As to meaning what, meaning this," he said, lifting a briefcase from my bed and setting it on the chair facing me. He opened it so I could see its contents.

"I know you killed Mr. Jones. You got away with it, but I know."

My heart was pounding, and I could feel myself sweating through my shirt.

"How do you know anything?"

He smiled. The smile didn't reach The Kestrel's eyes. "My organization makes it our business to know. Attend, please, to the items in the case."

He fished among them like a home-shopping network model.

"Here's the stun-gun, a little weed-clotted, photos of the burns from it on Mr. Jones's body, pictures of the pre-lake crash damage to Mr. Jones's car and—oh yes—the swatches of material from his car seat, still faintly stained with *your* blood."

Everything he mentioned he touched, each in its own separate plastic bag. There were stark photos of the battered BMW in a blank warehouse space and of Brightman's nude corpse, laid out on a steel table in an equally otherwise empty, blank room.

"Who are you? FBI? How did you get—"

The Kestrel held up his hands, palms out.

When I was quiet, he used them to gently close the case.

"I am the Kestrel. And all this was gathered after the authorities of the law were finished and off on another fool's errand. They didn't even bother retrieving the car. We did that. I am here to offer you a choice, Mr. Ketch. It's a gift from *The Fates*, this choice. You can either come with me, and in a short time, we will burn these items and they will never trouble you again. Or you can spurn my offer and I will see to it that you are charged for murder and away to rot in jail you will go."

"What do you want from me?" I said. Hackneyed, maybe, but what else do you say in this situation?

"From you? Nothing. I'm merely offering you the choice. Come with me and perhaps learn something useful about yourself. Useful, profitable, simple—in its way. Or stay here in Denmark and rot in prison."

I didn't say anything.

A knife, thick, matte-black and curved like a claw, fell out of his right sleeve, into his right hand. He stood before I could speak and swept it soundlessly through my bonds, which had been three extension cords.

"As to what I and my organization can provide, I suggest you visit your Dean Fletcher, tomorrow. Nine o'clock sharp. Then if you're still interested, simply press the call button on this phone."

He removed a small, thick black cell phone and placed it on my desk and stood, picking up the briefcase.

He looked at me briefly like I was a car he wasn't sure was worth it and left.

CHAPTER SIXTEEN

Broken Dean. The Thanatos Guild. Exit Jeromy. The Oldest Profession.

THE NEXT MORNING FELT WEIRD, like somehow the night before I'd been tripping on something, with a blurred idea of reality as part of the next day's hangover.

Part of me was curious and the rest of me teetered between fear, exhaustion, and resignation, to what, I couldn't know.

I went to Dean Fletcher's office, arriving just before nine, having decided to skip my classes for the day. Upon my entrance, Maria, my favorite secretary, looked...weird.

First of all, she wasn't really dressed for the office and wearing sweats that did nothing for her. Her hair was a mess and she looked like a woman who was doing laundry all day, like in a cheap commercial, *Stains, stains, stains! What am I going to do with these STAINS?* Second, as I entered, she walked very quickly to Fletcher's office door and said, "He's here," and closed the door.

Then she looked at me and almost but not quite ran out the door.

I was about to knock on the dean's office door when he jerked it open.

He looked even weirder.

Dean Fletcher hadn't shaved, was tie-less in just a loose-collared dress shirt and unbuttoned vest. He looked like he'd been up all night.

"Ketch. Sit down."

I did, my cane across my lap.

The dean's color wasn't good. He was very flushed.

"I am informing you that your scholarship has been fully restored. With an increase so as to facilitate payment in full for the remainder of your time at LSC. Further, you are now a graduate in good standing from LSC. Your diploma, ah, will be sent to you at the end of the spring semester."

"You're kidding," I said.

"Now get out of here," he said.

I don't know what made me do it, but I stood up and limped to his desk, leaning heavily on my cane as I bent to bring our faces closer.

The dean seemed to sink down in his seat.

"'*Sir*.'"

"I beg your pardon?" he said.

"Say: 'Please take your leave, sir,'" I said.

He stared at me, hollow-eyed, and his face mottled and spoke in a whisper.

"*Please take your leave sir*."

No point in lying, I liked that just fine.

* * *

"Kestrel," the voice said.

I was sitting on a bench in the quad.

"I want to know what the fuck this is all about."

"Capital! Go pack some clothes, just an overnight bag. And a suit, if you can manage it. I will pick you up at your dormitory in thirty minutes. Be ready."

"Jesus Christ," I said.

"And leave your cell phone behind. I'll know if you don't."

"Of course you will," I said.

* * *

The car was a Jaguar CX16, and the ride was extraordinary and a little nerve-wracking. The Kestrel drove pretty fast but also handled the car well. I didn't know a lot about cars, but this thing was fucking amazing.

"We are going to northeast New York, to Guild House. It's in the Adirondacks, in an area called the Emmons Plateau. We're driving straight through, save for the occasional stop for restrooms, coffee, dinner, and so on. All your questions will be answered shortly after we arrive. Don't ask me any now; I don't like repeating myself and it will all be made clear after you've met the rest of your flight."

"My what?" I said.

Your group. Now rest. Look at the scenery. Sleep," he said.

I went with the program.

Somewhere in the early part of the drive, the Kestrel took a pair of calls, almost back to back.

"Yes," he said, "you tell him there's only one choice."

And a little later—

"*No*. You tell her that this is the only option, other than the usual consequences."

I didn't bother asking but I got the idea that other people had spent some time in similar conversations to the one in my room last night, even as we were driving.

A month later, Mors would tell me that between sixteen thousand and seventeen thousand murders occur in America every year.

To paraphrase *Ghostbusters*, that's a big twinkie, as far as a talent pool to work with went.

We were driving through the dark when I awoke from a long nap, stiff and sore and needing to piss. It was near 10:30 at night and we'd reached a winding road that was gradually rising above a vast, black lake.

We went through a series of four gates, all of them electronic and opening for the Kestrel-mobile with the press of a button on his boxy cell.

My first view of Guild House left me breathless.

Amid a huge, rolling lawn, more like a golf course than anything you'd call a "lawn," really, and ringed all around by what amounted to forest, was a vast brick courtyard. The courtyard was lit with glass globes atop ornate wrought-iron poles, and in its center was a gigantic fountain with a giant, winged figure, its wings fully unfurled.

Beyond that, was a Chateau Novella Mansion, with virtually all of its windows lit a molten gold.

"Guild House," the Kestrel said as we he pulled onto the courtyard, swinging the wheel.

"Guild of what? Freemasons?"

He gave forth a single bark of laughter as he cut the engine next to the base of the fountain.

"Freemasons? Hardly. This is a house of *The Thanatos Guild*. Not the only one, certainly, but the primary one in North America."

"The Thanatos Guild," I repeated.

"We usually just call it Guild House," he said.

As we got out of the Jaguar, I saw a figure in one of the upstairs windows and several more in the downstairs. I paused to look up at the statue, the Kestrel standing behind me.

Standing above a group of partially submerged human shapes was a dark figure, a male nude with enormous, upraised, and fanned out wings, holding an upraised sword. The figures seemed to writhe beneath the roiling water and were cut from the same dark stone, which looked black. They reminded me of a painting I'd seen somewhere, *The Wrath of The Medusa*.

On closer inspection, in the glow of submerged lights I saw that all of the partially submerged figures were wounded in some way, dead or dying. An arrow jutted here, a spear there, a dagger, a terrible, carved gash.

And above them all, the winged youth, looking like a dark, winged David. On his face was the faintest of smiles.

The great sword he held upraised was gold.

"Who is he?" I said.

"Thanatos," the Kestrel replied, "the personification of death, in Greek mythology. And, some would say—mistakenly, the god of the Oath."

"Why mistakenly?" I said, but he just beckoned me follow, carrying my bag for me. *The god of the oath.*

I followed him into a spacious, well-appointed foyer where a slight dark-haired woman in a tasteful dark dress and necklace held out her hand, smiling slightly.

"You must be Daniel," she said. "My name is Yolanda. I'll show you to your room so you can rest and freshen up before the dinner."

I turned back but the Kestrel was gone.

The foyer, hallway beyond, and the broad, winding staircase were all carpeted a deep red. The furniture, lamps, artwork, sculpture were all tasteful and incredibly beautiful, though I couldn't have named much of it at that time.

I followed Yolanda up the stairs to the third floor and down a long hallway until the third door, which she opened with a swipe card.

She gestured.

"This is your room for tonight. Please feel free to make yourself at home," she said, handing me the key card. It was red and black, slashed sideways, with no other detail save for a magnetic strip.

"Dinner is at eight. Please be neither late nor early. Just come down to the first floor and someone will walk you to the dining room."

She turned to leave.

"Wait," I said, "can you tell me more about all this?"

Yolanda, I realized, was quite a bit older than I.

She smiled, shook her head.

"Be patient a bit longer, Daniel. Then you'll know just what to believe, do, and say."

"That'd be nice for change," I said.

She smiled at me, very natural, real, and pretty, and left.

The room was something else, huge, with windows overlooking the lawn, trees, and trails, only a little of which was lit by the windows facing that way.

There was a TV and remote. I tried it. It was pretty limited. Five channels of regular late news, PBS, and a blank white screen with black lettering that said: **Techniques 1–5. l. Temple 2. Nasion. 3. Philtrum 4. Coccyx 5. Russian Omelet. Instructor: Gardener/Solarium #3.**

"Russian Omelet" threw me, and at first I thought it was some kind of room service menu. Then I realized the *temple*, *nasion*, and *philtrum* were all parts of the head. The *coccyx*, the base of the spine, I thought.

Russian Omelet?

I set my duffel on the bed and after poking around a little more and finding a beer in the little fridge, took a shower.

* * *

Dressed in a jacket, tie, and best I could slap together of shirt, shoes, and pants, I made my way downstairs to the first floor to find another smiling woman waiting at the bottom of the stairs.

She was much older than Yolanda, with short white hair and a charcoal-colored pants suit.

"Good evening, Daniel. I'm Grace. Please come with me."

I did, following her down a long corridor, though what looked like a dark, outdoor chapel and inside again to a large vaulted room, high ceilinged, with vast wooden beams spanning it.

"The dining hall," she said, holding the door for me, "and I must ask you, Daniel, to speak to no one. The time for conversation will be soon but not yet. Simply stand behind your chair until he comes in."

I almost said "Thanks," but she held a finger to her lips and glided away.

As I stepped into the dining hall, I noticed other people coming in from separate doorways: from under a shadowed archway, a brightly lit area that seemed to lead to a kitchen, others. Some just ambled, or crept in; others briefly had their male or female handlers with them for a moment.

Then there were just the twelve of us, standing at the huge table, which was beautifully set for a dinner.

The room was quite cool, like a cave, seemingly made from huge blocks of marble. There were oil portraits lining the walls, portraying all manner of men and women, some in clothing dating back to pre-revolution America to stuff that would have looked at home in the forties and fifties. Oil lamps glowed in wall sconces; more candles were lit than I could count on the vast, Arthurian table. An array of platters plates and trays were laid out, most of them covered. Bottles of wine were also arranged, along with champagne set in ice-choked buckets and several crystal decanters.

There were twenty chairs at the table. I looked around.

There were six people on the far side of the table, standing behind their chairs, five on my side, counting me.

Everyone was young, but mostly an indeterminate youth. A couple were obviously past standard college-age, some by quite a bit.

Facing me: a light-skinned black man, medium height, glasses, my age. A slightly overweight but tough-looking girl with jet-black, curly hair. Glasses. A tall man, probably in his thirties, bone-pale and with white hair, very long. A skinny, short red-headed woman, also at least thirty, a big man in his late twenties, hard, balding with dark hair and beard down to stubble.

To my left (as I was at my end of the table): a tallish, college-aged boy with a crew-cut; a very slim Asian girl, also collegiate, tall with very long, black hair; a black woman, older, with her head clean-shaven (the only person smiling openly); a very short, fat kid, looking like he was still in high school, freckles and curly brown hair—and good ol me, tallish, with longish hair that tended to get in my eyes. Good shape. Big hands.

Nice teeth.

I turned around and was studying the oil portraits when there was a chime, a single, clear note, like you'd expect to hear in a monastery, calling the monks to Matins or vespers or whatever. I turned away from the portrait of a man who looked like a ship captain, or pirate.

The man I knew only as the Kestrel strode out of the shadows at the far end of the hall. As he reached the head of the table, others also walked in from all points of the compass.

I saw Grace, Yolanda, and several others, men and women visibly older than anyone else at the table, at least for the most part. There were now twenty-one people in the room, standing behind their chairs.

"Please be seated," the Kestrel said.

The Kestrel remained standing, as ever in a dark suit, hands behind his back. As he talked, he began to walk slowly around the table.

"Greetings, one and all. I, as some of you know, am the Kestrel. In conversation, 'Kestrel' will suffice. Some of the others some of you have met will stand, if they would. *Professor Artemis*"—who was Grace, to my surprise—"*Mr. Blue*," a short, jolly-looking man in a tux stood briefly, sketched a little salute, sat.

"*Mr. Quark*," a tiny, Asian man with black hair shot with grey. Up. Down.

"*Ms. Mercy*," and that was Yolanda.

"*Gardener*," a Garrison Keillor look-alike, rumpled and tousled, rose then sat.

"*The Nightingale*," a tiny old woman with dark glasses and a shawl, waved like a queen, not rising.

"*Iron Horse*," a middle-aged American Indian with long grey hair didn't rise either but nodded to the room, looking around gravely.

"*Dr. Yes*," a man in his forties with glasses, actually wearing a doctor's white coat stood, coughed into his fist, and sat.

"These people," the Kestrel said, "will be your instructors for the next three months. Some of them are also the scouts who took notice of your work and recognized your potential."

He stopped walking at the far end of the table from me.

"Look around you. Every new face in this room is a murderer. So am I. But I, like the people I just introduced, am an infinitely better one."

The Kestrel resumed walking.

"You, all of you, are the latest recruitment flight of the Thanatos Guild. You crossed a boundary, a personal Rubicon. You willingly strayed into a seemingly new and rarified land. But this land is as ancient as time. Some of you told yourselves you killed for revenge. Or for profit. Rage. Fear. Honor. Self-defense.

"The reasons don't interest the Guild. Only the ability. The ability to provide what the Guild has provided for—quite literally—hundreds of years. *Expedient murder*, for an agreed-upon price. Some of you were students. Some were simply private citizens. Some were in the armed services. Now, you are here. The Guild has seen to your obligations and offered you a clear path back to the status quo if you wish it. Or you can continue to work for us, that choice comes later. But first, there is this more immediate choice: For the next three months, you can learn to do what you were inclined to do, better, and then do it for the Guild. Three assigned assassinations, or slates, as we call them. Three each. Following the completion of your *Three*, you are free to go, with a handsome stipend, and all the evidence of your crimes erased. Or you can continue to work for the Guild, as the people I introduced have done."

"And what if we say, 'Fuck that, pal,'" someone said.

Heads turned.

The speaker was the college kid with the crew cut. He was wearing a red turtleneck and a loud, checkered jacket.

"I beg your pardon?" the Kestrel said.

The kid was all loose and raw-boned, the energy spilling off him showing itself in the little twitches of his head, his fingers.

"There's eleven new *recruits* here for your thanorexia team or whatever the fuck. That's thirty-three people you want iced, or is my fuckin' math off?" he said.

"What is your first name," the Kestrel said.

"Jeromy," he said, stressing the "O."

I can assure you—Jeromy, that thirty-three is a pittance, depending on the winds of politics and other social fabrications. And, as I said—"

"Yeah, yeah, what you said was a bunch of horseshit to me, Cockateel, or whatever the fuck you want to call yourself. I don't know how your spooky bitch caught me out, but I'm not killing for you or your fucked-up *Guild*, got it?"

"Indeed," the Kestrel said.

"Jeremy," someone said. I never found out who, things moved too fast, but it was a female voice.

"Jeromy," he said, "that's the way the slut spelled it out on the certificate and that's what I go by, not some dickhole moniker dreamed up by the secret squirrel-league of whateverthefuck. Now, somebody get me a ride back to Queens or you'll all fucking regret it."

He walked away from the table.

The Kestrel watched him stride jerkily across the big space, heels cracking on the gleaming slate floor.

"*Jeromy*," the Kestrel said, reaching into his jacket.

Jeromy turned around, starting to say something, and the Kestrel shot him, the bullet-hole appearing like a black mole in the center of his high forehead.

He fell backwards, kicked once, and was still.

When I turned back to the Kestrel, the gun was gone and his hands were behind his back again. Someone was crying, very softly. I didn't look to see who.

"I'm quite sure I didn't give the impression that this was a debate. You've killed, and you will kill again. Three, for the Guild. After that, your fates are your own. The only other alternative is to leave here and return to your previous lives, where, I can promise you, police, trial, and imprisonment await. And speak of the Guild at any point thereafter, you won't live to see the next sunrise," the Kestrel said.

He resumed his stroll even as two men in dark suits came out of an alcove and dragged Jeromy away into the shadows, like a stage play between acts.

"Never before in America—in the world—have so many eyes been watching us. You. Me. Cameras, satellites, everywhere there are eyes upon us all. But the Thanatos Guild uses the watchers and watches the watchmen. We are old. They say the oldest profession is prostitution. Not so. The oldest profession is murder," the Kestrel said.

"Now, let's dine together and get to know one another. Enjoyment, like so much else, is an act of willpower."

I watched him sit down.

Then I poured myself some wine.

And people began to talk, like at any party, in its careful, awkward first phase.

There was a breakfast the next morning, and as much as we were encouraged to eat, drink, and be merry the night before (as merry as you could get having seen someone get shot before the first course, that is), the morning meal felt guarded and quiet.

You could tell everyone was thinking it all over. Hard.

We had also been told that if and when we returned we'd be using new names, so it was important to me that the tall and oh so beautiful Asian woman asked me mine and said she'd share hers "if you return," as we walked, taking in the portraits. Probably my imagination, but I felt a little spark when we said goodnight. Something.

I was also surprised that the Kestrel was personally taking me back to Logan, "to settle your affairs," as they also say when you're about to die, I believe.

The drive back was the same drill as the drive to, mostly a silent affair save for endless classical music. The Kestrel did get chatty as we approached the campus.

"Pack what you wish and arrange for whatever contacts you need to maintain via email, whatever. Explain it however you like, student-exchange program, work-study. The Guild can supply faux documentation if it's absolutely necessary."

"I really don't have anyone to report to," I said.

"All the better," the Kestrel said.

He surprised me again by walking in with my bag, leaving me to my cast and cane, unburdened.

"On Thursday of this week, a woman named Flynn, just Flynn, will meet you at the entrance to Sparhawk Falls park. She'll transport you back to Guild house. Then we'll begin."

"Okay," I said.

The Kestrel considered me for a moment and then glanced around my basement room in Hannity one last time.

"Whatever may come, Daniel Ketch, it will be better than this banal little cell."

I got the impression that he didn't chat much like this with the recruits.

"Killing people will improve my living conditions, then?" He barked a laugh.

"Killing people is just a part of it. We all kill, Daniel. Anyone who's ever voted in an election has blood on their hands. They just prefer to think otherwise. We're all killers. A killer species, standing upon a mountain of naturally selected dead. What the Guild offers is a view of the world minus the rose-colored glasses. Clarity, Daniel. The Guild's lessons will be harsh at times, as you saw last night. But clarity is itself, also power. You and your fellows, myself and the other masters, we have a shared darkness inside us. Unbridled, it kills others—then its host. But *harnessed*, it can shape the world."

CHAPTER SEVENTEEN

Dagny. Bad Stars Over the New World.

I FIGURED AS FAR AS MY former teammates and RA pals went, maybe a simple disappearance would be best. Later, I'd regret that, but—another story for another time.

So, that was my decision at the time and decisiveness, even in a dark or ruthless manner, held a deep appeal for me.

I had packed my few belongings into two duffels, a leather satchel of the Master Chief's, a backpack, and was selecting three books to stuff in somewhere when there was a knock at my humble door.

I opened it to see Dagny Constantine.

"Hi Dan," she said, then "are you all right?"

The second was at seeing me with cane and cast.

She looked painfully good, no sign of her original injuries suffered at the hands of the late Mr. Jones.

"Yeah, I get the cast off, ah, tomorrow probably."

I wanted to hug her. I wanted her hair, her soft scented lips, her warm breasts nestled into my chest, my hands on her, but I knew we were no longer on the same map.

I was looking at her from the borderlands, at the edge of my spike-shard new coastline of the country of murder.

My new geography.

She paused, taking in the stripped-down room "Please, come in. How are you?" I said, leaning my cane on my desk.

The Stand, The Day of The Jackal, and *Stranger in a Strange Land* lay fanned out there, like a strange hand of cards.

She walked in, closing the door, and sat on the bed. I sat in my chair.

"I'm okay. Danny, I'm so sorry about what happened to that student at Grafton. I heard about it later, and I wish—I didn't know that was part of that night for you. I'm sorry. That was a night of, I don't know, bad stars."

Bad stars?

"Yes, I guess it was," I said.

Her eyes were huge and dark, playing off the dark wine color of her so soft-looking sweater.

"I'm sorry. I'm so nervous," she said.

"It's okay," I said, "I am too."

"Danny, I have to ask you a question. Before we can talk about anything else, I have to ask this. I have to."

"Ask it."

"Did you kill Brightman?"

"Yes," I said, "I did."

It's hard to explain what happened to her face, but it seemed to form new bones, somehow. It wasn't an angry thing, but still somehow dreadful. She nodded, looking down at the floor.

"Oh, Danny. How could you do that?"

"Well, it took a lot of planning. But"—I gestured to my foot—"he made me pay for the privilege."

She kept her eyes and head down, shaking her head slowly.

"How can you joke about it?"

"How can you think letting him get away with it is all right? I understand about you and your father, but then what? Then, he goes on to do it again? And even more, I don't know, emboldened because—"

"Don't you dare lay that on me!" she said, looking up, almost snarling.

"Did you just come here to ask me about that?" I said.

She shook her head.

"No. But why I came doesn't matter anymore now that you've answered. Where are you going?"

"Where did you go?" I said, ignoring her question.

"Home. Now I'm enrolled at Wellesley. I'm going to finish there, though it may take a while."

"Where are you going?" she said again.

"Where do you want me to go?" I said.

"If you've committed murder," she said, "I'd want you to get, I don't know! Help. Either from confessing and, and—"

"Confess? Wouldn't that involve my motive? And bring you and your father back into it?"

She stared at me, face unreadable.

"All right, yes. It would. But Brightman's *dead*; he can't—"

She stopped.

"You need help, Dan. If you did this, then—"

"I'm *getting* help," I said, "that's where I'm going. I'm going someplace that will help me do it better. Killing people like *Brightman*, the pricks who get away with it. The ones who make everything worse. I've been recruited to go to a school where they teach you how to be an assassin. I'm dead serious."

"Dan, you're not making any sense," she said.

She got up, and I didn't know what to do.

"Dagny. Dags," I said, "I love you. Please tell me that you still love me, tell me that's what you came here for and I'll—I won't go. We can try—"

She stopped, looked down again, and smoothed her cardigan over her stomach and hips.

"Please don't say that, Danny. I can't," she said.

"What? You can't hear me say I love you? You can't say you love me, still? Can you say that you still do? Just tell me that you still love me and there's a way to, to go somewhere else."

"I *can't*," she said. And with that, she left.

I might have imagined her voice breaking, but when you replay a memory, you often alter it.

An hour later I was sitting next to Flynn in an old Porsche. A beat-up Porsche, to be succinct.

Flynn was as chatty as a cinderblock and thin, with graying hair and wrap-around sunglasses. She called me "sir" more than once and offered to only smoke outside the car when we made a stop. I told her smoke away, and she offered me one. I took it, though smoking was a new thing to me then.

Flynn was fond of jazz and piano pieces, which is what we mainly listened to during the long drive to Guild house and the ancient country.

The New World.

Part Three

CHAPTER EIGHTEEN

The Horse with No Name-Mors 2.

***MORS DROVE THROUGH** the late autumn night surrounded by things he loved.*

Outside the speeding car leaves fled rattling ahead of him. The road winding through the woods of upstate New York was sparsely traveled at this time of night. The moon, a quarter full, was shining coldly, limning the ragged trees with its silver.

Mors loved that too, the pleasantly lonely sense of both movement and dislocation.

Mors also loved his more immediate surroundings, the almost sub-aural rumble of his lovingly restored and thoroughly customized 1950 Mercury, for one. He didn't have the opportunity to take her out much, and tonight it was heady to let her boom up the lonely highway like a black metal manta ray.

To complete his evening's pleasure, Mors pushed a button on the radio. A digitally remastered recording of Orson Welles' 1938 The War of The Worlds *broadcast began.*

It often just played whenever he drove, repeating on an endless loop.

"We know now that in the early years of the twentieth century this world was being watched closely by intelligences greater than man's—and yet as mortal as his own."

Mors found the old broadcast incredibly soothing. Since his childhood, he'd heard it at least, what? A thousand times, maybe.

Mors didn't know why it soothed him, and he didn't care, particularly. Introspection only suited him as far as it was necessary for his comfort, or his efficiency.

Beyond that, he found introspection pointless.

* * *

By the time Mors reached the last gate that marked the entrance to Guild house drive, the Martians had succumbed to earthly illnesses and the disc had continued on to the beginning again.

The last gate did not open to the car's transponder.

Mors snapped off the radio, shut off the engine, and got out.

While it was possible they'd changed something, some decision having been made about locking out the "nomads" of the tribe, he doubted it. True, the Guild and its shadowy upper echelon had been cagey about things with the "Thug" contingent before, but this didn't make any sense.

Especially since Mors, like most of those who had opted for independence as opposed to exclusive Guild-assigned work (a "hang-around-the-fort Indian" as Mors dubbed it, amusing only Ketch) would only ignore any such restrictions anyway.

Mors pulled on gloves and, after locking Mariah, climbed the fence.

Mors walked slowly across the jigsaw-fit flagstones of the courtyard, approaching the fountain and the looming statue of Thanatos.

Guild house was utterly dark. No lights in the courtyard, the building, no spots under the fountain's water.

And come to notice it, no fountain. The water lay in a still, leaf-scabbed pool.

Mors took out his gun from his black flight jacket, a GI American, matte-black.

He approached the main entrance, not in an overtly stealthy manner but cautiously. Cameras, cameras everywhere, but not a red light winked.

Even before training in the Tank room, Mors knew the weight of some-

one's visual attention on his skin. Be it camera or the naked eye, he felt it, like the tiniest raindrop.

Here he felt nothing.

Mors looked at the front entrance then back up at the statue of Thanatos, draped in cold moonlight.

He jogged all but silently along the south side of the building and came to the back, where there was a short set of stairs leading to a porch outside the great kitchen.

Mors peered in the door and then tapped the butt of his gun on the glass, breaking it.

He paused.

No alarm.

"Uh oh," he said.

He reached through the hole and unlocked the door.

It was cold inside. He knew it couldn't be—but it felt colder than the night outside. He fished a Knucklehead LED flashlight out of his jacket and played the beam about. The kitchen was a museum of gleaming steel surfaces. Mors could smell apples. There, on the cutting board the size of a bank president's desk, was a bowl of apples.

Yes, apples, but apples collapsed in on themselves with rot.

Mors opened one freezer. Full. Meat, mostly.

He shut it and continued. Out through the dining hall. The main one, where he and Ketch had first met the others of their flight, as well as the school "faculty."

He made his way past the gallery along one wall, splashing his light briefly across master assassins of the Victorian and Edwardian ages, many of whom he now knew, through study. Renard, The Reaper, The Scarecrow, Black Atticus, Blue-Luck Jack, Bettie Whyte—just some of the "secret names of the world's secret history."

Unlike Ketch, who'd confessed a certain slack-jawed astonishment at it all, Mors hadn't felt particularly blinkered by his Guild education. It merely confirmed his worldview.

He let himself into the theatre, a vast darkness that smelled of dust and wood and fabric.

Mors had a sudden unfurling of vivid memory. Eight years ago. Spring. With their flight of that year's talent, that year's box of unpolished, deadly little tools. All of them and the "faculty," house staff, the masters, whatever you want to call them, all seated in the theatre to see Waiting for Godot.

Most of their flight seemed to find it either boring or impenetrable, but both Mors and Ketch had enjoyed it.

Loved it, actually. Mors marked that night as the beginning of their friendship, though he didn't think about it much. Mors had no one else he'd use the word friend in reference to, though.

Even now, Ketch would discuss the play at the drop of a hat, and Mors had been one of the few to find it hilarious, in parts.

The Kestrel, Mr. Blue, Gardener, and Ms. Mercy had played the parts, and again, Mors simply felt his interior worldview confirmed. The world, the universe, was just chaos—temporarily and personally shaped by the observer.

His mother had taught him that, too. The hard way.

He walked down the center aisle and then exited through one of the doors near the stage.

More dark and cold and rug-muffled silence.

Mors trotted up three flights to the lecture halls and labs, frosty moonlight latticing the hallway.

Each room told him exactly nothing, until he came to the Tank room.

There was noise behind the steel door. A clicking, scrabbling, shuffling something that raised his hackles. The Tank room was the only place he'd ever—Mors shook that away in real disgust, annoyed to feel a sheen of sweat over his body.

He put his hand on the door and took his gun out silently.

Whatever was in that room was nothing to fear, fear me.

He set his hand on the wheel and spun it, the door opened easily and something big and black exploded out, slamming into his chest.

Mors almost fired into the mass just as it began to slobber all over his face.

"Brando? Brando, holy shit!"

Brando, a very large black lab despite being a little skinnier, licked and writhed and wagged his tail so violently that More had to struggle to get out from under him.

"Okay, okay! Easy, easy. That's a good boy. Good boy, Brando. It's okay. Good doggie."

And so on. Mars soothed him and then went in the Tank room.

Brando the lab, one of Guild house's four dogs, whined and hung back, refusing to enter.

More told him to stay and kept going, flashlight playing about the room.

The Tank room was so named for its three inhabitants, a clear plexiglass tank and two rivet-bristling stainless-steel tanks, all big enough to hold a pair of Clydesdales suspended in a small swimming pool's worth of water. The plastic tank and one of the steel tanks held extremely salty water, the other held some kind of thick, viscous gel.

Screens on crane-like black stands and other mounted equipment was gathered about the two steel tanks like a crowd of motionless giant praying mantises.

The faculty of Guild house were inside the clear, triple layered acrylic tank.

So were the other three dogs.

Mors shuddered once, violently, but whether at what he was seeing or the flash-memory of thousands upon thousands of tiny claws he couldn't say and wouldn't search inside to know.

The Tank was full of water, with Mr. Blue, Ms. Mercy, Mr. Quark, Dr. Yes, and Professor Artemis all suspended within it, along with Pasha, Orson, and Gandalf—the other dogs.

All of them were naked, blue-white in the flashlight wash, bloated, and a tangle of limbs, hair and humility, the dog's limbs among the human like a Lovecraft bookplate illustration.

Mors made himself circle the tank, illuminating the giant knot of dead bodies with the powerful flashlight, circling three full times, peering through the thick crystal-clear glass acrylic to fully identify each lifeless, distorted face.

He knew them well, even in this condition.

Four were missing. The Kestrel, obviously.

Gardener. He was jugged safely back at Dan's.

The Nightingale wasn't among the dead. Neither was Iron Horse. And each had a neat bullet hole in the forehead. How?

Why?

* * *

Mors found one answer as he searched each floor, Brando padding along happily at his side after he'd given him a bowl of water.

Iron Horse was in the second-floor library, sprawled in a huge pool of long-dried blood near an aquarium filled with dead fish. He had two bullet holes in his back, and one in the back of his head. Brando sniffed the edge of the blood-soak and then hung back, whining, pressing his skinny flanks against Mors.

Mors soothed the dog and then, snorting the high stench of rot, which was intense despite the cold, turned the stiff body over with a crackling ripping sound.

The old Indian had been shot once in the knee as well, perhaps the first shot, though it was impossible to say without an autopsy.

An autopsy would be unlikely.

Iron Horse had been knee-capped, probably the most painful wound a person could get and still live. He'd made his way across the library and had been shot twice in the back. He'd dragged a metal magazine rack down with him, magazines spilled all around him, under him, like fallen leaves.

He'd left a bloody handprint, livid in its dark, splattered imprimatur, heavy and complete in the center of a catalogue periodical.

TERRITORIAL SEED COMPANY
ALL THE PIECES TO YOUR GARDENING PUZZLE
SPRING 2012

Seeds
Plants
Garlic
Growing Supplies Growing Strong For 30 Years!

Mors picked up the catalogue, examining the handprint in its center.

He ran his big hand over the dry blood, the last mark of The Iron Horse.

Mors remembered liking the old Indian. His specialty was tracking. The silent stalk. Ambush techniques. Evading a larger force bent on your capture, if things went that way.

And sometimes they did.

"All THE PIECES OF YOUR GARDENING PUZZLE."

Mors slipped the catalogue inside his coat. Then he slid his belt off and used it as a makeshift leash for Brando, not wanting the hungry dog to go haring off when they got outside.

I wonder how he escaped the killer? *Some instinct, something told him that the dog's survival was a fluke, not a message.*

"You were always the alpha dog, big boy," Mors said, rubbing the lab's blocky head.

Mors was troubled. He'd only ever been really scared as an adult once before, and that had been here too.

CHAPTER NINETEEN

Kalorama Getaway. Roarke Call One. Buzzcock Wants In.

I MOVED INTO MY TOWNHOUSE in Kalorama in the Northwest Quadrangle of Washington, DC, and, after unpacking, decided to go about a few housekeeping chores while waiting for Buzzcock to call.

Compared to fall in Maine, it was tropical.

The townhouse was very nice, beautifully furnished, and fully stocked. Not that I didn't need some things.

It felt unsettling to be unarmed and on the other hand, a relief to be alone after a few days of constant company and talk. Particularly the last talk I had with Gardener.

"I have serious reservations about this, Daniel."

"Too late," I said, "you toasted on it."

Mors had left in the late afternoon, figuring to make it to Guild house in the middle of the night.

"I'm serious, Daniel. *Kidnapping* these three is not according the letter of the agreement."

"What agreement would that be, Gardener? This person, or people, haven't made any fucking agreement. They're blackmailing us. I thought we agreed that this was maybe the only way to smoke them out."

"You and *Mors* agreed," Gardener said, "and Mors—"

"Mors is Mors," I said. "Look, Gardener, we snatch these three, and then we negotiate. No Kestrel, no triple murder of Republican douchebags."

"And then what? What if they say, 'Forget it'? What if they say that—"

"Why are you so hung up on *they*, Gard?"

He sat down heavily on the couch.

"I don't know. I just can't conceive of anyone being able to best the Guild, to *know* the inner workings of the Guild, that wasn't a group. People who had the means, experience, and resources to learn about us."

"The Thanatos Guild is that secret? I wish you'd tell me more about it. I wish I'd had my head out of my ass enough to be more curious in the beginning."

"I can't tell you any more about it, and you don't want to know. You already know far more than is safe. Do you remember what we referred to your flight as, all flights actually, before *Perfectus*?"

"Tools," I said, "you'd call us '*Tools*.'"

"That's right," Gardener said, "and that was more than our version of West Point calling its cadets *Knobs*, or *Plebes*—or firemen calling their candidates *Proby*. You are tools, Daniel. And that's all you were ever meant to be."

I lit a cigarette, annoyed with myself for letting the habit return after three years of freedom.

"I have to say that really pisses me off, Gardener. I thought the Guild was more than that. More than a mill for just killing machines. The Kestrel used to say—"

"The Kestrel is a master manipulator," Gardener said, taking a drink. "I'm sorry. But that's the whole point of his screed."

Gardener didn't look well to me. He was drinking way too much, for one thing.

"I was given a *choice*, Gardener. To be a *Thug*, or a *Paladin*. *I'm a Paladin*. I believe in the Dark Bushido. It's what I've got."

Gardener's face looked like it was melting, he was frowning so deeply.

"The *Dark Bushido* is just a lie, Daniel," he said.

"Not to me it isn't. Look, I think the Kestrel is probably doomed. He's dead, or soon will be. But this is the only way I can think of to shake these people and open up a face to face."

"And what do you hope to accomplish with that?" Gardener said.

"Well, I hope to get some answers. They send a representative to a meeting—once they know we have Larry, Moe, and Curly jugged someplace—I plan on quizzing that person with a blowtorch."

"That's not funny, Daniel," he said.

"What made you think I was kidding?" I said. "I've killed more men than *Mors*, Gardener. They fuck with me, I'll see they pay for the privilege. Count on it."

Gardener shook his head but stopped arguing the point. "Lord Henry," I said.

"Yes, Mr. Ketch."

"Please allow designate Gardener to have access to all tiers of your duties until you are directed otherwise."

"I beg your pardon, sir, but I must ask you for a code to enable that."

"I know. Listen, Lord Henry: Moblis in Moblis," I said. There was a tone, a deep, buzzing basso profundo.

"Understood, sir," Lord Henry said.

"There you go, Gard," I said. "The helm is yours."

"And what, pray, am I to do with the helm? You seem to have your course set."

"I'm doing what I can think to do. All you seem to be able to offer is either 'I don't knows' or hopeless rollovers. You didn't want Mors to go to Guild house either, said it was a waste—"

"Because I told you, everyone in this thing has *gone to ground*. I can't reach anyone of the Guild masters. I call, and the house service is disconnected, a service that puts your *Lord Henry* to shame. What Mors hopes to accomplish is beyond my ken."

"Let Mors worry about that," I said. "In the meantime, Lord Henry is the system you have. Maybe you can work with it, *him*, to figure out something that can help us. Plus, you're safe here. Lord Henry can keep you safe. Better even than Guild house. Believe it."

"That you actually care about that is both rather ridiculous—and the reason I came to you, Dan."

* * *

Late that night, after Gardener was asleep and the house was quiet and dark.

"Mr. Ketch?"

"Yes."

"I'm sorry to disturb you, sir. I have Mr. Mors on the line. Voice-stress analysis indicates that there is some urgency."

"Mors sounds nervous," I said.

"As I understand '***nervous,' yes***," Lord Henry said.

"Patch him through."

The door was closed, and the armory was soundproof.

Mors began without preamble.

"Everyone at Guild house is dead," he said.

"*What*? Wait, let me get Gardener," I said. "He's up in—"

"No, Dan. If you're in private, stay that way."

"What the hell are you talking about; who's everyone?"

"Every master we had except for the Nightingale, Gardener, and the Kestrel," he said, "and Brando."

That threw me.

"Brando? Marlon Brando?"

"The *dog*, you idiot," Mars said.

Mors described his visit to Guild house and what he found there.

I sat down heavily. *All those people.*

And the fucking dogs.

We feel pain too, creatures such as we. The killers, the mercenaries in the cold cracks between the machinations that form your illusion of the world.

"Where's the Nightingale?" I said.

"How would I know? And don't talk to Gardener about it."

"What? Why?"

"Because," Mors said, "something's hinky here. If the Nightingale is still alive, which I doubt, she's in her eyrie. She's a scary old lady, but she got old by *being scary*. And smart. Leave her out of it."

"Yeah, but Gardener—" I said.

"Yeah, Gardener. I don't know. Something's not right. And I found something when I found Iron Horse. It might just be hoo-doo voodoo, but something's bugging me. Maybe about him, I don't know. You need to see what I'm talking about."

"Well, what the fuck did you find?" I said.

"I'll show you when I see you. In Washington," he said.

"When's your flight?"

"I'm driving," he said.

"Mors, Jesus, why? You—"

"I've got a fucking dog to take care of," he said.

Mors was the most bizarre human being I knew. Bizarre in that way that men who you've seen throw a sixty-year-old man off a highway overpass are when they also fuss over a scared and underfed black lab.

And people say we're psychopaths.

"Look," I said, "drop Brando off at a kennel; you can—"

"He's not going to a kennel," Mors said. "Let me think."

"Okay, don't hurt yourself," I said.

"Look, you lay low until fucking Buzzcock calls, then get our shit stowed, and I'll be there soon."

"Message received and understood," I said.

"Leave Gardener out of it for now," Mors said.

"All right, for Christ's sake!"

"Keep calm and carry on," he said.

He was gone.

* * *

I spent my first afternoon in Washington buying wine and a few other things I didn't have, though there was plenty of food in the fridge, pantry, and cabinets.

I was still feeling antsy, walking around without any weapon as yet, but once Buzzcock showed up that would be taken care of.

And, of course, there's unarmed, then there's *unarmed*, as anyone who'd spent time wired-up in the Tank room could attest. And the real reason I was feeling so out of sorts was more immediate. It was time to call my daughter. And I was afraid.

I had been given other gifts during my hours in the Tank room. My copy, maybe the only copy of *The New Assassin's Field Guide & Almanac*, was at home in a fireproof safe, in the Vault. But it was also in my head, intact.

> *From The New Assassin's Field Guide & Almanac.*
>
> *Chapter V. The Red World.*
>
> *Your life is often a reflection of all you fear. Need is fear, turned on its side. Thus, one must fear nothing and no one. Instead, be that which is needed and, when the occasion warrants, that which is feared.*
>
> *When fear threatens to infect the assumed mind, one must stay anchored to the present moment, realizing all else is illusion. Erase regret, erase anticipation, and focus upon the immediate action to be taken.*

Right.

Or maybe only sort of. The past couple days had shaken my faith in the whole calm, cool, and collected assassin thing.

But if one of the most dangerous men I knew was driving around looking for dog food, the least I could do was call my kid.

I lit a cigarette and picked up the scrambler and dialed. "Hello," Dagny said. "Hello?"

"Hi, Dagny. Ah, it's me. Dan."

"Dan! Oh, okay! Just a sec," she said.

Jesus!

"Hello?"

The voice (if you haven't talked to an eight-year-old girl lately) sounded like an elf. Bright, clear as crystal, and questing.

"Ummm, hi. Is this Rourke?"

"Yes, it is," she said.

"Hi. This is Dad. Dan. Daniel," I said.

"Hi," she said, then, "you're Dan Ketch. My father."

Oh boy.

"I guess that's right," I said. "How are you?"

"Do you smoke cigarettes?"

"Uh," I said and, like some old Dick Van Dyke routine, dropped my cigarette on my pants and tried to grab it in a fountain of stinging sparks.

"Why do you ask that?" I said, grinding the butt out in the ashtray.

"Because I can hear you smoking," she said.

"Well, I'm not smoking now," I said.

"You shouldn't smoke. It's very, very bad for you."

"That's true," I said. "You're right."

"Then why do you do it?" she said.

"That's a good question, Rourke. I don't know really. But I should quit, huh?"

"Yes, you should."

"What did you do today?"

"I helped take care of our horses, Woody and Buck. Buck only has one eye."

"No kidding," I said.

"Mm-hm," she said, "would you like to have lunch sometime here?"

"Ah, sure," I said, "if Dag—if Mommy says it's okay."

"Oh, she will," Rourke said. "She says you're very lonely and very dangerous but that you would *never* hurt us."

Okay. Everybody out of the pool.

"Well, that's true. I mean, I'm not dangerous, and I wouldn't ever—"

"Yes, you are," she said. "I can hear it in your voice. Not mean, but all claws and paws and jaws."

"Ah," I said.

"You're like talking to a lion," she said.

My mind was a complete blank.

"But that's okay. I like lions," Rourke said.

"Okay, honey," I said. "Can I talk to Mommy again?"

"Okay. Bye for now!"

"Bye," I said.

"Hello?" Dagny said.

"Hi. Listen, did you tell Rourke I was dangerous?"

"No. Well, not exactly. Danny, she reads voices. Facial things. It's pretty weird. Not always; sometimes it's—usually it's amazing."

"Okay," I said.

I lit another cigarette.

"Rourke *loved* talking with you. I can tell," she said.

"Good. That's good," I said.

"Listen, I have to go," Dagny said. "I'm sorry. We're having our roof fixed; there's a crew here. I know this is all, well, *a lot*. Will you call again next week? Or even during the week?"

"Sure," I said.

We said goodbye and hung up.

Claws and paws and jaws?

"Oh brother," I said to no one.

* * *

"Jesus Christ, what is this place, where all the Beltway douches go to mate?" Buzzcock said.

We were in Mehak, an Indian restaurant in Chinatown. I was having a Kingfisher Lager, Buzzcock, a rum and coke.

We were sharing garlic naan bread.

Mehak was a nice place, pretty quiet tonight, and a good place to talk. The lighting was sedate, laying a golden glow over everything. Buzzcock poked a small wooden statue of an Indian prince. *Arjuna*, I think.

"Fuck is that, Indian nutcracker?"

Rupert Buzzcock was swarthy, sweaty, balding in a bad way, not like Mors's craggy neatness, and only about five feet tall. He could stain any shirt, ruin any jacket or pants, or foul an atmosphere with a sour funk of old, lived-in cigarette smoke in mere minutes.

"It's a pretty popular restaurant, according to my realtor," I said.

He waved it away with one heavily ringed hand.

"So, what's the rumpus?"

Buzzcock was the only washout I knew of from the Guild who wasn't dead. Normally, you either did the Three and moved on to what I did, what Mors and the others did or—more rarely—went back to civilian life.

Usually the only other alternative was ending up like Jeromy.

I didn't know Buzzcock's story, but somehow, he'd achieved neither Thug, Paladin, or corpse status and instead was part of the shadowy infrastructure that worked with and lived off of the Guild, like a pilot fish darting among sharks.

And Buzzcock loved the lingo.

"Can't tell you, Rupert. You know that," I said.

"*Aww*, c'mon! I got everything you asked for; the room's almost finished—"

"And you'll be paid," I said.

"C'mon! Let me in on this! I'm good inna tight corner. I don't even need a cut."

"No. Thanks, Rupert."

"Who's the bunny?"

Oh brother. It was even worse when he used outdated lingo.

"Never mind, Rupert. Where's the gear?"

"Nearby. *Proteus*. Proteus, fuck is that, fucking Greek?"

"Where, goddamn it?"

"In a parking garage, where I stashed it after getting it at the airport. You know, I'm not fucking stupid. I *know* this is a two- or three-man show. I can tell just from the shit you asked for and that room. Lernme in. I need the legitimacy."

"Look, Buzzcock, you are in. In the way that's best for the Guild."

"Bullshit!" he said, slamming his fist on the table, making the silverware jump and all the other diners glance over.

"I bet Mors is in on it," Buzzcock said.

I said nothing and opened my dessert menu.

"Awright. Okay," he said, opening his own, "I know Bleach is in. I've got fucking eyes. Mors and his *Invisible Man* bullshit."

"What the fuck are you talking about? You've seen Bleach?"

This was alarming. It could be Rupert baiting me. Or coincidence, maybe overlapping ops.

But I didn't believe in coincidence.

And Bleach was very bad news.

Rupert kept perusing his desert choices, elaborately casual.

"I saw Bleach. Fucking douchebag doesn't *know* I saw him, but yeah. Yeah."

"Where?"

"On the metro. Riding the metro. Just yesterday. Riding the fuckin' metro like a big man in his stupid clothes."

A brief word about Bleach: His hair was yellow-white, a kind of dirty white, not albino by any means. I don't know why, but it didn't look right, like his hair was dead somehow.

Bleach was a very snappy dresser and a very ruthless (and cruel) killer. Pure Thug. He'd been in the same flight as Mors and me. We had never offered *naming* to each other. We'd recognized each other as immediate enemies.

It may sound funny coming from a contract killer, but Bleach was a monster. He specialized in vengeance killings. He had no boundaries in either his behavior or his appetites.

And hearing him mentioned in context with this clusterfuck I was trying to pull off made me deeply uneasy.

"Did you talk to him?"

"What? No! I just saw him in passing; he didn't see me. And now you're here, so I figured—"

"Rupert, listen to me. Stop figuring. Stop talking. Have a drink, have something to eat. You're really beginning to irritate me."

"Okay, all right! Jesus, relax. No harm meant, no harm done," he said.

After the waiter had come and gone (giving Rupert another look like I'd brought an orangutan in with me—a dirty, loud one), he cheered up after two glasses of Chivas.

"Hey. When'd you last get laid? 'Cause I know a joint—"

I sighed.

CHAPTER TWENTY

Lord of the Hyena. The Last Words of Cintilla Ruiz. Disclosure Agreements.

OUTSIDE, IT BEING WASHINGTON, the street was crowded with transvestites.

I kid, but not entirely. I learned later that there was an annual event called the DC Drag Queen Race. It was held on Halloween, but this was apparently a warm-up act, currently being run as a preview, check which heels were best, and so on.

Buzzcock, put-off by my refusal to discuss any plans for paid loving, was delighted, in a pretending-to-be-scandalized way, as we were almost run down by a huge group of men in wigs, dresses, and high heels, running as fast as they could manage.

"Jesus Christ, lookit these fuckin' fruits! Watch it you goddamn freak! Buncha fags."

"Actually, Rupe, I hear most transvestites like women," I said, stepping back from a trotting man in a bouffant hairdo, trailing a boa.

"Whaddaya talking about? They're queers! Jesus, lookatem!"

Well, the man squeezed the lemon of life, you had to give him that.

It was full night now and fall-chilly, even for Washington.

The air smelled like smoke and leaves.

I didn't want to partake in what Buzzcock called his "pussy hunt," but as he was taking me to where he's stashed the van (we called it such, less attention-grabbing than talking about "the ambulance") and its contents, I was thinking of treating him to another round before we parted. No hard feelings and all that—when there was a sudden shrieking of tires.

And then gunshots.

It was probably a sad commentary on what we'd both chosen to do for a living that Rupert and I hunched and then hit the ground flat while nearly everyone else turned to look, some aiming their camera phones.

Too much TV. Too many movies. Too many reality shows.

Screams all around. I had a disjointed weird thought about the "Drag race": did transvestites scream like men or women?

With my hands over my head, lying on the sidewalk, I craned my neck up to see what was happening. High heels skittered past me, and I saw one drag queen writhing on the ground, another lying across him, no, trying to drag him out of harm's way. Blood was pouring from his bare shoulder, his wig behind him in the street.

Further up the sidewalk were two people filming with their phones, their faces pinched and intent upon the little blue screens as opposed to the real-life gunship pulling a screeching U-turn just in front of the gate to Chinatown and coming back.

Behind the fallen queen and his rescuer, a Hispanic kid was scrambling a crabwalk to a shop doorway, already occupied by a cringing young woman almost climbing into the big carriage to protect a baby.

The kid glanced back at the screaming woman coolly, and drew his gun out, peering around the edge of the doorway.

The car was a dark blue station wagon, with a driver and two masked guys sitting on the front and back window frames and aiming over the hood as they came up the street for a second pass.

I got up.

Rupert squealed like a kid in first grade, terrified over his scariest teacher.

"*What the fuck are you doing?!*"

A good question. All I knew was that I was suddenly crazy with rage.

As the gang gunship accelerated, burning rubber, I took three strides toward the boy in the doorway. He was just standing up fully, his attention now divided between me and the approaching wagon.

"Hey—" he said, his gun low and vaguely pointed at the wagon, and as the car's big mill roared louder, I kicked him in the balls as hard as I could. I yanked the gun out of his hand as he went sideways and down, and before his hip hit the pavement, I kicked him in the stomach, barely able to hear the kid's high, keening "HOOOO—" before I stomped on the side of his head, bouncing it once off the bricks and shutting him up in mid "-OOH!"

The woman was draped entirely over the carriage, a dark form.

I stepped forward, the wagon now coming on almost parallel for their volley, and holding the kid's shitty Beretta in a two-handed stance, I shot the driver through the windshield, which instantly imploded, and then I shot the passenger-side window gunman.

The out of control car plowed left into a parking meter, sheering it off, and then came to a rumbling stop, engine still howling, against another car with a huge crunch.

Rupert was on the ground behind me almost gibbering like a cartoon squirrel "*Don't, don't, don't, don't!*"

The backseat shooter shot through the back window at me, the bullet droning through the air well to my right. One of the camera phone people, a man, screamed and went down hard.

The backseat shooter lunged out of the window, and I shot him twice in the chest.

I leaned down to the driver, whose face was pouring blood, safety glass stuck like quills to his forehead, nose, and lips, the steering wheel crushed into his sternum, and my shot a sucking wound, high on his left chest.

"*La concha de to madre*, you fuckin' with *Cintilla*, bitch. You call a fuckin' ambulance, you fuckin' shit cop, you get me help!"

"'Cintilla? That's your name?"

"Call my fucking ambulance, *pendejo*! Kiss your badge goodbye."

"No," I said, leaning in, "You see, Cintilla, I'm not a cop. *I'm a lion.* You and your friends? You're just jackals. Hyena. Fighting over scraps, fucking up the neighborhood."

"Call a fuckin' *ambulance*!" he screamed.

"You don't need one," I said and shot him.

I turned and walked back to the sidewalk where the camera-phone guy was fish-hooking in on himself in an ever-expanding pool of blood. I paused to stomp his phone to shards.

Now everyone was gone except Rupert, two drag-queens, the shot guy, mom and baby, and the kid who'd been the target.

There were always sirens, but these seemed on approach.

"Let's go, Rupert," I said, yanking him to his feet.

I looked back at the kid who was their target. He was stirring.

The woman draped over the carriage was peering around the side of her own hair. I gave her a thumbs up.

Rupert was screeching like an outraged nun.

"*Why the fuck did you do that? Look at what you did! You don't do that!*"

"Shut up and let's go," I said.

* * *

Rupert waited until we had inspected and unloaded the van before he finally needed to vent.

He came puffing into my living room and dropped the boxy case onto the coffee table with a significant thud, helping himself to a scotch I'd poured for him.

"Jesus Christ on a fuckin' *toboggan*, what the fuck was that about? No. *No!* Don't give me the scary killer how-dare-you-question-me look! I coulda been killed! That had nothing to do with us. You—me, we *both* coulda been pinched! Greased! Both!"

I was particularly pleased with the snatch vehicle Rupert had secured, a former Detroit Fire Department ambulance, now refitted for our needs and with all sorts of magnetic ID, easy slap on or take off, so I let him rant for a while.

Eventually he repeated the loop twice and then calmed down with another drink under his belt.

"Rupert, I don't like being in a firefight during an after-dinner stroll. I'm sick of hearing about people just lying on the floor while some asshole walks around shooting everyone. Or worse, standing around with their videophones, like they're in a fucking theme park."

"So you just run into a gang fight and kill everyone."

"I didn't kill everyone. I left that one kid they were gunning for alive."

"Huh. Why bother? Another witness," he said.

"I doubt it. We'll never hear about it again."

"Then why not ace him too? Fuck it. You think he'd thank you?"

"The proper term for a killing, Rupert, is '*slate*.' And I don't care if he thanks me. I didn't do it for him."

"Then why?" he said.

"Because some things are not to be tolerated."

Rupert shook his head.

"Jeez, you guys. *Paladins and Thugs*, whatta buncha bullshit. You're hitmen. That's all. Who cares about what your little fantasies of knighthood or samauraihood or whatever the fuck they are?"

"I care," I said. "Bow drop it. You're getting on my nerves."

"Awright, take it easy. I'm just talking about professionalism, Jesus."

I finished my drink and lit a cigarette.

"What do you have for me?"

Rupert got up and unlatched the case.

"Ho-kay. We got two Heckler and Koch P30s, two Les Baer 1911s, and a Korth. Annnnd a NAA Guardian," he said, gently lifting each gun and displaying it like shady salesman.

"Plus, these little babies," he said, holding out a slender, black gun that looked too insectile-frail to fire a bullet.

"The Murdock 950. Fires these," he said.

He held up a thin metal cartridge with a stubby needle on the end pointing up and a steel-ball body surrounded by a black plastic tri-fin. "You have six of these. Filled with one dose of *Immobilon*, or *etorphine* and *phenothioazine* mixed together, to be specific. It'll drop anybody in about five seconds, but—"

"Ah," I said, "but?"

"Well," Rupert said, "the size of the target matters. I mean, why don't cops carry tranq guns? Because they'd fucking kill people once a week, that's why. You dart a little kid with one of these, they're dead. Old lady, bad heart, like that? Sayonara. And listen, the target's a big guy, like you or Mors? It could take a few seconds. Minute, tops. The point is, get impatient and use two, you could end up with a corpse on your hands. Fair warning."

I picked up the dart gun and examined it.

"Also, you have to be within fifteen, maybe twenty feet, to be accurate. You know, it's funny, you asking for shit to knock people out. I mean, you usually just kill people, right?"

I looked at Rupert, but he seemed to be getting used to that particular look.

"Awright, geez. But—if this is something out of your usual line, maybe you need some help?"

"Nope," I said and pointed the dart gun at him.

"*Okay*! Okay, that's not funny. Jesus."

I put the gun down.

"What about the room?" I said.

"Almost done. I hadda sacrifice a neat job for a fast one, but it'll be fine. Wait'll you see the place. It's fucked." Being a hard-bitten assassin, I should have concluded our business at that point.

And if I wanted to be *particularly* hard-bitten, I'd have killed him and dumped his body in the Potomac, but I didn't want to be alone right now. I wasn't scared; it was more that I had a ritual to carry out and having company made it easier to get on with it.

"You hungry?" I said.

Rupert looked confused.

"We just ate, but yeah. Sure. Why?"

"Let's have a little something," I said, getting up to check the fridge and pantry.

* * *

Omyra Ruiz was a sallow, pinch-faced woman, known as a "party girl" and sometimes prostitute. During a robbery attempt (along with two hulking male cohorts), she beat an elderly woman to death with a golf club when the heist proved unprofitable.

She stoically maintained her innocence. Both of her accomplices refused to testify in her defense. Her last meal was pretty simple—fried oysters.

Her last words were: "I could have been more if all you good people hadn't kept me down."

* * *

"Jesus, this is delicious! We should have just stayed here," Rupert said.

"Glad you like it," I said.

The oysters were fresh from World Seafood and, oddly enough, the Master Chief's recipe. Simple as hell. Butter, 1 cup oysters, white wine, chopped green onion, three eggs, and a dash of chopped parsley.

Salt and pepper to taste.

I served it with a crusty loaf of bread, toasted in the oven and torn by hand.

"Tell me something," I said, "how is it that you're not a Paladin, you're not a Thug, but—"

Rupert's face darkened.

"But I'm still alive? Why should I tell you? You won't tell me anything. I ask about the rumpus, 'mind your business, Rupert.' I ask about Mors, 'shut up, Rupert.' I get you your shit, get a crew of reliable on the room, you nearly get my ass shot off in a street fight, like you decided suddenly you're Wyatt Fucking Earp or something."

He had a point, really.

"I made you a nice post-dinner, post gun-fight snack," I said.

"True," he said, "so—I will make you a deal. I will tell you why I'm the only Guild washout still breathing if you tell me something first. You know, like the *quid pro poe* thing."

"*Quid pro quo,*" I said. "Like what?"

Rupert drummed his fingers on the table, his plate all but licked clean.

"Awright. I wanna hear about your *Three*. I want to hear how Mors and you became buddies. I mean, most hitmen don't have nice little hitmen best friends, secret handshakes in the treehouse and like that. Unless you're queers, which—"

"Rupert. Have you ever had *any* friends?"

"Oh," he said, "trying to rub that in my face now?" *Gloriosky*.

He hurried past my look, which must have hurt. There's something extra terrible about the pity of a killer, I think. He threw his drink back.

"I want to hear about the fucking tiger," he said.

Everyone does, sooner or later.

"Okay, Rupert. That's a lot, but I'll tell you the story. Then it's your turn. And then, a miracle will have taken place."

"What miracle?"

"Then we'll be friends," I said.

To see the look of innocent surprise and the little fat kid hidden under the scruffy moon-face was both moving and a little awful. I thought of Fatty Farazzo in his unicorn cap.

And I felt bad about considering killing Buzzcock. The Potomac, cinderblocks, all that.

CHAPTER 21

Think Tank. Ant Farm. Jiufeng's Toes. The Razor Teds.

IT'S HARD TO JUST REMEMBER my time at Guild house in a clear, linear fashion, let alone tell it that way. I suspect that the Think Tank has something to do with that.

It was the clear one, though my first time inside it was encircled with glowing screens, computer equipment, cameras, lights, and other apparatus I couldn't identify, all of it webbed and netted in an incomprehensible tangle of cables and multicolored wires. One box had *Holographic Display* stenciled on it.

Before I got in, Dr. Yes and the Nightingale prepped me. Stood naked on the cold white floor as Dr. Yes attached sensors to my temples, chest, arms, shoulders, calves, and thighs.

"The glue on these is powerful. Let us take them off after the session. The spots stay sticky and can get bruised after a few immersions. Nothing to worry about, but they can look weird and need the proper care."

The Nightingale was a wizened little woman with very dark glasses that looked clunky and heavy enough for welding. In a white lab coat like the Doctor, she had me sit on the exam table once I was festooned with sensors and trailing wires.

They had the routine down pat, both taking turns talking as they both set a heavy helmet over my head that was mostly black, looked like hybrid of a diving helmet, fly's head, and carburetor. It enclosed my entire head and settled onto my shoulders with thick, black foam padding. I could still see and after a click, could hear them fine again, on earphones.

"It's awkward, I know," the Nightingale said, "but once you're in you won't even notice it.

"The Helm is a mural-phonic system, designed to generate a wide variety of virtual scenarios, teaching programs, and both subliminal and overt hypnotic audio and visual sequencing," Dr. Yes said.

"It's a teaching tool, Richard, let's not overwhelm them with techno-babble," the Nightingale said, patting my forearm with a very cold hand.

"The sensor pads will stimulate your muscles with electric pulses, as well as enhance some scenarios. The worst time is the first night after immersion. It's painful. But we'll help with that, and it's only a day or two," he continued.

"Later," the Nightingale said, "we'll also use different sedatives to work with various program modules, speed things along. Just allow *Cyberius* to guide you."

I don't remember that first climb up the steel scaffold, the metal grill painted a bright yellow, or getting sealed in.

I remember the voice in the helm. Soothing. Sexless. A computer-generated voice, yes, but with human inflection without being human at all. As I float in warm darkness and a series of black-and-white geometric patterns flare before my eyes, the tiny red word *Calibration* flashing for a few seconds before the patterns began to speed up.

"Answer each question simply and quickly. There is no wrong answer. At the end of this you will be given a choice of names."

Maybe they'd already given us drugs. I can't say. The questions were very strange, and I cannot remember my answers.

Not one.

"Explain the meaning of the word 'IF.'"

"What are the nine uses for rage?"

"The dog is running toward you, do you run toward it?"

"Is the headstone in the sun, the rain, mossy, or under snow?"

"What would the zebra choose for its eulogy after the lions ate it?"

"What is the color of fear?"

It seemed a long time in the "Think Tank," as I learned it was called.

I saw pictures, films—new and ancient—of the previous flights of the past century, unsmiling posed groups and portraits, some as few as three and others as large as a softball team.

From any time period or fashion, it was the eyes that were unsettling. Eyes like mine.

Each flight had a name, supposedly absolutely meaningless.

Just a word.

Sabre.

Magenta.

Robur.

Braille.

Narthex.

Manta.

"You are now a member of Patience Flight. Consider the list of names and choose one. It will be your only name here."

I do remember having to be helped from the tank. After I chose Proteus as my name, there was a brief demonstration of how the sticky pads worked.

It started simply, with an obviously cartoon image of a path in a forest.

"Walk," Cyberius said in my ears.

Then the simulations got progressively more detailed and astonishing. Desert. Ice field. Beach. Mars. The Moon.

And all the while, the voice calmly encouraging yet, somehow, implacable.

"Jog."

I jogged across desert.

"Run."

I ran through a rainforest.

"Sprint."

I sprinted across hard sand. Not actually running, but the electric stimulation made my muscles writhe as if I were.

It was exhilarating. Then, excruciating.

* * *

That night at dinner. Or maybe the third night. Or the fourth, I met all the new people.

The handsome, bespectacled black guy was *D'jall.* The heavy girl with black hair was *Lamia*. The Scottish guy with the weird white-blond hair was *Bleach. Black-Annie* was the diminutive redhead girl, *Mors* was the balding, scruffy big guy.

Jiufeng was the Asian woman who was almost my height and shook hands in a lingering fashion. *Rubik* ("with a 'K,'" he both pointed out and underlined on his nametag) was the short, high-school kid. Miskali was the bald black woman in her thirties.

The nametags made it both silly and very real. We talked about what they meant, or politely refused to.

My nametag said *Proteus.*

"Poseidon's son" seemed to satisfy anybody who asked.

We took classes, as a whole flight, as pairs, trios, individuals, that were never on any college curriculum, classes on weapons, wars, battle techniques and histories of wars, explosives, safe-cracking, hotwiring vehicles, disarming alarm systems and unlocking doors. I met Gardener and learned that a "Russian Omelet" is a good way to break someone's back and that it usually kills them.

I learned that a "*Rasputin*" was a slate-attempt that goes incredibly, unpredictably wrong, the target simply refusing to die. I learned that to be "Straw-dogged" was when your target was holed-up and trying to actively keep you out.

I knew I was changing into Proteus when I listened with a laughing group in the dining hall to a particularly grisly Rasputin story and actually found it funny.

In the Think Tank, as my body was drugged and exercised and new reflexes and eye-hand coordination neural pathways were carved into the meat of my brain, I'd sometimes listen to lectures recorded by the Kestrel and the other masters, both long past and present. The voices, old and young, male and female, blended into a dry litany.

Murder is everywhere. This culture, Western culture, prefers to pretend otherwise, but our entertainments prove otherwise. Our literature, our fantasies, large and small, our politics, our worship, all lead inexorably to the bullet or the blade. Sports as cloaked gladiatorial matches, so many ways that societies seek to hide or romanticize this truth can't make it any less so. The homicide rate in America is among the highest of the industrialized nations. In one year, 14,748 murders, with minor variations for decade after decade.

If murder stems from the right brain, the borderland of madness, magic, the Dionysian realm, then you may consider the Thuggee path; if it's born of your reason, your logic, your Apollonian left-brain, some of you will choose to be among the Paladins.

Both are welcome. Useful. And above all, necessary.

The Thanatos Guild was centuries old and providing this vital, shadowed service to the machinations of man long before any other group or so-called "secret society." The Guild's warriors have shaped nations, brought down empires, sparked wars and snuffed them, both as easily as you might blow out a candle.

And though you may think yourselves as base predators, consider and study what befalls an ecosystem that loses its top-tier predators. It implodes. It dies.

"Food for thought," the Kestrel said during a discussion over real food, one late night, the dining hall smelling like peppermint from so many people slathered in ointment for inflamed musculature.

The food was always quite good.

And nobody else was shot before dessert, which was a relief.

* * *

But not all training took place in the tank room or the classroom. Sometimes you needed the real thing.

Various flights had given it various nicknames, *The Kill-Zone, Maze of Death, The Mousetrap, The Rattrap, Murderville, Elysium Flats*, but the official name was *The Ant Farm.*

On the outside, it looked like a college athletic center but somewhat bigger, a building the size of an aircraft hangar, set far back from the main building across the snow-blanketed lawn. Inside, it was a vast warren of simulacrum homes, offices, street settings, basements, and backyards, all roofless and easily observed from above by the steel catwalks that crisscrossed the entire, huge space.

When a scenario was running, the sections being used were the only ones lit. It made for a disturbing tableau when you observed from above. Just as jarring was being in a scenario and the moment it ended, having the world above explode into blazing rows of klieg lights.

And eventually, many were run in complete darkness with the observers wearing night-goggles, careful to snatch them off before the lights went on. Temporary blindness hurts.

Mors and I had already chatted over *Godot* together, *We are all born mad, some remain so*, but it was an incident in the Ant Farm that made us friends.

And made Bleach my nemesis.

The Kestrel was addressing the observer group while I stood alone below them, pulling on my foam rubber armor.

"We borrowed the name of an old con for this next exercise," the Kestrel said from the scaffolding above me. "You may have heard of it. *Two Brothers and A Stranger*. But in this case, it's not a con but a survival exercise. Below us, we have 'The Stranger,' our own Proteus."

Above me on the grilled catwalk alongside him were Black Annie,

Djall, Rubik, and Jiufeng, all with night-vision gear slid up on their foreheads or dangling around their necks. The group was in casual clothing, which I envied, as the padded armor was hot, especially under the lights.

Fifteen feet below, I was standing in the section of the Ant Farm that formed a two-story house, it's false streets, lampposts, hedges, trees all eerily authentic, and looking up at my classmates through the roofless master bedroom.

I noticed that I was almost directly below Jiufeng, and that from this angle, her body in bright red-and-green spandex was particularly inspiring, especially her ample curves.

She was leaning on the bright yellow rail, and I noticed she was also barefoot, her toes in a neat row gripping the edge of the platform.

She saw me looking up at her and made a truly goofy face and wiggled her toes at me, then laughed.

I grinned and looked away, forcing myself to wonder about who she'd killed, how and why and that she was here to get better at it. That happened a lot at Guild house, at breakfast, outside jogging on the outdoor track, during the evening news in the lounge when whoever might be hanging out there; these were the moments it snuck up on you.

This person is a murderer. They have killed and have chosen to turn pro. And after the initial inner shudder, you have a second one when you re-realize it about yourself.

It made a heated argument over the rules of *Monopoly* in the lounge—popcorn, sweats, and jammies and all that—take on an entirely different tone, let me tell you, than the typical college lounge spat.

"It's certainly not a regular occurrence, but on occasion you may arrive at a site and cross paths with another contractor, an occurrence that, as you might suspect, can be fatal for *all* parties involved. Not that it will be another Guild member, *that* is unheard of. We have our words."

I checked my pistol. Each scenario began with being given an equipment list and signing out whatever was required from the armory, be it guns, rope, lockpicks, goggles, you name it. We were all becoming experts at field stripping quite an incredible array of weapons, for both familiarity with the odd and also to choose our preferences. Today's show and tell was a Glock semi—auto, fully loaded with Baton Rounds, which basically boil down to rubber bullets, in layman's talk, and man oh man, did they fucking hurt, padded armor or no. You also had to know exactly what you were doing and stay on top of your increasingly lethal *Think-tanked* reflexes. A shot to the head with one of these rubber rounds would kill you just like lead.

"So, what do I do, as the, ah, *stranger*?" I said. Everyone looked down now, and Jiufeng winked at me, along with another toe show.

Dagny who?

"My. Well, Lord Proteus, your job is to be today's slate."

"Terrific," I said.

Polite laughter, just like in a normal school.

"Mr. Mors is going to be on approach when we go to Full Night. He believes he is on a routine slate, the objective being to slate an unknowing target. He believes the main objective is scaling the building due to alarm scenarios and street visibility. Mr. Bleach will approach from the opposite quadrant"—he gestured off to his right—"and his understanding of the scenario is that it is his lockpicking skills that are the primary point. Neither knows of the other. Neither know that the target is forewarned and forearmed."

"Ah," I said.

This was good, two of the scarier people I knew were coming to kill me.

Mors and I were circling some kind of friendliness, hard to say why, but Bleach was a different story.

Tall and whipcord thin, Bleach was all ropy muscle and gristle. He had an almost incomprehensible Glaswegian accent and long white-blond hair, like dirty ivory. He was almost always tricked out in a suit and tie, smiled more than any normal human ever would, and had supposedly already killed three people, even before being scouted.

Bleach had also bragged of beheading a dog and leaving it in a pot of boiling water at some gang leader's house in Glasgow, back when he was part of some gang, *The Razor Teds*, if memory serves. None of the women liked him either, it seemed.

Not a nice guy, even for a killer.

"Let us begin," the Kestrel said.

I nodded and looked around the master bedroom. Four large windows, pile carpet, tasteful bedroom set.

The Kestrel murmured into a walkie-talkie, presumably telling handlers on either end of the Ant Farm to "release the hounds."

"Full Night," he said, and the kliegs all thudded off, one by one, the blackness approaching from every direction until the only real light was the interior of the first floor below me.

And bad men were coming through the dead streets.

CHAPTER 22

My House My Rules. The Longshanks Solution.

JUST FOR SOMETHING TO DO, I decided to scramble around the house and turn all the interior lights off and all exterior lights on. Looking out the windows, you'd think you were in a real house on a leafy, vaguely autumnal street.

I saw no sign of my expected company and decided to try out an idea I'd just had.

I went to the dark kitchen, sweating now in my body armor and slipped outside.

Across the "street" from my house was a squat brick building that I knew actually housed a generator. I slipped into the pool of shadows under a scalloped doorway, out of the yellow glow of the nearest streetlight. I went into what Mr. Quark called "the statue crouch" and became still. Already part of a landscape for when Stan and Ollie eventually showed up.

I didn't have to wait long. Mors arrived first, just a glimpse of a dark shape near the fake hedges lining the back of home sweet home. His only big mistake was when he strapped on the climbing spikes, not the putting on, but climbing about six feet and then making this huge scraping sound when a shingle ripped loose, and Mors slid back down four feet.

Invisible Man my ass, I thought, knowing Mors was already enraged by his fuck-up. But he kept climbing, silent now and as swift as a spider monkey.

I stepped out of the shadows and sort of crept-ran into my backyard, trying to step properly on the plastic leaves, that is—silently, as Iron Horse had us learning to do on every surface imaginable, in every kind of shoe.

And I had to hand it to him, the back-porch deck sliding door lock had already been cracked, and Bleach was inside.

Seeing nothing in my shadowy living room, I slipped inside the same door, figuring I could catch Bleach on the stairs and put a round between his shoulder blades. Then, while he was dry-heaving and unable to breathe for a few excruciating seconds, I'd enjoy the show and just wait for Mors to try for me.

Which, as we'd learned in the Nightingale's plant-choked lecture hall, was a very difficult wait.

"The high ground works better outside," she said.

And that would have all been swell, if I hadn't heard a war erupt upstairs above me. A loud explosion shattered the silence of the Ant Farm, then thudding footsteps and breaking glass and then two more shots

Looking back, I should have stuck to the script and, being the *stranger* and all, run like hell away from my house.

But Jiufeng, unseen, was watching me. Gettit?

I was sick of being heartsick. Time to live in the moment, surrender to circumstance. All that.

* * *

What happened was sort of weird, really.

Bleach had cased the house and headed upstairs, fully kitted out in night goggles and found every room empty. In the meantime, Mors had reached the window and was about to cut the glass when Bleach saw his heat signature, along with the goggles around his neck, which you'd think was a tip-off that whatever was going on this guy wasn't the target.

But Bleach being Bleach shot Mors in the face. Or at least, tried to.

The rubber bullet smashed the window and whacked Mors in the shoulder, effectively "killing" that arm for the day. With powdered glass in one eye and a lot more driven into his cheeks and forehead, Mors slipped and fell a rocketing eight feet until he was able to drive the spikes in again and grab a hold with his left, as shingles clattered down around him. His right arm hung, useless, and his gun was still in a web holster on his armor.

Bleach smashed the rest of the window out with his pistol and leaned out and shot twice more as Mors clambered around the edge of the house, driving the climbing spikes in hard and grabbing the drainpipe with his good hand, ripping it away from the siding.

The first shot rang off the drainpipe; the second missed entirely.

Not that I knew any of that at the moment. I was creeping up the stairs to the master bedroom, more careful than ever now that the shooting had stopped.

I crawled from the stairs to the door and even in the gloom could see Bleach framed in the window by streetlight, still leaning out. I stood and moved as quietly as I could across the carpet.

He was laughing.

"So this is your idea of what a target would do, eh? This isnae a square go, mate."

"Fuck you," Mors said, still clinging to the twisted drainpipe and only able to see from one eye, blood covering half his face.

"Fuck me, is it? Awright. I always thought you were the biggest snotter in the place," Bleach said and pointed his pistol at Mors's head.

"Hey!" I yelled, and as Bleach spun toward me, I punched him in the face, twisting with my torso, hips. and legs the way the Master Chief had taught me for years.

The punch took Bleach clean off his feet and his gun went clattering.

He was already up on one knee, snarling “Shitebag!” when the light exploded biblically over our heads.

“Enough!” the Kestrel thundered.

Bleach wasn’t having it and came for me anyway. I raised both fists. and the shot exploded much louder than the rubber rounds, the bullet tearing a clot of carpeting up off the floor exactly between the two of us.

“The exercise is over,” the Kestrel said. I stepped back from the hole in the carpet, glancing up my classmates who were all at the railing, looking more like startled kids than killers for the moment. The Kestrel lowered his gun.

“There is a solution to the scenario, but that wasn’t it.” the Kestrel said, “Where’s Mors?”

“Here,” Mors said.

I hadn’t heard him even come up the stairs from outside. His face was half masked with blood, bits of glass still in his hair and face, his right eye screwed shut.

Bleach wasn’t standing up very straight, but he spit blood off to the side and grinned at Mors, his teeth filmed red.

“Ah, I see. The bawbag *and* his buddy. Weel, no worries, Morsey. It only takes one eye to meet your true love but both eyes closed to keep her.”

We were all getting much faster reflexes, but Mors was still a prodigy. He grabbed Bleach by the shoulders with loud clap of palms on rubber, spun, and threw him out the window.

Bleach smashed through the frame and wailed once as he fell. The thud seemed a long time coming.

“Jesus Christ!” I said.

Mors touched his hurt eye gingerly, squinting up at the observation platform.

“The Longshanks solution,” he said.

No one said anything. Even the Kestrel seemed speechless.

“What,”, Mors said, “nobody here has seen fucking *Braveheart*?”

* * *

Early evening. It was one of those busy days when a buffet was laid out for dinner, serve yourself, eat when you want.

I was in the north rec room on the second floor with Jiufeng, Black Annie, Rubik and the Nightingale, the other three watching *Glengarry, Glennross* and the Nightingale and I were over near a fireplace big enough to roast a Clydesdale in.

Mors had been taken off to the infirmary and then to some mysterious meeting with the masters. It looked like his eye would be fine, but that was all the Nightingale would tell me.

Bleach was *still* in the infirmary with a broken collarbone, two broken ribs, and a concussion.

He'd landed badly.

There was a keystone on the fireplace arch that intrigued me, carved out of grey marble. It was a circular, Celtic-style knot surrounded by a ring of spheres like huge pearls and overlaid with a human skull in its center. Cut into the stone around the carving were the words: *Scrie Mori Sors Prima Viris, Sed Proxima Cogni.*

"Do you read Latin?"

I turned to the Nightingale, sitting tiny and all but sunk into a leather chair, knitting something from red yarn. She usually wore huge sweaters and pants and sneakers and looked like someone's old nana putting around, always in the heavy black visor sunglasses.

I wondered how she could see her knitting in the cozy gloom of the lamps and firelight.

"Not much, no," I said.

With a little old lady grunt, she got up and joined me at the keystone, having to crane her neck to look up at it.

She traced the arc of letters around the sigil with one wizened finger.

"*Man's first happiness is to know how to die, his second—to be forced to die,*" she recited.

"That's tough to swallow," I said.

She cackled, patting my arm.

"It is! But it's wise and true, as you will undoubtedly realize when you're no longer a young idiot. Marcus Annaeus Lucanus. He was among the first of our order. A skilled arsonist."

"Arsonist?"

"Oh yes," she said, "it's one of the master methods, though not one I have any skill in. Too difficult to aim and control."

I looked back at the keystone, wanting to ask more questions. A thousand.

Who have you killed, old woman, and why? How?

What is the Thanatos Guild's history?

How deep does all this go?

"What's going to happen to Mors exactly?"

"Ah, young Mors. You are all dangerous people. That's why no form of serious physical altercation will be tolerated here. Such things are dealt with severely. Mors is facing a consequence for his actions. If he endures, he'll rejoin the rest of you soon. If not—"

She spread her tiny hands.

"What about Bleach? Same deal?"

"Of course not. I'd say he was already suffering for his poor choices, wouldn't you?"

"I guess. Can I ask what Mors is, ah, going to be enduring?"

"His fears. The questions Cyberius asked the first time you were in the Think Tank tell us a great deal about the individual and his shadows. Mors is facing his fears, wondering if he can make it through the siege perilous, or escape it. Or, perhaps, against all hope, be rescued from it?"

"I don't get it," I said.

She laughed and patted me again before going to resume her knitting.

"And I can't 'get it' for you. We'll all have to see what comes, yes?"

I ran my hand over the sigil again, the stone a warm as a living thing from the birch logs crackling below.

I went to join the others watching the movie.

CHAPTER 23

Mors Three.

*"**WHAT?**" Mors said.*

"Strip down," Ms. Mercy said. She wasn't smiling. Neither she nor Mr. Blue looked uncertain or angry, just flatly alert. Mors knew the look.

Both were armed.

The clear acrylic tank before him was empty of liquid and gleaming clean. The port couplings were all sealed, no hoses or wiring connected. The tank was illuminated from within and mounted atop it was a gleaming, stainless-steel funnel the size of a cement mixer.

Mors glanced around the tank room, the stitches on his face and the corner of his eye tugging slightly. He considered trying to fight his way out. Mercy's gun was pointed at his midsection, Blue's at his head.

Mors stripped out of his clothes and stood naked before the tank. Like all of Patience flight now, he was bruised and had many areas marked with imperfect circles of adhesive, now black despite attempts to scrub them off, like the scars of a squid's tentacle's suckers.

Mr. Blue pressed a switch on the floor with his foot, and the cylinder slid open.

"Get in, please."

Mors stepped inside.

"When the tank closes, it's locked. If you can endure until it's finished, your consequence will cease and you'll resume training. If you find you can't do this, press down hard on the red disc on the floor there. That's the panic button. Your consequence will cease."

"And then what?" Mors said.

"Maybe death. Some form of imprisonment, more likely." Mr. Blue pressed the floor switch again, and the cylinder door hissed shut on its cylindrical track.

They both made to leave, tucking their guns away. At the door, Ms. Mercy turned back.

"Luck," she said.

The door shut behind them.

The floor of the cylinder was cold, polished steel, seamed in sections and stenciled with a large, black "1," the circular border lined with black and yellow "caution" hashmarks. The red disc, framed in black rubber, was off center, almost at the edge of the of the circle behind him.

Mors could feel cool air blowing down on him suddenly from above. He looked up and saw only a grill and behind it, just a black metal panel.

He squatted and carefully ran his fingers lightly over the big red button.

There was a whirring sound above him and Mors stood in an instant. A distant thud, and then there was a stench, acrid and rotten, wafting down from above. Something hit his shoulder lightly. Mors bent to examine it and saw it was a large cricket, crawling busily across the panic button.

Then a second one fell onto the steel.

And a third.

CHAPTER 24

Killer Romance. Mors Four. The Code of the Dark Bushido.

DURING THE FIRST TWO WEEKS at Guild house I had tried to reach Dagny by cell phone, email, scrambler phone, and good ol' landline. I was rebuffed by who I assumed was a butler, then a sister, twice more by mom, and then Dagny herself.

Sort of.

She answered on my final call, maybe because I was calling from a number she'd never seen.

"Hello?"

"Dagny, please don't hang up."

And she didn't. She breathed, and I could hear windchimes, either because she was outside or the window was open.

"Dagny. Please let me see you. For just one face-to-face talk, that's all I'm asking."

More silence except for the chimes.

An intake of her breath, and then she hung up.

That was when I quit. I had just learned in one of the Nightingale's classes what the words to the gates of hell were and understood them perfectly now.

Abandon All Hope, Ye Who Enter Here.

I bet there were windchimes in Hell, hanging in the dead and twisted forest of suicides, there to make things even worse with their sound of backyards and summer breezes. Their random tunes of lost hopes and utterly broken hearts.

* * *

When the others left the lounge and Jiufeng and I were alone, she asked me if I'd ever seen *Bladerunner*.

"Years ago," I said.

We were both in typical hanging-around-the-dorm outfits, me in sweatpants and a long-sleeved T-shirt and heavy socks, Jiufeng in black yoga pants and a turtleneck that looked comfortably ancient and leopard-print slippers.

"Wanna watch it with me?"

"Sure," I said.

As the movie began, I was in one of the big leather chairs and Jiufeng was on the floor, stretching. We both had the sticky, crusty rings of adhesive on the backs of our hands and sides of our necks.

Jiufeng groaned as she twisted her torso in some yoga pose that looked more torturous than fetching.

"Good grief, I'm so fucking sore," she said.

"When were you last in?" I said.

"Yesterday morning."

"What module?"

"Capture/Evasion. Then it switches to some abs thing that made me feel like a rug that's been beaten with a rake."

She rolled one pantleg up and examined a large bruise in the center of her sticky calf.

I was troubled over whatever the hell they were doing to Mors, feeling the reality of what I was becoming really sinking in (as well as what I'd truly lost), and here I was, before the roaring fireplace, all alone with easily one of the most exotically beautiful women I'd ever known in real life.

The fact that the only name I knew her by was that of a nine-headed Chinese monster didn't seem anymore fucked up than anything else in my life so far.

We watched about half the movie and then Jiufeng paused it, asking me if I had "tank-time" ahead for the weekend, this being Friday. I told her I had the day to myself, actually, mandatory rest and recreation.

"Me too! Wait here a sec," she said, and ran lightly off into the shadowed hallway, long black pony tail bouncing.

One nice thing about assassin school is that you have a bit more freedom than regular college. The kitchen, for one thing, was open to all at all times.

And you could have an adult beverage if you liked, with the understanding that if you fucked up, it was your ass. 'Nuff said.

Jiufeng thumped back up the stairs and reappeared with two juice glasses and two bottles of wine.

"Okay! Let's resume," she said, asking me if I wanted red or white.

"Red. Either, really."

And she sat back on the floor with hers, but this time sat with her back to the couch, my legs to either side of her.

Gloriosky!

We watched Deckard's rainy rooftop fight with the replicant Roy Batty, polishing off the first bottle pretty quickly.

By the time Edward James Almos was leaving his unicorn origami sculpture, we'd opened the white.

The movie ended. Jiufeng switched the TV mode to radio, and Bach's cello something or other played softly as the logs in the fireplace crumbled in a freshet of sparks.

"Alrighty," I said, "I'm asking. How did you end up here?" Jiufeng propped an arm up over my leg, still facing away toward the fire and the blank screen.

"How? Hm. All right. I'll show you mine if you show me *yours*. You first."

"Okay. I killed the guy who raped my girlfriend. And then she left me and won't speak to me."

She turned around quick, ponytail whipping over one shoulder, still between my legs and sitting back on her folded feet, rested both arms on my thighs.

"Oh my God, I killed a rapist! It wasn't as personal, but he was a guy who raped three women at—where I was."

"Well," I said, "that's something."

"Yes, it is," she said.

Jiufeng reached back for her glass and finished her drink. Then she held my hands.

"I like you, Proteus. Tell me your real name."

"You first, this time," I said, even as I was beginning to lose all coherent thought. This was a lapful of beautiful girl, and dangerous weapon, which was a heady mix.

"Baozhai," she said.

I repeated it.

"What does it mean?" I said.

"*Precious hairpin*," she said, and we both laughed.

"I'm serious!" she said. "Now you."

"Daniel. Dan. And I actually know what it means. It's—oh, God Is My Judge. I wish I hadn't remembered that. Yours is better."

"Less fraught," she said.

And then she took my face in her hands and kissed me.

It was a kiss to remember when you were old. And she had a scent, not just soap and shampoo, but sweat too, from the day and wood smoke from the fire. I understood "chemistry" as more than a concept, as I *liked* the scent of her sweat, the animal scent of her, the taste of her.

It wasn't a loving kiss, more make-out session as it was swiftly becoming, an avalanche of kisses and bites and even licks, Jiufeng breathing hard now in little moans and coos and at the same time pulling the hair at the back of my head almost but not quite hard enough to hurt.

Jiufeng fumbled between my legs as my hands found the firm roundness of her breasts, deliciously braless beneath her shirt and her nipples peaked and hard and hot. As I reached beneath her shirt and her hand caressed my crotch, she stopped me suddenly, grabbing my wrists.

"P-*Dan*," she said breathlessly, "let's go to my room. Or yours."

I knew this might be a mistake, but life had become much more immediate.

"Your room, Hairpin," I said.

Jiufeng laughed and grabbed the other bottle.

"I'm sweaty and dirty," she said. "Do you want to shower first? I mean, together?"

"No," I said, "later."

She grinned and stood and pulled me up off the couch.

"I had a feeling about you, Danny-boy," she said.

Happiness, too, is inevitable.

I read that someplace. I don't remember where.

* * *

Mors Four.

Mors couldn't find the button. He'd screamed until his throat felt like something had broken in it. He'd vomited at one point, the sheer mass of scrabbling, hopping, chirping crickets gave off a noxious, rotten stench; he'd never realized insects could smell like anything, worse than shit, somehow. A rotten insect reek of creatures that fed off of death and decay.

When the trickle of crickets had gradually become a torrent (and Mors was pretty sure they were getting bigger now too) he'd already crushed hundreds, first deliberately and then, simply inevitably as he stumbled around the tank.

That had been an hour, maybe hours, ago. Now the writhing, insanely hopping, clicking, chirping, glistening mass of living insect flesh was almost up to his neck. Mors was treading crickets, his feet caked with several inches of their crushed dead bodies.

And he'd found that crickets bite; he had to keep plunging one hand down into the spiky mass to tuck his genitals between his thighs. He could feel crickets writhing spikily in the crack of his ass. Most were almost black, shiny-carapaced, big as his thumbnail, and many much bigger. But smaller brown ones leapt the highest and kept getting into his ears.

And then the giants dropped.

Cook Strait Giant Wetas. New Zealand crickets, each as big as a rat.

Mors gathered what tiny scraps of self-control he had around him, tears, sweat, bile and cricket guts be damned and took in a whooping breath and attempted to dive to the bottom of the tank and press, punch, pound the panic button. Pound and stomp and even headbutt it, anything to just get out.

But he couldn't find it. Couldn't orient himself to where it had been. Couldn't immerse himself to any greater depth to find it. Couldn't feel anything but the slime and popcorn-shell crunch of writhing bodies beneath his feet, all over him.

The huge crickets were warm and pulpy and frantic. He was almost up to his eyebrows in them all, and now one of the huge ones climbed across his mouth. Another scrabbled for purchase on his stubbled scalp, its abdomen a sickly hot balloon, its feet clawed and needle sharp.

And in that moment, he was the newly forged Mors no longer. He was Albert Collins Edwards.

Screaming for the mother who would never, ever come.

* * *

I'd contemplate later why, even during the most frantic and animalistic of our lovemaking, Jiufeng preferred me to call her that and, even in the throes of orgasm, called me only "Danny" or "Dan."

I'd considered myself no prude and an experienced lover, but it's a learning curve. I did things with Jiufeng I'd only read about, and I was covered with welts on my back, ass, and thighs from her nails, short though they were. She'd asked me at one point on top, and deep inside her, to bite her, and I had, struggling not to let my conscious mind completely go to fragments and actually hurt her.

It was a near thing.

We lay in a sweaty tangle of sheets in her dark, cool room, yellow candles flickering on one table, smelling of vanilla.

In the quiet as our breathing eased, she snuggled up to my chest and glided one smooth foot up and down my leg.

"Man," she said. One word, but it helped something torn in me close up a little.

Men, after all, are as predictable and stupid as draught horses.

We had just turned to each other and re-tangled our arms and legs, kissing in a more exploratory, less savage fashion when there were a series of dull thuds above us. The music she'd put on was long over, and I heard the thuds almost immediately repeat. No rhythm to them, just sporadic thuds, one loud enough to actually shiver the window frame.

I sat up in bed a little.

"What the hell is that?"

"Mors, probably," Jieufeng said.

"What?"

"My room is directly under the Tank room. *Consequencing* is done in the tank, according to Grace. God knows what they're putting him through given the shit they do to us when we follow the program."

I was thinking about what the Kestrel said to us after Mors and Bleach had been taken away following the incident in the Ant Farm.

Consider why we showed you Godot. *You are apart from almost all of contemporary society. The rest tolerate a system that lets others do the dirty work for them. But where will you turn when your back's against the wall? The code of the Dark Bushido is simply this: consider your fellow Guild members—if not friends—then at the least, brothers.*"

"Come with me," I said.

"Where?"

"I'm going to the Tank room."

"What for? You want to end up in there too?"

I got out of bed, groping for my clothes.

"Come with me or not," I said.

* * *

The Tank room was locked.

And the sporadic thudding was much louder but more intermittent.

"We shouldn't be here. I'm serious," Jiufeng said. Behind the heavy metal door, the thudding continued. It sounded like a horse kicking at its stall. A horse during a fire, or scenting the slaughter truck.

A fire extinguisher hung at the end of the hallway. I grabbed it. Jiufeng grabbed my wrist.

"Damn it, Dan, wait. Do you want to end up in there? Or worse?"

"*Baozhai*, please listen to me. I think everything here is a test. *Everything*. I think we're supposed to be learning more than just how to kill. I think we're supposed to—like today—also show we have restraint. Even mercy. I think we're supposed to save him."

"And what if you're wrong?"

"Nothing new there," I said, and swung the fire extinguisher up and brought it down on the door handle, once, twice, and finally shearing the handle off on the third blow.

"God *damn* it!" Jiufeng said, grabbing the back of her neck with both hands but standing fast.

I kicked the door open.

The tank room was brightly lit, the center tank filled with a glistening, writhing black-brown mass that moved and shifted. From within came muffled sounds. Screams? Sobs? There was a great thump as a large hand, outlined in crushed insects and gore, slammed against the thick acrylic.

"There's a switch!" Jiufeng said, first stomping on it with her foot, then kneeling to press it down with both hands.

The switch plate began flashing an angry red, but nothing happened.

I swung the heavy extinguisher from the hips at the tank, a home-run swing.

It bounced off the glass. But the man inside must have heard it, and suddenly two fists slammed against the glass, one of them crushing a cricket the size of a squirrel into viscous pulp.

I swung again in concert with the impact of the fists. And again.

A crack shrieked across the cylinder like a lightning bolt. On the third blow, Jiufeng joined me, swinging a heavy metal stool by the legs. More cracks snaked across the glass like the root structure of a crystal tree.

On the fifth blow, the three of us shared the glass exploded outward, along with an avalanche of crickets, ichor, and stench.

Jiufeng smashed the lower section of the glass, and a human shape rose up like a monster in some old movie.

Mors, his eyes and teeth startling white, the rest of him a mottled red and brown, slathered with slime, blood, and still twitching insect parts, stood unsteadily.

Jiufeng made a squeal of disgust and slammed the stool down onto one of the monster crickets. Others of all sizes ran crazily across the floor to all corners of the tank room.

Mors was coughing and alternately drawing in great sobs of breath, wiping his face with one hand.

Others had gathered in the doorway and the hall beyond. Dijall, in bright orange pajamas, Black Annie, Rubik, with a night mask pushed up on his head, Miskali in big slippers that looked like a bear's paws.

And several of the masters, all still impeccably dressed.

The Kestrel, Ms. Mercy, and the Nightingale pushed through the gawkers and came into the tank room, unarmed, to my relief.

Leaning on Jiufeng, Mors staggered off the dais, crickets still crawling everywhere all over a crushed mass of insect flesh that was over a foot deep in places.

Mors spit and wiped his mouth. His stitches had pulled open, and he was bleeding freely.

"Thank you," he said.

* * *

"Fucking *A*," Rupert said, "what did they do to you guys after that?"

"Nothing, really," I said.

"Nothing!"

"Well, Mors was in the infirmary for a night, some other section than Bleach. Jiufeng and I were given the task of using vacuum backpacks to get as many crickets as we could, though you could hear them chirping all over the mansion for about a month after that. It sounded like we were outdoors. We had to work with Yes, Quark, and Mercy to dismantle the shattered tank and help install its replacement. Grunt work, mostly."

"And that's it?"

"Pretty much," I said.

"Jesus fuck, *why*?" Rupert said.

He sounded almost as outraged as when I'd taken on the street shooting.

I lit a cigarette.

"No one ever said. But I think it was because we'd pulled together in the whole Dark Bushido thing."

"Balls."

My apartment door closed, and Rupert and I almost leapt out of our seats.

A large black lab trotted into the room, tail wagging furiously, a leather belt loosely around his neck, dragging on the floor behind him, tongue out and smiling in that way dogs can. He arrowed right for Rupert, who cringed away.

Mors tossed his keys onto the table and poured himself a drink and sat down.

"I was just telling Rupert about the Night of the Crickets. He's surprised we weren't all put to death after."

More shrugged.

"Why would they put me to death? I never did hit the button."

Brando has climbed up onto the couch, licking Rupert's face.

"Goddamnit, stop! Okay, tell me about the tiger."

"Oh, brother," Mors said.

"Later," I said, "we need to hit the hay."

"We had a fucking deal!" Rupert wailed, now scratching the big black lab behind the ears.

"The deal isn't that we talk all fucking night; I'm drunk and tired. We'll have another slumber party later. Now go home, and we'll call you tomorrow," I said.

"And take the dog," Mors said. "He likes you."

Rupert looked rather pleased at that.

CHAPTER 25

Rourke Call Two.

"HI, DADDY."

"Hi, honey."

"Mommy says I can call you Daddy if I want and you say it's okay."

"It's definitely okay," I said.

"Good. 'Cause it's true," she said.

"It is. What are you doing today?"

"Right now, I'm talking to you," she said.

"Right, right."

"Later today we're taking a walk on the beach. Right now, we're going to the indoor pool. Mom and me and Mrs. Bustamonte an' Clark an' Shea."

"Well, that sounds fun. Do you swim?"

"Oh yes, I swim! I started swimming lessons when I was a baby," Roarke said.

"What, you mean like when little babies that can't talk or walk are shown swimming around underwater with their eyes open and stuff?"

"Yes! Like that. *I* did that!"

"That's terrifying," I said.

"Oh no, Daddy, it's great! I'm a great swimmer 'cause of that."

"I bet you are. But it's still scary."

"No, no, it was good. Do you swim?"

"I do," I said.

"We should go swimming some time," Roarke said.

"All right. We will."

"Don't say it if you don't mean it," she said.

"I won't. I'm not."

"Are you and Mommy friends?"

"Um. I don't—I mean, yes, yes, I think so."

"Mommy says she thinks of you as a *possible* friend."

"Oh?"

"Yes. She said, 'The jury's out'; she said that to Uncle Malcolm."

"Who's Uncle Malcolm?"

"Mom's boyfriend," she said.

"Oh I see. Well, what does Uncle Malcolm say?"

"He says, '*Jesus, Daggy, if the guy's willin' to make an effort, he can't be all bad*' is what he said yesterday morning."

The inflection of the man through the eight-year-old mouth was powerfully eerie. I just *saw* Malcolm for a sec. I'd recognize his voice if I heard it again.

Jesus, Daggy.

Daggy.

"Well, don't worry about it, we'll figure it all out as we go."

"You know what Superman says?"

"Nope," I said, "what does he say?"

"He says, '*There's always a way*,'" Rourke said.

"That's a good way to look at things," I said.

"Superman says, he says this to a girl once. He says, '*You're much stronger than you think*.'"

"I like that," I said.

"Me too. It was very nice to talk with you, Daddy. I'd like to talk longer next time, but for now I really have to go."

"I understand. Have a good time at the pool and the beach."

"Okay, I'll talk to you again soon," she said.

"Okay. Be careful swimming. Don't get in the way of anyone training their babies to swim in the ocean."

"There are no babies at the beach swimming in the ocean!" She laughed.

"Well. Be safe," I said.

"I'll be fine, Daddy, I'm a really good swimmer. Bye bye."

"Bye bye, Rourke," I said.

CHAPTER 26

Prefatory Matters. Today's Tom Sawyer. The Plan.

GARDENER LOOKED GLUMMER, if anything, on the flat screen television.

"The New Alexandrian's All Hallow's Dinner will be held at the Willard Intercontinental hotel in Washington, DC. All three are arriving with their own security details, all three in gun cars, as I'm sure surprises none of us. It's on a Thursday evening, and the event is being announced as a costume ball with a Halloween theme. The function room will be completely redecorated according to the theme, complete with a live band. The entire building will be swept by dogs during the afternoon. Video cameras will be keyed to an individual recorder in the ballroom ceiling. They are all slaved to a primary time-code generator, making a permanent record of the party. Metro police will be stationed at all key interior positions. Private security will be stationed throughout the crowd, at the ballroom doors and the lobby. A metal detector will be placed within the frame of the entrance door. Both printed invitations and photo ID's will be checked. A second metal detector is going to be set within the frame of the main entrance to the function room.

"There will be several speeches, followed by dinner, then dancing. I would imagine a great deal of political hob-knobbing both before and particularly after dinner.

And of course, it's *deeply* troubling to hear our compatriot Mr. Bleach is in the area," Gardener finished.

"Well. That sounds like a lovely party," Mors said.

"We're fucked," Rupert said.

"Boys, boys," I said, "take heart."

Despite his hangover, Buzzcock looked positively delighted to be included in "The Rumpus." He'd been in a brief funk after Mors arrived, steadfastly refusing to tell his tale of why he'd retained his connection to the Guild even after he'd washed out of the program. We'd never hear it, sadly.

"Not until I hear about the fuckin' tiger," he said.

But he'd brightened considerably when I now decided we'd include him in the plan.

Mors hadn't protested; he seemed distracted, but drawing him out was impossible.

"It's your party" was all he would say.

Mors had unpacked, including dog food for Brando and a collar. After we sent Rupert home with the dog, we'd both gone to bed.

The next morning while we were waiting for Mors to come with coffee, Mars told me of what he'd found at Guild House. "Jesus Fucking Christ."

Mors nodded.

"This is all wrong. Bleach here. Gardener just wandering onto your property that way. It's fucked."

"Expound on 'fucked.'"

He pulled something out of his bag and threw it on the table. A seed catalogue, stained with rusty blood.

"This was under Iron Horse's hand in the library," he said.

"I'm lost."

"Look at the handprint. It's plastered right under the word *gardening*."

"Oh, come on," I said.

"Did you have Iron Horse for training?"

"Not much," I said, "no. He was more 'hands' than guns."

"He was one of the most cunning men I ever knew. I think Gardener's in on this whole thing. Part of it, somehow. He got everyone in the tank room and killed them. Or killed them and put them there, after, I dunno. After that, he gunned down Iron Horse. Horse grabbed that catalogue to leave a clue to who killed him."

"Gardener. Gardener killed the whole staff of Guild house? For Christ's sake, these guys were all expert assassins!"

"So what?" Mors said, "I could kill you, right now. Then Buzzcock, easy."

"Well, Buzzcock," I said.

"I'm serious," Mors said. "I don't know how or why, but I think he's in this. He killed them all. Or helped."

"Except the Nightingale," I said.

"Except the Nightingale," he agreed.

I just couldn't imagine it.

"Look," I said, "I respect your judgement. But we're supposed to talk with Gardener today, anyway. Can we just see what he has to say and chew this over? I can't see it, Mors."

Mors said nothing.

When Rupert arrived, I'd hooked up the Kirby box and we listened to Gardener's specs on the party.

"I assume you need two invitations?" Gardener said on the screen.

"Just one," I said.

Gardener signed off.

* * *

AFTER RUPERT HAD BEEN SENT to finish overseeing things at the Crystal City Motel, I sat with Mors at the dining room table with the three folders Gardener had given me.

"So. Share your thoughts, Estragon."

Mors shook his head.

"I understand that we'll probably need Buzzcock, but if he fucks anything up, I'll kill him myself."

"Me too," I said. "We'll kill him twice. You still suspect Gardener?"

"I dunno. Something's hinky."

I reached over and picked up the Kirby box, a portable device the Guild had provided that had all sorts of nifty applications.

"Lord Henry?"

"**Yes, Mr. Ketch.**"

"Abraxas," I said.

There was a pause, then a tone.

"**Understood, sir.**"

"Excellent. Now, please list all calls made by Gardener since my departure."

"**Yes, sir. Gardener has made six calls since your departure, all of them on his scrambler phone. One call was to his niece in West Virginia, the other five calls were to Pratt Industries in Lively, Texas.**"

"Lord Henry, please play all of those calls except the call to his niece."

Mors raised his eyebrows.

"Snooper scope," I said, "he can listen in on anything."

"**I cannot comply, Mr. Ketch. All calls were electronically washed.**"

"Washed?"

"**Yes, sir. A low-grade sonic pulse that disrupted my system's ability to voice record. The only exception was the identification extrapolated from the greeting during each call.**"

There was a hiss and then a woman's voice, saying:

"*Pratt Industries, how—*" and then a high-pitched sound like a katydid.

"Christ," I said, "does the listener hear that?"

"**No, sir,**" Lord Henry said, placidly, "**it is an ultra-sonic wave. It can only be heard on the recording.**"

"Great. But the niece's call isn't washed?"

"**No, sir. Do you wish to hear the call?**"

"Is it filled with seething, irrefutable proof that Gardener is the father of all our sorrows?"

"**I'm afraid not, sir. It is primarily a brief discussion of where Gardener and his niece, Ashley, will be meeting for dinner in Washington this upcoming Christmas.**"

"Shit," I said.

Mors said nothing.

* * *

My new home in Kalorama came with a nice backyard complete with brick courtyard, overgrown mess of a former garden, a pair of ornate metal chairs and a glass table.

Mors had gone on an errand for the upcoming festivities, and Rupert had driven to Carver Massachusetts to drop Brando off with his mother, not planning to be back until the following night.

The slim trees overgrowing my garden and whose roots were buckling the brick courtyard were ash. I took a cleaver from my well-appointed kitchen to chop a sapling down and cut the section I needed, a piece shaped like a capital "Y" and about the span of the palm of my hand.

Mors had leant me a knife, one of those stainless-steel multi-tool gadgets that had every little bell and whistle besides a laser. I stripped the bark and smoothed the edges of the "Y" and then used the auger blade to bore neat holes in the top of each arm.

It was a lovely day, though more like spring than Maine winter. An old woman in a sari opened her window on the second floor of the house next to mine and seeing me look up, waved, smiling.

I waved back, then resumed my augering, taking care not to cut myself.

The scrambler buzzed like an angry bee.

"Ketch."

"Sugar was easy," Mors said. "I got the potassium chlorate from a chemistry student who wanted thirty bucks, which you owe me. But where the fuck do I get sulfuric acid?"

"Ohhh, let's see. Any home improvement store. Cost you twelve bucks, maybe," I said.

"Why do I want it?"

"Cleaning a drain," I said.

"That'll be forty bucks you owe me, plus aggravation. I can't drive five fucking feet without a herd of Asians walking in front of my car, jacked into their iPods or texting. Oblivious."

"That sounds racist, Mors. And stop being so tight-fisted, for Christ's sake you're a rich bad guy."

"Principle," he said and hung up.

I'd finished my augering. I took two thick rubber bands off the table and looped them through the holes and then back through the loops. Then I did the same thing with each band and a small leather square I'd cut from an old glove.

Today's Tom Sawyer, himself.

* * *

"Ho-kay, gents," I said, "pulling this off in the ball, on the way to the ball, or in their separate hotel rooms will either get us all killed or thrown in jail. Agreed? I mean, the point is to make sure no one gets hurt."

"Uh-huh," Mors said.

"Wait. We're not killing anybody?" Rupert said.

Two weeks now before The New Alexandrian's party and Mors, Rupert, and I sat waiting for Gardener to call, laying our final plans on how to kidnap three of the bigger right-wing shit-heads in Ye Grande Olde Pissing Match.

I say this with no real rancor toward Republicans, per se, I just had no use for either religious or political fanatics or those who use such throwbacks for their own ends.

Our targets encompassed either or both combined.

"I assume your plan has become more specific," Mors said.

"You are correct. Between security, Metro bulls, and high-tech surveillance, getting in and snatching those three, let alone killing them—is all but impossible. But snatching them as they attempt to flee a threat, that's doable. At the predetermined time, I will set in motion a disturbance that ensures that all the guests will decide to haul ass. The truly important and self-important alike will not just run pell-mell to any exit, they will make their egress point to a pre-planned escape route. In this case, the loading dock area behind the kitchens."

"What will they be fleeing?" Mors said.

"The oldest thing that cramps every caveman echo in the brain with terror: fire," I said. "So, as the bunnies run out the various egress points, you two and myself will deal with any security they may have, subdue them, and take them in the ambulance to our holding pen. Simple."

Mors and Rupert looked at each other before looking back at me. Not a good sign.

"Look, boys, it will take a little bit of improvisation, but it's not that complicated."

"How are you getting them all in one spot? Asking them to line up?" Mors said.

"No-oh," I said, "they'll all be sitting at the same table for honored speakers. When disaster strikes—"

"Which you're causing," Rupert said.

"That's right. I will. But Collins, Mitchell, and Chandler will not know that. To them, I will be the heroic voice of reason and leadership in a crisis. They, and any security that might tag along—work-for-hire, all—will instinctively follow the strongest personality. And that, gents, will be me."

"How?" Rupert said.

"Have a little faith, Rupert. Look, we're all under the shadow of this thing. And if what you suspect is true, then all the more reason to keep things a little fluid."

"*I'm* not under any shadow," Rupert said, "and what does he suspect?"

"Shut up," Mors and I said.

He fumed.

"Right," Rupert said, "it's just '*Shut up, Rupert,*' '*Take the dog, Rupert,*' '*Go get the room finished, Rupert.*' I thought I was part of the team, but you two have to keep me in the dark while the grown-ups talk. Jeez."

"Jeez?" Mors said.

"Yeah," I said. "Cripes."

"Fuck you," Rupert said, then looked nervously at Mors.

"All right, Rupert," I said, and told him of the whole thing, the Kestrel's kidnapping and my plan to kidnap as opposed to killing the targets as I'd been told. Mors frowned at that but then surprised me by telling Rupert of his trip to Guild house and what he'd found there.

"Holy shit, they're all *dead*?" Rupert said, whey faced.

Mors lit a cigarette.

"And you think *Gardener's* involved?"

"I do," Mors said.

Rupert then looked at me for confirmation.

"I wasn't sure, but this Washington dinner thing, his calls to Pratt Industries in Texas. It's owned by the Pratt twins. *Agatha and Maxwell Pratt*, uber rich, prominent backers of uber-conservative organizations, candidates—"

"Tea party," Mors said.

"But," Rupert said, "if Gardener's the one who set this up, if he killed all the masters, snatched the Kestrel, why the fuck are we trusting him for anything?"

"Relax, boys. I've got Lord Henry keeping a secret eye on him. The note told me to kill these clowns; the kidnap plan is mine. Because it's all I can think to do to smoke out whoever they are. If it's really Gardener, we'll find out all the sooner."

"It's the stupidest plan I ever heard," Rupert said, "and the Kestrel's dead already."

"The Kestrel would want us to do something, not just roll over," I said. "Besides, killing these three would be *big*, more's the pity. I'm not going to be—"

"**I have an incoming video call from Gardener, sir**," Lord Henry's voice intoned from the Kirby box, making Rupert jump.

"Patch it through, but leave the video feed from this end off," I said.

"**Understood. Patching call through in three**."

Gardener appeared on the TV, squinting at what, for him, was a black screen.

"Daniel? Are you there?"

"I am, Gard, I'm sorry. The video feed on this end is screwed up somehow. I can see you; you're not getting anything on your end?"

"Just your voice, I'm afraid."

"I'll get Lord Henry on it, just go ahead," I said.

Gardener hesitated, looking flustered. It might have been the typical fussiness of someone who had spent much of his time as a teacher of one kind or another. Or not. When I had told Lord Henry "*Abraxas*," he was not only recording everything he was able, he was processing everything he "saw and heard," vocal tone and frequency for stress and what's known as "the psychological tremor" in Gardener's vocal chords, as well as his facial tics, his rate of eye-blink, all that.

Like his cousin, *Cyberius*, who ferreted out exactly how to break Mors, Lord Henry could not be lied to.

"All right, Daniel. Your invitation to The New Alexandrian's function is being delivered by courier today. It wasn't all that difficult, really. You will also receive your false identification packet."

Gardener paused to look up at the ceiling, fingers laced over his midriff in my living room. I could hear music in the background. Jazz.

It occurred to me that with a word, I could maybe kill Gardener, even from five hundred miles away.

But that wouldn't solve anything.

Yet.

"Thanks," I said.

"I will assume that I can't make a last-ditch effort to, ah, persuade you to just go ahead with what they want. In fact, I might be able to be more helpful than the trifle I've done, if the ground were more, say, familiar."

"You mean a slate. Kill them," I said.

"Yes, Daniel. I mean doing what they told us to do, slating them all. I'm sure Mors would assist you if you asked."

Gardener's eyes came back to the screen, almost as if he could see us. But the little green light on the Kirby box wasn't glowing.

"I'm sticking with Plan B, Gardener," I said.

"Yes," Gardener said, "of course. I suppose you think me cowardly in my dotage. There is one more thing I must pass on to you. I'm sure I don't need to remind you that All Hallow's is a mere two weeks away."

"Yeah," I said, "so?"

"I've tried to contact my peers at Guild house with no luck at all. Very strange. Everyone's gone to their hidey-holes, it would seem. But I have received another communication from our would-be masters."

"What is it?"

"I have no idea, only that it must go from their hand to yours. The message says it will be a further motivator and aid to you, as well as a reminder to stick what's been asked of you."

Mors looked vindicated; Rupert looked like he was riveted to a good movie.

"There's no time to send it to you, but I can recall it all too easily. You are to go to the Lincoln Memorial at eleven thirty p.m. tomorrow night. Alone. A representative of these people will give you what they want you to have. They said it will—'make the job easier.'"

"That doesn't sound too good, Gardener."

"I know, Daniel. I know how you feel. But it's highly unlikely they'd hurt you when they want you to carry out their aims. I rather fear that it will be further proof of their detention of the Kestrel. Maybe something else, but—"

"What, you mean someone wants to meet me in the middle of the night to hand me the Kestrel's tongue in a Ziplock bag now?"

"I don't know, Dan. Perhaps something like that. Or maybe it's information that will help you do the job."

"Well, find out," I said.

We signed off.

"Lord Henry?"

Gardener's face came back onscreen with a schematic overlay that looked like a football coach's chalk talk.

"**According to facial analysis, Gardener deconstructed over sixty-seven 'tells' regarding both his discomfort and his honesty relative to—**"

"Skip the seminar, please. Was he lying?"

"**Yes, Mr. Ketch. Though about what is unknown.**"

"What are you gonna do?" Rupert said.

"I'm going to go, of course. Want to come along?"

CHAPTER 27

Rintrah Roars.

THAT NIGHT, MORS WENT TO "walk the course," which was his phrase for familiarizing himself with an area. The puppet masters could tell me "come alone" all they want, but—of course—fuck that. Mors intended to position himself and, incredibly, Buzzcock, in the park to keep an eye on me.

And twin crosshairs on whomever showed up.

So while Mors was prowling around the Lincoln Memorial and frightening tourists, Rupert and I had stripped and cleaned every piece of equipment we'd be using during the rumpus and whatever came after.

When we'd finished, Rupert poured himself a scotch and I had a cigarette. I had quit for four years and was trying to limit myself to only five a day, but it was hard. I told myself I'd quit again once this was over.

"So," Rupert said, "tell me about the tiger."

"Rupert—"

"You could get killed tomorrow night!"

"Jesus Christ, Rupert!"

"Well?" he said.

Well? What the hell.

"After you did your Three, you were free to choose," I said.

Rupert got comfortable, short of corking his mouth with his thumb.

* * *

Of course, you could still cull assignments through the Guild. It was always there, even if you went primarily with freelancing, like Mors and a few of the others had planned.

Thugs, mostly.

The Kestrel accompanied me for my first, a politico who'd raped some law clerk in Florida during a retreat. The law clerk never filed a complaint and instead went home to Vermont, sank into a depression and killed herself.

Anyway, I'd been sick with fear, the Kestrel and I in a zodiac boat in a Florida marina at night, awaiting the target to exit some kind of exclusive naughty party being held on a whale of a boat at dockside.

I remember the slate was a big man, big gut, big pompadour of blue-white hair. I had vomited off the side of the boat an hour or so before he exited, the Kestrel and I both in night-work gear. But when he emerged from the party and staggered down the dock, the ramp lit with rows of tiny electric lanterns, I centered the crosshairs on his head, let my breath out slowly, and squeezed the trigger.

One shot. One splash. The Kestrel fired up the motor, and we were out of the water and speeding down the highway in less than twenty minutes. The months of training, the countless hours in the Tank, it had all taken. My body was hard, my reflexes phenomenal.

Except for the one bout of sickness, I didn't flinch. I didn't mentally "repeat" over it. The guy didn't seem very real beyond being a nuisance that needed eradicating.

Brightman Jones had been *real*. That crazy night on the ice was real.

This was work.

A week off to stay at a largely deserted Guild house. Everyone in our flight was doing their three, people came and went, and there wasn't much by way of dinners together or chit-chat. We were discouraged from losing focus.

My Second was weirder.

A priest, living in self-imposed exile in Hawaii. His dossier was a nightmare landscape of abuses and ruined lives, but I was sort of disturbed to find I had very little sense of righteous mission. It was a job. Just a job.

I found him where I expected to find him, walking his usual predawn walk down Kuana'oa Beach. The sunrise was just beginning when I met him halfway on his walk, coming from the opposite direction.

He just stopped, an old man in a track suit, and looked at me, speaking quietly without preamble.

"There's sea turtles out there," he said, "in the bay."

"I didn't know that," I said.

"Manta rays, too. That's why there's no motorized recreation allowed here."

"No kidding. I'm not from around here," I said.

"I know you aren't. Just go ahead and do it. Please."

I shot him before the sunrise could reveal anymore of his expression. What little I saw was plenty.

And then, my Third. "The bitch kitty of the litter," as the Master Chief would say.

Your Third had all sorts of little conditions. Not just the Kestrel's, as I learned later from some of my peers, but any sempai. They did it to fuck with you and make you adapt. Be creative. Improvise. Apply all you'd learned.

The first two, my choice of weapon, tactics, "Pounce" (your method of approach), my "Plan B" (if things went into *Rasputin* territory) all that—was up to me.

But your Third, your sempai chooses all that for you.

The Kestrel, being a true bastard, had chosen my Third with all sorts of treats. As I had chosen my future *eyrie*, or home base, to be the coastal Maine area, my slate was in York, Maine.

He chose the weapon as well. Which is how I came to be driving down 95 toward Maine with that last little "fuck you" sitting next to me in a black hockey bag. A Lee-Enfield bolt action rifle.

Great gun. British used them for a century. Like, a century ago. It was a heavy, old, archaic piece of crap to use on my third and final obligation.

"Reassess. Adapt. Improvise. When these all fail, be audacious," the Nightingale said, on many occasions.

So, I would adapt to the ancient rifle.

It was after that slate that I discovered the almanac and my ritual of the last meal. That also has made remembering the name of the men I've killed, effortless.

Dr. Martin Castello.

According to the dossier, Dr. Castello was involved in some form of sex-trade ring. Apparently the good doctor founded a school for troubled adolescents and then ran some kind of naughty business out of it, misusing society's bungled and botched. Dr. Castello was apparently the latest wonder boy in modern education, so he was addressing the graduating class of Nubble Light Academy (home of The Fightin' Lobsters).

Then, according to the shadowy sources the Guild has in spades, Dr. Secret Pimp would attend a lobster dinner for some rich kids and then be going home to Castle Castello; his wife and daughters were off overnight to some hootenanny at Wheaton College.

I decided to attend graduation. Observe. Wait for it to get late. And then kill Martin Castello in his house with the goddamned Lee-Enfield (oh yeah, they'd check) and that would be that.

* * *

Graduation followed a basic script as old as time. But what was with all the speeches?

The big gymnasium at NLA in quaint little York was crammed with families, friends, teachers, and the high school band, with the teachers in black robes and the grads in blue and gold. The mayor, the school board, the principal, an astronaut, and all three thousand people gave a speech.

Well, not really. But *Christ*.

The class president, the valedictorian, the valedictorian's retarded *brother*, the captain of the football team, everybody but the fucking janitor all gave the same, clichéd speech, either about their pitch-perfect future or so riddled with class in-jokes that it was already stale when the first draft was written.

Sitting there, in a nice suit, even noticing that I'd caught the eye of this pretty lady, or that I began to feel a sort of slow-motion rage writhe through me, a slit-eyed judging of a world that life with the Master Chief had denied me.

Not the killing of him. The living with him.

The scholarships were typical. Endless standing ovations as the have-nots clapped their sheep's trotters for the haves getting to have even more. Talented scholars, natural athletes, and ass-kissers getting more of what dough, genes, and luck had already given them plenty of. Some football shithead was actually called "a hero."

The astronaut was a hero.

The principal referred to a coach as "a hero."

The Lee-Enfield was in my rental and would have attracted attention, but I was tempted to go get it and shoot myself.

There was a kid in a tank-like electric wheelchair with long black hair, almost totally paralyzed. He sat through the whole hot-air palooza quietly paying attention. Once in a while, a female staff member would help him sip water.

That kid should have gotten a standing ovation for one straight hour until our hands hurt. Then everybody could go home and get their diplomas and scholarships in the fucking mail.

Anyway, then Dr. Martin Castello, public pillar and secret pimp, made his speech.

And here was an interesting thing, people *hated* this guy.

One of the Tank modules was called *Dynamic Observational Mechanics*. It involved the usual drugs and weightless mind-kneading and it made you learn to see. *Everything*.

Everything you needed to, anyway.

As Dr. Castello began his screed (referring to himself as, get this, "*The Man from Vermont*," whatever that was supposed to mean), I scanned the teaching staff on their lower dais. Whispers. Smirks. Hands cupping their mouths. I lip-read naughty words. Registered eye-bar indexes, all that.

I grokked that over half the room thought this guy was an asshole.

And they didn't even know the truth.

He looked like you'd expect, silver-haired, steel-rim glasses, nice suit stuffed with his Little-Man Complex, and the layer of see-my-success fat over his morning treadmill plug of a body. He spoke for almost an hour. Astonishing.

At one point he referenced playing his saxophone at a staff meeting recently.

These poor people.

In a perfect world I would have shot him there. During the inevitable standing ovation, the principal could have played swooning nurse to the astronaut's smooching sailor as the mortar boards pin-wheeled through the air, occasionally braining a grandmother.

Then I'd take the wheelchair kid out to get laid.

But reality "is". All that.

* * *

In the movies, cartoons too, there's a trope in which a character screams the word "NO" and the cry is shown to echo through the streets. The cities. The solar system. The known galaxy. *NOOOOOOO!* Get me?

It is usually pretty funny.

The Island of Doctor Castello (actually a private cove near picturesque marshland, much like my own future home) was supposed to be dark and drowsing at this late hour. Instead, *this* is the donkey-derby I found.

The property was lurching with blue lights, amber lights, red lights, spotlights, and, dig this, *The Southeast Maine Special Response Special Weapons and Tactics Team.*

(Yes, it's *that* long and with the word "special" in it twice).

The question was, Why in the blue holy fuck was the SMSRSW&TT here at my slate's home? Along with every other Yorkie asshat with a light on his vehicle, (maybe even including the high-school groundskeeper)?

It seemed that someone had tipped off the doctor about an hour or so before that *The Very Bad Man* was coming.

Who did this? The Kestrel. It was his style.

I will never prove this.

Now, one might think: "Abort," but it was impossible in this case. Failure during any part of your Three meant death. Aborting a job happens, sure. But it wasn't an option during the Three. It is—by design—a make-or-break-type thing.

Straw-dogged.

Which was exactly what Dr. Castello had done. He knew his town had dumped who knows how much tourist dough into the Special *Special* squad and their accessories. Knowing the local hondos would just have to roll out with all their gadgets, Castello had (I read the following morning) called in a suicide threat.

Which was very survival-clever of him.

"*I'm going to kill myself! I have a gun!*"

New York? Go ahead.

York, Maine? The entire town had come to him. He knew I'd never get to him now.

What to do?

* * *

Stealing a Bengal tiger was not the utter cluster-fuck one might rightly assume it would be. Unlike a city zoo, New York's Wild Kingdom was a nice little place about eight miles from Castello's Last Stand. No electric fences except around the paddocks. No guards.

Well. Maybe now there are.

The idea came from all those hours with the Nightingale and her lectures about Greek fire and siege engines and fire ships.

Hellburner, they used to call them. Designed to panic the enemy and make them break formation.

Running, climbing a fence, and running again with my Beretta at the ready (I only had to use the Lee for the actual slate), I reached the white blockhouses behind the big cat paddocks.

Ala a Guild lockpicking seminar, in no time at all I was standing before one Dr. Lanford, working late at a centrifuge.

I pointed my Beretta at his nose and said, "Good evening," while the centrifuge rumbled behind him, and I asked him his name.

I introduced myself for the first time, professionally, as Proteus.

I was wearing no mask, just long hair and a ball cap.

"Dr. Lanford, let me be simple and direct. I need one of your tigers. I need to transport it. Now, I don't want to hurt you or your cat. But if you do not help me quickly, efficiently and cooperatively, I will shoot you through both knees and both elbows, and if you live, it will be in crippled agony for the rest of your life. *Help* me not to do this. Keep everything in perspective."

Shortly, Dr. Steven Lanford darted Rintrah (their older male Bengal tiger), and we loaded 583 pounds of *Panthera Tigris Tigris* onto a bright blue plastic forklift and into "The Cat Van."

That's the for-real, actual name of their big, fairly new high-tech ambulance for big, scary animals.

Dr. Lanford drove pretty well with a gun in his armpit and killed the lights when I told him, easing the Cat Van to a stop in the shadows pooled beneath the pines at the top of Castello's driveway. It was a long, relatively straight slope leading down through the overhanging trees to where the lights of York's most special pulsed feverishly.

The van was quiet in neutral, but we were over a hundred yards away, anyway. Dr. Lanford was understandably nervous. So, as he set about injecting a stimulant into the slumbering mass of muscle, claws, paws and jaws, I asked him to share some tiger facts with me.

I learned that Rintrah was a seven-year-old Bengal tiger. There were less than four hundred like him left in the wild.

Rintrah could kill a 1,980-pound water buffalo, easy as pie.

He also smelled like piss and corn chips. Strange but true! That was my own discovery.

Dr. Lanford inquired periodically if I was going to kill him. I assured him that that was up to him, but? So far, so good!

Rintrah was stirring. I instructed the doc to exit with me.

In the glove box I found a bottle of fuel line cleaner. Dr. Lanford became extremely agitated when I began to splash it over the ambulance roof and—admirably—tried to interfere. Killing him would have been easier and maybe smarter, but I hit him once, hard, with the Beretta and dragged him into a comfy copse of bushes.

Sociopath my ass.

I reviewed The Nightingale's lectures and diagrams about siege engines, all that. One would think it archaic stuff, but here I was, combining two medieval ideas with my own twist for modernity's sake.

The Fire Ship combined with *The Tortoise*.

And an added bonus.

I checked Dr. Lanford's pulse (which was good and strong), and then watched the Special Squad swan about in the strobe lights below for a bit and then hauled the hockey bag out of the van. I rummaged in it for four "hinge pops."

They look like sticky, grey glue-sticks with a red tack in each end.

Then I hunted for a branch and broke it to arm-length, something that looked like a capital "L."

There was a thick, syrupy rumbling from behind the van's doors. Rintrah wakes.

I pressed the hinge pops in place on the back doors of the van and pocketed the tiny transmitter and then slung the Lee-Enfield over my shoulder.

I lit an entire pack of matches and threw them up onto the van roof, the sudden flames erupting with a thud. Then I jammed the stick between the gas pedal and the steering wheel, released the parking brake, and stepped back into the murk near Dr. Lanford as the van rumbled away.

I lit a cigarette, held it in my teeth, and held the little transmitter at the ready.

As the fire ship rolled majestically down the drive, roof engulfed with blazing yellow-orange flame, tires bouncing over roots and rocks, the Special Specials were momentarily ass-to.

But the roaring flames and rumbling tires were attention grabbers and the crowd of uniforms and civilians turned to see the Fire-ship, one nitwit firing a shot amid simultaneous, contradictory orders.

Every window of the Castello Mcmansion was lit, including the front yard spots, so even at the top of the drive I could see everything easily enough.

As regular cops, civilians, and helmeted members of the Special Squad ran from their posts around the front of the house, the flame-wreathed van bounced over a big rock and then rammed a big pine tree about twenty feet from the front door, blowing out both back windows.

After some initial hesitation, having seen too many cars explode on TV, the Special Squad et al cautiously doused the already guttering flames with Castello's garden hose and lots of efficient knees-bent running-about behavior.

As some of the squad now approached the smoldering vehicle, guns at the ready, there was a lot of smoke hanging low over the area.

I pressed the detonator, and the hinge pops blew with a loud syncopated bang. The doors yawned open with their own weight, trailing smoke and embers. One squadling leaned into the dark rectangle, gun raised. All concerned, man and beast, were motionless and crouched. I was in pre-wince, smoking handless ala Master Chief style, and I confess the man's helmet and flak jacket were a comfort.

It was satisfyingly predictable. Cinematic, even. One helmeted head engulfed by eight hundred pounds of confused, pissed-off Bengal tiger. Man down, tiger loose, one really never knows what a day will bring. Below me in the smoke and steam there were wild, flailing shadows amid the blue, red, and amber strobes, spastic nightmare keystone cops scattering, like a school play in breakdown behind a scrim.

Screams and shots and one basso profundo roar.

I spit my smoke out and trotted off into the darkness to my left, bearing the heavy Lee-Enfield.

* * *

There was an O. Henry moment when Rintrah bounded briefly across my path, but he was also preoccupied with the man he was chasing, following his *panthers tigris tigris* nature.

Cats love to chase spastic, jerky things, as we all know. I was glad to see that Rintrah hadn't been shot yet.

I reached the back deck easily, all the real action momentarily elsewhere. I raked Castello's candy-easy lock with an electric pick and then slipped into the spacious Castello mudroom, locking the door behind me.

Far off now, I heard another pair of roars that seemed to vibrate the door, then another high-pitched scream and a volley of shots.

Hang in there, Rintrah.

The Castello kitchen was cool and big and smelled of apples and, more faintly, cigars.

Now, where would he be? I'd thought this over for a while. Upstairs? No. Treed cat. Remodeled basement rumpus room? No. Dead end.

Rintrah and York's finest were still raising hell outside, but I moved as silently as possible as I headed toward the deep center of the house.

It was miles from any Ant-Farm scenario.

I found the Pervert from Vermont in his tasteful living room, catalogue-sharp in his striped pajamas, comfy-looking silk robe, and leather slippers.

He was also accessorized with a Bulldog .44 magnum, which he held loosely in one hand as he peered out the light-leaping window.

A fallen king in his Ikea kingdom.

A fire blazed in the gas fireplace, ceramic logs that looked real but never actually burned.

I raised the Lee-Enfield and crunched the bolt, click-clack, American shorthand for "*You're it.*"

Amateurs with overpowered handguns couldn't rattle me as newborn Proteus, but I did feel a pang of almost pity as Castello whipped around without even lifting the heavy pistol to point it.

"Wait! *Wait*. I'm sorry. Tell whoever—Wait. *Oh God, I'll give you anything, anything you want*!" he screamed.

"You can't," I said. "You don't have it."

Bang.

Never mind the movies, overkill, all that. Once gets it thoroughly done with the Lee-Enfield. No need to check, trust me.

The gun was "clean," but I tossed it in the fireplace anyway and left.

Slipping away was simple. I ran through the woods, emerging an hour later at the Park n' Ride on 236, where my second vehicle had been stashed.

By Mors, as I found out later. I had been assigned to do similar back-up work over the past two months of finals.

I read later that despite the mystery of what the hell happened that night, Dr. Castello's secret life was fully revealed by both an anonymous mailing of incriminating papers and examination of the modern subconscious, his hard drive.

Far more important, Rintrah, though wounded, survived. Embraced by the community, he was hailed as a tiger-victim-hero. Safe forever in a zoo with its brand-new guards.

Some cops, locals, and "Special" people were maimed by Rintrah, but it was nothing too bad, and besides, they'd be speaking at next year's graduation, I was sure.

Worst case was two cops who shot each other in the melee, but not too badly, according to the *Portland Press Herald*.

Dr. Lanford, though concussed, was fine. His description of me was "a tall white man, lanky, with a hat."

Lovely. And thus, I was in. A graduate.

CHAPTER 28

The Anubis Club. A Chance Meeting. Bibliothecae de Ossuarium. The Mysterious Mr. Fell.

MORS CAME BACK and Rupert left, and Mors went to bed.

I stayed up awhile, sitting outside in my courtyard, listening to the dead leaves shower down and rattle across the bricks in the muggy, Virginia fall. It was windy, but the wind was warm. Thunder muttered far off, and heat lightning flickered across the western horizon.

I thought about Rintrah. And Rourke calling me a lion.

Claws and paws and jaws.

I hadn't told Rupert about the dinner or the club, the Thanatos Guild version of graduation and prom night, combined.

I didn't want to hurt him. And I had my secrets, too.

* * *

I hadn't seen the Master Chief for a long time, but he was on the helicopter with us as we headed for Rhode Island.

The members of Patience flight were aboard an Augusta Westland 139 helicopter, marveling at its plush leather interior and all of us dressed to the nines in clothes bought with our first real pay as professional assassins.

The Kestrel was our only chaperone, and he spent most of the flight in the cockpit.

We were told that most of the masters of Guild house would be attending the evening, but that this trip was for us, the remaining members of Patience, sipping champagne as the sleek, black chopper hammered its way through the sky at over 180 miles an hour.

The AW139 seated fifteen. I was sitting next to Jiufeng, talking about Ray Charles, when I saw the Master Chief, leaning on the bulkhead next to the cockpit door, just gazing out the windows as evening fell beneath us.

"Are you okay? Pro?" Jiufeng said.

"Yes. I'm fine, just had a little stomach flip," I said. We went back to talking, and when I looked again, he was gone.

I had slept with Jiufeng twice more, prior to our respective launches into the world of high-end expedient murder.

"This isn't 'in love,' Dan. You got that, right?" she said the last time we were alone together.

"Oh, I got it," I said.

"I like you, and we're phenomenal in bed together, but I don't think love is going to be a part of our lives for a while, you know what I mean?"

I ran my hand over her smooth skin, kneading the muscles of her back.

"Bonzai, I'm way ahead of you. I don't plan on love being in my life at all, anymore. Easier that way."

"Bonzai" was a joke between us, one we didn't use outside the confines of a bedroom.

We'd kept things as discreet as possible, but like my quiet friendship with Mors, it was obvious we were close.

Bleach, on the other hand, was close to no one, though he maintained a smirking, sardonic manner toward everyone but Mors and me.

On the chopper, he sat as far from us as possible, chatting with Rubik as they handed some computer game back and forth.

* * *

"Welcome, all, to the Anubis Club," the Kestrel said.

The club was located in Federal Hill in Providence, surrounded by grounds only a little less vast than those around Guild house and ringed by an imposing wall of grey stone.

We walked through a light mist away from the helicopter pad, with several men and women in white dinner jackets coming to meet us and walk with us holding umbrellas over the heads of our female members.

The interior of the club was, if anything, more ornate than Guild house, a richly lit museum-like atmosphere of sculpture, paintings, and mellow lighting. A string quartet was playing, and within ten minutes of being on the other side of doors that would have been at home in a medieval keep, we were all holding drinks and eating hors d'oeuvres.

The club was already crowded with at a glance, about thirty men and women I'd never seen before, along with the staff of Guild house, all in the finest evening wear.

Dressed entirely in black and holding a drink, the Kestrel turned from a group of people he'd been talking with animatedly and approached me where I was examining a bronze statue of a Spartan warrior with Mors.

I hadn't seen him since I'd returned from York.

"Proteus, join me for a moment," he said, taking my arm. He nodded to Mors and walked me slowly to the group he'd been with.

"Daniel, I must say, your solution to your last slate was—"

He stopped halfway back to his group and made me halt with him as he startled me by both barking out a loud laugh and stamping one foot.

"A *tiger*! What on earth made you think of it?"

I couldn't help smiling. And don't think you're oh so clever in noticing that here I was, getting the long-awaited praise from this *Dark Father*. I know myself pretty well, especially after the Think Tank.

But it *was* pretty nice.

"Did you tip him off?" I said.

The Kestrel just smiled and shook his head, either in denial or dismissal of the subject.

"A bloody tiger from the local zoo. A fire ship assault on a straw-dogged target. *Inspired* madness, Daniel. I honestly don't know what to think of you."

He took my shoulder and squeezed it.

"Well. Enough of that. Come with me a moment."

The Kestrel took me to a trio of two men and one woman. The oldest of the two men was in his sixties, barrel-chested and with a thick head of steel-grey hair, almost my height. He wore glasses and was tan and hale looking in an Armani suit. The second man was obviously his son, similar suit and face but a little taller and quite a bit fatter. The woman was an elegant beauty, dripping with jewels and cool charm, grey but vibrant and with a tasteful amount of tan cleavage showing.

"Proteus," the Kestrel said as we approached, "I'd like you to meet Arthur Constantine, his lovely wife Crystal, and his oldest son, Nicholas. Mr. Constantine provided our marvelous transport this evening."

It took an effort not to reel at what I'd just heard, as well as at a sudden yammering in my head of a savage voice *They Don't Know You!* as I took Crystal Constantine's hand first and bowed ever so slightly.

"It's a pleasure to meet you, Mrs. Constantine," I said, and she smiled exactly like her daughter. Mr. Constantine's handshake was firm, his hand slightly bigger than mine, and mine are pretty big. Nicholas's hand was softer and sweaty, and I noticed he had on way too much cologne.

"I've heard some pretty interesting things about your, er, class, flight, whatever the hell they're calling it nowadays," Arthur Constantine said, "and what was it, again, *Prospero*?"

"Proteus," I said.

"Right. Me, I don't go in for all the spy stuff, but hell, given your line of work, I get it. If you ever work for me, maybe you can trust me with your real name?"

"Anything's possible," I said.

This struck him as funny, God knows why, and he laughed and took a drink.

"I have lived by those words," he said, "and even though we're not supposed to talk about it, I'm paying for almost half of this little *celebrazione*."

He leaned closer to me, even doing a little double take over his shoulder as if we might be overheard.

"You're the crazy sonofabitch that used the tiger, am I right?"

"Yes, sir. I am," I said.

He snorted laughter and nudged me with an elbow.

"Fucking fabulous. Someday I could— Let me just say that I have used the Guild to solve some problems in the past. I may ask for you specifically, some day. I value innovation. I respect it."

I nodded, rapidly losing each thread of the conversation. The Kestrel, meanwhile, was chatting with the wife and son, apparently running interference for me so this conversation could take place.

Constantine shook my hand again, squeezing hard this time.

"I'll let you get back to your night. I don't want to monopolize. But someday, I hope you can do something for me. After, we'll break bread together and I can learn your real name, ah, *Proteus*, all right?"

"Yes, sir. Who knows what the future holds?" I said, but he was still all smiles, and I couldn't help smiling too, though I also saw the Master Chief leaning on the plinth of a marble statue of a Griffin, lighting a cigarette about twenty feet away.

To make things more surreal, I saw Mors sharing a very uncharacteristic laugh with Jiufeng and Black Annie over at a buffet table, and the string quartet had just begun a lovely arrangement of *The Spinners* "I'll Be Around."

I made my farewells to the Constantines and, on impulse, bent to kiss Crystal Constantine's hand in parting.

"*My goodness,*" she said, and I left them all smiling, even the Kestrel. Crystal shared her daughter's eyes and mouth.

I walked straight to the bar and ordered a scotch, no ice, no water and downed it.

Bleach was leaning with his back against the bar, hands dangling.

"Easy, there, dick-dome. Ye'll get yerself muntit."

"Bleach, whatever you just said, would 'fuck off' still be the correct response?" I said.

"Fancy a damn', now? Soon enough, *Tiger boy.* Ul wham yeh, yeh fuckin' rocket. You n' yer pal."

"Eat me," I said and ordered a second drink.

Bleach stayed in his relaxed pose and nodded serenely, as if our exchange was only too proper. Pleasant, even.

The evening was quite enjoyable. I drank with some of the masters, even shared a dance with Jiufeng and, later, Ms. Mercy. We were informed that we'd be put up for the night at the nearby Hotel Providence, with cars to transport us when we saw fit throughout the night.

We were also encouraged to explore the club, and after I'd eaten enough and drunk way too much, I set off to poke around.

Upstairs I found a warren of rooms, one, a vast dining hall with all the furniture draped with cloths, the walls lined with two centuries of oil portraits, another that was full of ancient torture implements, all museum quality and discreetly labeled and explained on ornate brass plates. Another room was filled with a collection of meteorites, all in glass cases.

In another, there was a stuffed wooly mammoth.

At the end of a long, softly lit hallway, I found an oaken door with a filigreed copper plate.

Bibliothecae de Ossuarium.

My Latin wasn't great, but better than it had ever been before after sitting through three of the Nightingale's seminars.

"*The Library of Bones.*"

I tried the doorknob, expecting it to be locked, but the door opened silently on well-oiled hinges.

The plaque wasn't lying. Unlike the other rooms, this one was softly lit by shaded reading lamps, chandeliers and far across the vaulted space, a large fireplace, a real one, exuding the soft tang of woodsmoke.

And all about was an enormous library of books that looked to be from old to very old to ancient.

The entire room—knit into the construction of the hardwood shelves, running across top of the bookcases and sometimes intertwined overhead and even the frames of the huge chandeliers overhead—was nothing but bones.

The chandeliers, hung with ornate gas globes, were formed of intertwined antlers of both animals I knew and many I didn't. The shelves were festooned with bones of every description, none of them labeled, as well as complete skeletons of every kind, all wired and posed (and often interactively with their neighbors). Sabretooth tigers clashed in frozen, rampant leaps overhead, dinosaurs snarled, and necks, tails, and wings spanned over the entire ceiling, looking for all the world in most cases like the remains of dragons. The shelves were decorated with all manner of delicate fish, fowl, cat, dog, and other smaller animal skeletons, some of them as small as rats and mice. Skeletal horses pranced and reared across the stacks.

And posed throughout, some riding, some fighting, stabbing, spearing as well as being gored, engulfed, and even eaten, were the bleached white skeletons of men.

And maybe women. Probably, though I wasn't enough of an anatomist to tell the difference.

The gas lamps were almost certainly electric but designed to flicker slightly, so the entire vast web of bones appeared to shift and ripple slightly, as if about to break into a mass writhe of movement and frantic struggle.

I was examining a skull with a rusted iron spike rammed neatly through its temples when a man cleared his voice nearby.

I jumped.

Sitting at the edge of the crackling fireplace was a skeleton in an evening suit, holding a newspaper in its lap.

Closer examination revealed it wasn't a skeleton but an elegantly tuxedoed man who had sometime in the past been terribly, horribly burned.

He beckoned me over with one withered hand.

"Hello," he said, his voice metallic and raspy, either from injury or disuse.

"Hello," I said, approaching him but keeping my distance.

"Mr. Fell," he said, extending his hand. I walked closer and bent to shake it. It felt like a dry leather glove.

"Proteus," I said.

"Ah, yeth. I have heard of you. One of the Kethtrel's bright starth. Thit, for a moment. I came up here to read. I know my appearanth, even among thuch hard cathes as your fellowth, can be upthetting."

"Oh," I said, "not at all."

His eyes crinkled in amusement, maybe; it was hard to tell in a face so ruined that his eye sockets and mouth looked crudely cut from a block of melted tallow. He had no hair, not even eyelashes.

"A kind one. Thank you, Proteuth, but I know my own fathe all too well."

Despite his impediment, his accent was a melodical British and filled with lilts amid the raspiness.

I decided to be direct and hoped I wouldn't offend.

"Sir, pardon my asking but, what happened to you?"

He laughed, wheezing, and reached down to sip a drink he'd set on the floor near the fire.

"What happened? I wath in a plane crath. Long ago. A job I had completed...went wrong. I burned. Terrible thing, burning. It leavthe you with high blood prethure, did you know that?"

"No, I didn't," I said.

"You know burning, I think. I can thee it in your fathe, but it wathn't you that burned, wath it?"

Nothing surprised me in this bone museum. I simply went with it.

"I burned someone, once. But I didn't mean to. At least, I don't think I did," I said.

Mr. Fell nodded.

"Thothe are the mithtakes that thtay with uth. The oneth when we really don't want to know our own mindth. Don't want to or thimply can't know."

"Yes," I said. I couldn't think of anything else.

I was about to sit for whatever the rest of the conversation was going to be, but Mr. Fell held up a hand.

"Go back to your party, boy. I enjoyed meeting you. But I am tired and will retire thoon. Before you go, thelect a book."

"We can take these books?"

He shrugged. It was a glimpse, that shrug, of a very cool customer.

"I don't know. But no one keepth track of them anymore. Help yourthelf."

I nodded and ambled off through the library of books and bones, disquieted.

I returned to the skull pierced long ago by the iron spike. Beneath it were rows of shelves of leatherbound books, the leather—green, brown, or black—was cracked and ornate in some cases as decoratively as a woodcarving.

The first book I picked up was labeled *The Codex Seraphinianus.* I flipped through it and found it was written in an absolutely unknown language. It was illustrated with grotesque anatomical studies of things that simply don't, can't, exist.

I put it back.

The next was *The World Guide to Subterranean Monasteries.*

I flipped through it and found it was mostly maps. Some of them depicted huge, vaulted city spaces that looked for all the world like Escher prints come to life.

The pages were crumbling, but there was no copyright or publishing house.

I returned it and slid a thin volume out, the cover ornate though the leather was chipped and scuffed. There was a tiny brass lock on the side, broken and heavily tarnished.

The cover had the same hand-tooled design in old leather that was on the keystone of the fireplace back at Guild house, complete with a small silver skull, ringed with stones.

I opened it to the title page.

The New Assassin's Field Guide and Almanac.

The copyright was 1917, London, England.

That was the only information. No author listed. No publishing house.

I flipped through pages and read some random snatches.

"*The Strategies of Realistic Exits, Conventionality and the Unexpected.*"

"*The Red World: Your life is a reflection of all you Fear. Need is fear, turned on its side. Fear Nothing. Fear No One. Be instead, That Which Is Feared.*"

"*Killing with the Mind: Gullivar Faust's Treatise on Time Malleability and Applications In The Warrior's Trade and Exercises.*"

I closed the book and turned back to the fireplace.

Mr. Fell was gone.

CHAPTER 29

The New Assassin's Field Guide and Almanac.

I RETURNED TO THE PARTY with the book stuffed down the back of my pants. I was mildly distressed to learn that Jiufeng had already left, and when I arrived at the Providence Hotel I found that she was not there.

Jiufeng had already left for her first independent slate, I learned much later, in Copenhagen.

Jiufeng, you see, was a Thug. That philosophy of assassination was always in higher demand than those of the Paladin's, we who liked to think we were actually making a moral choice, however much of a rationalization that might be.

I was disappointed but not quite hurt. In my room, locked or not made little difference to such as we, she had left me an origami unicorn made of silver foil.

I knew what it meant, and I have it still.

I wouldn't see her again for seven and a half years.

And in my heart of hearts, I was somewhat relieved to have the rest of the night to myself. I was sobering up and ordered a pot of coffee and food to my room and spent the hours between one a.m. and sunrise with the book.

The book that shaped the following years of my life.

Written in the margins of the old, brown text, there were occasional, largely cryptic notes, written in a spidery copperplate in faded *green* ink.

The first was on the opening page, which read:

> *The New Assassin's Field Guide and Almanac*
> *By -N.-*
> *The Complete Guide to Secretive Murder,*
> *Methodology, and Employments*

The first note was directly beneath that but written on a slant.

Trust? Trust is a smooth pretty stone on the beach, my lord. However long it may take, it will turn to sand in your fist.

I won't rewrite the entire book, no fear. It was less than two hundred pages long. But I'll give you some of the chapter titles as well as "the green notes" to give you an idea. I can say that for that moment, that night, I was transfixed.

A convert, you might say.

And maybe that was the point, I'm still not sure.

"Our Predatory Origins and Heritage." "The Illusion of Self." "Multi-faceted Form Creation." "The Palace of Mentational Mechanics." "The Way of The Blade." "History's Secret Servants." The Dangers and Uses of Compassion." "The Wolf's Eye." "Masks for All Lights." "Concentration, Mentation, and Time Fluidity." "Love and Other Sufferings." "Beyond All Hate." "Impossibilities."

And the aforementioned treatise: *"Gullivar Faust's Treatise on Time Malleability and Application in The Warrior's Trade and Exercises."*

And these from various chapters:

Romance, like all religions, is for fools, weaklings, and the unsuitable. All structures of the human heart fail all save those who use those structures to yoke their weaker fellows. To maximize one's viability in this veil of illusions and manipulations, one must sever all such from your life. Romance only that of thine own life, to seek anything else is to court a phantom, insubstantial and as destructive as Hamlet's father's shade.

Doubt All but Thine Own Self.

The Church, all Churches, are made of Stone, shaped by Man's Geometries and Empty of All Save That Which Controls Man. Respect Its Dangers and Its Opportunities For Employ.

All that Truly Matters in this Life is Wealth and Power Over Life and Death. The Assassin Uses one to accrue the other. Any other concern is Hollow Conceit, fodder for well-fed Monks, Fat Politicians, and Wealthy Fools to debate as dogs will fight over a bone.

And of the green notes, there were these, among others:

Love is a lie. Honor a choice. God is the biggest lie of them all. Mourn this, and then BE FREE.

And as I read, and drank coffee, and stalked about my luxurious room and the sky grew grey with dawn, it was as though something in me was dying as something else was born.

I thought of how when Dagny and I were kissing and I was inside her, her mouth would suddenly taste like rain. Summer, thunderstorm rain.

I thought of her father, and his plans to know my name someday.

I thought of Didi and Gogo and how they seemed to be trapped forever in Eliot's *Wasteland*, and that for me—like them—it was too late, too late, too late. Godot would never come.

I would kill child molesters. Rapists. The crazy, greedy, and the cruel. The ones who thought they got away with it, until I arrived.

I would never fear any monster again, never worry over fate or love or friendship.

I was a *friend* of monsters. Even beloved by them, in their way.

Maybe someone else could luck into the sweet lie lyrics of bullshit that the bibles and radios and songs and shows all tell us, after I'd put a bullet in their boogeymen.

I would study this fucking book and everything it alluded to. I would follow the trail and see the world for what it was, not what I'd once so wished it to be. *I'd fucking tried* to be something other than what the Master Chief pounded out on his anvil, but I'd tried in the wrong direction.

Now, I'd become a man that even *he'd* fear.

I wondered, while the sun rose, what Dagny was doing right then. Sleeping, probably. Only a few miles away, maybe. Would her father kiss her on the cheek at breakfast in the morning? Say he'd met an interesting man, the night before?

I wondered who Bonzai would be killing in Copehagen.

We were, all of us, in The Wasteland.

Beyond confused companionship, there was nothing else.

The field guide had filled me with its—what? The closest I could come was *Zen Nihilism*. I'd found my muse.

I'd had enough of love and other weaknesses.

* * *

Yeah, *I know*. But I was twenty-one. You know how it is.

CHAPTER 30

No Man's Land. Mors Five and Six. Rourke Call Three. Rupert's Vision. The Bell Tolls for Ace Towing.

THE MEETING WASN'T SCHEDULED until eleven thirty that night, fifteen minutes before the park closed.

I was curious how a site that big *could* be closed, but I didn't dwell on it.

Being well-versed in defensive as well as offensive techniques in all aspects of human conflict, we were there almost three hours early. Tourists of every stripe swarmed the Lincoln Memorial and the Mall beyond. It was a bright fall day and unusually cold for what was usually a festering swamp, the brilliant leaves on all the trees pinch-hitting for the sun, veiled behind a gun-metal sky that promised rain.

Mors and I stood beneath the statue of Lincoln, seated inside the great Doric-style temple.

"Where's Rupert?" I said.

"Getting something to eat at that Indian place."

"You really think I needed a sweep, back-up, all that?" Mors shrugged.

"You'd rather meet this douchebag without us, be my guest. Better safe than sorry. Remember that Tad Williams book the Nightingale made us all read?"

"Yeah," I said, "*Confident, cocky, lazy, dead.*"

Mors huddled in his flight jacket and sighed.

"Personally, I don't see why you don't just slate these assholes like they want and call it a deal. You'd be doing the whole country a favor," he said.

"Are you in a bad mood?"

"I hate Washington," Mors said. "The whole goddamn city is the world's largest necropolis since Egypt. A graveyard for the entire country's most fucked-up dreams."

"Don't hold back," I said.

"I'm not," Mors said. "I don't. Look, Danny, we *kill people. For money*. You think that makes you some kind of hero because of your area."

"I don't think I'm a hero, Mors. But I think child molesters, rapists, child pornographers, and terrorists and their backers and their ilk, yeah, they're better in the ground."

"But you've slated others," he said.

"Occasionally. Maybe at first. I'll never know. But I specialize, yes."

"Well, how do you always know? You only know what the dossier says. And you really buy this Dark Bushido shit. Honor among bastards."

"Jesus Christ, Mors, *yeah*, I do. You'd still be under six feet of fucking crickets if I didn't. What's your point?"

Mors glared at me, then gathered himself.

He nodded toward the statue of Lincoln, eternally on his throne.

"Would you have slated *him*?" he said.

"No, Mors, I wouldn't."

"Why? Because he was a good man?"

"Well, yes, actually. I mean, look around. This whole edifice is dedicated to his goodness," I said.

Mors laughed, which was always scary since his sense of humor was pitched a little differently than most humans.

"Danny, Danny. As Bugs would say, you're such a maroon. Who do you think slated Lincoln? *We did*. The Guild," he said.

"Don't fuck with me right now, Mors. I'm not in the mood."

"Booth was *Guild*, you ever look at the portraits in the old hall?"

"I've looked at them," I said.

"Well, he's there. We did *that*," he said, gesturing to the statue, "And do you think this place would even be here if he hadn't been slated? *Killing him's what made him great*."

A trio of Japanese tourists glanced at us uneasily and moved away.

"Shut up, Mors," I said.

He glanced back, then continued in a lower voice.

"You saved my ass, *Vladimir*. I'll never forget it. But I'm here to tell you there aren't any good guys. Maybe not even any bad guys. There's just perspective. Wake up."

"Thanks, Dad," I said.

"Yeah," Mors said, "that's half your problem. Look, I'll stick with this until it's over. And you're my—friend. Maybe the only one. But the Kestrel isn't your dad. Don't kid yourself. We're not knights, Danny."

I looked out over the crowd below us, the Washington monument a ways off and the capital beyond that. The area where the reflecting pool normally would be was a sea of churned earth and construction equipment.

"Then what are we, Mors? According to you?"

"Death," he said, "made to order. Fate and who wins will take care of the definitions."

I lit a cigarette, ignoring the scowls from a group of students, all in their school windbreakers.

Mors sighed again.

"I'm going to get Rupert. Then we'll come in over there, along those two parallel lines of trees. I'll be halfway along the construction area, there."

More gestured to the left of where the reflecting pool normally was. The area looked like a socket missing a tooth, completely enclosed by chainlink fence, drained and ugly with board walkways. I'd read that the facelift was supposed to take three years.

"Numb-nuts will be opposite me on the right. We'll both have scopes, and we'll move up bit by bit before your appointment. I'll have the Blaser. Buzzcock will have the Ashbury; he's used one before. Try to keep the conversation near this pillar," Mors said, gesturing to the column we were standing near on the right side of the chamber.

"Okay," I said, "and Mors, thank you for doing this."

Mors shrugged again, hands deep in his jacket pockets. "Nothing to be done," he said, and turned to walk down the stairs.

* * *

I had brought something to eat and read with me in a leather satchel and sat it beside me on a bench facing Independence Ave.

An hour to go.

After Mors had left, I'd walked the whole park, then sat and read.

I'd brought crackers, a tin of sardines and a bottle of iced tea along with a copy of O'Neill's *The Iceman Cometh* I'd bought at Second Story Books on Dupont Circle.

I'd never seen the play and had come to learn it was rarely performed. I was about halfway through, well into the part where Hickey's return to Harry Hope's bar is boding ill for its inhabitants and their desperately important pipe dreams about tomorrows that will never come. Reading it was sort of compulsive. I knew where it was going and dreaded it, but you couldn't look away.

Pretty fucking good for a play I was reading like a book, written in 1939.

I tried to focus on the book, the lunch, the moment, all that, but it was hard. Aside from the Rumpus we'd be pulling off (or not) soon, I was shook by what Mors had said.

The Kestrel wasn't my father. Check.

I was trying to do—something. Prove something. To whom?

I was a father. Yes indeed. At least biologically.

But what did that mean? Had it really changed my internal weathervane at all? A sea-change of the soul? I couldn't say.

I didn't know.

I killed people for money. Granted, people whom many say they'd kill, given the chance. But what did I think of myself as?

Claw and paws and jaws.

"Existential crap," I said out loud. Then kept reading a play that made it worse.

"That's the stuff, Harry! Of course you'll try to show me! That's what I want you to do!" Helpless dread.

Helpless dread. So says Eugene O'Neill.

* * *

Fifteen to go, I walked back toward the Lincoln Memorial, my satchel over my shoulder. I was cold and stiff. I stretched a little and took stock. My Walther was a reassuring presence under my coat. I was wearing jeans, a canvas jacket, and running shoes with a Red Sox baseball cap to keep off the rain, which had started about ten and was coming down harder.

Approaching the memorial, I looked over to the Washington Monument, glowing in the rain. The reflecting pool construction site was long deserted now and a long expanse of rain-swept muck, shadowy, and bleak looking.

It looked like a set for *No Man's Land* in a World War One movie, complete with trenches.

The memorial itself was sparsely attended now, a few knots of people inside the temple, the seated statue of Lincoln glowing white, the rest of the building and the columns lit an ivory yellow.

There was a row of cement blocks lining the enclosing fence and, to the right, a prefab shack that looked like it would serve fried clams back in Maine, displaying various military insignia.

There were two park service kiosks off to my right, the larger one dark, now, the smaller, closer one lit but seemingly unoccupied.

A police car sat off to the far right of the monument road, engines idling, wipers off.

Two high lampposts with three big spotlights apiece stood at each corner of the courtyard, the rain heavy gold streaks in their beams.

My scrambler's alarm buzzed in my pocket.

Time to attend.

I stayed near the construction fence a moment longer and held my phone to me ear, pressing the call button. Whispering.

"Mors? Are you in position?"

Nothing but static, mixing with the rain?

"Rupert?"

Nothing.

What the fuck?

The whole system was "slaved" to Lord Henry, who also should have been listening in.

"Lord Henry."

Three strikes. Well, I didn't think I was in immediate danger and knew my friends were watching, communications snafu or no.

I crossed the flagstone courtyard and went up each platform of stairs, then trotted up the main stairs, couples and trios passing me with umbrellas on the way down.

Once at the top, there was no one in the huge, vaulted space of the temple but me and Abe.

I went in, shivering. The marble surrounding me seemed to generate cold and radiate it.

Lincoln sat in eternal weariness, it seemed, looking off slightly to his right. I'd read somewhere that his hands were posed in sign language for the initials "A" and "L."

I turned. The dark, rainy park was empty.

It was 11:41.

I was at the edge of the stairway when the park service kiosk that was still lit exploded into flame.

I saw the cop exit his car and, jerking a glance back at me, run to the building and then U-turned abruptly back to his own car as flames engulfed the building despite the heavy rain.

A bullet screamed off the column to my immediate right and droned off into the dark as I dove to the stairs, hunched against the sting of marble chips hitting the side of my face and neck. The shot echoed only slightly out of synch with the impact.

The enclosure was a deathtrap, the stairs and courtyard open exposure.

I pushed off the stairs into a headlong run, almost falling on the wet marble. A second shot caromed off a stair behind me, but I was already pelting across the courtyard toward the fence.

Behind me there was another shot, and a man screamed, then another shot hit the insignia shack as I ducked between it and the fence and then climbed up and over the chainlinks, flipping up and over it and down into the thick mud.

No man's land was inky dark with all the spotlights pointing toward the memorial.

I ripped the satchel off and threw it away—so long, Eugene—and pulled out my gun.

A huge explosion hammered the night air and compressed my eardrums, a fireball rolling up and in on itself, throwing my shadow across the muddy landscape.

The police car.

I ran through the board-strewn mud and sand piles toward a chemical toilet, then zig-zagged across a huge lake of muck and stopped to crouch behind a cement mixer that was sitting at a weird, canted angle.

The kiosk and car were both burning brightly in the rain, with no sign of the cop or lingering tourists.

I thought I could hear sirens, but the rain became an absolute deluge, plastering my hair to my face, my hat long gone.

Where the fuck were Buzzcock and Mors? Or were they—?

No, no, no. Can't think that.

I was about as wet and muddy as one could get. I crawled on my belly with my elbows away from the cement mixer and under a wooden platform where it was relatively dry and sheltered.

Whatever this was, whoever, it wouldn't be long. Sirens were definitely coming this way, and this was, big or not, an enclosed space.

Over a third of a mile, but still a cage.

They'd have to come for me or give it up, soon, before the cops, firetrucks, et al showed up.

"Hoo-hooo, ye eejit! Come out, come out and we'll have a square go of it, awright? This is dead manky down here, this is."

Well.

I guess Bleach had decided the same thing.

* * *

Mors Five.

Mors checked his watch, a thick Invicta chronograph.

Plenty of time to get in position.

"Let's go," he said.

Rupert got up and dumped his tray and joined Mors in Mariah.

"Now this is a sweet ride. You restore this baby yourself?"

"Whadda you think she's worth?" Rupert said.

"Dunno," Mors said.

Mors swung Mariah onto Constitution Avenue, frowning at the police cars coming and going, watching his speed.

"How long'd it take to get her up and running?" Rupert said.

Mors was silent.

"What's her max? One ten? One twenty?"

Mors said nothing.

"Jesus. What is this? The silent treatment? What, is discussing your fuckin' car off limits or offensive or somethin'?"

Mors surprised them both by sharing his thought.

"I don't like this," Mors said.

"What?"

"This whole thing. Better we'd been dug in hours ago. But it's the fucking National Mall, and even at night, it'd be tricky. Couldn't get us in position during the day."

Rupert hadn't heard Mors talk so much to anyone but Ketch.

"Um. Do you think it's a set-up?"

"Everything's a set-up," Mors said.

Mors pulled off Independence Ave. and parked illegally near the walkway heading toward the World War One Memorial.

Outside, they checked for tourists and cops, but it had started to rain, and the park was deserted.

Mors opened the trunk and handed Rupert his gun.

"Okay," Mors said, "the rain is going to fuck this up even worse, but we're going in. Go straight ahead until you see the fence around the pool construction. Follow it until you have a good clear line on the steps and get yourself settled. I'll check in after I'm in position. Don't use your phone except to answer me or Ketch. Unless you see something."

"Okay," Rupert said, "okay, I'm on it."

Mors took Rupert's shoulder in one large hand.

"Keep your shit together, Buzzcock."

Rupert felt almost elated.

"I will!"

Rupert trotted off into the rainy dark.

Mors watched him and sighed, then jogged back the way they'd come, checking his watch once.

He got back to where he'd parked.

But Mariah was gone.

* * *

Rupert refrained from using his phone as long as he could stand it, but when the rain really began to pound he found his view of the memorial hopelessly fucked up, water filling the scope like a shot glass. He thought he'd seen Ketch's jacket and cap, but he'd lost him in the haze of heavy rain.

He keyed his phone.

"Mors!"

Static.

"Ketch!"

Nothing.

Then, not far off, there was a whump, and firelight glowed through the trees, smoke starting to roil up to the left of the memorial, even in the rain.

"Shit!"

Rupert tried his phone again.

When he couldn't reach anyone, he began to trot toward the memorial. When the second explosion came, he fell, then got up and began to sprint as a huge fireball boiled up on itself into the rainy sky.

Rupert was scared but elated, too. If he saved Ketch, got into some action, these guys would see he was one of them.

One of the elite.

* * *

The rain might have let up, but the wind had become wildly violent, so it was hard to tell.

I'd glimpsed Bleach but couldn't make the shot, running across a series of planks over a mud-choked culvert for my next cover, a pile of concrete pipes amid a forest of metal rods bundled together with wire.

Bleach kept calling out to me.

"Dinnae just hide over there like a fart in a trance, Proteus! Mebbe ye'll get hoachie, look, I'm nae far a'tall!"

A shot. A bullet rang off the reinforcing rod about six feet from where I was.

Sirens everywhere now. And strobing lights through the rain.

"C'mon, yeh tosser! The gendarms are about. Come for me and let's just sort it out afore the fun's over. C'mon!"

I saw the Master Chief in a wash of some far-off cop's spotlight, standing in his peacoat, pointing to my left, face placid and calm.

All right. It's as good a time as any to go crazy.

I went toward where he was pointing, down on my belly again in the mud.

"What is this, Bleach?" I yelled, despite the risk. I tried to crawl faster, after, and clambered around the edge of the pipes and into another culvert that was three feet deep with muddy, churning water.

A shot—close enough to see the flash—and a bullet splattered mud six feet behind me.

"Oh, yeh mean who's put up the cally dosh for your arse? Wouldn't yeh like t'know that, hey?"

The Master Chief was standing atop the mud, next to a huge concrete ring the size of above-ground swimming pool. He looked at me and flipped his cigarette into the pool.

The concrete pool was less than half full of muddy water, the interior had four holes a little larger than a man at four points of the compass.

Pipes.

I jumped down into the enclosure, finding the water to be about waist high and hard concrete under foot.

I looked up, and the Master Chief was gone.

One thing they didn't teach at the Guild was hydraulics and drainage design, but I couldn't see any other options.

Bleach called out over the storm and the sirens, like he was the neighborhood bully hunting a smaller kid in a junkyard.

"Prooooteusl, here, y'heid case, show yerself an' let's get it over and done. Ah cannae be arsed to chase yeh aul night in this boggin' pit."

I splashed over to the edge of the ring and fired twice toward the sound of his voice. He fired back almost instantly, chipping the far edge of the concrete with a whine.

I dove for the far pipe, hoping it stayed in a straight line running the length of the reflecting pool bed.

And that the end wasn't blocked.

I have always had a touch of claustrophobia, which I was lucky enough to have kept a lid on in the tank room. There was a steady stream of brackish water about five inches deep coursing through the pipe and flowing over my arms and around my shoulders as I crawled forward.

I was breathing hard, gasping really, and not just from the effort. There was enough clearance that I could maybe get almost on my knees with my back pressed tight against the curve of pipe above me.

I strained to look back after thirty feet of crawling and saw only vague darkness, then a flash of a spotlight, washing past the pipe entrance, impossible to tell from what distance.

I heard Bleach yelling something else but couldn't make it out. Farther away, maybe.

The water was cold and smelled rancid, and my teeth were chattering. Ahead of me was just blackness. I squirmed onto my side and dug the scrambler out of my inside pocket. It was wet and the display window was cracked, but these bastards are tough and being submerged doesn't do much. But I wasn't making a call; I needed a light.

I thumbed the display button twice, and cracked or not, the LED screen gave forth it's flashlight mode.

Ahead of me was straight, concrete pipe, stretching off into a far-off darkness of immeasurable length. But the pool was, what, over two thousand feet in length?

A third of a mile, more or less, since I'd run into No Man's Land quite a ways when all the excitement started.

If Bleach found either end of the pipe, I was dead. I'd either be shot through the top of my head or, worse, up through my ass.

I crawled faster through the cold running muck, my gun clutched in one hand, the scrambler in flashlight mode in the other. I had to bear down hard, mentally, not to panic, not to allow myself to be overwhelmed by questions that did me not one fucking bit of good in my current situation. *What happened to the phone? Were Mors and Rupert dead? And what the fuck was Bleach doing here? Never mind whether my hallucination of the Master Chief actually might have helped me out. Maybe.*

Or helped me into a perfect corner.

Concentrate on surviving the night. Solve this.

That was the scenario.

The scrambler vibrated in my hand. I stopped crawling and answered, relief flooding me in an almost nauseating wave. The Calvary, at last.

"*Where the fuck have you been?*" I said in a strangled whisper.

"Hi, Daddy."

"Jesus, ah, *hi honey!* It's—boy, it's late."

"I know. It's raining here. I'm sorry to call after bedtime."

"It's okay. It's—are you okay?"

"Yes," Rourke said.

"How did you get this number?" I said.

I had stopped crawling and was lying in the water. I made myself go forward again.

"I saw it on the screen when we talked last and remembered it."

"Right. Of course you did. Where's Mommy?"

"Asleep. I would probably be in trouble for calling you late, but I was scared."

"It's okay," I said. "I'm, um, sorry you had a nightmare."

"It was very scary. I had a nightmare about an elephant."

"No kidding. Well, I'm glad it's over. I mean, it wasn't real."

"I know that, Daddy. I was just scared," Rourke said.

"I understand. Everybody gets scared."

"Yes. Daddy? Could you sing me a song?"

"Well. I mean, sure I could. Softly," I said, feeling a slight breeze blowing toward me now. But no light yet but my own.

"Do you have a roommate, is that why you're whispering?" she said.

"Yes. Yes, I do. And I don't want to wake him up."

"Okay," Rourke said, "do you know America?"

"You mean like the country?" I said.

"No!" Rourke laughed, "the *band*; it's a band mommy likes."

"Oh. Yes, then. I know that band."

"Do you know the song 'A Horse with No Name'?"

"Yeah. I know that one," I said.

"Could you sing it to me so I can back to sleep? ...Daddy?"

"Okay. Yes, honey. But super softly, okay?"

"Oh, sure," she said.

I definitely felt a breeze and could smell fresher air.

I wracked my brain for a moment, and then it came to me, hearing the tune on the radio a hundred times, the Master Chief a fan of seventies rock stations.

"'*On the first part of the journey*.' Umm. "'*I was looking at all the life, there were plants and birds and rocks and things, there was sand and hills and rings. The first thing I met was—*' *Shit*. I mean, shoot."

"A fly," Rourke said.

"'*A fly with a buzz, and the sky, with no clouds. The heat was hot and the ground was dry but the air was full of sound. I've been through the desert on a horse with no name, it felt good to be out of the rain. In the desert, you can remember your name, 'cause there ain't no one for to give you no pain.*'"

"Ah."

"Go on, Daddy," she said, "you have a good voice, even whispering."

"'*La la la la la la la la la,*'" I sang.

"Uh oh! I think Mommy's up. Gotta go," Roarke said.

"Okay," I said.

"Thank you for singing to me, Daddy."

"You're welcome. Do you feel better?"

"Yes, I do. Goodnight!"

"Goodnight, Rourke," I said.

I crawled a little farther and saw a flash of light. And definitely wind. I also saw a rat trundling ahead of me until it was lost in the shadows.

I shimmied faster, my gun clutched in my fist, the scrambler stuffed back in my pocket. It was dim, but I could see the proverbial light at the end of the tunnel.

I also heard sirens, not close, and Bleach, much closer, calling from somewhere above me, but I couldn't see the opening.

"Hiding, is it? Why, Proteus, I'm black affronted, I am. Should've packed yer tiger, hey? I awready drilled yer pal."

A frantic five-minute crawl, maybe longer, and I came to the other end. I squirmed out and promptly fell about ten feet into a pool of mud and leaves, in an enclosure identical to the pipe I'd climbed into.

I could see an aluminum ladder against the edge of the concrete pool and gun at the ready, climbed it, absolutely black with muck from crown to heels.

I peeked over the top of the pipe. Bleach was standing about twelve feet away, "ass to" as the Master Chief would say.

Bleach was wearing a dark nylon jacket, and his ivory hair was plastered around his head under a scally cap. His pistol was bright silver in the swooping glare of the cop's spotlights, though we were far enough away to not be very distinctive among the looming shapes of earth-moving gear. Someone blared something over a loud-speaker, sounding like the dialogue between songs on Pink Floyd's "The Wall."

I climbed up onto the wet ground and centered my aim, two handed. I whistled. Loud.

Bleach spun, gun up, and I fired even as I saw the flash of his shot.

The bullet shattered glass to my left, and I saw Bleach go down, his gun spinning off into the dark. He was clutching his right hand, black blood spouting in a freshet.

"*Aw, 'gabby! Yeh fuckin' cunt! Yer teas oot! Fuckin' fook!*" I aimed for the killshot as Bleach danced, his hand under his armpit and his gun in the muck.

And the spotlights married, swinging toward me and I could see the figures behind them, running toward us.

"*Freeze!*"

I turned and ran.

* * *

Mors Six.

He had been standing in the space that Mariah had apparently been fucking teleported from, in a white-hot, teeth-gritted rage, when Mors heard the first explosion and saw its glow refracted in the heavy rain.

Mors ran for the footpath that went past the Vietnam Woman's Memorial, his boots pounding the wet pavement.

He keyed his phone and hissed Ketch's name. Then Buzzcock's. God damn it!

Mors stepped up his speed as the second explosion clapped the air, this time thudding through his chest.

The fireball rose like a refrain of all the wars the site was consecrated to.

Mors skidded to a halt.

He couldn't just run into a goddamn battle.

Was Ketch already dead? Mors tried the phone again.

Nothing.

Mors crept near the construction enclosure. The rain began to hammer down loudly now, along with the increasing whoop and warble of sirens. Mors could see cops, an ambulance and now firetrucks. The firemen were pulling hoses toward the burning kiosk, which was already no longer a building but a bonfire. The shell of the police car was burning much more brightly, ignoring the rain and boiling black smoke into the sky.

* * *

Rupert threw his rifle into the brush and slipped his Glock out and held it at his side. He crept along the West bank of the Potomac, staying as low as he could and still see the fire and strobing lights.

Rupert thought he'd heard gunshots and tried the useless piece of shit scrambler for the hundredth fucking useless time.

Cops, firetrucks, gunshots, and fire, all great shit to stay as far away from as possible, *Rupert thought.*

But these were the big boys. And Ketch and Mors were counting on him. Needing him. He'd get Ketch out of this mess, beat Mors to the punch, and earn his fucking bones. Hook his little fucking wagon to their stars and they could be a team.

Rupert had already envisioned it all, like a movie preview. "The Trio of Death," maybe, or "Death's Trio"?

The rain was driving into Rupert's face now. He could see a small statue to his left. He decided to risk getting closer. Be had to at least see what the fuck was going on.

Rupert reached the statue, some guy sitting in a throne with an angel standing over him. Good omen?

Rupert eased his way around the edge of the seated figure and heard the shot that killed him. A sledgehammer blow to the chest and a wet ripping as the bullet punched through his back and went on through the rain into the Potomac.

He fell to his knees hard enough to break bone, but he didn't feel it. Then he couldn't feel anything.

* * *

Mors stayed in the rainy shadows, watching the lights of the emergency vehicles. After a long silence, save for all the cops, there had been two more shots. Now the police were swarming the enclosure, a section of fence cut away. Powerful flashlights, and some kind of SUV churning mud.

Time to get lost.

Mors walked (walk, when things go to shit, never run, unless absolutely necessary) hands in his coat, his pistol gripped through the slit pocket inside his jacket, the rain cold and stinging on his scruffy pate.

He stuck to the shadows and walked along the street around the back of the memorial, then hit Ohio Drive and walked past the bridge and into the park again, staying at the edge of the rain-swept Potomac.

With the hubbub to his left and moving swiftly away from him, he walked easily along the river's edge until he saw a statue in the gloom.

A figure like a bundle of dirty rags was at the base of a statue of a seated figure. At first Mors thought it was a bum, but no one would be sleeping on cold marble in a downpour. Mors mounted the little stairway to the statue.

Looming over all was a nude woman with a cloak. It reminded Mors uncomfortably of the statue of Thanatos, back at Guild house. The woman appeared to be shielding the seated figure from the rain.

Mors read the legend VISION in the faint strobe of the emergency lights and the glow of the memorial. The seated man was John Ericson.

The bundle of rags was Rupert Buzzcock.

He knelt. Felt for Rupert's pulse.

Mors gently pulled him over onto his back. The fat little man's expression was open-mouthed surprise, the rain fell onto his open eyes.

Mors swept them closed.

"Buzzcock," he muttered.

* * *

"Washington, DC, PD, how may I direct your call."

"I...think my car was stolen," Mors said, cringing at even having to do this.

"What's the license, model, and last location of the vehicle, sir?"

Mors writhed in the phone booth, but what could he do? He had to know before acting.

"Nineteen fifty Mercury, license number PSII164, Massachusetts plates. It was parked—ahm—near the Vietnam Women's Memorial."

"Not stolen, sir," the bored sounding cop on phone duty said, "towed."

"Towed."

"Yes,sir. Ace Towing Company. 202-555-1564."

"Thanks."

"Goodnight, sir."

Mors blew air out in a gust and hung up the phone. Just the idea of Mariah in some cop impound lot, with what was both inside and built into her, made his skin crawl. The keychain fob in his fist was a little brass elephant. It could be twisted in such a way to detonate the car.

He was very glad not to have to do that. She'd been years of work in the making.

Now that at least one crisis was in hand he could think a little. Meeting just a set-up. Buzzcock dead. Ketch likely dead. Gardener cozy in Maine. Future uncertain at best.

VISION.

Mors took out his scrambler phone, startled to find it was working fine now. He dialed Ace Towing.

"Yeah," some guy said. There was music in the background.

"You got my car. Nineteen fifty Merc. Black."

"Yeah, we got it."

"How much?"

"One fifty," the guy said.

"Where are you?"

* * *

Mors had the cab drop him off at the end of Park St. It had stopped raining and was chill now; he could see his breath. The area was a largely abandoned industrial park on the outskirts of Arlington, bleak and overgrown. Warehouse buildings all in a state of shit-ass decrepitude, witch grass and weeds growing amid the mud and cracked asphalt.

Most of the buildings were dark with no service or security lights. Empty.

He walked down the main road, over a set of tracks toward an area lit with light poles. As he walked, a tow truck came flying up the road past him, heading out. Music was playing in the cab, something by ZZ Top.

They beeped as they went by.

Beep! Beep! A jeering tone.

Mors kept walking.

Ace Towing was shack with a fenced-in dirt lot behind it, the fence chained and padlocked with a Titus lock the size of his fist. Mors could see Mariah and maybe twelve or thirteen other cars in the far corner of the lot, looking like penned animals huddling together for warmth.

The light poles gave off a sick orange glow.

A second tow truck was uncoupling from a dented Elentra, one guy in a do-rag at the car, the driver in the truck.

Mors went to the shack's tiny scalloped window, the hole in the thick, dirty plastic even tinier.

A fat guy with a red afro and long red sideburns was in the booth, watching a huge old computer monitor. There was some kind of virtual card game on the screen.

The fat guy had a red, fleshy moon face and turned away from the game with a half-mast lidded "Yeah," when Mors tapped on the glass. A newspaper article headlined "Predators with Tow Trucks?" was taped to the wall, with a red, devil-horned smiley face drawn on it.

"I want my car," Mors said. He could smell pot.

The fat guy smirked.

"Then you pay me one-fifty," he said.

"No. I don't," Mors said, and shot him twice through the window.

Mors walked six steps to the lot on his right. The guy in the do-rag had stepped toward the shack, wide-eyed, the Titus padlock in one hand.

Mors shot him.

The tow truck lurched forward, spraying mud and gravel. Mors shot the driver twice through the windshield and the truck ground to a halt, still running choppily.

Mors started Mariah with the elephant fob switch and lit a cigarette. He enjoyed half of it, leaning back against the tow truck until the second truck came grinding back down the road, still blaring music, George Thorogood's "I Drink Alone," towing an electric-blue Element SUV. Mors flipped the cigarette away.

He shot the driver through the windshield. The assistant flung the door open, and before his second foot could hit the dirt, Mors shot him twice.

George Thorogood ground into "Move It on Over."

He got into Mariah and drove out of the lot.

CHAPTER 31

Homecoming. Party Prep.

IT TOOK ME A WHILE to get home.

When the police swarmed into the construction pool, I had quite a lead on them, which was aided by the fact that they either split their forces to chase Bleach too or hung back because of caution, before chasing anybody.

It gave me just enough of a lead to loop around to my left past another cluster of construction equipment and climb the fence and drop into the park past the far end of the pond near the Vietnam Women's Memorial.

I'd wrenched my right ankle jumping down from the fence and was absolutely covered with muck.

I half-hobbled, half-ran, lying down once in the scrub when a metro cruiser went by with its lights on and siren off. I made it to Constitution Ave. and limped all the way to the DAR museum.

I checked the scrambler phone. Surprise, surprise, it was working again, though the battery was all but dead. Damaged, somehow, during the festivities.

It had enough juice to call for a cab, then winked out.

When the cabbie arrived, at first he wouldn't let me get in I was so filthy.

But money talks.

By the time I got back to the townhouse it was almost two a.m.

The house was dark except for an exterior light, as I had left it. I went around back, and though aching with sprained everything and adrenaline spent, I got my gun out, reloaded during my cab ride, and crept-limped through the dark courtyard toward the back entrance.

I heard nothing, saw nothing, except for the mellow glow of lit windows in the surrounding houses, one window on the second floor festively framed with hot red pepper Christmas lights.

I put my key in the back door when I heard the distinctive click that, as I said, meant you're it.

"Hold it," a voice said.

I was pitifully slow bringing my gun up.

Then Mors said, "*Si vis pacem, para helium.*"

"Jesus, Mors—!"

He came out of the shadows under the porch stairway, gun dangling.

"I knew it was you; I just didn't want you to shoot first or anything," he said.

And then he astonished me by hugging me. Hard.

Gloriosky!

* * *

By three a.m. I was clean, had ice on my ankle and was sitting with a beer in front of a gas fire. Mors was at the living room coffee table, cleaning both of our disassembled pieces.

"I feel like absolute shit about Rupert," I said.

"You didn't shoot him. I won't say I told you so about Gardener."

"Thanks. I fucked it up with Bleach. He's still out there."

"Maybe we can use this. Rupert won't be identified any time soon. Gardener knows you had me in on this. Let him think it was me who got slated. Buzzcock was out of his league and that's that. But maybe if Gardener thinks I'm dead, he'll plan on you being alone now. That could help. Maybe."

I was past exhausted but angry enough to stay awake. I'd never seen Mors tired.

Well. Once.

It was close to dawn as I poured my flat beer down the drain and made coffee.

The previous hours had been spent in the ugly business of tracking down Buzzcock's mother and telling her of her son. Mors surprised me by insisting on making the actual call.

After putting coffee on, I didn't want to be anywhere near that sad errand, so I left Mors on the balcony and switched on the television, taking care to check all the connections to the Kirby box.

We'd checked our phones earlier; they were functioning fine, now, for any app, including walkie-talkie.

Now I had questions for Lord Henry's vast, cold brain, but I wanted to wait for Mors before connecting. I watched the early local news.

There were leading reports on every station about the "disturbance" at the Lincoln Memorial. The fires, the discovery of an unknown man's body, and the shooting death of a policeman were all mentioned as well as the possibility of a home-grown terrorist plot gone afoul.

On another station, a white supremacist plot was anonymously reported as well as a Tea-Party splinter group called *The Hardcore Raiders.*

I was relieved at the idiot bullshit for once as it muddied the waters.

The next report about "a night of unprecedented violence for the metro area" erased my relief.

Five people, the entire staff of some skanky towing company, killed in cold blood. Both the mob and some kind of drug-running nest were speculated.

At first I thought of Bleach, but the times didn't match.

And Mors had expressed his incredulous rage that Mariah had been towed, leaving him too late and rifle-less for when the meeting went south.

Mors came back inside, closing the slider behind him. "Can I ask you a question?"

"You just did," he said.

I decided I didn't want to know.

"Forget it," I said.

Mors showed no curiosity about my question; he poured himself a cup of coffee as the sky turned pink with dawn.

"Rupert's mother is going to keep Brando. She wants him."

"Good," I said, "that's good."

I turned on the Kirby box and the flat screen went blank.

"Lord Henry."

"**Yes, Mr. Ketch.**"

"What happened to our scrambler phone service last night?"

"**I shut off all scrambler-phone access to the units slaved to my system from the hours of eleven twenty p.m. to twelve fifty a.m. as I was directed to do by Gardener.**"

Mors drank his coffee back in a gulp and threw his mug into the kitchen where it shattered into a thousand pieces like a porcelain bomb.

I glanced at him, but he looked as placid as ever, the gesture his only lapse in temper and, as far as he was concerned, over now, and in the ever-receding past. I thought about the towing company again.

Nothing to be done, as the sad refrain from Godot went. "Lord Henry, listen to me: *Gilgamesh*."

There was a deep bass thrum that buzzed angrily from the television speakers.

"**Understood, sir.**"

"That's all for now, Lord Henry."

"**Yes, sir.**"

Save for a tiny green tell-tale, all the lights on the Kirby box went out.

Mors lit a cigarette and I joined him as we went out onto the balcony to smoke them.

"What's 'Gilgamesh' mean?" he said.

"Trigger code. Lord Henry's a copy program of Cyberius, you know, the computer at—"

"I know what Cyberius is," Mors said.

Curtly, I thought.

Of course. Cyberius had been the device that figured out the easiest way to break him.

"Lord Henry, like Cyberius, is an incredibly complex program. When we left, I still trusted Gardener. I thought he might be freaking out because he was scared, not that he was actually betraying us. Looks like I was wrong. And Rupert paid for my stupid mistake. I gave Gardener access to Lord Henry, which is to say my whole house, defense systems, the phone satellite hook-up, the works. You were right, Mors. Gardener's in this. I'd never have believed it, but I do now. But I still think we should go ahead with my plan to smoke this out. Gardener can't be in this alone. Where's the profit?"

"Lord Henry," I continued, "can be reprogrammed, redirected, re-tasked, by various trigger codes. 'Moblis in Mobli' made him accept Gardener as another master equal to me. 'Gilgamesh' made him split in two. Two separate programs that can run simultaneously, each undetected by the other. Like a split personality. It's risky, but it will blow our cover if I do something drastic like take away Gardener's access. Now, Lord Henry is programmed to keep serving Gardener's ends but also ours. We won't lose our phones again, though if Gardener tells him too, it will look on his end like service has been cut off. And we can continue to monitor his calls without him peeking at ours."

Mors nodded.

I lit another cigarette, hating the harsh taste.

"Fucking Rupert. Jesus," I said.

"You didn't shoot him," Mors said, "but you still want to go ahead with snatching these clowns?"

I nodded.

"Gardener, and whoever's behind him, wants those three dead. We go ahead with the grab and stash, the ball's in our court."

"Maybe," More said, "but you started this whole thing to help the Kestrel. If he's even still alive, they might send you his head for fucking around."

"Yeah. But like I said, he'd wants us to try, not just cave in and obey."

"The Dark Bushido," Mors said, "honor among bastards?"

"Call it that."

"What about Bleach?"

I stretched my neck, gingerly. The biggest cuts peppering it from the marble shrapnel at the memorial I'd closed with butterfly strips, and they itched.

"I hurt him. Maybe pretty badly. And I think they'll hold him back now. Last night was their shot, and they fucked it up. Whether it was Gardener or his, I don't know, *blackmailers*, whatever's going on. As far as they know, they missed me and got you. Now I think they'll see if I'll just obey. I'm telling Gardener you're dead. He'll know I'm alone now. Let's do the snatch and then we'll have all their targets in one place. That's when they'll move on me next."

"Then what?" he said.

"Then we find out who the authors of our sorrows are and make them sorry," I said.

Mors ground his cigarette out.

"Good plan. You have prearrangements for a funeral?"

"Help me do this, Mors. We'll prepare for Halloween. I'm calling Gardener now; you stay out of camera range and pay attention."

* * *

The week leading up to Halloween passed busily and was tropical in its swampy heat.

Adjustments to what I'd planned as a two-man job, then tightened up as a three-man job only to find it was a two-man job again, with Gardener believing it to be a one-man job, were myriad.

Gardener expressed his shock (shock!) at Mors's death and the attempt on my life and Bleach's involvement as well as absolute ignorance as to why the scrambler phones went down.

"I'm so sorry about Mors, Daniel. I know he was your friend. These people are obviously professionals and more than likely they had some way of jamming your phones. Who knows what else they can do? They know all about our organization, thus their access to Bleach and his turning. I must ask again, are you sure this abduction scheme is the best course?"

I sat saying nothing. Gardener's gloomy countenance looked back at me.

"All right. Then do you want tell me where you'll be taking three people for an extended period? Alone? Or even how you think you can pull this off?"

"It's better you don't know, Gard. Especially if it goes south," I said.

Gardener looked sadder than ever.

"You needn't protect me, Daniel. We're all that's left of the Guild. We're in this together," he said.

"You'll just have to trust me, Gardener."

We signed off.

Mors came out of the kitchen, eating a ham sandwich and handed me an Amstel Light. He set his own down on the coffee table and sat.

"Lord Henry," I said, "analysis and report on Gardener's activities, if you please."

"**At once, sir. Gardener is still lying and quite anxious when speaking with you. Insofar as I can monitor his activities here, he has been drinking an unusual amount of alcohol. He has also had female companionship here from an escort service—**"

"Christ," I said.

"There's escorts in the Maine boondocks?" Mors said.

"Please continue, Lord Henry. Sorry."

"Not at all, sir. He has had female companionship on three separate occasions. He has made three calls to the Pratts', which I am still unable to monitor, all under five minutes in length. I have filmed all such, as well as sexual activities, should lip reading be of service to you."

"You can read lips?" I said, non-plussed.

"**Alas, Mr. Ketch, I regret to say I cannot. There is an upgrade available, but all such access to my sister programs at Guild house are currently offline. And I should mention that the majority of Gardener's calls are either in the dark in your study, or his head is down, often propped by his left hand.**"

"Thank you, Lord Henry. Keep it up. And did you send the funds to Wanda Buzzcock?"

"**That I did, sir. She has deposited the sum in a Bank of America account in Hartford.**"

"That's all. Thank you," I said.

"**Goodnight, sir.**"

"Gardener getting laid on film. Kee-rist," Mors said.

"Out of my head," I said.

* * *

Mors was fascinated that I'd arranged to have milk actually delivered to the front door. It did give both of us an old-fashioned feeling of simpler times we'd never lived through.

It also gave us bottles.

I had eight of them lined up on the fence that faced our courtyard.

I tried shooting both standing and sitting. Standing worked way better, though it might draw more attention if I wasn't quick when the time came.

I stood near the outdoor table and reached back into my waistband and slipped the slingshot out with my left hand and the big glass marble from my right pocket and loaded the slingshot smoothly, drew, aimed, and fired at the first bottle.

I missed by four inches, the marble exploding against the brick wall behind the fence.

I reset everything and tried again.

The first milk bottle exploded into shards this time.

After I could shatter eight in a row, Mors handed me the five eighths of a dram glass phial we'd gotten a case of via Rupert's efforts, this one loaded with tap water and a smaller glass marble.

The marble inside the phial provided enough mass to shatter a milk bottle on the second try.

After that we were out of milk bottles and switched to what I'd actually be using, a clear glass jar with a flat black lid.

Success on the first try. Then, with Mors resetting the jars and loading more marbles into more phials of tap water for me, I practiced for another hour and a half.

Ball bearings would have been better, but metal detectors lucked that up.

I've always had excellent aim, even with things like skipping stones, throwing cards in a hat, darts, all that. I only missed twice during the next fifteen shots. I was rather pleased.

"Troubling" was all Mors would say.

CHAPTER 32

The New Alexandrians. Chinese Ghost Festival. The Fall of Captain Caine.

THE NEW ALEXANDRIAN'S Annual Halloween Ball.

It was blatantly, unashamedly, proudly a playdate for the rich and the powerful, with plenty of entertainment for whatever groove your taste ran in.

Twenty minutes into my arrival at the party I was reminded of a dozen films, books, and even plays.

That's the legacy of being raised by an alcoholic. If you've a fairly high-functioning brain, you read, read, read, see every movie you can, go to (or even act) in the theatre.

All in a desperate effort to both escape and to learn how to ape life. Normalcy. Romance. Courage.

Of course, using that as your template, you get it all wrong. And being thoroughly American, I had fully absorbed the Culture of the Gun.

And again, no excuses here, my friends. Just telling it like it is.

So anyway, *Casablanca, The Mikado, Rocky Horror Picture Show*, all that and more was before me at The New Alexandrian's Halloween Ball.

Mors (and poor Rupert) had put my outfit together: high black leather boots, fake sword and scabbard, black cloak, tri-corn hat, and a ceramic mask; I was fully tricked-out in a highwayman's costume.

Security had been a snap, not designed to detect a phial of sulfuric acid, a bottle of premixed potassium chlorate and sugar and a homemade slingshot and some marbles, all securely tucked away in my get-up.

The Willard Intercontinental Hotel was transformed, utterly. The ballroom was done up throughout like a medieval Chinese warlord's castle. Partial ruins (made of plastic, I assumed) complete with moss and verdigris were set about the huge function hall and lining the far walls. The walls themselves were festooned with guttering wall sconce torches, huge silk tapestries depicting tigers, dragons, and other animals of the Chinese zodiac.

Dragons, though, were the primary motif, carved in relief all over the "stone" arches and walls, as well as golden dragons—near life-sized—twined in a row of serpentine arches vaulting over the entire open space.

Crossed samurai swords, suits of samurai armor draped in cobwebs and worn by skeletons in action poses, and several fountains under-lit with colored spots decorated the ballroom.

Both individual and joined rows of tables and chairs were set throughout. There also appeared to be two bars at either end of the gallery with waitstaff in all manner of costume coming and going.

I had no assigned seat and picked up an illustrated place card at a table with the evening's events, theme, a menu, all tastefully gushed over in an elegantly calligraphed list.

-The New Alexandrian's 45th Annual Hallowe'en Ball-

The Mystic Orient Celebrates the Chinese

-Ghost Festival-

6–7:30 p.m. Drinks, Entertainment & Hob-knobbing

8:00 p.m. Keynote address Vincent Becke Mitchell

Dancing & Dining throughout & Unmasking © 12:00 a.m.

The room was rapidly filling with large milling and re-milling knots of costumed revelers, all privileged to be here at $5,000 a ticket, a percentage of which—of course—would be going to some charity none of them gave a rat's ass about.

On the far wall of the ballroom there was a truly Nazi-size blue, silver, and gold banner, styled as a coat of arms depicting a flaming golden sword severing an ornate Celtic-style Gordian knot with the continents of the world outlined in the weave.

An elaborately stylized "A" was embossed in silver and gold at opposite corners of the banner like a gigantic playing card.

The live band was playing with a black-clad, bosomy blonde belting out "I've Got You Under My Skin."

I went to the nearest of the two bars and got a drink. The tiny earpiece I was wearing put Mors effectively on my shoulder.

"*Mr. and Mrs. Collins just arrived and should be in sight, shortly. Chandler's come with some bimbo and is still working the crowd outside, having his picture taken. The sprinkler system is slaved to Lord Henry. And Kissinger's here.*"

"Oh, good," I murmured like a ventriloquist, "we can nab him if all else fails."

"*Fuck Kissinger, Mitchell's here. Stag.*"

"Thunderbirds are go," I said.

* * * * *

While my quarry were either entering the ballroom or still wading through security or pausing to glad-hand their fellow big-pigs, I made my way across the floor toward to the banner.

My slingshot was taped to the upper inside of my left glove cuff and the phial of sulfuric acid to my right's.

The jar of sugar and potassium chlorate was snug inside a pouch sewn in the inner lining of my cloak.

Now all I needed to do was attach it, unnoticed and unseen, to the banner, without being caught or putting it where someone would notice.

And place it in such a way that from, oh, maybe thirty feet (or less) away, I could hit and shatter it with one Tom-Sawyer shot.

And do this without being noticed. Or tackled. Or shot.

I looked up at the banner of The New Alexandrians.

Rourke had made me begin to question everything, the whole idea of man as ignoble predator, Zen-nihilism, all that.

The Gun Gods.

Looking up at the garish, somehow sneering banner, I could feel the added pull of strange, quirky little Rourke.

She didn't belong in this worldview. In fact, thinking of her while looking at the strident blue and gold shout of *The New Alexandrian's* banner felt obscene, somehow.

I set her aside and got my head in the game.

The New Alexandrians were an ultra-conservative club, sometimes referred to as a think- tank, other times a bohemian indulgence, other times a fascist, racist, hard-right Republican enclave. I'd read of their religious fervor. I'd heard them uphold Ayn Rand as a leading light and at the same time realized that no one could have possibly read her, given her contempt for organized religion.

Just skimmed for what fit, I supposed.

But, like all whores, the main thing that united the New Alexandrians was *money*.

While gazing up at the banner I reached carefully with my left hand behind myself and under my cloak, which hid the movement. I slid the glass tube of mixed powder out of the pouch, taking care to avoid the crown of fish hooks I'd taped in place around the top, hooks out and curving downward.

The vial was seven inches long and about the thickness of a standard flashlight, painted the same royal blue as the banner, hooks and all.

From The New Assassin's Field Guide and Almanac: "Hesitation and furtiveness is highly visible, owing to the echo of our predatory natures. Conversely, boldness is often less noticed by the naked eye."

I flipped the vial like one would flick a switchblade. It hit the banner with a soft *whump*, the cloth hanging about eight inches out from the wall, and slid down maybe three inches before the hooks caught.

I turned away, cloak swirling, and limped several paces back toward the gathering horde, helping myself to a glass of champagne from a black silk-clad waiter and then turned back to admire my handiwork and mark my target.

The vial of potassium-chlorate and sugar was all but invisible, hanging directly below the pommel of the flame-wreathed sword.

I fixed its position in my mind, then turned back to survey the ever-roiling crowd.

Beneath a faux-stone archway, dripping fake moss and cobwebs, was the main table for some of the most prominent guests.

Kathleen Collins was in an elaborate black dress that looked like Scarlett O'Hara would wear it in mourning, her brunette hair elaborately styled around a silver-whiskered black cat mask. Her husband, Henry Collins, was seated next to her. Like many of the attendees, he'd eschewed any costume and was wearing a double-breasted tux.

My brain's tank-induced training brought up their dossiers with little conscious effort.

Kathleen Collins, congresswoman from Texas, had spoken of perhaps running for the presidency "someday". Self-proclaimed "Constitutional Conservative." Right-to-lifer. Author of *The Christian Wife's Duty*. She believed America was founded on biblical principles. Mother of five. Religious beliefs somewhere in the yahoo area of dominionism. Though she claimed to have been "misunderstood," she had referred to interracial marriages as "unequal yoking."

She missed pretty in some brittle fashion, with a smile that looked like it could bite and a laugh that seemed like it could veer into a scream, each with only a minor adjustment.

Hubby Henry looked like a typical stuffed-shirt stooge, graying hair stylishly cut. Former preacher who now ran some rescue center for troubled youth. Author of *The Godless Curriculum* and *The Bread of Heaven*. He had played the drums on David Letterman once, and, according to the dossier, fucked children under his care and had as yet, no formal complaints lodged against him.

Next to Mr. Collins was the oh so famous Jeffery Chandler. Former disc jockey, former pro-football team promoter, former wife-beater, and former drug addict. Now he was the smug and schmaltzy head of a fifty-million dollar empire. Chandler had ducked charges for beating his wife with a garden hose one night on their front lawn, while drunk. More recently, he'd ducked drug charges.

Constitutional stalwart, he mostly snuggled down into the laps of hard right conservatives, a yapping, pissing lap dog to power.

A proponent of "Family Values," he had none of his own and, now in the aftermath of his fourth divorce, was accompanied by a blonde, uber-boobed rent-a-wench who looked like she might be challenged by even the word "idea."

Now being seated with great fanfare was Vincent Becke Mitchell, top-gun Republican political advisor and strategist, Mitchell charged fifty thousand dollars per speaking engagement. He was often on TV and talk-radio, referred to as "The Ringmaster." He was also the chief advisor to "American Core," a Christian family group that was associated with "Focus on the Family."

According to the dossier, Mitchell also had a powerful appetite for cocaine and crystal meth and a penchant for being urinated on by male prostitutes, but hey, to each his own.

The Great Man was now being seated between the Collins and Chandler. There were three other couples at the table, but I didn't recognize them or know their place in the hierarchy.

All I needed to do now was have them insist that I join them and then have them willing to follow me when calamity struck.

And, of course, cause the calamity.

* * *

I hung back from the table, sipping my drink.

The Chinese Ghost Festival was in full swing. Performances intercut with the band, ghouls in Hopping Ghost masks sword fought, there was an interesting version of the woman-in-the-basket and silk-garbed waiters and waitresses glided here and there with food and drink, and when the band played, it continued in its classics mode.

After a big, smoky pyrotechnic routine with a huger Chinese dragon costume that ended up eating three of the waitstaff, one politico, and then (quite impressively) itself, starting with its own tail.

Then, as the band swung into an instrumental of *Stardust*, I waited for the next approaching waitress to reach the royal table. She had a tray heavily laden with a variety of drinks—wine, mixed drinks, beers, martinis, and more.

My limp was mostly fake as my ankle was feeling better, but since I'd arrived, I'd put on a pretty obvious hitch in my step. As I limped toward the table, I was delighted to see a second waiter moved in from the left with two trays laden with the first of five promised courses.

The second tray looked like a magazine cover for *Gourmet*.

Baked king prawns with chili peppers, Thai mussels and seafood broth, satay chicken skewers, the works.

I limped forward and let my leg buckle and, throwing myself headlong, managed to collide with both servers.

Hard.

As the food went flying directly up and all over the table in front of Mitchell, I flailed, saying "*Aaaagh*!" and (in what looked like a falling man's attempt to catch himself), actually punched the underside of the waitress's tray, sending drinks everywhere (mostly on the waitress's head and shoulders).

And down the three of us went in a scrum of booze, silk, and victuals.

Henry Collins actually blurted "Jesus Christ!" and I glimpsed his wife's head snap around to glare at him.

But Mitchell actually got up to help.

I sat up, all apologies, trying both to pat the wet waitress, ascertain that she and the waiter were okay and trying manfully to regain my feet.

Mitchell was helping the waitress, and I yanked the little waiter up only to cry out and fall again myself.

"Sir, are you injured?" he said, food still sliding down his chest and arms.

I swung my left leg out in front of me with my cloak puddled on the floor behind me and my sword and scabbard skewed beneath it.

"No! No—this was, *argh*, my fault," I said.

I pulled the pant leg up to the knee, revealing a plastic doll-skin-colored sheath that had a metal bar running up one side toward my knee and the other and down into my sock.

I had the table's attention, Kathleen Collins even had her hand daintily up to her mouth, eyes wide.

"My fault entirely, I'm so sorry. Just got home from Afghanistan. Salang."

I gasped in pain as I fumbled at the leg, pretending to adjust it.

"Salang, the gift that keeps on taking," I said, with a little chuckle.

I pretended to be going through a grit-teethed struggle with my "prosthesis"—feigning pain that would bring Ann Coulter to sympathetic tears.

"Afghanistan," Mitchell said, glancing at my leg and then hurriedly looking back at my masked face.

"What's your name, son?"

"Jack," I said, "Jack Caine, sir."

Mitchell made to help me, and Chandler got up and hurried around the table to join him along with the waitress to help me up.

"Where are you sitting?" Mitchell said.

"Actually, I hadn't chosen a place yet, sir. I, ah, came here alone. Sort of a, I guess, massively failed experiment in a little socializing. I was just coming over to your table—before ruining your dinner to, well, get yours and Mrs. Collins's and Mr. Chandler's autographs."

I straightened to my full height and adjusted my tricorn.

"I apologize again, ma'am, sirs, for making such a mess and such an ass of myself. Enjoy the rest of your evening."

I made to turn away, giving an embarrassed little wave.

"Wait," Mitchell said, "what's your rank, soldier?"

"Captain, sir," I said.

"Captain Caine, I insist that you join us," he said, pulling out the chair between him and Kathleen Collins.

There was a general murmur of assent.

"Well. I'd be absolutely honored," I said.

Mrs. Collins patted my arm as I made a show of reluctantly sitting down.

Voila.

* * *

As heroic, wounded, self-deprecating, and lonely Captain Caine, everybody thought I was just swell. My tank-trained radar also picked up on a few interesting things: Kathleen Collins didn't really care much for hubby Henry. In fact, she treated him like an annoying idiot.

She also wanted to get laid.

Vincent Becke Mitchell was a world-class alcoholic, and Jeffery Chandler, whose radio show I considered the modern equivalent of Himmler's speech at Poznan, was surprisingly good dinner company for an asshole.

In fact, my overall impression of Chandler was that as an absolute scam artist. He basically wanted to be *anything*; it didn't matter what. Political gadfly, talk and/or television host, thriller writer, religious leader, whatever worked and made him noticed and rich. He seemed a little wide-eyed to be at the adult table at last.

I liked him a little for that.

Not that it mattered. I'd killed people I'd liked, before.

"Captain Caine, I don't want to pry or bring up painful memories, but I do want to thank you for your service," Kathleen said.

"Not at all, ma'am," I said, "it's what I signed up for."

"And I must second that, Captain," Mitchell said. "My deepest thanks. I only wish there were more young men like you for God's holy tasks."

Oh, I'll bet you do.

"Yes, sir," I said.

Henry and Jeff were picking over the latest platter to come our way, fillet steak, braised mushrooms, and little cups of sweet corn soup.

I only picked at my food, not wanting to be sluggish with a full stomach at game time, but it was a challenge.

"You know, Captain," Mitchell said, "if you would ever consider it, I'd very much like to feature you and your story—as much as you'd feel comfortable with—in a public appearance with me when I campaign next year."

"Campaign?"

"Oh, yes. I have determined after a long period of reflection and prayer that the time has come for me to stop just whispering in the king's ear and make a go for the throne, so to speak. It's a ways off, but I'd be honored if you could appear with me at some point as an example of what's best in America. What we're all about."

"I'd be happy too," I said.

Like most of the table, except for naughty pussy-cat Kathleen and myself, my three new buddy-roos were in various styles of tuxedo.

But just past Chandler's bunny-girl was a tall woman in a high-necked jacket that glittered an iridescent scaly green and gold. She had a molded-to-her-face imitation jade face mask that left her eyes and nose comfortably free but curved up over her forehead and formed a frilled cowl like a triceratops.

She was eating with chopsticks, expertly, and occasionally offering a morsel with them to her companion.

He was tall, wearing a black suit and red tie, and wearing a full-faced lacquered red devil mask. He didn't remove it even to eat, though he did raise a drink with a straw occasionally to sip from.

Weird.

Of course, the room was *full* of weird, (being a gathering of politicians and the New Dumb). But when you kill people for a living, you pay attention to weird.

"Mr. Mitchell," I said.

"Vincent, please, Captain," he said, laying a hand on my arm.

"All right, Vincent." I lowered my voice and head a little. "Just curious, sir, but, who's the Devil?"

Mitchell glanced at him and bellowed laughter, patting me.

"Why, that's Lucas! My bodyguard. Lucas and Yushi are my security detail. No worries, Captain, you're among friends here."

Swell.

* * *

There was an after-dinner show where various cobweb-festooned armored samurai fought all around us with various impressive ghouls, complete with live background music from the band and a scream-inducing blackout at the climax, severed heads, and so on at lights up.

Then it was speech time.

Chandler went first, basically warming the crowd up, reminding them that "wealth is their birthright" and that America "can not only survive but, better, thrive, with adherence to strict conservative values."

He questioned the courage, patriotism, and sanity of anyone who had any other view and basically banged the God, Guns, and Gays washtub to clear everyone's arteries a bit.

"Red Meat Rhetoric" Mors called it once, pointing out that Chandler, Beck, Hannity, Limbaugh, Savage, et al, seemed awfully gung-ho when it came to the military but, for all the brown-nosing, never actually *served*. In anything. Ever.

And in all draft-related cases, avoided it at all cost.

Anyway, this bunch ate it up, seeming to miss the fascism and gave Chandler a big hand.

Kat-woman was next, stepping up to the New Alexandrian's silver-and-gold podium amid the bombast of Chandler's introduction.

"And now, a true lady, a true patriot, a hero, who'd like to see America return to the biblical principles upon which it was founded—Congresswoman *Kathleen Collins*!"

Collins kept her cat mask on and got lots of laughs amid the applause.

"My fellow New Alexandrians, my fellow Americans, my fellow movers and shakers—it's our year to *shake* and *move*!"

It pretty much goes on like that.

I tuned out, figuring that after the speeches would be more drinking and dancing. And drinking.

Then would be the best time to let the wild rumpus start.

I glanced at Lucas the devil and Yoshi. They were both watching Collins' Ode to the Ubermensch, seemingly neither with derision nor applauding approval.

Pros, I supposed. Doing their job.

The devil mask began to turn in my direction, and I looked back to Collins.

"—and before we get to the specifics of that battle plan, I'd like to introduce my husband, the man who keeps the beat while I march, Mr. Henry Collins!"

Twin spots swung over to the band where amid laughter and wild applause Henry Collins was adjusting his glasses and sitting down behind a drum set.

"Dear sweet Jesus," Vincent Becke Mitchell moaned next to me.

Then a middle-aged Asian waiter took to the microphone and shrieked: *"Hee-hee-hee-hee-heeeh! Wipeout-tuh!"*

And Collins and some of the band began overt butchery of "The Sufaris" best known tune.

It was the one time Mors spoke in my earpiece before showtime.

"*What the fuck is going on in there?*"

I tapped the earpiece twice, and outside in the ambulance Mors heard the two beeps that meant all was well.

But all wasn't all *that* well. While Lucas the devil had a mask that covered his whole head (which combined with the suit made him look like a really scary freak), Yoshi's left the lower half of her face, like my own, uncovered. *A familiar jawline.*

The Mr. and Mrs. Collins show was mercifully drawing to a close, with a more than tipsy Kathleen Collins doing some kind of Dominionist bump and grind to her hubby and the band's wind-up of "Wipeout."

As Mitchell straightened his tie, he winked at me and said, "Well, showtime," I was sure of one thing.

I might not know who was under the Lucifer mask, but his companion in security was my old schoolmate and one-time lover, Jiufeng.

CHAPTER 33

Minowski Space. Captain Caine Takes Charge. Mr. Joy.

MITCHELL WAS MAGNETIC, I'll give him that.

"Happy Halloween, New Alexandrians! You know, it's said that All Hallow's Eve is a Satanic holiday and it's not. It's not. It's Celtic. It's a time when the veil between this world and the next was supposed to be very thin. And this is true now, my friends. This is reality, now. Not just on Halloween but now for our country. But the veil isn't between the living and the dead; it's between calamity and prosperity. It's between—"

Applause interrupted him.

While he paused, head down and smiling, Kathleen Collins pressed a breast against my forearm and whispered in my ear.

"Oh, Captain my Captain, where are you bivouacked tonight? Do you live here in DC?"

"I do," I said, then the applause died out and Mitchell continued.

"It's between abject failure and triumphant success! It's between settling for a dismal present or rising up to greet a glorious future!"

More applause but he rammed right over it.

"With God's grace, my friends, we can return this country to its roots and thus sow the seeds of prosperity. You know, you see most tree roots, they're like a lightning bolt, ever which a' way. But the tree of American liberty and success has only three roots: *Faith. Family. Freedom.*"

The crowd loved it, *huge* applause, cheers, whistles. Kathleen Collins snuggled up to me. Henry Collins threw back a martini. Jeffery Chandler lip-locked with his bimbo. Lucifer sucked at his straw, and *Ms. Yoshi* watched the speech impassively while nibbling at a cherry.

"Faith, Family, Freedom! That's the E=MC squared of prosperity. *'F' to the third.* 'F' to the third! 'F' to the third!"

The crowd took it up, chanting.

F to the third! F to the third! F to the third!

Mors in my ear: "*Jesus H. Fuck, where are you, Nuremberg?*"

Ms. Yushi/Jiufeng turned then and looked at me.

Directly.

I saluted with my finger, and she looked away, her head moving like an owl's. Then the devil turned to look at me, and this time I held his gaze, even though I couldn't see his eyes shadowed by the brow of the ugly mask.

He flashed me the peace sign.

Could things get any weirder?

F to the third!

Anyway, you get the idea. Mitchell told the rich, drunk, well-stuffed members of the New Alexandrians that they deserved to be rich, drunk, and stuffed and that their destiny was to be richer, drunker, and routinely re-stuffed and—if they voted for the right guys (and very likely, the white guys)—they'd get it and live forever in the bargain. Huzzah!

Mitchell wrapped it up by basically repeating the same sentiments in several different configurations, attacking the current administration and anybody who disagreed with his vaguely feel-good, fascist Christian no-cost capitalism.

Waiters and waitresses appeared in full force as if on cue, trays laden with more booze of every description and the band revved into its swing mode with Cole Porter's "Begin the Beguine."

I excused myself a little abruptly from the offended-looking Mrs. Collins and limped toward The Devil and Ms. Schizo.

"Pardon me," I said, "but would you care to dance?"

She surprised me by taking my offered hand and rising. Next to her, Satan, as always, was inscrutable.

We swung onto the floor amid roughly thirty other couples and black-clad waitstaff and continued dancing right into "Moonlight Serenade."

Her grip and hold was firm, and she snuggled right up to me. She smelled like lilacs and something spicy.

"You move well for a one-legged man, Proteus," she said.

We were, as before, of a height.

"And you, *Jiufeng*, for a security goon."

Her face was impossible to read with the lacquered mask.

"Goon? Hmm. I've never been called a goon before. And what do you think you're doing, *Captain Caine*? Exactly?"

I leaned in close.

"Me? I'm here trying to save the Kestrel's life. Are you part of this shit-show?"

She moved even closer, clunking her mask against mine.

"Do you remember watching *Glenngarry, Glenn Ross*?"

"Oh, yes," I said.

"Then consider me being here from *Mitch & Murray*. Get it?"

I considered.

"Okay," I said. "I hope I know my Mamet well enough to interpret that. Because '*I'm going anyway*.'"

"Who's stopping you? I just hope it's good," she said.

We had danced, with me leading to a spot on the dance floor about twenty feet from the New Alexandrian's banner. As the band swung into "String of Pearls," I kept my left arm around Jiufeng's warm waist and dipped my other hand into the little pouch Nana Mors had sewn into the inside of my cloak, and then palmed the slingshot and the vial.

I released Jiufeng but cocked my face even closer to her, almost as if we were about to kiss. She didn't move back.

"If you're part of this, I'll have to kill you," I said.

"Mm," Jiufeng said, "or die trying."

She stepped back and turned to walk back to the devil's table.

Well. One way to find out.

There was no time left for chit-chat or questions. I tapped my earpiece three times.

"*Roger that. Moving into position,*" Mors said.

Amid the swirling, swaying pirates, mummies, vampires, werewolves, tuxes, gypsies, and samurai, I knocked the ampule in the slingshot pouch, feeling the little rattle of the marble inside.

As I raised the slingshot and pulled back, some little guy dressed as a bishop said "Hey!" though he was smiling.

I could almost hear his thought *Geez, should I raise any alarm over a slingshot?*

Then I let it all fall away as willed adrenaline surged into my system and time slowed to the space between heartbeats and something the now lamentably dead Mr. Quark said in one of his lectures about mental focus unspooled through my head.

"*Minowski space, I believe, can be accessed mentally—in that moment where the light cones of past and future can be halted for all intents and purposes from the observers' point of view on the hypersurface of the present.*"

Well. Maybe you had to be there.

* * *

Let's keep it simple.

TWANG!

When you know, you know. (And if I didn't know, then I'd missed and all would be lost).

I about-faced smartly after loosing the shot and had taken a half-step toward my table when the explosion boomed through the great hall and every shadow, including mine, ran up the walls of the faux temple in a purple-white flash, brighter than daylight.

Then the flames became more normal and terrifying yellow-orange as the New Alexandrians banner roared in a reverse waterfall of flame and some of DC's best and brightest began screaming.

I ran for the table as the stampede began. The potassium chlorate, sugar and sulphuric acid created one hell of a fireball and the banner was almost consumed, roiling up even as it was devoured by an almost solid-looking wave of flame that hit the ceiling and spread across like a tsunami.

I might have used too much.

I ripped off my mask and ran around the right end of the table and grabbed Kathleen Collins by the arm.

"All of you follow me. Now!"

Collins, her husband, Mitchell, Chandler, and his eye-candy all got up and came with me. Jiufeng and the devil hesitated for a beat, then joined us, Satan bringing up the rear.

"This way!" I said in brave Captain Caine's best commanding bark, striding forward as the fireflies of glowing ash began to fall around us.

No one seemed to notice the captain's limp had miraculously healed, of a sudden.

Keeping Lord Henry's helpful schematic of the layout firmly in mind, I shepherded my little herd through the kitchen doors behind one Styrofoam Mandarin arch, bulling my way past exiting cooks and waitstaff with Kathleen Collins going "Oh! Oh! Oh!" in a steady counterpoint next to me.

We made our trotting way past a row of stainless steel freezers to a raw-looking cinderblock room cluttered with stacks of slashed and broken down boxes bundled with wire, a huge trash compactor and—just where it was supposed to be—a corrugated steel roll-up door.

I turned to Chandler.

"Roll it up!"

"Okay! I'm on it!"

Chandler started yanking the chain like one of Blackbeard's crew.

"I'm calling my driver, Captain, where—?"

Mitchell had his phone to his ear. I plucked it out of his hand and tossed it in the compactor bay.

"*Wha-*?"

Mitchell looked odd, sputtering.

"Sprinklers, Mors," I said, holding my right hand to my ear.

"*Roger that*," Mors said.

Kathleen Collins pulled her mask off.

"Captain Caine, who are you talking to?"

Chandler and his escort were absorbed with the door chain and had wanged it up into its sheath like a huge window shade.

A large concrete bunker of an underground lot was below us, with a large ambulance backed up to the loading dock with its amber and red lights rotating in silent fury, panel doors open.

Mors hopped out of the van wearing his usual black flight jacket and tossed me one dart gun with his left while he aimed the one held in his right and shot Chandler in the thigh.

Chandler had just squealed out the word "Hey!" as Mors then shot Chandler's date in one ample hip and then Mitchell in the shoulder.

Chandler then screamed in concert with Collins even as both Mitchell and the girl collapsed like two hammered steers. I shoved Kathleen hard away from me, and as she stumbled out of one high heel, Mors shot her, the dart's bright yellow tail of fluff appearing high on her right thigh.

Her eyes rolled up double zeros as she caved in on herself, her dress collapsing like a circus tent.

At any moment I was expecting the Devil and Ms. Jieufeng to shoot me, but they were both back near the bindles of stacked cardboard. Both had removed their masks. Mr. Devil was turned away from me, tossing his mask into the crusher. Jieufeng had her pistol out and was looking at me calmly, the gun held loose at her side.

Henry Collins screamed and jumped off the dock, landed badly, sprawling, and then got up again, breaking into a limping run.

Mors shrugged, indicating "After you" in the gesture.

I steadied myself with a two-handed grip and fired. A bright orange ball appeared on Collins' ample ass.

He went down by degrees as he kept lurching forward, like a dying rhino. He made it to a concrete support pylon and, after bouncing off it, collapsed in a heap.

Mors hopped down and ambled after him.

It took us less than three sweaty, heaving minutes to get the congresswoman, Mitchell, and Chandler strapped into the leather chairs that were bolted to the ambulance floor instead of the standard medical ware.

Mors hogtied our bonus baby, Henry, with plastic shackles and shoved him across the ambulance floor, under Chandler's chair.

"What about the cookie?" Mors said.

"Leave her. Him, we might need, but she's a tourist."

"Lucky her," Mors said, dragging Chandler's unconscious date away from the edge of the dock.

We gagged and blindfolded all four of them and pulled the darts free, discarding them on the van floor.

"*Hold it, motherfucker*!"

I looked up from the ambulance interior to see some security goon in a sober suit, drawing down on me.

Apparently, he dashed in past the bindles on his mission for God and glory and didn't see Jiufeng and her former Devil pal—a thin-faced man with a messy head of strawberry-blond hair.

He was lighting a cigarette, head cocked and squinting against the lighter's flame as Jiufeng shot sober-suit in the back.

He fell, arms outflung, head thrown back, to crunch into the cement.

I was surprised to see the yellow beanbag projectile next to his shoulder. How strangely non-lethal of my old classmate.

Jiufeng winked at me and tucked her gun away and did a smart about-face and walked back up the way we'd come with her curtain of shining black hair swinging prettily.

I hopped out of the ambulance and slammed its doors shut. Mors stood next to me, both of us looking up at the stranger. Mors had his gun out and was pointing it up at him though his target was unarmed.

"Easy, lads. We're on the same side," he said, exhaling smoke.

"Who the fuck're you?" Mors said.

"You can call me *Mr. Joy*," he said, in a clipped, English accent, "*Si vis pacem, para bellum*, and so on."

The reply leapt from me though Mors didn't lower his gun.

"*Si vis pacem, para pactum*," I said.

Mr. Joy gestured with the cigarette, which looked thicker than a normal one.

"You don't honor the words, Sir Mors?"

Mors kept his gun trained on Mr. Joy. Sirens were closer now, and I was sweating.

"Why didn't Jiufeng identify?" Mors said.

Mr. Joy exhaled a silver-blue cloud, as relaxed as if we were in a living room.

"Because we were waiting to see what you were doing, matey-boy. We had our suspicions, but one must be sure, yes? So, before we are overrun, what are you doing?"

"We're trying to save the Kestrel," I said.

"If he's still alive," Mors said.

"Capital!" Mr. Joy said, "Oh, that's grand."

He tossed a phone to me as Mors lowered his gun. Standard issue scrambler phone.

"When you have the next move on the board completed, call me on that. Perhaps I can help you along."

"Who sent you?" I said.

"The home office, chum. The Thanatos Guild you know—or rather, quite lamentably, knew, is only a branch office. Me, I'm from Europe.

You know, where the history comes from." He pitched his cigarette off into the garage.

"On your bike, lads," he said.

He shot his cuffs and walked back into what I figured must have been an atmosphere of smoky, steamy downpour (ala the restored sprinkler system), freaked-out cops, and soaking wet right-wing hotshots.

"I'm tired, honey," I said to Mors. "Let's go back to the motel."

Mors didn't laugh. And the bastard says *I* have no sense of humor.

CHAPTER 34

Group Icebreakers. A Rat in The Rosebush. Kestrel Locus Classicus.

EMERGENCY FLASHERS CLEARING THE WAY quite handily, Mors eased our way past all manner of DC. Metro cops, firetrucks, and news vans and into the night.

The distance between the hotel and the Crystal City Motel was about eight miles. Traffic continued to considerately move aside as Mors sped through the city with all the literal bells and whistles running, but as we approached the last mile or so, we shut down everything but standard running lights and slowed to a more ho-hum speed.

Mors cut the lights as we turned down the ramp and parked alongside the battered fence that enclosed the entire area. I got out and opened the gate that Rupert had earlier cut the chains to.

One night, over Chinese, Rupert had informed us that the motel he'd found had actually still been a going concern as late as 2006.

Not anymore. *Just like poor Rupert.*

Mors eased the dark ambulance into the central courtyard, cans and glass and grit crunching loudly under the tires.

It was an abandoned ruin that looked like it had last been thriving around the time the pyramids were being finished. The huge and boxy main sign that once flagged travelers was now sitting in the center of the courtyard like a rust-caked dinosaur. Mors got out with me to grab a dun-colored tarp that Rupert had left stowed on top of the sign and helped me drape the ambulance with it.

I noticed in the gloom that along with all the wine and whiskey bottle shards and Red Bull cans, take-out containers, and every other kind of human trash, the courtyard was full of shattered television sets. Glass was glittering everywhere, not one window on the ground or upper floors wasn't broken. A couple of windows were boarded up; most weren't.

"What a fucking shithole," Mors said.

"Yeah, but the price was right. It's a fixer-upper."

"Wonderful how close we are to the Pentagon," Mors said, a wee bit sarcastically.

"You mean you never heard of hiding in plain sight? Think positive," I said.

"At least tell me we're not hauling the Four Stooges up to the second floor."

"No, we're not. See the manager's little bungalow?"

After we did a quick reconnoiter to make sure no homeless crackheads were shacked up in any of the ruins (and, weirdly, all of the mattresses were still in the filthy rooms, along with disassembled bedframes and sets of drawers), we opened the ambulance and, one by one, carried our favorite *F to the Thirders* into The House that Buzzcock Rebuilt.

From the outside, the reception office and quarters were a wreck in a sea of shit, weeds, and shattered asphalt, complete with bracken-filled hot tub.

But inside, Rupert had crafted a stark and spartanly functional holding cell.

There were three rooms, all of raw, pine-wood paneling, floor, and walls. Mors started a small but powerful Briggs and Stratton generator in the bathroom and three lamps glowed.

Rupert had cut vent holes, small and near the ceiling.

The room had three cots with blankets and sleeping bags. There was a couch and three chairs. The little fridge was stocked with water and TV dinners. A cheap microwave was sitting on one of two card tables alongside a small portable radio. Next to that was the Kirby Box.

To round things out were two chemical toilets.

Not the most pleasant accommodations, but then again, the idea was to keep them alive. Comfort wasn't all that important. We checked the vitals on our reluctant campers as we cut their bonds. Mrs. Collins, Chandler, and Mitchell were on their cots while Mr. Collins was laid out on an unzipped sleeping bag. Both the Collins and Mitchell seemed to be coming to groggy consciousness, but Chandler didn't look so good and remained out and off the air. His complexion was chalky, lips slightly blue, and his heartbeat sounded thready.

I changed out of my highwayman costume and into my own night-work clothes as Mors lit a cigarette, leaning back against the dirty sink.

"Rupert did a good job," he said.

"Yeah," I said and sighed.

Not much of an epitaph.

"Mors," I said, "has it ever occurred to you that we're not, in almost any way, nice people?"

Mors squinted at me, one eye shut against the raftering smoke. I'd only seen Mors and the Master Chief smoke comfortably, hands-free like that.

"What the fuck are you talking about now?"

"Nothing," I said.

* * *

As they awoke to find two scary bad men in black standing over them with guns, the valedictorians of New Alexandrian High went through various mental adjustments to their situation.

Kathleen Collins was the first to come around.

"Captain Caine? What is this about? Oww, my leg! Who is that? Why do you have guns pointed at us, you—you *son of a bitch! Don't you dare point a gun at—wait!* Is there a terrorist attack?!"

Mr. Collins was just sitting there like a great stunned toad, upright on his cot.

Vincent Becke Mitchell chimed in.

"What is the meaning of this, Captain Caine? Are we in some sort of safe-house?"

More smiled at me as he spoke around his cigarette and removed a second pistol from his jacket.

"*Captain Caine*, you realize, might come up later if we get out of this," he said.

"Shut up," I said.

"Who is this man?" Mitchell said, and at the same time, Henry Collins burst out in great blubbering sobs.

"Awww, gawwwd! It's us you're afterrr! You're the terrorists! Oh Lord! Oh Lord! Awww gawwd! Listen! Listen! I, we, I have money and, and—"

"You won't get away with this," Mitchell said, rising from his cot, "and I can assure you, you scum, that—"

"Oh my God!" Kathleen blurted over him. "Who are you? What—"

Chandler sat up like a clockwork scarecrow and, still looking like a corpse, began urking and hurking and hulping.

"*Kee-rist*," Mors said, spitting his cigarette out over his shoulder into the sink.

I stepped forward and yanked Chandler up by the back of his jacket and walked him scuffling and urking toward the sink where he bent and promptly vomited all of his expensive meal. And then some.

Mors grimaced and tucked one pistol under his arm and snapped the cap off of a gallon of water and—now that Chandler was in the spitting aftermath stage—poured the jug first over Chandler's head and then the rest into the sink to wash the puke down the drain.

"Now, you listen to me, you sons of bitches," Mitchell began, "I *demand*—"

Mors left his right-hand pistol under his left armpit and punched Mitchell in the nose with a speed-blurred jab. Mitchell sat down hard on the floor, blood spurting through his hands as they gripped his face.

Mors turned and grabbed Chandler and yanked him backwards.

"*Siddown*," he said.

I threw Chandler a towel and pointed my gun at Mitchell, who was squinting up me as he nursed his crushed nose.

Kathleen seemed to be the least hungover from the drugging and spoke directly to Mors. Truth to power.

"I don't know what this is about, but we are, all of us, the future heart and soul of America, you bastards. And if you think you're going to get away with this, you're sadly—"

Mors cocked both pistols. Unnecessary, but it sounded nice.

"Shut the fuck up, lady. Now. I'd shoot all three of you idiots on general principles and sleep like a lamb. But it's his show. Be grateful. And shut up."

All three looked at me, either blearily, like Henry Collins or outraged cockatiel-ish, like Collins and Mitchell.

"My name is Proteus. And what I say, goes, as far as you're all concerned. My goal, much as it pains me, is to keep you alive. Keep your lips zipped. Watch TV. Irritate me once, and I'll turn you over to Mr. Mors. As he said, he'd much rather kill you. It's showtime, campers."

* * *

I kept my eye on the company and switched on the TV. It came on in the middle of a local newscast.

"*—kidnapped amid what authorities are labeling a deliberate act of arson via some form of chemical explosive. Congresswoman Kathleen Collins and her husband, Henry Collins, as well as radio personality Jeffrey Chandler and Vincent Beck Mitchell, well-known Republican con—*"

"Lord Henry, please open a face-to-face connection with Gardener." I said, "Working Protocol, if you please."

"***Yes, Proteus,***" Lord Henry said in George Sander's somehow acidic intonation.

Mors kept both pistols trained on our guests. Chandler was looking perkier and pop-eyed with fear. Mitchell had Chandler's damp towel clamped on his bloody nose, now sitting on a cot. Henry Collins was still sitting on the floor, his eyes closed and his lips silently moving in what I assumed was prayer.

All had maintained silence as ordered, save for Kathleen, who had quietly asked Mors for one of his cigarettes. Mors shrugged and flipped her one, then a pack of matches.

Gardener's face resolved on the tiny black-and-white screen. He was wearing a wrinkled open-collared shirt, and while his hair always looked slightly unkempt in a professorial way, now it looked dirty. Greasy.

There was a drink in front of him, and he was smoking.

"D-ah, *Proteus*, did you get them?"

"Take a gander," I said and shifted the Kirby box so that the lens could take in the foursome, Mors and I both out of sight.

"Wait," Gardener said, "aren't they *dead*?"

Both Henry and Chandler sucked wind at this. Kathleen smoked, looking vaguely reptilian, while Mitchell tended to his nose, only glancing at the screen.

"Nope," I said, "and they're not going to be. Not tonight, anyway. Where's the Kestrel, Gardener?"

"What? Wait. Proteus, you have the key to the Kestrel *right there*. Just do what these people want. You can't—"

"Again, Gard, nope. *No*. It's over. Where's the Kestrel?"

Gardener's face twisted in a way I'd never seen.

"Where's the Kestrel? How would I know?"

"You know," I said. "Lord Henry, please list Gardener's most frequent contact number."

"**555-620-1134**," Lord Henry said, "**There have been a total seventeen calls to the Pratts' since Gardener arrived at this house.**"

"Wait a minute," Gardener said, looking truly flummoxed, like Clinton when asked about the cigar. "I don't, I haven't—Now, you listen to me, Proteus—"

"No, you listen to me, you traitorous piece of shit. You cooked up this fucking deal with the Pratt twins. You betrayed your order. You killed the masters of Guild house, but Iron Horse was able to nail your ass to the barn door even as he died in the library where you shot him."

Gardener looked ivory pale, even on the shitty little black-and-white television.

"I don't know what you're talking about, Daniel. Now, we have to keep it together. These people who have the Kestrel, if you have the—"

"Lord Henry?" I said.

"**He's lying. Stress analysis and diphthong**—"

"Enough. And it's *Proteus*, you fucking asshole. Want me to use your alias? Like I'd even know it. How much money did you get to fuck over your order? How much? Even the Dark Bushido has more honor and dignity than the shit you've tried to pull. Have you killed the Kestrel yet? Try telling the truth just to sample a new taste in your bullshit-filled mouth."

Gardener, always cool, or charmingly befuddled, exploded.

"These are *powerful* people, you stupid little bastard. *These are powerful people!* You think you can threaten me? Confront me? With your fucking deluded, twisted idea of integrity among monsters? You're a *hitman, Daniel*! You're a tool! You're nothing!! And you either kill those assholes or you'll be getting the Kestrel's balls for your first mail-call in jail. Do you understand me, you delusional little bastard? These are the people who move the world. Do you really think—"

Mors stepped fully into view.

"Shut up, you conniving cunt. We're coming for you. You're already dead."

Our captive audience watched the whole thing as if they were seeing a really good play. All that Chandler was missing was a bag of popcorn.

Gardener, for his part, looked momentarily petrified.

The Thanatos Guild (or what I'd come recently to think of as the Northeast American franchise thereof) was a steam-press forge for able murderers, yes, but Mors—even by Guild house standards—had become something of an anomaly. After the tank, he'd even frightened some of the masters with whatever the experience had calcified within him.

"So," Gardener said, recovering his composure with a visible effort, "Mr. Mors. Back from the dead to stand by your brother. Well, stand by him, by all means. *I know where you are*, fools. If you won't kill those buffoonish wastes of skin, there are those who will. Die with them, by all means. It will serve the big picture."

Mors looked at me, a question.

"The *ambulance*," I said through my teeth. "It was figured into this weeks ago. A transponder, something."

"Then that's it," Mors said, "slate everyone, starting with them."

"*No*, Mors," I said.

Gardener laughed.

"Try to run. I've already got that figured. Or better yet, *Proteus*, try running with your little field trip in tow. You two clowns, trying to run with four drugged captives. I'd like that. But it's moot. They're already on their way."

Gardener raised his scrambler and waggled it.

"All I had to do was press a button. Run. Stay put. Either way you're done."

I knew it was pointless, but I screamed at the television.

"If you could do it this way, why did you involve the Guild at all?"

Gardener looked haggard now. And crazy.

"Because, my boy, my patrons wanted no direct part in this. And because the Guild *will* make for a rich, nine days wonder when the trail leads back to them. An ancient nest of assassins? *Perfect*. But even now, that can still serve. You just won't be around to see it, you naïve, pathetic fool."

The television went black.

"Lord Henry," I said.

"*Lord Henry*!"

No response. The Kirby box was dead, no telltale lights.

"What the fuck did he do?" I said.

A flash of Kiku's face in the garden.

Beware love.

"Never mind," Mors said. "We need to get out there."

He pulled Mr. Joy's scrambler phone from his jacket and tossed it to me, dexterous with just his thumb free, the other gun never leaving our audience, passive though they appeared.

"Call our pal," Mors said. "Maybe Mr. Wizard can help us out of this mess."

I hit the call button as Mors pointed both pistols at the four and got them settled.

"Don't get up. Don't move. 'Captain Caine' has his way; you'll live to keep ass-banging America. But make one move you're not told to, I'll end you."

I stepped outside into a chilly downpour amid muttering thunder. The scrambler Joy had given me was much smaller and thinner than the models Mors and I were used to. A delicate flip phone with a glass touchscreen; it looked like a high-tech dragonfly. After I'd pressed "call," it lit up a molten green.

There was a tone and then Mr. Joy's plummy voice.

"Hello, Proteus."

"Hello, Mr. Joy. I assume you know the Guild master, Gardener, one of my flight's instructors?"

"Indeed I do," he said, "not well, mind, but I know him. Is he our rat in the rosebush?"

"He is," I said, "at least one of them. His new partners, bosses, whatever, are the Pratt brothers, are you familiar?"

"I read Forbes," Mr. Joy said.

"They have the Kestrel, and I have the people they want dead. I'd hoped to force their hand—"

"And now you have," Mr. Joy said, "and they're coming for you and yours in that shitpit you're sequestered in?"

"Yes, so Gardener has threatened," I said, "but how—"

"Two can track a transponder, old thing," he said.

"Can you help us?"

"Oh, I can," Mr. Joy said, "I have, at my disposal, a Cobra attack helicopter. The problem is we are in a city with the most heavily monitored airspace on earth, especially since 9/11. No luck there. But chin up. Jiufeng and I are on our way, post haste. Hold the fort and keep your charges safe from harm; Thanatos doesn't need the kind of scrutiny their deaths would arouse. Now, attend: we are coming. And in case I'm not alive to tell you this—the Kestrel is most definitely alive. Take a gander and then you'd best get into a defensive position, you and Sir Mors."

The digital screen on the latest scrambler phone was gee-whiz perfect. On it was a holographic red-wire framework of grids with various tiny concentric pulsing circles of yellow and green. It was the layout of a large, multifloored house, shot from above.

It took me a moment, I confess.

"That's my house," I said.

"Indeed," Mr. Joy said, "and this image is approximately six hours old, taken by a Telcom military satellite, briefly slaved to a contractor employed by the Guild. Within are the bio-signatures of five people, two in your regular living areas and three in the subsection. I believe you call it the Vault?"

Gardener, Gardener's helper, or bodyguard.

Or keeper.

And three in the vault. Omi and Kiku.

"And the Kestrel," I said.

"Hide in plain sight," Mr. Joy said.

"The bastard has the Kestrel in my house? How? Never mind. So can't you—you're from the Guild, the Home Office, can't you send someone?"

"Who, dear Proteus? We're an organization of single agent providers, not an army. Busy, busy. Besides, who better to storm your castle than you? You know where all the boards creak, yes? Let's attend to one trouble at a time. Surviving the night, say. Jiufeng and I are on our way to you. Travel time plus a distraction for the local gendarmes will slow us. Suggest you secure your chicks and get outside with Mors to man the battlements. Luck, my brother."

Joy was gone.

* * *

I went back into the cell.

"We're locking you in. Don't make a sound. No banging on the walls, yelling, nothing."

Mitchell spoke up, voice froggy with his new, thicker nose.

"I don't understand any of this. You kidnapped us."

"With luck, you never will either. We're the lesser of two evils, Vincent. I grabbed you as a chess move. But the people coming here want you dead. Now shut the fuck up and do what I said. *Nothing.* And if it's not Mors, me, or a cop that opens that door in a little while, try to be a good Christian."

"Meaning what?" Mitchell said.

"Repent."

CHAPTER 35

Shootout at the Crystal City Motel.

LIKE BUFORD AT GETTYSBURG, we decided the high ground was key. Mors positioned himself on the balcony directly above and catawampus to the reception cottage.

Rupert *had* done well in constructing the holding cell; from outside it was utterly dark.

After ducking under the tarp to doublecheck that the keys were still in the ambulance, I took a position behind the fallen Crystal City Motel sign sitting in the center of the courtyard.

Thunder rumbled and a rafter of heat lightning rippled across the sky as it began to rain. It wasn't October in Maine, that was for sure. It was muggy and close. While I welcomed the rain and the thunderstorm breeze that was picking up, I wasn't crazy about the distracting noise.

I also knew that Mors wouldn't give a shit. Our nightwork clothes (mine a natty and way too hot leather jacket and Mors's lighter bomber) blended in nicely with the general murk.

Other than the approaching storm, it was quiet. The traffic on the parallel highway was almost nil. There was a rattle of fireworks in a nearby neighborhood. Halloween revels. A dog barking, probably spooked by the fireworks.

Then after a silent mortar flash of lightning, a boom of thunder exploded over everything, and the warmish rain began to fall in earnest.

* * *

Mors.

Mors actually welcomed the storm. He'd had an idea, and the noise-wash of the thunder and rain made it easier, though he went about it quietly anyway.

Not all the old TVs had been thrown into the courtyard. Mors did a quick sweep of all the rooms facing the balcony, all open, all trashed. Beer bottles, signs of squatters, needles, pipes, shit. But all the dressers, mattresses, and two intact televisions were still in rooms where the floors hadn't been ripped out or collapsed.

Plus, one disassembled bedframe.

Mors crept to the end of the balcony near a stairway and gently leaned one long metal bar from a bedframe against the support beam.

He carried one television down to the other end of the balcony and set it down gently as thunder crashed and the storm intensified. He yanked the cord and lifted the black TV, letting it dangle for a moment, satisfied that the weight wouldn't be enough to rip the cord out.

He set it down and then made a double loop big enough for his fist and knotted it, leaving it on top of the set.

The second TV he set next to where he stood at the center of the balcony. Then he took out both pistols and stepped back into the shadow of the splintered door behind him.

Even in the next, brighter octopus of lightning, he was invisible.

The Invisible Man.

* * *

I was thinking about some of the men I'd killed, fairly recent slates before *this* mess. There'd been a murderer, pardoned by some jackass governor in Mississippi. I'd been contracted to kill the governor, too, but risk assessment just didn't pan out.

I'd been present when Mors slated a woman, despite my Paladin preference. A real monster, killed her entire family with an icepick and then set up a new identity running a yarn store. Emily something, I think.

I didn't want to die in Virginia. I thought of Rourke again. And Dagny. Then cursed myself for the willful distraction.

I didn't want to die here, though. If I had to die, I wanted to be in Maine. New England. Home. Where I could at least smell the ocean instead of this fucking ass-swamp of a city of hustling, grinning, glad-handing egg-suck dogs.

The rain was really falling now; I was getting soaked to the skin. Then amid the soft roar of downpour, I heard a bottle roll. That was all, but it was enough. The careless stupid move of the amateur hard ass.

Goons, then. Hired hard babies, not people like Mors and me.

I uncoiled from behind the sign and peered around the edge. A truly large man was barely moving beneath the second-floor balcony. He had a shotgun and a long black leather coat. Lightning reflected off the coat's wet sheen and his bald head.

He made his way step by step, quiet and cautious, and a second guy came into view, this one crouched low and much smaller. He had a hoodie up over his face, black fingerless gloves, and pistol in hand, creeping along on trench-coat shotgun's left, exposed to the rain.

I put my hand to my ear.

"Two," I said, the word vibrating along my jaw to transmit however faintly to Mors.

"*Four,*" he replied instantly, "*repeat, four. Two more on approach from Old Jeff Davis highway, coming from behind construction junk.*"

I couldn't see them unless I broke cover.

Then another guy, another trench coat and shotgun combo, this one with a ballcap, gun held at port arms as he crept around the opposite side of the motel, maybe forty yards from Shotgun One and Gollum.

"Oh, let's make it five," I sub-vocalized, "two shotguns."

Mors and I hadn't needed to chit-chat about wanting to avoid a long, loud shootout. Washington would respond. The storm was a gift, but the fewer bangs, the better.

We waited as the creeper kept creeping. Our count stayed at five. The two from the abandoned highway were climbing through a hole in the fence, both big, neckless guys, one in a suit, hair plastered to his blocky skull the other in a sleeveless sweatshirt and with spiral designs shaved into his head.

Hired pistoleros, both.

There was another soundless but huge shutter flash of lightning, the spreading bolt like an instantly growing root system of some huge, unseen tree above the clouds. All five froze on their approach in the blue-white glare.

In the silent heartbeat before the thunder roar, Mors said in my ear, "*Five, then. Let's go.*"

But there were six.

I saw the Master Chief, hands in his peacoat, standing grim atop the brackish, rain-spiked water of the hot tub.

The thunderclap exploded and rolled like a cannonade. Rolled with it, first running in a low scuttle from behind the sign and Kirk-rolled, coming up on one knee and fired at the shotgun and ballcap, who'd just made it around the far corner of the building. Center mass hit. His head went up, cap tumbling, shotgun thrown up and out as I swung around and shot neckless suit twice in the chest. The shotgun clattered to the wet tarmac even as the second man was caving in, firing once, wild, into the storm above us. I fired again at shaved-head design and missed, just as a fusillade of shots from the two under the balcony droned through the wet air past the right side of my head, another ricocheted off the sign and another hit the pavement directly in front of me, sending chips of tarmac.

There was a sharp pain in my thigh.

Tiger-head was running at me, firing in a two handed grip, and while I tried to run too, my thigh seized up in hot agony, and I fell, sprawling in a great splash in the thin lake the lot had become.

There was a flash from the upper balcony and tiger-head's face disappeared in a red-black spray.

He fell with a splash as I scrambled, kicking on my side like Curly of the Stooges, managing to resume cover behind the battered sign.

The heavy rain was beating a meaningless tattoo on the big metal box of the sign and another shot winged off it as I resumed my spot.

Three men dead or dying in the rain as the thunder fell to a receding mutter. Gollum had run to the far stairway, almost stomping on his dead or dying comrade as he snatched up the shotgun and hit the stairs behind with only one loud stomp, then nothing.

Bald trench coat had run back into the dark hallway beneath the dark hallway beneath the other side of the balcony.

The rain pounded. There was another fusillade of lightning, but it was farther off now. Then, a block, maybe two blocks away, an explosion hammered through the air. An unmistakable gasoline fireball roiled up into view, orange light erupting and then fading.

"*Whatthehellwasthat?*" Mors said in my ear.

"I dunno," I said, "Joy, maybe."

"*You hit?*"

"No, well. Yeah. Road shrapnel."

"*Bad?*"

"No," I said. Though it was bad enough, maybe.

"You've got one coming up. My left. Maybe two. Right stair hallway's where he faded."

"*So both stairs?*" Mors said.

"Let's assume," I said.

"*Take the hallway one, you're closer.*"

The sirens, what sounded like cops, firetrucks, the works, were getting louder. And fainter, the sounds of people yelling, forming on whatever Joy had blown up.

And then, to quote the great Billy West on *Futurama*, "Good news, everyone! *Bad news...*"

The Master Chief was gone, but a sixth goon had come after all. Another suit, this one tall and thin, came through the torn chainlink fence, crouched low and cautious.

I pressed my hand to my thigh. My pants were shredded, blood was running down into one shoe, and a piece of road was stuck in the muscle.

I tried to stand up, and boy oh boy, did it hurt.

There was a huge crash on the balcony, and I strained to straighten up and peek as Suit Two sprinted for cover on the same side of the building as one of the trench coats had fallen near.

* * *

Mors.

Mors could see from his perch that whatever had blown up was now not only burning merry hell, rain or no, but judging from the flashes, it was surrounded by firetrucks, cops, and fucking fucking fuck, here comes a goddamn helicopter out of the west.

It wouldn't be long before cops came over to see what some old lady was saying about hearing shots over at the old motel. Guaranteed.

So. No more bang-bang, if it could be helped.

Mors sighed, and with a quick scan of the shadowed balcony hall to his left, empty, he tucked his pistols away in his jacket webbing and crept silent and swift down the other way toward the stair.

He reached the TV and slipped a knife out of his left pocket and put his right hand through the looped cord. He lifted the TV silently as he stood up straight.

Mors waited. He could have waited with the heavy television dangling from his fist for an hour or two, but convergence was happening.

And while Dan was likely on the fuck at the other end, he was also hurt. So let's move things along.

Deliberately, Mors just barely cleared his throat, the way you would if you just had to but were trying to do it quietly. As he did, he bent his knees slightly and swung the big TV back like a big, blocky pendulum.

The little guy in the sodden hoodie erupted off the top step where he'd been crouching, bringing the shotgun up, teeth bared, eyes slit against the shot he was about fire just as Mors swung the television up and over like a circus strongman and imploded the tube with hoodie's skull.

Wearing the television, hoodie dropped the shotgun and before he could fall back, Mors yanked him savagely forward with the cord and buried the knife in his chest.

One wild sepia-toned memory flash of watching Robot Monster *with his drunk and slatternly mother.*

He caught the dead man by his television-ensconced head and eased him down with a soft clunk.

* * *

I limped to the edge of the balcony overhang near the stairs and caught just a glimpse of leather jacket flapping around the rusty support post.

"Mors," I sub-voxed.

"You hear that?"

"Yes. All well?"

"Yup."

"Good. Next guy's on his way up to you. Going around back. Number six is late to the party."

"Understood."

I ran-limped behind the building. The storm was moving off, and the rain was letting up. The helicopter hovering over the fire was providing a steady low thumping of rotors against the wet air and provided me with a little cover noise.

I stopped about ten feet from the corner and seeing no one yet, attempted to pull the shard of asphalt from my thigh.

Pain to the tenth. No way, José.

I heard something to my right and whirled, pistol up, to see a lumpy, shambling scarecrow. Staggering, obviously drunk, in filthy layered clothes, with the ragged brim of a baseball cap poking out of an upturned hood, a bum with a bag-wrapped bottle in his left hand weaved steadily toward me.

Shit.

I hesitated and then continued to slide toward the far end of the building. The drunk just kept staggering toward me.

Then the suit came around the corner, firing.

I drove off my good left leg, diving down toward the pavement like it was a pool.

The bullet whined off the wall above me.

But I didn't think I could move that fast again.

The tall suit was a cool one. He steadied his gun with two hands as he lunged forward and as I was bringing my gun up. But I knew I'd never make it before getting shot.

Then the homeless guy threw his bottle down, the smash distracting both of us, and the guy suddenly ran flapping toward us.

The suit was only off his mark for a second, his attention (but not his gun) shifted toward the bum on approach.

I was about to use the moment when the shambling homeless man straightened gracefully, drawing his gun, and put two shots in Mr. Suit, one in the chest and one in the head.

He approached and stood over both of us, lying in our separate filthy puddles and swept the cap and hood off to shake out long, shiny black hair and reveal the cool, remote face I'd kissed long ago.

"*Si vi pacem, para bellum,*" Jiufeng said.

Bad protocol, I know, but I could only nod and lower my pistol.

* * *

Mors.

Mors figured if it worked once, it'll work again. These idiots are amateurs.

Slowly and silently, he took the bar from the bedframe away from the wall and raised up like a baseball bat and cleared his throat again in phony, timid stealth.

And the bald guy in the trench coat popped up like a creepy Jack-In-The-Box even before Mors could finish or move, firing his shotgun. The bullet would have gone through the bigger man's chest but, instead, caromed off the descending bar with an earsplitting ringing tone, the impact-vibration of the ricochet breaking both of Mors's hands even as he lost his grip on the bar, and it clanged to the floor.

Mors clawed for his pistol with his shattered left—the marginally less-damaged hand, but the bald guy was racking the slide on the shotgun, and this, Mors knew, was it.

It. The Day of the Cricket.

The bald guy knew it too, sneering at Mors with contempt at the lesser predator just as his forehead exploded, stinging Mors's face with macerated bone fragments and blood.

The dead man collapsed onto his own shotgun and fell bonelessly, sliding back down the stairs on his belly with his trench coat and pantlegs rucking up around his calves as he skidded down into the dark.

Mr. Joy, wearing his own nightwork get-up, sidestepped the big man's avalanche like a matador and looked down at Mors, still crouched over his ruined hands.

"No worries, mate. You're safe as mice."

CHAPTER 36

Duck, Duck, Goose. The Legacy of Lady Bird Johnson.

SO THE BAD GUYS had killed the even worse guys.

We gathered at the tarp-shrouded ambulance, Joy and Jiufeng just as perky as could be, me limping and with a pressure bandage in place (after Jiufeng clamped one hand over my mouth and yanked the shard of asphalt out of my thigh) and Mors white-faced and groggy with two shattered hands that had already swollen to blue-black Mickey Mouse gloves.

Oh, and the Metro cops had arrived, just in time for the Four Freshmen to smash a chair leg through the wood paneling over the sink.

Kathleen had marshaled them to the task, I had no doubt.

"Good," Mr. Joy said, looking at the hole, "let those gits make a ruckus; it will slow the police down."

But, alas, it didn't. We were just getting into the ambulance, Joy behind the wheel (at his insistence) when a Arlington cop car slewed sideways next to the hole in the fence, and two cops got out, guns drawn, one screaming a bull-throated "Freeze!" while his partner jabbered into a radio.

Almost instantly, the helicopter swung away from whatever Joy and Jiufeng had blown up and came toward us, its spotlight Martian-like in its approaching cone through the rain.

We did not freeze. I climbed in last, hauling my damaged leg in with both hands just as one of the cops shot Jiufeng.

"*Suff*-ering *fuck*-ing *CATS*!" Mr. Joy screamed in rage as he slammed the ambulance in gear, tires screaming.

I grabbed Jiufeng as she fell, her hands to her right upper chest. Another bullet punched into the door, and another shattered the back window. Joy drove through the fence, flattening it in a ringing crash as the windshield crazed with cracks and turned a crazy, screeching right onto the "Old" Jefferson Davis Highway.

I was trying to hold my hand over the blood-pumping hole in Jiufeng's chest as the ambulance boomed up the decrepit road.

"Right, gents, hang on. Ketch, patch her up as best can; we will not be in this bloody van for long."

I found a roll of gauze in the huge glove box, and Mors kicked a roll of duct tape that had been on the floor toward me. I wrapped her up as best I could with the van rocketing down the bumpy, very much long abandoned road.

A police car was maybe two bus-lengths behind us and gaining. Joy had the pedal to the floor and was passing ninety as we screamed past the abandoned Clark Street Playhouse and then a confusing row of construction vehicles and equipment, all of which were easy enough to glimpse as we were framed by the helicopter's spotlight as it momentarily overshot us.

We flashed past a soccer field on our right, then a blocky collection of public storage buildings and more construction equipment on our left. The Washington Monument glowed a long ways off, implacable and declamatory.

Joy almost took us down a dirt road labeled DO NOT ENTER and then flung Mors out of his seat and Jiufeng and I sideways against a panel door with a berserk left onto the 395 South and North entrance.

The cops behind us followed but lost ground fishtailing wildly. The chopper wheeled about and pinned us in the spotlight again, pacing us easily until we went into a long, low tunnel that opened a heart-in-mouth moment later with the Pentagon dead ahead like the world's largest medieval prison.

"Awright, gents, listen to your engine driver. Fasten your seatbelts. Ketch, strap her in; nothing more to be done."

He spoke in tight plumminess, but Joy's face and the back of his neck were slick with a sheen of sweat.

I did as he said though Jieufeng looked dead now, head lolling all the way down, her black hair like a caul over her face. I had to belt Mors in too, as his ruined hands weren't obeying.

"Get in a seat, damn you!" Joy said.

I did, momentarily blinded by the wash of the helicopter's spot. Jiufeng lolled and jounced. I flashed on the origami unicorn she'd left me, once.

"Last thing, gents, keep your mouths closed; goose shit is best left unswallowed."

I had time for a single "Wha—?" and Joy abruptly jerked the ambulance in a very sharp right just past an enormous, flapping underlit American flag, almost tipping us over as the ambulance keeled up on just two wheels and then resettled with a teeth-clicking crash.

It rammed through low hedges and something vital beneath the floor was ripped away as we bottomed out on a low concrete barrier. The ambulance careened down and off a swampy looking drop-off too steep to call a hill and too short to call a cliff. The helicopter beam was still cascading over us, even as a sickening weightless sensation told me we were entirely airborne and—as a bonus—slowly flipping upside down.

"*HOOOLLLLLLLD!*" Joy screamed.

Impact. Roof first into the Potomac.

* * *

I lost some time there. Then the ambulance was drifting, now upside down, now sideways, now sinking sideways as cold, swamp-stenchy water gushed in through sprung panels and broken windows.

Mors was bleeding from a head wound and hanging upside down, groping feebly at his seatbelt.

I released myself with a splash and then him, making a bad job of easing him gently to stand on the now submerged roof of the ambulance.

Joy was a mess. He'd broken the windshield with his head in a huge starburst pattern that lit up electric white in the helicopter's intermittent beam, which had resumed and intensified. Joy's face was a mask of blood, weirdly echoing his original appearance as red-masked Lucifer.

Jiufeng was worse than that. She was gone. Her seat had ripped entirely loose of its moorings and with the water now chest-high, entirely out of sight.

"Get out. Both of you, get out. Help him, I've got 'er," Joy said and submerged.

The van pitched sharply left now and began sinking in earnest.

Mors used his right elbow to pull himself over the back seat and disappeared under the murky water, diving down to the windowless back doors.

In another whirling swoop of the spotlight I turned back to the front, and there was no Joy to be seen.

I dove, keeping my mouth shut tight. Opening my eyes showed me light-shot murk and pain at whatever crap infected this part of the Potomac. I swam blind, once feeling the tread of a boot above me. I surfaced next to Mors, the blatting of the helicopter loud directly above us, the water white with the frosty cone of light jittering all around.

There was also a chorus, a cacophony, of honking.

"Can you swim?"

"Yeh," Mors said. "Cold water feels good."

Lucky you, I thought. I was so cold I wanted to scream. I yanked Mors along with me, and we got out of the spotlight momentarily, and fool's errand or not, we began swimming toward the little marina across from us, maybe less than a football field's distance from us.

Even as the helicopter seemed to veer away from us slightly, the eerie honking intensified in a sudden, explosive wave of what sounded like applause mixed with the sound of snapping, shook-out laundry sheets.

The night's little miracle.

Mors and I were floundering toward the marina among a vast flock of slumbering geese. *Hundreds of geese.* No doubt, hanging around this close to the Pentagon and a marina accounted for their tolerance for some commotion, but when the helicopter had veered away from the drifting, mostly submerged ambulance and pinned us once again in its beam, the geese had had enough.

In a rippling, clapping, honking wave, the geese took off and either disturbed by the chopper's wind-wash or disoriented by the spotlight, they flew directly up at the machine.

"Iss like warrath' worlss...." Mors said.

"What? Close your mouth and swim, goddamnit!"

I'm not sure what happened, exactly. The reverse avalanche of big fucking geese into the sky didn't last long but hadn't geese taken down jet planes before? The helicopter avoided the dispersing flock and wheeled away, rotors thudding, making a big, looping arc back over land, almost back to the motel, and then it returned.

But not to us.

Maybe it was the buoys, easy to confuse with the heads of floating men. Or maybe it was Joy or Jiuefeng's bodies.

The ambulance was no longer visible, but the chopper hovered motionless now nearer the shore, perhaps pinpointing where it sank.

We made it to slime covered pylons under a dock on the far-left side of the marina. Mors couldn't climb the pulpy, rotten ladder that was nailed into the pylons by himself so I boosted him up, trying to spit as much goose-shit water out as I could.

The helicopter was drifting further away now, its beam pointed stridently down. A boat with flashing blue-and-red lights was approaching the spotlight from the right.

Converging on the ambulance. Or bodies.

I was shivering so violently it was like St. Vitus dance. Limp-running, crouched low and dragging Mors along beside me, I looked like Jerry Lewis running while having a seizure.

In contrast, Mors wasn't shivering at all and seemed groggily indifferent. Shock.

I stopped us in a little clot of trees on the edge of the largely empty parking lot. We were in the shadows.

"We have to -g-get a car, Muh-muh-*Mors*," I said.

Mors nodded and spat, leaning over awkwardly, his broken hands loosely splayed on his knees, his fingers lumpy purple and white starfish on the ends of each wrist.

I kept my hand on his shoulder and tried to scan the dark, the only light the Washington Monument far off in the skeletal trees and one weak bulb illuminating a sign at the edge of the parking lot. **The Lady Bird Johnson Marina.**

Well, all right.

Near us was a BMW and a gleaming new Maxima. At the far end of the lot, parked next to a hangar-like building, was a decrepit-looking tow truck. I didn't need to see it up close to determine it was a rusty piece of shit.

"Mors. *Mors*, listen to me."

"M'lissinen'," he said, still folded over.

"We gotta get warm and we gotta get away. We h-have three cars to choose from."

Both of us had sat through all manner of classes they'd never have at dear old Eton. Lock-picking, safe-peeling, car-theft, engine-jumping and so on. Mors was better at all of it. I would be his hands, but he'd know better which one would be the easiest to boost.

"What are they?"

"H-hokay," I said, "We gotta BMW, we got a M-m-maxima, and we got a fucking old tow truck. Looks like a Holmes. From the fifties."

Mors looked up and smiled, which was always disconcerting on its own.

"The Holmes," he said.

* * *

The tow truck was a rusty, filthy, stinking piece of shit that nearly gave me a rupture to both steer and shift. Its waning life was clearly being spent as an unregistered, uninspected, uninspectable runabout, strictly for the marina grounds.

Belching oily smoke as we drove it onto the road, with the top two floors of the fucking Pentagon right there, I didn't think we'd get far in it before being pulled over. On the bright side, the truck had a heater of sorts and, in the filthy, trash-crammed dash shelf, an open plastic bag of hard candy. We both crunched one after the other, the fuel spilling in and fending off hypothermia.

Fully expecting to be seeing cops behind us at any minute, I drove us lurching, grinding, and bellowing smoke through a weirdly quiet and indifferent city, finally parking the wreck behind an abandoned gas station maybe a mile and a half west of the townhouse.

No one bothered us as we walked through the night, the rain coming in spats. The few whose paths we crossed stared at our wet, filthy clothes, my bloody thigh bandage, Mors's white, shocky pallor, his hands tucked under his armpits, and our green, shit-smeared faces and gave us wide berth.

We looked like bad news walking, best not to look too closely.

* * *

From *The New Assassin's Field Guide and Almanac: "Do not ever rely upon the public medicos. Be prepared for injuries, no matter how grievous."*

Recalling that part of the almanacs made me think of Mr. Joy's jaunty Englishness. Not a priority but it did seem a clue to the book's country of origin.

But that was for another day, if other days were ahead.

Mors and I reached the townhouse, and once there, I used my kit to fix us up with bandages, antibiotics, and two shots of morphine for Mors and his smashed hands. Following showers, we were sitting in my living room while I was doing my best to splint and wrap Mors's hands when the Kirby box chirped.

No reassuring greeting from Lord Henry this time, just the cool green light indicating a waiting video call via the scrambled frequency. I finished Mors's right hand and then poured us both a knock of brandy and then switched the screen on. Mr. Joy's face filled the screen, a rather upscale hotel room partially visible behind him.

"Greetings, gentlemen. May we stipulate that we're comrades in arms, rogues together, rakes at the gates of hell and thus no need for Latin folderol?"

I turned the Kirby box lens to take us both in at the dining room table.

"Jieufeng?" I said.

Joy smiled, tight and without reaching his eyes. His hair was still damp, and a swatch of bandage covered his left brow, giving him a piratical look.

"Jury's out, I'm afraid. She's alive. Just."

"Where is she?" I said.

Joy's crooked smile faded, and now his face matched his eyes.

"Need to know, old son. Be satisfied she's alive. And how is Mr. Mors?"

Mors answered for himself.

"My hands are wrecked and I feel like shit."

Joy nodded.

"I have arranged for a car to pick you up in twenty minutes at the curb. You can avail yourself of the same attention and accommodations as Jiufeng's."

Mors said nothing, sipping his brandy by holding it in his bandaged palms.

"Yes, well. And you, Proteus. What are your intentions?"

I thought about it one more time.

"My intentions are to drive to Maine, creep my own house, rescue my people and the Kestrel," I said. "Can the Guild help me?"

Joy was shaking his head before I even finished.

"Watch the news. The kidnapping attempt on The Gang of Four is anywhere and everywhere. As is the arson attempt. Quite the upsetting mess as far as a shadow agency is concerned. I can't help you anymore than I already have, though I might be along *after* you finish. Assuming you finish."

I said nothing.

"And come now, who better to storm his own castle than the king, hm? You know where all the boards creak and which garden gnome the keys are under. And time is of the essence."

"He sounded berserk last we spoke. He's probably killed them all and run," I said.

Joy shrugged. It was a Mors shrug. A killer's shrug. I imagined I shrugged the same way, nowadays.

"Indeed, he may have. Or—he might hold the cards he has left in the hopes of playing them to some advantage. After all, Gardener has now failed his wealthy, wicked patrons and betrayed the ancient order of assassins he knows far less than all about and in whose employ Leland Parish Clay has spent his life since he stopped being a philosophy professor at Wheaton."

"Leland Clay? That's Gardener's real name?"

Joy shook his head gingerly and sipped something amber from his own glass. He was wearing a very white dress shirt, sloppily buttoned.

"Long ago. But the Guild knows all of us. You, Proteus, are Daniel Francis Ketch. You, Mors, are—"

Broken hands or no, Mors threw his glass with deadly aim at the television screen, which imploded loudly.

I turned to look at him, too flabbergasted to form speech.

Mors was groping on the table clumsily. He held up his key ring in one bandaged hand. A small ornate elephant swung, catching the light with little heliographs.

Mors sighed a weirdly long sigh.

"Take Mariah. She's all gassed up. But wait until that blabby prick sends the car for me. I'm fuckin' hurtin'."

* * *

Thirty minutes later I was sipping coffee and hurtling through the Virginia night, following Mariah's built-in GPS directions just to be safe, given the fatigue factor.

Mariah looked like the result of a three-way orgy between a torpedo, coffin, and tank, but once inside, I found her quite comfortable and a near perfect ride.

The only sticking point was that once inside, the radio would only play Orson Welles' 1938 radio broadcast of *The War of the Worlds*, complete and uncut. I couldn't find any other radio or music. Given the time it would take to drive from Washington, DC, to Maine meant I'd end up listening to it ten times or more.

Ladies and gentlemen, the director of the Mercury Theatre and—

As Mariah glided onto the freeway, I snapped it off. I tried to arrange myself as comfortably as possible, despite various aches and the tight wrapping on my thigh. I was dressed for nightwork. Mors had reviewed the arsenal inside Mariah and how to get to it.

Nightwork. But not tonight. Tonight was already over, and thin grey dawn was coming on. It would be a drive through the day and into the next night's work, with maybe time for a wee nap once I was in the New England area.

I snapped the radio back on. The show had rolled on. So it wasn't a CD, I guess. More like a live broadcast, really.

"Yet across an immense ethereal gulf, minds that are to our minds, as ours are to the beasts in the jungle, intellects vast, cool and unsympathetic, regarded this earth with envious eyes—and slowly and surely drew their plans against us.'

CHAPTER 37

Deadly Built-Ins of the Old Place.

BY THE TIME I REACHED Hampton Beach, it was late afternoon on a cold, grey day. I was probably another thirty minutes or so from my house, but I needed both rest and nightfall before going home. I eased Mariah off the highway and onto the coastal road, parking in a small, empty lot across from the seawall.

I was very tired. It was high tide, and the waves were large and laden with seaweed, the sea beyond them grey like spoiled meat. I remembered summers here when I was a kid, nice if pedestrian memories. Now, it seemed a dead place, like all off-season resort beaches I suppose, redolent of lost summers and echo-scented with all the things you'd ever regret losing for the rest of your life.

I turned off *The War of the Worlds* and eased the seat back and mentally bookmarked waking in four hours, another little trick from my time at Guild house. It occurred to me that it was Iron Horse who had taught that to me. Little mental tricks of autohypnosis. How to shrug off fatigue or quiet pain or set an alarm clock in the head.

I wondered who shot him as he fled through the library, seeking his final symbolic clue for whomever might find him and understand.

I fell asleep musing over the irony of professors of murder, mourned only by their deadly students.

* * *

A word or two about my home. True, my nasty business paid for my dream home, but with that trade came all sorts of potential threats both real and imagined.

I wanted to relax when at home. Completely.

So, with the help of Guild consultants, I crafted a mini Normandy Beach just beneath the visible surface of my grounds with all the most modern defense measures and some good old-fashioned medieval smash-mouth, all run by an entity that was about as close to Clarke and Kubrick's HAL as you could get on the private market. Artificial intelligence is still a dream, but I liked to imagine that Lord Henry had about a caterpillar's level of self-awareness.

That said, I'd been the idiot who'd turned the keys over to Gardener. And of course, I could switch him back over completely to his rightful lord and master with a phone call, but I had something else in mind.

On the grounds in virtually a hundred places, Lord Henry "saw" all through crystalline lenses in wavelengths far beyond the scope of the human eye. Say you climbed the gate or just smashed through it, there was an array of tracking devices specifically designed to digitally target the human retina. The laser arrays then emit a green diode-pumped solid-state laser beam directly into the eyes being tracked. It only fires twice before it essentially destroys itself, but the first strike causes permanent blindness.

If you somehow managed to get past that, the next welcome mat was an array of well-placed, pressure sensitive bounding mines—basically a Guild-adapted rip-off of the M16APM mine—which, when triggered, launches about four feet in the air and then explodes in a high velocity shockwave of steel ball bearings and "shredder" stars.

And of course, guns. Primarily, "Jack-In-The-Box" machine guns on accordion pneumo-turrets, capable of firing, I don't know, a jillion rounds a second.

Overkill really.

* * *

After my nap, I got out of Mariah and went through a series of elaborate stretches in the now dusk shadowed lot. I was pretty sore from the past few days, especially my thigh and right ankle. After stretching, I took my time driving to Wells, parking Mariah on the marsh road about half a mile from my driveway.

I had considered using Mariah as a siege-engine in an assault on my own home. Though tight-lipped about all the details of her refit, Mors had told me enough to know that Mariah was, among other things, a rolling bomb with the concussive force to destroy half my front lawn and most of the house with it. But that would be like using a bazooka to kill a fly. Besides, she was Mors's most treasured possession.

Limping worse than I'd have liked, dressed for nightwork and carrying one of Gaston Glock's creations, Model 35, with its seventeen rounds (just in case), I approached my gate, walking slowly down the dark, tree-shrouded dirt and gravel drive. I glimpsed the Master Chief walking with me, hands in pockets, head bent ruminatively. But he was mostly visible in the corner of my eye. When I looked directly over at him, he'd disappear.

CHAPTER 38

Home Invasion.

I STOOD IN THE DARK, a dark man, eight feet from the stylized front gate. One more step would wake the cyber-hounds, if Gardener was still here and still had something worth holding onto.

I exhaled and assumed The Now, which was actually easier to do when you were sort of overtaxed. Time fell away. I enjoyed the breeze that lifted the hair from my brow. The remaining leaves rustled dryly. Fall sluggish moths now moved like bubbles in sepia-toned syrup, slowly pinwheeling about the big, ornate light-globes that bracketed the gate.

I walked forward, triggering the pressure-plate sensor running across the driveway. I felt the insectile weight of a dragonfly's eye's worth of facets turning their deadly, single-minded attention upon me.

And not even the somehow comforting cyber sock puppet of Lord Henry, no. This was *Abraxas One*, Gardener's "Man of All Work" ala my own stupidity.

Side-time is what this assumed perception was called, both in the almanac and by my instructors at the Guild, a slowing of one's perception of the one-way flow of time we're all stuck in. Everyone has experienced it, during a car accident, or sports play, or birth, or battle. That one kiss. But in this case, it was a summoned and controlled thing.

And even as I relaxed into that strange, *all-the-time-in-the-worrrrrld-duh* state of syrupy hyper-awareness, was that a slowly blinking array of identically green fireflies, spread throughout the branches of the largely leafless maple branches above and across from me? And weren't they blinking in unison now, inexorably speeding up, with Abraxas on full alert? Full alert for me?

Sunk in side-time, I could see the spread of fairy-light lasers blinking ever faster as they built up the charge that would sear my retinas even through closed lids. I imagined the mines all punching up through the soil in unison, the gun turrets hatching out of the ground and bushes and swinging their blind barrel eyes' attention on my head.

Beyond the trees I could see that virtually all of the house lights were on, my dream home alight like a cabin cruiser at sea. Or a fortress, prepped for attack. In the waxy flow of frame-by-frame perception, I felt a chill as I saw a male form pass the second-floor windows. A body-English I knew.

Speaking felt thunderously deliberate and overloud.

"*Thermidor-Omnibus-Vertigo-Morpheus*," I said.

A ratcheting, glass-pack bass tone issued from the speakers mounted behind each lantern, almost rattling the glass globes and visibly making the lights gutter, momentarily.

When Lord Henry spoke, he sounded almost sad, though that was surely my imagination.

"Understood, Mr. Ketch. Farewell, sir."

It was a silent event, but I liked imagining the mood inside as the power shut off with an unwinding moan. Defense systems deactivated. No phones. No eyes. All the doors in the entire house unlocking with a unified crunching chorus. The house and grounds went black. System crash. Lights out.

* * *

In the sudden inky darkness I sped my perspective up, reassuming the world as we usually see it rather than it actually is. I drew Proteus, the trickster self, over me like a cloak. I could see around corners. Through walls. Into minds, hearts, souls.

I was Proteus. And I could do anything.

I stepped silently through the now unlocked gate and then ran to my left, following the beautifully crafted rock wall enclosing the property. I wasn't sprinting, just a steady, quiet lope, barely limping at all.

Except for the wind coming off the marshes, it was silent, my house and grounds dark and Lord Henry as dead as if I'd shot him. Or worse, made him commit seppuku. You see, that last command trigger didn't just shut him off, it erased him.

I ran past the back deck and into the darkest part of the yard, the trees there providing a canopy of intertwined branches that would block even most moonlight, if there'd been any that night. On the southeast corner of the house was a clay drainpipe held to the brick with iron brackets. I ran to the corner of the house and pulled my gloves from my jacket pocket. Manchester United goalie gloves, perfect for climbing slippery drainpipes, along with the thick rubber soles of my rock-climbing boots.

Despite my injured right leg, I climbed fairly quickly, reaching the second floor and then the third without any trouble. Now, above me and to my left was the underside of the deck, supported by a row of four thick beams as struts. I reached up to the closest one and hauled myself up crouch on it, the angle straining my ankles and my back against the house. Below me, under the furthest edge of the deck was the window to my second-floor study.

In the webbing pockets of my bomber jacket was compact set of Viper 4 Nightvision goggles, a set of lockpicks and a glass cutter. I slid the glass cutter out, making sure the other gear, including my gun, were secure before starting work on the window.

I gathered myself, breathing deeply, and then twisted around and, hooking my legs around the support strut, hung upside down, my head level with the top windowpane and my hands able to reach the middle one. The cutter had a carbide wheel blade on one end and a suction cup on the other. With blood rushing to my head, I ran the cutter around the pane close to the wood, the gritting bite of the blade seemed very loud in the night, though it really just made a soft scraping sound, not much louder than drawing a wooden match across a brick.

I licked the suction cup and set it firmly on the pane, ready to tap the glass loose when the sliding door opening onto the deck slid in its track and footsteps creaked steadily across the boards, approaching me.

I froze, blood pounding now in my temples and blood-congested face.

The footsteps stopped. There was a crackle of cellophane, a gritting snap, and then a whiff of cigarette smoke. Some expensive blend. Dunhill. Silk cut. Turkish, maybe.

The footsteps resumed, now walking away from me, now stopping again. Then coming back to directly above me.

I strained to look up, my arms still outstretched to the pane of glass below. I thought I could just see the darker shadow of the form above me through the cracks in the boards of the deck, but that might have been my imagination. There was a rustle of cloth and another creek as he leaned out over the railing, but not looking down.

I could see a plume of smoke and in the fall evening breeze, a slight swirl of white hair.

Bleach.

The cigarette spiraled out over the railing, trailing sparks as it fell down past me.

My head was pounding now, my eyeballs felt like they were going to pop out of their sockets from hydrostatic pressure, my arms were burning, my calves, my thigh feeling hot and wet as the wound there was being pulled open against the tape. The hand holding the cutter had begun to tremble and was refusing my mental command to be still.

I wondered if I could shoot him up through the floor with any hope of a crippling wound when the footsteps withdrew back across the deck and the slider hissed closed on its track again.

I forced myself to count to ten and then tapped the glass with one gloved finger, and the cut pane came free with a quiet snap, securely attached to the cutter's suction cup.

Oh, the cleverness of me, I thought just as my numb hand lost its numb grip on both the cutter and pane and both tumbled from my grasp, aerodynamically odd enough in its shape to not just fall with a thump to the grass but shatter loudly on the bricks all the way down.

The fusillade of gunshots ripped across the deck from above, smashing huge, ragged holes in an arc above me and sending a hailstorm of splinters ricocheting around me, tearing my clothes and stinging my body.

I wasn't sure if I was hit or not, but the adrenaline rush gave me enough of a boost to wrench myself up and grab the support strut and hug it to my armpit while releasing my legs, like a swimmer spinning at the end of a lap to kick off the wall.

I heard Bleach walk back onto the deck. Dropping to the ground wasn't an option unless I wanted to break both legs.

He raked another deafening spray of gunfire across the deck, several shots screaming off the brickwork directly in front of me and smashing the middle struts in a spray of pulverized flinders.

An uzi, I thought. Maybe even a mini, but both could cut me in half, just as they had over half of the struts holding this end of the deck up.

"Proteus, Proteus, me old jobby jabber. Didja know the word *'aha'* comes from the fourteenth century? Middle English, that."

The deck creaked ominously. I wasn't in a very good spot for a gunfight, and he knew it, but he didn't quite dare to take a peek over the railing.

"C'mon, ya fud. Say somethin'. My hand's still gowpin' from our last waltz, but no hard feelin's, hm? Maybe we can work it out, awright?"

The window I'd been working on was below me at a considerable angle, but it had come to the Moment of Decision, as the fundies say. I let myself hang down from the strut and kicked away hard from the wall so I'd have plenty of momentum in my swing. As I swung forward and released my grip, Bleach fired his third sweep, this time in a straight line following where the deck meets the wall.

A mistake on his part as that was about all that end of the deck could take. With a rending crack of splintering wood, the overhanging section of deck ripped away from the side of the house and fell like a drawbridge even as I went feet first through the second floor window, Bleach's scream of "Fucking cuuunt!" followed me, his last burst of gunfire streaking upward into the cold night sky.

A moment later there was an impact of debris I could feel through the soles of my feet, even up here. There was no way to know if Bleach was down there too, hopefully underneath it.

I stepped into the pitch-black hallway and slipped the goggles over my head, thumbing them on. Stopped, listened, looked around. The second floor in the ghost-green light of the goggles was quite the mess. Several empty wine bottles, piles of newspapers, a half empty bottle of Glenfiddich Rare that cost more than the average used car, all were in a scree of tidal-like flotsam down the hallway. There were also several items of feminine apparel that I'd have remembered were they in my wardrobe.

I stepped on something that rolled under my foot. It was a short leather whip; I think it was called a quirt. It was stained, the dried blood appearing dark green in the goggles' spectrum.

Jesus, Gardener.

There was a sudden breeze that stirred the newspapers in a fall-leaves rustle. Either the upstairs deck door was still open or had just been opened.

Assume the worst, always.

I spun, gun up, at movement I'd caught in the corner of my eye. There, about five feet away, even more ghostly in the infrared spectrum, was the Master Chief. His eyes glowed like a cat's in oncoming headlights as he lifted one hand from his peacoat pocket and pressed one finger to his lips in a "*Shhh*" gesture.

I froze. Was this it? The final stress-induced cracks coming so quickly now that I'd end up so distracted by worsening psychosis I'd be easy prey for the killers in my house?

My father continued to look at me, a shimmering green phantom with an ever-placid expression, right hand in his coat pocket, the left in its "Shhh" position. Then the flatly glowing metallic eyes cut to the right, and he dropped his hand sharply and pointed at the floor.

I hunched my neck and fell to my knees just as the gunshot exploded, deafening me even as the flash projected two nova-white flares of light into my retinas. I threw myself sideways as I swept out with my right leg, hard, knocking the shooter off his feet. Even as I ripped the goggles off I heard the back of his head hit the floor before his heels. I rose in a crouch, gun at the ready and blind as a bastard.

"Augh, ya mauchit, keeching swamp donkey, my loupin' heid!" I blinked, crabbing backwards down the hall. White dots and blue dots, flaring suns, streaked and throbbed before me in the blackness.

"Awright, yeh fook," Bleach said through gritted teeth, taking aim, I assumed.

Well, fuck it. I couldn't see anyway, so I closed my eyes and fired five times in a sweep toward the voice of Glasgow and at the same time lunged up and forward as hard as I could.

I collided with Bleach, my head hitting his stomach and his gun, driving the air out of him and both of us down onto the floor, Bleach apparently unhurt by my shots.

"*Fucker*!" Bleach snarled as we grappled without finesse. I'd knocked his gun loose, breaking the bridge of my nose doing it. I still had my gun, but he had my wrist in an iron grip, the gun jammed down into my own thigh. I still couldn't see anything but lens-flare dots, but I didn't need to see to know the layout of my own house. I dug into the carpet with the thick rubber treads of the climbing boots and bulldozed both of us toward the stairs. In a moment of like minds, we headbutted each other at the same time, but I had the better angle. Eight pounds of skull crushed Bleach's nose, and now we had that in common as well.

Bleach twisted around and must have seen we were approaching the precipice of the stairway.

"Stop, ya fuckin' pure mad dafty!"

"Hey," I said, "my house, my rules."

I drove us off the edge of the stair top and down we went. I put my right shoulder into it and actually rolled over Bleach once on the way down, slamming and thudding and—my wrist still in his clutch—my gun barrel snapping banisters as we fell. I'd steeled myself for the pain, but it still hurt my back and my stitched thigh the worst; something tore there, and I felt hot wetness spreading as I kicked off the last few risers and cartwheeled again over Bleach and hit the landing hard, losing both his grip and my gun at last.

We were sprawled at the bottom of the stairs. Despite my still blinkered vision, I could now see Bleach's shadowy form amid the streaks and flares scarring my sight. Bleach twisted around and grabbed a fistful of my hair, yanking my head back while clawing to grab my throat with the other. When he couldn't get a good purchase, he drew his free hand back to chop a killing blow, and I snapped my head forward to catch the strike and bit as hard as I could into the unraveling bandage there. Bitter blood flooded my mouth as Bleach shrieked like an animal. I drove my knee into his groin and yanked him down to the floor, releasing his hand and spitting blood as I tried to get on top of him. Bleach twisted around, face to the floor, and tried to squirm away, but I grabbed his head under the chin with both hands.

I heard Rourke's tiny, pretty voice.

Claws and paws and jaws.

I drove my knee into his back and yanked upward, breaking his neck. I wrenched his head around to the right, breaking him further. Bleach bucked galvanically, twice, and was still. I rolled off him onto the carpet, breathing like a bellows.

I rolled onto my stomach and, still seeing spots in my vision, found my gun a few feet from his hand. I stood up unsteadily; everything hurt. Bleach's head was at a very unnatural angle, and one of his arms looked oddly canted. Broken collar bone, maybe.

Just to be safe, I shot him twice in each shoulder blade and once in the back of the head.

Rasputin was a fag.

*   *   *

It wasn't a complete surprise, I mean, it's not like Bleach and I had been fighting quietly so as not to wake the house.

"Drop your gun, Daniel. Hands on your head. And I fully intend to kill you, so if you're in a rush, irritate me by trying something, *please*."

I dropped my gun with a clunk. I laced my hands over my head. To be honest, I don't think I could have tried anything, anyway.

In Which Several Things Are Resolved for Good or Ill, Depending on One's Point of View.

I ENJOYED RESTING FOR A MOMENT while Gardener breathed heavily behind me. Blood was running down my leg and making one sock sodden and my nose hurt, though I had rediagnosed the damage to a fracture as opposed to a full break.

Hey, you have to appreciate the little things.

"Get the fucking lights back on. Right now. Or I will kill you. Right now."

"*Phos*," I said. The lights went on, all of them. The sudden brightness made me squint, as I was still slightly glare-blind from a gunshot filtered through amplified night-vision.

Bleach groaned in a wet rattle, making us both jump. It was, however, the groan of a very dead man, settling. It happens.

"Now, get that fucking computer and the phones back up and running."

"I can't," I said, "I'm serious. Lord Henry is destroyed."

Gardener didn't say anything but jammed the rifle hard into my spine then withdrew it and repeated the painful action at the base of my neck.

"This isn't the time to—"

"When I shut the computer down, it self-destructed. I can get the lights on and the heat and all that, but the only phones are the scramblers. What, you didn't plug yours in to charge? Too busy beating up whores and fucking over your comrades?"

Gardener shoved me in the back.

"Head for the vault, idiot."

"Ask me nicely, fuckface."

He hit me in the side of the head with the barrel and then drove the butt into my right shoulder, twice.

"Stand up straight! Now walk!"

We reached the sub-basement, and the vault door was open. That was no surprise to me, as Lord Henry's self-destruct code also opened all the locks. There were two bodies sprawled just inside the doorway of the room, both face down. Omi and Kiku.

I groaned "No" and was disconcerted to hear Gardener doing it in concert with me. Not that he gave a shit about the dead Toranagas. He had other worries.

The Kestrel was out.

Gardener banged the barrel back against my neck.

"Get in—*get in there*! Now keep walking. Stop. Keep your hands on your head!"

"It's not going to work, Leland," I said.

"*What?* Shut up."

"That's your name, isn't it? Professor Leland Parish Clay? "Shut up, you fucking stupid asshole. You idiot. How do you know that?"

"I know all kinds of stuff, *Leland*. More about the Guild, now, than you do. It's a franchise. You have the home office's attention now. It's over."

"I said shut up!"

"And if the Kestrel is out and you haven't hurt him too bad, you're fucked, *Professor Clay*, whether you kill me or not."

"Shut up! I'll blow your fucking head off!"

"I'm going to turn around, Leland," I said.

"You fucking move and I'll kill you," he said. His voice sounded thick, almost as if he were sobbing.

"Then kill me, you poor, doomed douchebag. He's already behind you. I just want to watch and see your face."

"*You shut the fuck up right now! You are not in charge*!"

"Ah, Gardener," the Kestrel said, "but Daniel's right."

Gardener screamed like an eleven-year-old girl even before the Kestrel shot him in the back of the left knee. Then he yanked him backward roughly by the hair as the rifle clattered to the floor, landing on Omi's leg.

Omi said, quite distinctly, "Ow."

* * *

Some of the following is a little blurry in my memory. The Kestrel explained that when the lights went out and the lock of vault's door thudded open, he decided to take Omi and Kiku out of the equation. Two precise blows to the neck of each.

"For your sake, Mr. and Mrs. Toranaga, I know your warrior spirits. And for you, Daniel, naturally. They're your staff."

"They're my friends," I said.

Omi made coffee, and Kiku bandaged the mostly screaming and moaning Gardener, sans pain killers.

I myself tended to the Kestrel in the well-lit, fresh-brewed-coffee-scented, Gardener-screaming kitchen.

The Kestrel was a mess.

One eye, the left, was gone. It gave me a moment of odd displacement to realize it was in a bottle, down in the vault. The bandage was professional but old and clotted with gore. Two of his fingers were gone from his left hand, the wound equally as tended and neglected. As I was repacking the eye-socket, the Kestrel watched Kiku, feeling her way carefully, bandaging his now cleaned and disinfected hand.

"Why," the Kestrel said to Kiku's scalp, "did you save me?"

I thought about it.

"Because I like you," I said, "you're important to me."

The Kestrel then looked at me with his fierce remaining eye.

"Well then," he said, "well. Thank you, Daniel."

Bandaged, the Kestrel stood and turned and yanked Gardener to his feet, keening, leading him roughly to the double sink. "Questions, Gardener. You will answer them," the Kestrel said. He jammed Gardener's hand into the garbage disposal in the left sink.

"Wait! These are wealthy people; we can, they can deal! It's worth it."

"No deals, Gardener," the Kestrel said, "just questions and answers. Who are these people of wealth?"

"The Pratt twins. The Pratts! They wanted to fix the elections, solidify the tea party influence, drive up sympathy for the right with the murder of three prominent conservatives. Further the imbalance without another war, or..."

"Who killed Guild House?"

"A team the Pratts sent, with Bleach as their leader. Ex-muscle from Division, the Shop, gang hitters."

"Were you there?"

"...Yes."

I lit a cigarette as Omi set a cup of coffee on the table for me as well as two codeine tablets.

"Why were they nude?" I said.

Zabu appeared, slinking around the corner, and jumped up onto the table, sniffing at my cup. I ran one hand over his back, smoothing his fur.

"Just, just to be freakish. Bleach's idea. Confuse the issue, false clues."

"Who killed Iron Horse?"

Mors would be pissed if I didn't check.

"I did," Gardener said. "I asked him to meet me in Special Collections because he wasn't there yet when the team arrived and dealt with, with the others."

"Money good?" I said.

"More than you'd even know what to do with," he said.

"How badly is the Guild compromised?" the Kestrel said, placing his diminished hand on the disposal switch. "Be precise."

"They know we exist. They know only about Guild house, the New England house, no others. The house safe and files are all intact, computer, all of that. Figured I could bargain with it piece by piece, didn't want to give it all away. They know *your* name, Ketch," he said, smiling. He was drooling into the sink, standing at a crooked angle on his shattered knee.

"And that's it," he said.

"Bad enough." The Kestrel sighed.

"How could you kill all your comrades?" I said.

Gardener exploded at the Kestrel like a rabid rat.

"I told you the truth! Now will you fucking *get me away from Huck Finn here and get me some medical attention?!*"

"Of course," the Kestrel said. He pressed a comforting palm upon Gardner's shoulder, which also kept his hand inside the drain—and switched the disposal on.

Eye for an eye, that sort of thing.

It wasn't easy to watch, so I didn't. Or listen to, but then it rarely is when someone gets what's coming to them.

Shortly after that, Professor Leland Clay was dead. Twilight Kingdom bound.

* * *

By the time a clean-up crew had been summoned and the Kestrel had patched a call via Kirby box from Mr. Joy to the Pratts, I was both drugged and drunk, on top of exhausted. "Exhaustipated," as Dagny used to say. I'd seen the Pratts on television, magazines, we all had. But I was pretty sure nobody had seen them like this, both in their stylish jammies, both looking like abruptly awakened baby owls. Agatha

Pratt was in some African robe with her face caked with night cream, Maxwell in actual blue pajamas, white hair in a crow's nest.

The Kestrel and I saw what the Pratt twins were seeing from their respective homes, a gaunt, strawberry-blond man in a black suit and tie on the screen, sitting in a featureless grey room, a neat white butterfly closure on his left brow partially obscured by his unruly hair.

And I had to admit, Mr. Joy *did* have a way with words.

"So now we come to it. You stole a cobra from the king's basket and drowned the others, only to find there are many more cobras and many more baskets than you could have ever imagined."

Offscreen, one of the power broker twins, Maxwell, began to speak in rolling Texan tones.

"Despite this complete misunderstanding I'm confident that if we can—"

Joy overrode him without raising his voice.

"You're dead. Your enterprise is dead. Your family. Your allies. You were all dead the day you set this scheme in motion; it just took a while for the echo of your foolishness to bounce back to you. Pratt family? *We'll be seeing you.*"

The screen went blank.

The Kestrel sat in a most un-Kestrel like position, one hand over his bandaged eye, slumped in one of my living room chairs, pantlegs riding up his calves and a drink cradled in his spider-like intact hand.

"I quit, by the way," I said.

The Kestrel had laid his head back on the plush leather, his remaining eye closed.

"Hm. I don't think Guild members just quit, Daniel. It's unheard of."

I was quiet for a minute.

"I've heard of people being '*Sunsetted*'."

"That," the Kestrel said, "is only in the most unique of cases."

"Maybe you can put in a word," I said, "pull some strings."

He kept his head back, eyes closed, saying nothing.

Epilogue

THERE'S A BEACH IN WELLS, MAINE, that's actually Wells Harbor. It's free. Rarely crowded. No waves but plenty of water.

I sat in my beach chair reading *A Clockwork Orange*. It was the British edition, with the missing twenty-first chapter that the American version doesn't have, the one where Alex, droog, murderer, and rapist, has begun to carry a picture of an infant secreted on his person, his violent nature perhaps becoming something he's simply growing out of.

Mors preferred the American version.

It was a perfect November day, oddly warm enough to make it comfortable for sweatpants, bandages, and a long-sleeved T-shirt.

Dagny Constantine walked down the wooden boards to the beach, her brown hair longer than I'd ever seen it. I decided to focus fully on my daughter, for now.

Rourke was a beautiful little blond girl, taller than I expected, with long straight hair that stirred in the breeze. I got up, setting the book on the blanket and wishing for the tenth time that morning that I didn't have a black eye and tape across the bridge of my nose.

I thought I saw the Master Chief over on a bench near the unpaved parking lot, but it was just an old gent in a dark sweater.

Dagny and Rourke came within five feet, then Dagny stopped while Rourke walked forward, coming right up to me, shading her eyes with one hand.

"Hi, Daddy," she said.

"Hi."

"You look different than I thought you would," she said.

I squatted down to be closer to eye level with her.

"You don't," I said.

Rourke smiled at me.